Camp
Koinonia

Camp Koinonia

A NOVEL

JOHN E. OLT

TRUSTED
BOOKS
A DIVISION OF DEEP RIVER BOOKS

Trusted Books is an imprint of Deep River Books. The views expressed or implied in this work are those of the author. To learn more about Deep River Books, go online to www.DeepRiverBooks.com.

The author of this book has waived a portion of the publisher's recommended professional editing services. As such, any related errors found in this finished product are not the responsibility of the publisher.

Unless otherwise noted, all Scriptures are taken from the *Holy Bible, New International Version*®, *NIV*®. Copyright © 1973, 1978, 1984 by Biblica, Inc.™ Used by permission of Zondervan. All rights reserved worldwide. www.zondervan.com

ISBN 13: 978-1-63269-242-9
Library of Congress Catalog Card Number: 2011963640

To my happy campers:
my wife, Krista, and my sons, Jay and Andrew

Contents

Acknowledgments

THANKS TO CAROL Thorne, Warren and Cheryl Kemple, Ruth Brown, and Laurie Hartman for their thorough and thoughtful editing of *Camp Koinonia*.

I would also like to recognize the Friends Book Club of Post Road Christian Church in Indianapolis, Indiana, for their critiquing of my manuscript.

Koinonia (koy-nohn-ee'-ah): A Greek word meaning to be drawn together by intimate participation. It is often used to describe the idealized state of fellowship, prayer, and service within the early Christian church.

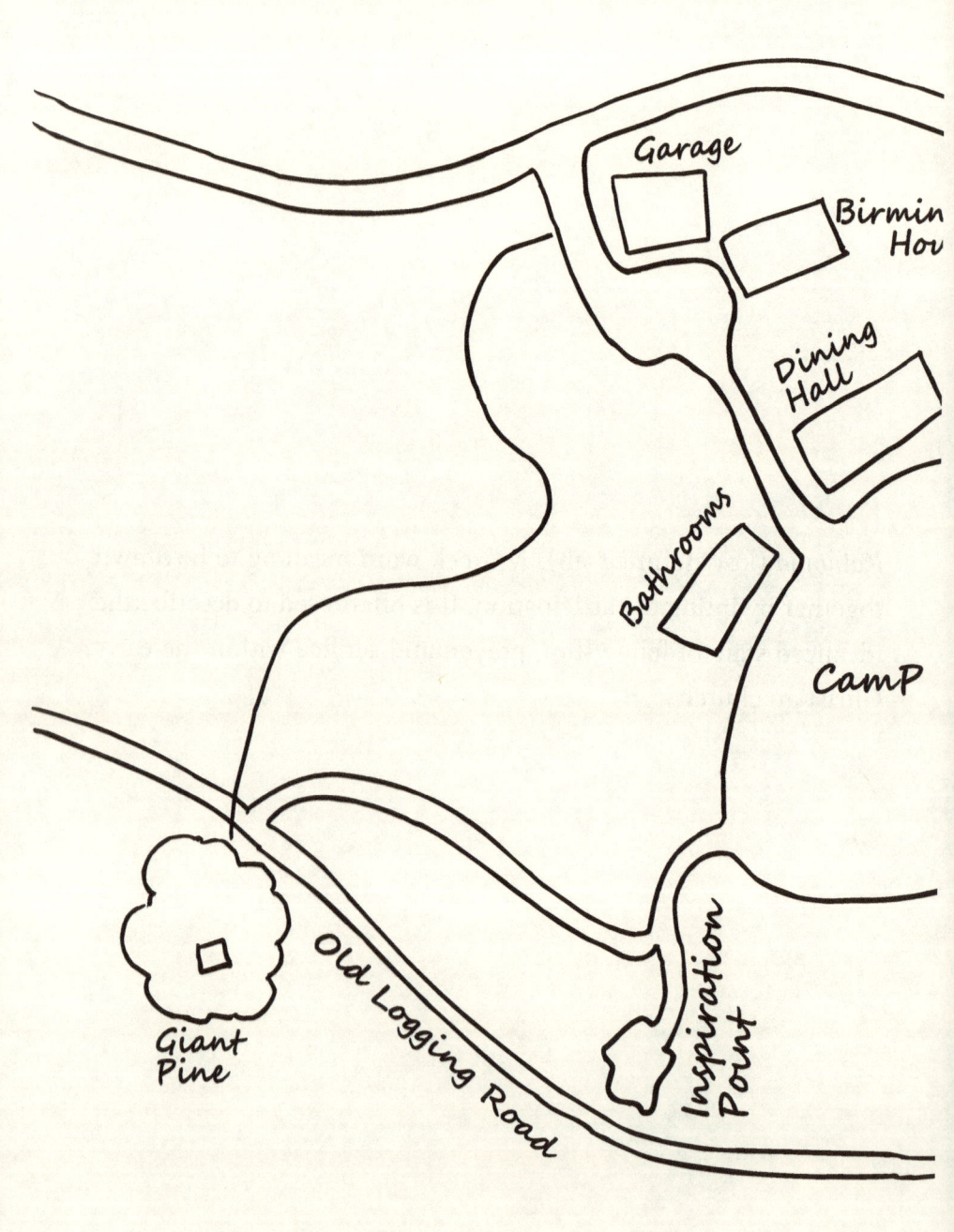

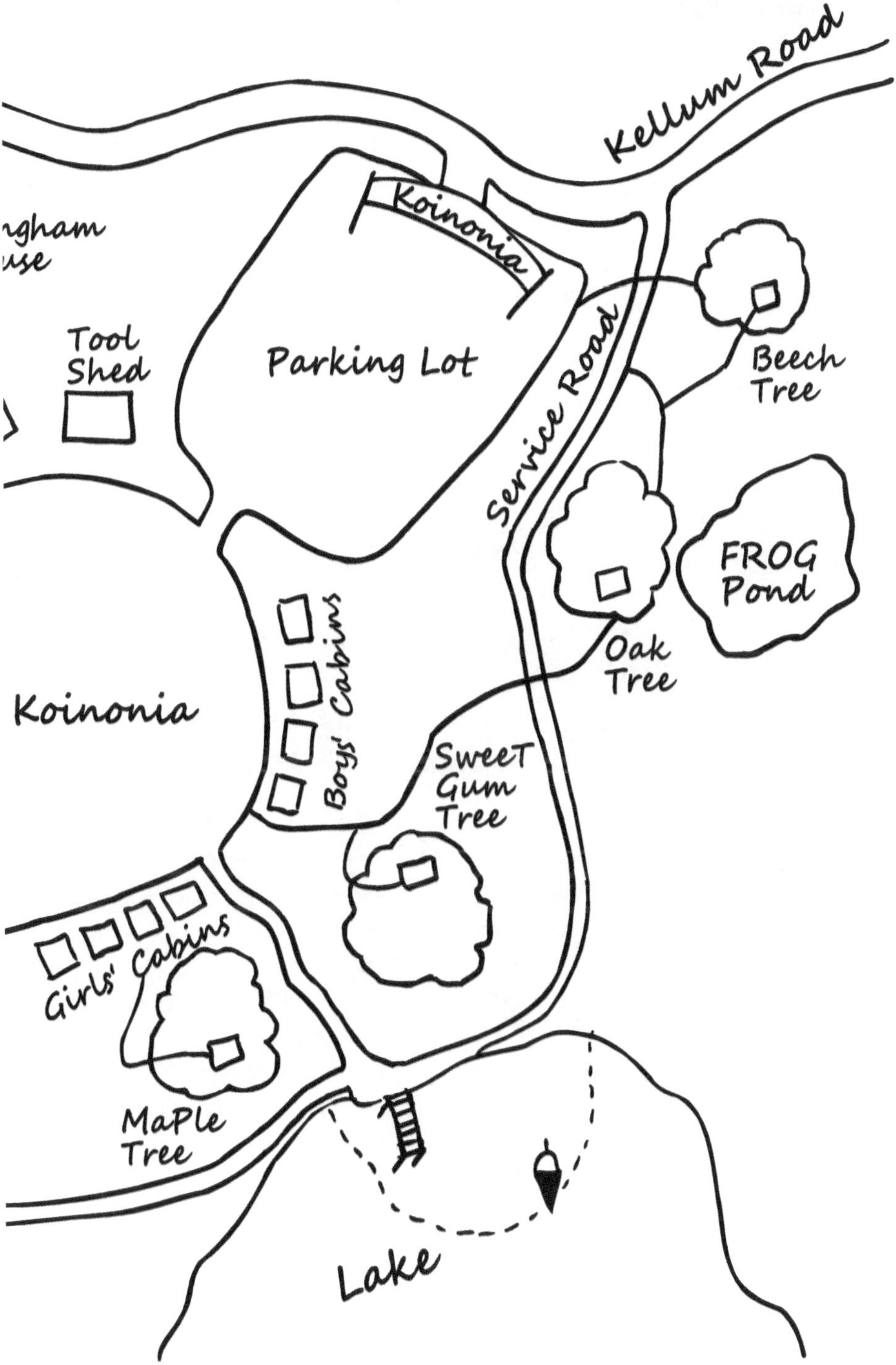

Kellum Road
Koinonia
nghham
use
Tool
Shed
Parking Lot
Service Road
Beech
Tree
FROG
Pond
Oak
Tree
Koinonia
Boys' Cabins
Sweet
Gum
Tree
Girls' Cabins
Maple
Tree
Lake

PART ONE

Camp Koinonia

> They devoted themselves to the apostles' teaching and to the fellowship, to the breaking of bread and to prayer ... All the believers were together and had everything in common.
>
> —Acts 2:42, 44

CHAPTER 1

Newcomer

JAKE VEERED OFF Kellum Road and into Camp Koinonia. His car coasted under the archway that supported the camp's name. Through the midnight calm, he eased across the camp yard. A light shining through a cabin's window beckoned him from across the green. He stopped his car in front of it, climbed out, and stretched. Jake took a long, deep breath. He could smell the pine forest that waved in the breeze. An unseen army of crickets and tree frogs sang their chorus to welcome him.

Jake had only been at camp for one minute, and already, he felt at home. He surveyed the camp yard. He felt like Nehemiah on the day that the Old Testament builder first surveyed the dilapidated walls and gates of ancient Jerusalem. God had entrusted Nehemiah with two tasks: first to rebuild the fortress and second to instruct his people in the ways of the Lord. Jake's mission would be much the same.

As if asleep, the other cabins lay dark and silent off to each side. He could sense the love that had gone into building them. They were old and beaten but not defeated. Jake knew that his top priority for the next seven days would be to get the facilities in shape for this season's first wave of campers. As he gazed at the moonlit cabins, he could see that they would need a fresh coat of paint.

Jake was looking forward to the rejuvenation of Camp Koinonia. From mid-June to mid-August, this would be his mission field. He had faith that the Lord would equip him for whatever was to come.

With a creak and a thud, the screen door's spring closed the door behind him. Jake walked into the large room that held four sets of bunk beds. He dropped his two large suitcases on the floor of the inner room, where a simple bed had been freshly made. *This must be where the counselor sleeps.* The bed sheets had been pulled back for him. On a small table that held the lamp, there was a plate of cookies and a note written in elegant cursive. It said:

> Dear Jake,
>   Welcome to Camp Koinonia! Thank you for joining us. I look forward to working with you this summer.
>   God bless you.
>   Sincerely,
>   Barbara Birmingham

Mmmm, cookies … homemade … chocolate chip. Jake stuffed the first two cookies in his mouth and then another two. *Wow that really hit the spot. I better save a few for tomorrow.* He quickly unpacked. After setting his alarm clock for 6:00 A.M., Jake slid between the heavy, stiff sheets. Through the screened window, he listened to the breeze rustle the trees. He loved the sound of the forest at night. Jake appreciated the difference between loneliness and solitude. He was alone but not lonely. Closing his eyes, he mused about the French trappers who had trekked through these woods 300 years ago. All they had were the hard ground to sleep on and their muskets to keep them company. He counted his blessings. Sleep came quickly.

Buzz. Buzz. Buzz. Jake snapped the alarm clock off the table. 6:00 A.M. *Saturday, I have got to get up.* He looked out his window. The camp yard was alive with the sound of the morning birds. *Breakfast won't be for a couple of hours.*

Jake reviewed the phone conversation he'd had yesterday afternoon with Mrs. Birmingham while stuck behind a wreck on the interstate. Her instructions were clear and concise: "After you get settled in, clean the four boys' cabins. Make a list of any repairs and the supplies that will be needed to fix them. Then start on the bathroom and shower facility. Miss Ella will provide meals for you at 8:00, 11:30, and 4:30." Jake appreciated the clarity of these marching orders. He realized that he would be working alone.

OK, first things first, check the sink and toilet to make sure the water is on. Mmmm, only cold water, but at least it works. I can live with that. Next, make a survey of the four cabins; then prioritize the clean-up effort.

Mrs. Birmingham watched her face in the mirror as a tear rolled down her cheek. She prayed, *Heavenly Father, thank you for giving me this day. Thank you, thank you, thank you for bringing the help I so desperately prayed for. Although my arthritis may inhibit me, I find my strength in You. Jesus you are the only one who knows the number of my days. I will serve you with all of my strength, all my heart, and all my soul. Amen.*

With both hands, the elderly matriarch of Camp Koinonia raised her brush to her head and fought through the painful strokes. Determined not to let the pain make her cry, she focused her energy on not dropping the brush, because dropping the brush would require a cumbersome and painful retrieval. The clanging of a large, cast-iron skillet as it slid around the stove burner in the next room let her know that breakfast would soon be ready. She peeked out into the kitchen.

"Good morning, Mrs. Birmingham!" Mindy flipped the bacon strips once more and then placed them on the paper towel. She broke two eggs over the skillet and added a touch of salt and pepper. She looked down at Champ, Mrs. Birmingham's Airedale watchdog, who was sitting next to the stove, watching her. "Ok … just a little piece." Mindy snapped the end off of a piece of bacon and flipped it in the air. Champ jockeyed to catch the morsel in mid air.

"The bacon smells heavenly. I'll be out in a few minutes," said Mrs. Birmingham. She placed the brush on the vanity and dobbed her cheeks with a tissue.

"Orange juice or grape juice?" Mindy asked as she placed the glasses on the table.

"I'll have orange juice this morning." Mrs. Birmingham walked slowly out of the adjacent bedroom and into the kitchen.

Glancing over to Mrs. Birmingham, Mindy said, "You look great today. Did you sleep well?" She flipped the eggs.

"Yes, I did sleep well. But in my condition, it would be next to impossible to look great. But you ... you look *great*." Mrs. Birmingham arrived at the table and took a sip of her orange juice. She grinned to herself as she noticed Mindy's fresh polo shirt, makeup, and earrings. She wondered if Mindy's clean up was in anticipation of the new arrival, Jake Olson. These adornments had been absent during the first three days of Mindy's stay. But that could be expected considering the sad state of Mrs. Birmingham's health and house on the day that Mindy arrived. Mindy had spent the entire time restoring the old house to order and nursing Mrs. Birmingham back to health.

Mrs. Birmingham took a seat at the table. "Have you heard anything from our new senior counselor?

"No ... I'll let him settle in. You have your doctor's appointment at 8:00. After that, you said you wanted to stop by the bank, and then on the way home, I would like to pick up a few supplies for the camp. I plan to go down to meet him after lunch." Mindy slid the eggs and bacon onto the plates and placed the plates onto the table.

"It was very nice of you to go to the trouble of making his bed and baking those cookies for him. I'm not sure how late he pulled into camp, but I'm sure he appreciated your acts of kindness." Mrs. Birmingham folded her hands to pray.

Mindy sat at the table. "From what I understand, the new guy is coming from a small, Christian college in the middle of an Indiana corn field. I just wanted him to feel welcome." Folding her hands

4

and closing her eyes, Mindy waited for Mrs. Birmingham to say the blessing.

"Heavenly Father, thank you for this day and for the great and mighty things you will do at Camp Koinonia this summer. Send your angels to protect the staff and campers. Bless this food to our bodies. Amen." Mrs. Birmingham studied the young woman who continued to pray silently from the other side of the table. She had known Mindy since she was a baby. Mindy's grandparents had been instrumental in helping her and her late husband, Carl, found Camp Koinonia. Mindy's mother still served on the camp's governing board.

Mrs. Birmingham thought back to earlier that week, when Mindy had arrived, and how Mindy had been assisted from behind by a tall man with a radiant face in a brilliant, white robe. Together they lifted her off the couch where she had collapsed and eased her into Mindy's car. That trip to the doctor may have very well saved her life. She had decided not to mention the angel to Mindy, thinking that the angel would reveal himself to her on his own accord.

"Mindy, I see your mother's face when I look at you. Your mother was the artist; but it was from your father that you inherited the blessing of the servant leader. Mindy, I want to thank you from the bottom of my heart. If you had not taken me to the doctor three days ago, I might have gotten weak enough to die."

Mindy blushed. "You're welcome. It was an honor to help you. It's I who want to thank you. I feel in my soul something incredible is going to happen at Camp Koinonia this summer. I want you to know how much I appreciate your inviting me to be a part of it." Mindy picked up her fork and knife. "So how did you find this newcomer?"

"Dr. Daniel Ransokoff, a former camp counselor, who is now the professor of Business Marketing at Taylor University, presented his class with a case study about a youth camp that was failing. When Jake Olson received the top grade in the class, Daniel sent me a copy of Jake's report. The report went way above and beyond the requirements of the assignment." Mrs. Birmingham bit into her first piece of bacon.

"Jake wrote a report on how to revive a failing camp. How does it compare to my report?" Mindy's voice revealed a twinge of jealousy.

"Both reports are excellent. Yours is written from an insider's point of view: upgrading the menu, camp uniforms, and curriculum while preserving the camp's traditions. You are the only one who could have provided that analysis.

Jake's report was from the point of view of an outside consultant. He recommended computerized databases for campers, counselors, suppliers, and donors for tracking and fundraising. He had some excellent ideas for an interactive website; an automated, twenty-four-hour phone number; and some targeted marketing campaigns. He even presented an elaborate decision tree for how and when to incorporate the family business or sell out to an outside company."

"Sell out to an outside company?" Mindy straightened in her chair.

"It's just an option. If we don't turn the camp around this summer, we'll have to consider our options. Now listen, Mindy, I know you've spent many summers at Camp Koinonia. When Jake suggests new ways of doing things, I don't want us to refuse just because it's something we've never tried before."

"I know … you're right. We all need to work together." Mindy finished the last of her egg. "So you hired him based on a written report?"

"No, I spoke to him on the phone in Danny's office. I could tell the hand of the Lord was on him. He accepted my offer on the spot."

After they both finished their breakfast, Mindy cleared the plates.

"Did you hear anything about that meteor shower that will be visible tonight?" Mrs. Birmingham pointed to the newspaper sitting on the kitchen counter.

"Yeah, I saw the article in the paper. It said the debris that was falling into the atmosphere was once-in-a-lifetime occurrence." Mindy noted the newspaper stack she had readied for the trash can.

"Have you ever been down the old logging road that leads back to the lookout bluff?"

"My dad took me there when I was young."

"I bet you can see the shower from there. Maybe you and Jake can take a hike back there to watch it." Mrs. Birmingham watched for Mindy's reaction.

"Ah, I don't know. I'll see if he's interested. I thought campers weren't allowed back there."

"That's true, for various reasons, one of which is that the cliffs on the sides of the bluffs are steep and too dangerous for children. Why don't you walk back there in the daylight so you can get to know the bluff?"

Mindy turned to observe Mrs. Birmingham's reaction. "So how did you select me for this summer? Did my mom talk you into it?"

"No, no! I had to cling to the Lord. I let the Holy Spirit direct my path. I was too weak to think straight. I prayed and prayed, and then finally, the names came to me. You were the first to be invited. You and Jake and all six of the cabin counselors came to me through prayer."

Mindy smiled as she rinsed the plates in the sink and then glanced at the clock. "Come on. We better get going."

As Jake finished his lunch, Mindy walked into the dining hall. They introduced themselves. Mindy's smile was quick. Her eyes were bright and glowing with charm. When she offered to show him around, Jake responded immediately, "Sure, let's go." Jake gathered his plate and utensils. They both walked to the kitchen area, where Miss Ella inventoried the food supplies. "Thank you for the great lunch. Would you like for me to wash my dishes before I go?"

"No. You have plenty of cleaning and fixing to do, but not the dishes." Miss Ella opened her arms wide to give Mindy a hug. "Welcome back, Mindy! You know you have always been my favorite camper."

"Thank you, Miss Ella. It is truly great to be back. Thanks for brainstorming with me on how to update the camp's menu. I couldn't have completed that part of the report without you." Mindy commented on how a number of food selections that they had recommended had been delivered earlier that morning.

"I'm not sure how Mrs. Birmingham talked this boy into coming to our camp, but he's the hardest working kid I've seen in years. Mrs. Birmingham asked me to bring Jake up to speed about the camp. I've been talking his ear off over breakfast and lunch about what changes I've seen in my eighteen years as the camp's cook." Miss Ella smiled at Jake and then at Mindy. "Well, you two better get going. We only have a week until the campers arrive."

CHAPTER 2

Inspiration Point

AS MINDY LED Jake through the camp yard toward the old logging road, she pointed to one of cabins that the girls would be staying in. "That will be my cabin. Now that Mrs. Birmingham is feeling better, I'll start cleaning it and the other three girls' cabins later today or tomorrow. I probably won't sleep in it until the campers arrive. We're lucky that we have small bathrooms in the counselors' room, even if they are only piped for cold water. Of course, there is plenty of hot water in the shower building."

Jake nodded, "Let me know if you need any help with your cabins."

"Thanks." Mindy grinned at Jake.

They walked under the thick canopy made of tree limbs that shaded them from the mid-June sun. There was still a path where the tires had worn through the forest floor; yet weeds grew along its sides. Jake had experienced this type of path before. His grandfather's tracker had mowed paths through the family's woods and around their small lake in southern Indiana each summer, just in time for the grandkids' annual visit.

"Where does this path lead?" Jake asked.

"To a lookout," Mindy replied. "My dad took me there a couple of times during my first years at camp. It had been a secluded refuge for my mom and dad when they were counselors."

"So you are a legacy camper."

"Oh yes, my grandmother and grandfather on my mom's side helped the Birminghams launch this camp."

They walked out of the forest into an opening. A stunning panorama of the surrounding hills and forest opened before them.

Jake, in awe, admired the view. "This place is now my *favorite* place. What do you call it?"

"Inspiration Point."

"It's breathtaking," he said.

Jake soaked in the view of the far-off hills covered with lush, green trees. The Holy Spirit welled up inside of him. As he moved away from Mindy and closer to the bluff's edge, he saw Mindy smile with approval. They turned away from each other, both taking a few moments to pray. Quietly but fervently, Jake whispered a prayer, "Jehovah, Almighty Creator … thank you for these natural wonders." Waves of tingling flowed over his skin.

After a few moments, Jake turned to face Mindy, who was sitting on the bluff, looking over the vast Wisconsin forest in the valley below.

"Have you ever seen a meteor shower?" Mindy asked.

"Sure, why?"

"There's going to be one tonight." Mindy turned back to gaze at the northeast sky.

"Yeah, I remember hearing about it. It'll be best viewed from the northeast from midnight until 4:00." Jake took his bearing from the sun and pointed to the northeast, exactly the direction Mindy was already facing. *Impressive,* he thought. Mindy's knowledge of the meteor shower astonished Jake. He liked people who were well-informed, and Mindy certainly seemed to know what she was talking about. He was already looking forward to working with her this summer.

"It looks clear enough. Do you think we should watch it?" she asked.

"Absolutely. Do you prefer getting up at 2:00 or staying up until after midnight?"

She smiled. "Let's stay up. If it clouds over, we'll know it by 10:00 or 11:00. On the other hand, if big ones really start falling, we can stay up as long as we can stay awake."

"What did you say your major was?" Jake inquired.

"I'm studying American and English literature with a biology minor at Northwestern. I'll be a junior. And you?"

"Business at Taylor University; I'll be a senior."

"So where is Taylor?" Mindy turned to face Jake.

"Taylor University is halfway between Indianapolis, which is in the center of the state, and Indiana's northern border. It's in a small town called Upland. Taylor is not very big, about 2,000 students, but it has been around since before the Civil War." Jake looked at Mindy. "So you go to a Big Ten school, home of the Kellogg School of Management."

"Yes ... so what made you want to go to Taylor?" She asked.

"I've had in the back of my mind that I wanted to be a missionary. I've always been good at organizing and motivating people. Studying business at Taylor was my best option." Jake glanced at Mindy. "Why did you choose Northwestern?"

"I don't know. My dad went there. My friends go there. It was close to home." Mindy stood and dusted off her pants.

As they walked back into the woods, Mindy asked, "So, where did you go to high school?"

"I went to Fort Wayne High. I wrestled there," he replied. "I was team captain my senior year. By some twist of fate, my class elected me class president for the last two years of high school." Jake tried to sound humble; yet he hoped she would be impressed.

"Oh, so you were a glamour boy."

"No. Far from it," he said. "And you?"

"My older sister, Kathy, was the glamour girl in our family. She was a basketball star, volleyball star, and homecoming queen. As for me, like you say ... I was ... 'far from it.' I was the smart one; you know ... the wallflower, the late bloomer. I read a lot, enjoyed swimming. I was a lifeguard and taught children's Sunday school.

I was honored when Mrs. Birmingham invited me to be part of this year's camp."

"So, a wrestler, huh?" She crouched into the "get ready" stance that wrestlers do when they are ready to start a match. "Were you any good?"

Seeing Mindy's playful grin, Jake reminisced back to a youth group picnic, years ago, where his high school sweetheart, Sally, had smiled the same way. And he thought about how surprised Sally was when he'd gently grabbed her elbow, ducked his head under her arm pit, grabbed her leg, and lifted her onto his shoulders. "A fireman's carry … an airplane spin, and finally … a bone crushing body slam." Jake had narrated to Sally as he gently lifted her off the ground, spun her around, and laid her gently back on the grass. Breaking away from his daydream, he refocused on Mindy.

Mindy swayed back and forth in her stance.

Jake couldn't resist. He grinned, assumed the wrestling stance, softly grabbed Mindy's wrist, and made a half step lunge. His shot was only deep enough to let her know that if he had wanted to, he could have taken her down, but it was not close enough to touch her. "Good? I won my share of matches." His voice conveyed humor without a hint of boasting. "From your stance, you look like a champ."

"I dated a wrestler in high school," Mindy stated. "By the way, the only champ around here is a dog."

"A dog?"

"Mrs. Birmingham's Airedale is named Champ."

"Oh."

"What does Mrs. Birmingham have on your agenda for this afternoon?" Mindy asked.

"Cleaning the boys' cabins. Someone cleaned my room before I got here. The rest of the cabins are pits."

Mindy smiled. "Someone cleaned your bedroom in the cabin?"

"Mrs. Birmingham mentioned in my phone call that 'Missy' would leave the light on for me. Maybe *she* cleaned it for me. Who is Missy?" Jake asked.

"Oh, I think you'll be getting to know her quite well this summer."

Jake grinned, realizing that Missy was Mindy and that it was her handiwork. "Thanks, I really appreciate it. I ate half the cookies the minute I got here and the rest first thing this morning."

"If you don't mind, I would appreciate it if you would call me Mindy. Missy is a pet name that my family uses."

Jake nodded in acceptance.

Mindy turned onto the path that led to the house. "I'll be working in the house, reviewing the attendance rosters with Mrs. Birmingham. I'll check in with you after dinner."

They parted to pursue their afternoon's work.

A few steps up the path, Mindy glanced over her shoulder, just in time to catch Jake looking back over his. They blushed, then turned away. *This newcomer seems like a great guy. It's a miracle how this once-in-a-lifetime meteor shower marks our first day together. I've got to get back to the kitchen and dig out that newspaper article. I need to make sure I have the facts right.*

The setting sun yielded to a warm, clear night. Mindy knocked at Jake's cabin door.

"Are you ready?" she asked with a voice full of anticipation.

"Yes." He pulled a small, stuffed pack to his shoulder, noticing that Mindy arrived empty-handed. Secretly, he was happy. He hoped to impress her with his foresight. His pack contained a plastic ground cloth, two bottles of water, two packs of Peanut M&Ms, two small citronella candles, and even a pack of gum.

They strolled into the tunnel made by the trees branches. As they arrived at Inspiration Point, the twilight revealed its first orbs of light. "That's Saturn, and that's Venus." Jake pointed to the two bright bodies of light.

"Wow. That's interesting how God reveals His planets just before He brings out the stars," Mindy replied.

"What's that?" Jake looked at the dark-green, canvas bag sitting on the ground.

"It's my stuff." Out of the old army duffle bag she pulled a large Army blanket and camouflage parachute. A clove of garlic fell to the ground.

"Hey … is that a vintage Vietnam era tiger stripe parachute? Is your dad in the Army?" he asked.

"No, he is an insurance executive."

"Where did you get the blanket and parachute?"

"It was passed down to me by Judy Berry, my older sister's best friend. Judy and Kathy have been friends for as long as they have known each other. This stuff belonged to Judy's boyfriend, Bill. In the daytime, the parachute was used as a ground cloth for campers who picnicked in the woods. At night, the counselors, as a prank, would scare the campers by wearing it over their heads, pretending to be a ghost. It was *really* scary. Even with a flashlight, you could only see a blob in the woods." Mindy spread the parachute on the ground, broke apart the clove of garlic and rubbed it into the rocks around them. She then threw a few bits of garlic on the ground behind them.

"Afraid of vampires?" asked Jake.

"Yes … but the garlic is to keep the varmints away."

Not wanting to be outdone, Jake pulled out the water, treats, and candles from his pack. "I'll light these and set them behind our heads so the light won't affect our eyes."

"Great." She turned her head but not before Jake saw her broad smile.

"Did Judy give you anything else?"

"Oh, yeah, she gave me a map."

"A treasure map?"

"Yes. It shows the location of the five benches. Judy's boyfriend, Bill, loved working with wood and loved big trees, so he built benches and stationed them under the five biggest trees in the woods. In the daylight, they served as hiking destinations."

"And, at night?"

"For late-night rendezvous." Mindy raised her eyebrows and gave Jake a mischievous look.

Jake and Mindy lay down on their backs as the first meteor pierced the night sky. Within a few minutes, one meteor after another streaked through the heavens.

"Wow. Did you see that?" She settled her head into the rolled-up duffle bag.

"Yeah. This is going to be a great light show." Jake felt euphoria settling into his body. *Is it the meteor shower or the encounter with Mindy or do I just feel great after a hard day of work?* He turned to face her. "Isn't it amazing that simple beings can know the time and place to watch rocks fall out of the sky? Yet, we are only the observers, only specks on this earth. God made those marvels in the heavens at the beginning of time, knowing they would fall in front of us tonight." Jake nestled his head back onto his backpack.

Mindy grinned at the lecture. "There is a weekend near the middle of each camp season where there are no campers scheduled. It is a time to recuperate and repair anything that needs to be fixed. It would be a good time for you to invite your parents out to see the camp. Maybe your girlfriend would like to come for a visit. She could stay with me in my cabin if she wanted," Mindy said.

Jake smiled. "Thanks for the offer, but my parents won't be coming to camp, and ... well ... I don't have a girlfriend." Jake looked away. A heart tug tightened in his chest. Although it surfaced only every once in a while, he knew what it was about. He did not want to talk about it.

"I'm sorry, Jake. I have to admit I was curious about your having a girlfriend. But I didn't mean to bring up a tender subject."

"It's OK. I guess I'm one of those hopeless romantics." Jake recovered from the dip in his mood. "I used to rationalize it by thinking that Taylor girls only wanted to go out with boys who had money. That's not fair or accurate. I have to admit that it was my preoccupation with *not* having much money that kept me from pursuing a girlfriend. Taylor girls are intelligent and beautiful, but there was no spark in me for them."

Jake sat up. "I'm the middle of three sons. My parents are pretty frugal; they made all three boys the same offer. As far as college, we could go anywhere we wanted. They would pay for the room and board, and we would pay the tuition. I decided to go to Taylor, thinking that someday I would go to the mission field. To offset the cost of a private school, I took a job in the campus library."

A reluctant grin formed across Jake's face. "Everybody else in the work/study program wanted to be an intramural referee or give tours of the campus on the CREW staff. I tell you, the library has a lot of advantages; it's warm in the winter and cool in the summer. I have learned a tremendous amount about organizing files and data and where and how to search to find information."

"You know," Jake's grin revealed his delight, "there's a table and chairs in the archive section, right in front of the shelf that holds the Wall Street Journals. I've made that spot my study haven. Only the library staff can get back there. Every night when I study, I pull the latest copy of the WSJ off the shelf and read it on my study break. I put it back, of course." Jake laughed to himself. "Library assistant is one of the best jobs on campus."

Jake cocked his head to one side, looked off into the distance, then turned to face Mindy. "Something just dawned on me. For my three years at Taylor ... I was never lonely. I have always had lots of friends, guys and girls, but I mean never lonely in a romantic sense. I think it goes back to Sally, my girlfriend in high school."

Jake checked for any hint of laughter on Mindy's face. "It's not like we had a fight and broke up. It's not like we snuck off and had affairs behind each other's backs. No, it wasn't like that. It was like fate pulled us apart and spun us around and then we wandered off in different directions. She graduated early to spend a year as an exchange student in Belgium the year I went off to college."

Jake bit his lip while he gathered his thoughts. "Saying 'good-bye' ... yet knowing that we were *not* breaking up, that really tangled my emotions. We both hoped to be together again, but deep inside, we knew it probably wouldn't happen. I felt horrible. It still haunts me every once in awhile.

"We kept in touch for a while … then I didn't hear much from her … then nothing. Somehow, my love for her occupied a part of my heart long after I knew I would never see her again. I stayed in love with the image of her that I carried around with me.

"We were like two lovers in a drama," Jake asserted, "where the woman goes off to be a nurse in a foreign war and the man stays behind to support the local war effort. As the war ends, the woman doesn't return home. Yet, her name is never documented as a casualty. In the absence of closure, the man left behind clings to the hope of reunion. Because when hope for the missing loved one dies … despair sets in." Jake sat looking off into the distance.

He gently shook his head and shoulders. "All of a sudden, this hope I have been holding on to has gone sour, and it is trying to get out. It is difficult to describe, but I can feel it."

Jake turned away. "I am sorry for going on like this. I have never talked to anyone about this before. Maybe it's been bottled up, waiting for the right person to let the genie out of its bottle. It's funny how I've opened up to you." Jake took a deep breath. "You must think I'm a nerd—no money, no girlfriend, working in the library. But you know, if I am, I'm a nerd for the Lord. I came here in answer to a calling by the Holy Spirit."

Jake sighed. The tightness in his chest vanished. He could breath more easily now. He peeked out of the corner of his eye to see Mindy's reaction.

Mindy sat motionless, watching him. "Jake, that was the most touching and honest thing I have ever heard a guy tell me. No, I definitely don't think you are a nerd. Thank you for sharing your heart with me. I want you to know how much I appreciate your coming to Camp Koinonia."

Mindy inhaled a long, deep breath. "My story is not as touching as yours, but it's a heartache all the same. I dated Keith in high school. I went to Northwestern; he went to the University of Chicago. He partied a little in high school, but he fell off the deep end at college. Each year it got worse. It was like you said; I stayed in love with the *image* of Keith that I carried around in my heart.

"It was easy for me to do when I didn't see him very often. This spring was a disaster; he gave me a hard time for deciding to spend the summer at camp. He wanted me to stay and party with him and his buddies." Mindy looked down. "He pressured me to do things I didn't want to do. We had the 'big fight' and broke up. I know it was for the best. It pains me to see him rot away. But that is his choice."

Mindy made eye contact with Jake. "I'm not so sure that despair has to linger when hope dries up ... I want to believe that when the hope for one is gone ... the heart is ripened for another."

Jake and Mindy shared a glance. Grins grew out of their melancholy moods. They had transcended the barriers that strangers maintain. From this point forward, they would be friends.

"I'll tell you something else. I dream of someday being the director of Camp Koinonia. No one knows it. It's something I've known deep inside for about a year now. It's like God's once again chosen an unlikely candidate for some great work He has planned. I have even written a report on how to turn the camp around."

Jake sat silently, waiting, making sure she had all the time she needed to speak her mind. "A report?" Jake asked. "I'd like to read it. I was assigned a case study at Taylor. It was about restoring a summer camp that had failed. I think it was a Holy Spirit thing. I had no idea at the time that I would be working here this summer. I can assure you I have no ambition to be the next director. I see my assignment lasting only one summer. I'll support your dream in every way I can."

"It's a deal." She held her hand out for them to shake.

"It's a deal."

They settled onto their backs to watch the meteors fall. After only a few minutes, Mindy yawned.

"Are you getting sleepy?" Jake asked.

"Yes. I'm ready to go if you are."

They packed the parachute and gear and headed back down the path through the woods.

Mindy walked beside Jake until they arrived at Mrs. Birmingham's back porch door. With sleepy eyes, Mindy turned to Jake. "Jake, do you think *I'm* a nerd?"

"Well I don't know much about you … but you don't *look* like a nerd." Jake watched her face.

When she looked into his eyes, she could feel his sincerity. She could tell his comment was intended to be a compliment. Mindy smiled back.

His extended glance assured her that he liked what he saw. That was important to her. She had known that there would be a young man in the role opposite hers. She had prayed that they would get along, that they could trust each other, and that they would work well together.

Mindy had known for years that Mrs. Birmingham's policy was that "romantic entanglements between counselors and campers were strictly forbidden." Yet deep in her heart, Mindy yearned for Jake to like her, to think of her as beautiful.

She suspected that the topic of nerds would never come up again, and even if they were nerds, they were nerds for the Lord. That thought made her smile. "Thanks, good night." Mindy opened the screen door to step inside. Champ noted her presence with one quiet bark as he scampered to the door to meet her.

"You're welcome. Good night."

Jake waited for the door to shut securely, then turned his flashlight down the path to his cabin. He cast his eyes to the sky and whispered, "I can't believe I went on and on like that out on that bluff. There must be some kind of truth serum oozing out of those rocks." He chuckled. "Thank you, Lord, for bringing me to Camp Koinonia, for Mindy, for the meteor shower ... and for the perfect weather."

CHAPTER 3

Tornado

DURING LUNCH THE next day, Mindy stopped in to see Jake in the dining hall. Even though he was dirty and sweaty from his morning's work, he was glad to see her.

"Good morning," Mindy said.

"Good morning," Jake returned.

"Looks like you're getting a lot done." She eyed his soiled shirt. "I see the clouds rolled in."

"And they brought in this humidity."

"Let me guess, you ate breakfast with full gospel choir music blasting over the intercom."

"Yeah!"

"That is kind of a tradition on Sundays at camp."

"Miss Ella and I ate breakfast together. She played a sermon on CD, and we finished with prayer." Jake folded his napkin and placed it on his plate. "Did you and Mrs. Birmingham go to church together?"

"No. She wasn't feeling well this morning. She read Psalms while I worked out of my book of devotions."

"I'll be ready for an inspection from the chief by dinner time. Does Mrs. Birmingham ever come down to the camp, or does she always stay up on the plantation?"

21

"Listen!" she snapped. "Mrs. Birmingham has been very ill and depressed. When I got here a few days ago, she was so weak that she could hardly stand. She lost her husband last year. She is crippled by arthritis. I spent the first two days getting her to her doctors and cleaning her house. She didn't want *you* to see her that way. She's frail, Jake. She still has her dignity and her courage. Mrs. Birmingham has been a pillar in this community for many years. She is a humble and generous servant. She'd be crushed if she thought you had accused her of being pompous."

Jake, with eyebrows raised, stared at Mindy in silence. Obviously, he had struck a very tender nerve. "I am sorry … I had no idea. Is there anything I can do for her?"

"No." Mindy's gaze dropped to the floor. "I'm the one who should be sorry. I shouldn't have lashed out at you like that. I want you to know she feels terrible about you staying down in the camp all by yourself. She's getting stronger every day. She still can't walk down to the camp. I know she's been eager to have you up to the house for dinner … maybe tomorrow." She raised her eyes to Jake's. "Please forgive me. Mrs. Birmingham's been like a great aunt to me for many years. I guess I'm a little too defensive."

"You're forgiven. Thank you for sharing. Give her my best, and tell her that I made a before-and-after video of all the work I've done. Whenever she's ready, I'd like to share it with her." Jake's voice rolled with increasing vigor. "If it's any comfort to her, I am a huge fan of Henry David Thoreau and his solitude experience at Walden Pond. I'm not suffering. I'm the happiest when I'm being productive. I'm having the time of my life." They traded smiles and parted.

Jake labored at a feverish pace for the rest of the afternoon. After dinner, he decided to wash up in the lake. He'd been unable to get the shower facility's hot-water heater to work. Jake hoped that the camp's retired facilities manager, Bob Peterson, could help him fix it. Yesterday's shower was bitterly cold. Jake had endured cold showers while he was on mission trips to Mexico, but this Wisconsin tap water was *really cold.* Anyway, he reasoned, the scenery was much better down at the dock.

As he bathed, he noticed the black clouds rolling in from the north. His upbringing in Indiana had made him leery of hot, muggy days that were followed by fast-moving cold fronts. *Tornados!* He wondered, *Could they form this far north?* He gathered his towel, Ivory soap, and shampoo and returned to his cabin. Quickly, he flipped open his laptop and clicked through his favorites to the local news and weather home page. He could hear gusts of wind whipping and tossing the trees, and then there was a bright flash. *CRACK! BOOM!* A pounding hail storm blasted his cabin. He watched in horror as the radar weather map appeared. A tornado had formed only a few miles away and was bearing down on the camp.

Jake snatched his pack, threw in his laptop, cell phone, camera, all three of his flashlights, a few bottles of water, and two hand fulls of fruit. He jerked on his raincoat and pulled the hood over his head as he dashed out of his cabin. Jake ran to the big house on top of the hill.

Champ barked from inside the house. Jake ran up to the back screen door and pounded impatiently. He waited for what seemed an eternity. Finally, a silhouette appeared in the door.

"Yes, child. What is it?" Mrs. Birmingham asked.

"A tornado is heading this way! There isn't anyone in the camp. We need to find Mindy and get to the basement!"

Mrs. Birmingham swung open the door and motioned for Jake to come in.

Mindy bounded down the back stairs. "Jake! What's the matter?"

"There's a tornado! It's about to hit this house!"

Mrs. Birmingham whispered something to Mindy. Mindy ran through the house.

Mrs. Birmingham pointed to the door across the room. "The door to the basement is over here."

Mindy returned with a ring of keys. Mrs. Birmingham selected the key and unlocked the door. "You two go ahead. I'll be down in a minute."

"We are not leaving you up here," Mindy said, glancing out the window at the raging storm.

Realizing that Mrs. Birmingham was not able to get down the stairs, Jake grabbed the sturdy oak chair from the dining room table. "Here, sit on this! We'll carry you down."

Mrs. Birmingham complied.

"Mindy, you stabilize the top of the chair, and I'll lift the base." As he stepped backward down the stairs, Jake reminded Mindy, "Close the door securely. Tornados can suck people out of open doors."

Jake and Mindy placed Mrs. Birmingham in the center of the basement. "Let me refresh my memory about what's down here," Mrs. Birmingham whispered as she surveyed the room. "There's that old, worn couch and matching chair, a long tabletop for a desk, and at least a dozen metal bookshelves filled with books. A little bit off to the side is an armless rocking chair. To one side of the chair sits a floor lamp, and on the other side, there's a short table with Carl's reading glasses. This must be where Carl did his best reading." After only a flicker of warning, the basement plunged into darkness.

"Stay calm," Jake said as he fumbled for the zipper on his pack. With a click of the flashlight, he could tell that the small beam of light brought reassurance to Mindy and Mrs. Birmingham. He handed the first flashlight to Mrs. Birmingham. Then he pulled out the second flashlight and gave it to Mindy. "We need to start praying ... I will be right over there." He took a few steps and dropped to his knees. "Jesus, all powerful and merciful God ... protect us ..."

Mindy dropped to her knees next to him. Rain and wind pounded the house. Sweat seeped from Jake's face as the terrifying roar of a tornado permeated the underground cavity. The old exterior walls above them groaned under the storm's pressure. Jake reached over and put his arm around Mindy's shoulders. He could feel her trembling. Jake closed his eyes. He prayed fervently. He realized that their lives depended on it.

Jake was not sure what happened next. He had perceived a barrage of disturbing images in his mind, but it had all gone blank. He wasn't sure if he had died or been knocked unconscious. He could feel nothing … then, in an instant, he could feel warmth, then peace, and then euphoria. He stayed motionless for a while. And then he slowly became aware that he was kneeling on the basement floor. His arm was still around Mindy. He rose. Mrs. Birmingham was weeping quietly on Carl's chair. They had been spared.

"Praise the Lord!" Jake quickly went upstairs to survey the damage. He found nothing out of place. *It's a miracle. If this stillness was the result of passing through the eye of the twister … then we would have been blown apart by the storm's other side by now. By the grace of God, the storm has vanished.* He headed back to the basement, and Mrs. Birmingham met him at the door. She had climbed the stairs without assistance. Mindy followed closely behind.

"Carl bought these special candles years ago; they will burn for a long time." Mrs. Birmingham lit the two hurricane candles that were sitting on the bookshelf adjacent to the basement door. "Mindy, why don't you take one, and I'll use the other. Jake, I would like for you to spend the night in the house with us. Mindy, will you show him to the master bedroom?"

"Thank you, Mrs. Birmingham," Jake said.

Mrs. Birmingham smiled at her two young helpers. An extraordinary brightness illuminated her eyes, "No," she corrected him gently. "Thank *you* … and God bless you both. Good night."

Mindy and Jake looked at Mrs. Birmingham and then at each other. Mrs. Birmingham disappeared around the corner. She was headed for her bedroom on the other side of the kitchen. Although he couldn't immediately confirm it, it appeared to Jake that the crippling effects of Mrs. Birmingham's arthritis had disappeared.

Mindy led Jake up the stairs as she explained, "This first bedroom was originally for the Birmingham's twin daughters. I've been sleeping there since I arrived last week. The next bedroom is the master bedroom. That's where you'll be sleeping. It may be a little musty. It hasn't been slept in for a while. The bathroom's at the end of the hall."

Mindy stopped in the middle of the hall. "Mrs. Birmingham had the first floor family room, next to the kitchen, converted into a bedroom when her husband, Carl, became ill. As Mrs. Birmingham's condition worsened, she also was unable to climb the stairs, so she made the first floor bedroom her own."

Jake looked at Mindy's face, which was illuminated by candle light. "Even when the power is out, there is usually enough water in the pipes to flush the toilet a few times. If you have to go, you can go first." He nodded towards the bathroom. "Maybe we should put the candle in your room so we are not walking around with it."

Mindy handed Jake the candle, then switched on Jake's flashlight and headed for the bathroom. Jake entered the first bedroom, noting the two beds that sat across the room from each other. He set the candle on the table next to Mindy's bed, then went to explore the master bedroom.

In a few minutes, Jake heard Mindy's door to the hall open and close. Jake untied his hiking boots, pulled them off, and slipped off his socks. With his flashlight in hand, he made his way to the bathroom.

Upon his return, he noticed a dim glow from the master bedroom. Jake walked in to find Mindy sitting on the bed, her face pensive, nervous. She sat with her back against the bed's headboard, her legs drawn up to her chest, and her arms wrapped around her knees.

"Mindy ... are you OK?" Jake asked.

"Jake, can I talk to you about something?"

"Sure." Jake sat on the bed's edge.

"Did you see anything when we were praying?"

"Yes," Jake replied, "I saw what it must be like to stand inside the eye of a tornado. Somehow I witnessed the power and destruction, and yet I was not harmed by it. I could see trees being ripped apart, limbs and debris swirled all around. And then it was like the Lord pulled me up through the eye. The next thing I saw was the tornado from the air ... like I was floating on a cloud. I realized the tornado was heading directly for the house. Then it all went black. When I woke up, I knew we had been spared."

He pondered for a moment. "You know … there was more … I was left with the impression that God has sent us to Camp Koinonia for more than just preparing the place for this year's campers. I get the distinct impression that Camp Koinonia will develop into a training ground for a new generation of Christian leaders."

Mindy sat, stunned by what she had heard. She had experienced the exact visual pictures as Jake but without the perception of new understanding. "I saw all that, but I did not hear anything. Why didn't God speak to me? While we were in the basement, God told Mrs. Birmingham that she would have renewed health so that she could oversee the camp's rejuvenation. Why did He leave me out?"

"God communicates in many ways, revealing His Word through the Bible, through experiences, and even through the voices of other people. How can you say that God left you out? Wasn't it His miracle that spared your life? Don't you think He's been preparing you for this mission during all those years of teaching Sunday school and being a camp counselor? What about the inspiration to write the Camp Koinonia improvement paper?"

Jake continued, "Mindy, I wouldn't say that God has left you out. I would say that you are right in the middle of it. He has His hand upon you. You need only to yield to it." Jake's eye connected with Mindy's. Her posture relaxed as her anxiety waned. "Would you like me to massage the tension out of your shoulders?"

Mindy nodded as she maneuvered to turn her back to Jake. He applied his hands to her shoulders, squeezing softly at first and then firmly. He could feel her muscles soften as her tension melted away. He massaged up her neck as her head dipped forward. Jake stepped back. Her eyes were closed; yet she smiled contently. He could tell that she felt secure.

Mindy stretched out on top of the comforter. Jake moved to the foot of the bed. "They say the feet are a storehouse of tension. This may tickle." He touched her toes. They felt as cold as ice. He cupped his hands around them until they warmed. As he massaged from her ankles to her toes, he could feel her squirm and giggle quietly. Within minutes, Mindy was asleep.

Jake turned and blew out the candle. He stood for a minute, allowing his eyes to adjust to the dark. He walked to the window to open the curtain and raise the shade. *There*, he thought. *That will let the morning sun in.* He lingered at the window, watching the gentle rain. Then from the bed across the room, he heard the whimper of a pathetic murmur. It sounded like the plea of a small child trapped in a nightmare.

"No, no ... don't leave me here ... don't leave me in the dark. Please, Lord, don't leave me here all alone."

Jake flipped on his flashlight and approached the bed. "Mindy ... it's Jake ... I'm right here." She was sound asleep. He noticed her body had curled into the fetal position. *I bet she's cold.* Jake hustled into the next bedroom and returned carrying the down comforter he had snatched from Mindy's bed. He slipped it over Mindy, carefully covering her feet and shoulders. Then he left the flashlight turned on as he propped it up on the night stand next to Mindy. *These batteries will last for at least three or four hours. If she wakes up in the middle of the night, she'll be able to see that she's safe.*

For just an instant, Jake perceived himself as a man who was a number of years older and the girl before him as a child. Overwhelming love filled him. He now knew how fathers felt when they tuck their young daughters into bed. As he watched Mindy sleep, the words of Jesus came to him. *"Blessed are the pure in heart for they will see God."*

Jake whispered to himself, "Someday ... I hope I have a little daughter just like Mindy." Jake walked to the other bedroom and plopped down on the bed. His weary body slumped from exhaustion.

"Thank you, all powerful and merciful Lord, for sparing us from the tornado. I am your humble servant. My head is bowed, and my hands are lifted up. Reveal to me the tasks that will draw me closer to you.

The Lord in heaven smiled upon his two young servants. He, and only He, knew the plans He had laid out for them.

CHAPTER 4

Benches

EVEN THOUGH MRS. Birmingham's house had been spared from the tornado, the rest of Camp Koinonia was less fortunate. Tree limbs and debris from the buildings that had been torn apart marked the widespread destruction that littered the camp yard. Jake concluded from his early morning survey of the camp that it would take a miracle for the facilities to be ready for the campers by the coming weekend.

Mrs. Birmingham, Mindy, and Jake fasted and prayed all Monday morning, seeking God's supernatural provision and asking for the Holy Spirit to guide them into action. Then they took Jake's list of things that were damaged by the tornado and combined it with the reports that Jake and Mindy had prepared earlier that year to form a master plan for Camp Koinonia's rejuvenation. After that, an urgent plea for aid and assistance was sent to the surrounding communities and the families of former counselors and campers.

A wellspring of support mounted in the nearby towns that were not affected by the storm. Help started arriving within a few hours. Jake orchestrated the work projects on the cabins and camp facilities. Miss Ella provided meals and refreshments to the crews of workers, and Mrs. Birmingham and Mindy managed the control center in the house. The elderly master and her young apprentice directed the flow of funds to ensure that money was matched to the required materials and services. Master schedule updates were compiled every two hours.

Throughout Monday afternoon and evening and all day on Tuesday and Wednesday, the miraculous in-pouring of workers, money, and resources transformed the rag-tag camp into a viable facility.

Early Thursday morning, Mindy drove Mrs. Birmingham around the camp yard so she could see the amazing results that the rejuvenation team had accomplished. At the end of her tour, through her tears of joy, Mrs. Birmingham rejoiced, "Hallelujah! You are the all-powerful, all-knowing God. You are the one who protects us. You are the one who provides for our needs. Thank you, thank you, Lord, our Abba Father."

The four core campers shared breakfast in the newly renovated dining hall. Mrs. Birmingham cleared her throat. "Here is a little token of our appreciation that the camp's board voted on yesterday evening." Mrs. Birmingham presented Miss Ella, Mindy, and Jake with bonus checks. "Why don't we all take the rest of the day off?" Mrs. Birmingham smiled at the pleasantly stunned group. "The campers will be here in a few days. I think we could all use a little free time."

Jake and Mindy glanced at each other, thanked their boss graciously, then disappeared into the kitchen to rinse off their plates and deposit them into the dishwasher. They had been waiting for the chance to initiate their plans. In the cool of the morning, they would hike to the benches, and in the afternoon, they would go into town.

Jake beamed with anticipation, "OK, let's see the map."

Mindy pulled a folded, white piece of paper from her pocket. It was the fast-food bag on which Judy Berry had drawn a simple map containing Mrs. Birmingham's house, the two rows of cabins, and a series of paths that led to the large trees. Tree figures were drawn to represent each tree's canopy, and small rectangles marked the locations of the benches.

Jake studied the map. He saw that the "Giant Pine" bench was out past Inspiration Point. The "maple tree" bench was nestled behind the girls' cabins, and the "sweet gum" bench sat down a short path, just beyond the boys' cabins. The ancient "oak tree" bench was located at the Frog Pond, and finally, there was the "beech tree" bench in the middle of the Pine Grove.

Mindy smiled and nodded. She was obviously eager to get the expedition under way.

"We will set our mark point for the compass over there, where the mouth of the trail leads behind the last men's cabin," Jake asserted.

In Jake's small backpack were two bottles of water, a couple of bags of Peanut M&Ms, and some fresh fruit. He felt his pocket to make sure that he had his small camera. Mindy put Judy's map back into the pocket of her hiking shorts.

Like most paths through the woods, there was only enough room to walk single file. Jake turned towards Mindy and said, "So tell me about Judy Berry."

"I bumped into her while shopping the day before I came to camp. She drew me the map over lunch," Mindy said as she walked behind Jake. "Judy and my sister Kathy have been best friends since childhood. They were together at camp when they were young and served as cabin counselors in high school. The campers called my sister 'The General' ... and called Judy 'Juice.'"

"Juice?" Jake inquired.

"Judy was a riot, crazy ... in a fun way, always dreaming up pranks. All the *cool* girls wanted to be in Judy's cabin. But all the mothers wanted their daughters under the watchful eye of The General."

"And whose cabin were you in?"

"At first I was in with Kathy. Later they let me stay in with Judy. I think they put me in there so they would have a set of eyes behind the scenes. But I never ratted on her ... that would have ruined everything."

"What's with *The General*?" he asked.

"Well, if I were as sure about *anything* as she is about *everything*, I would be a confident girl. Kathy is tall and beautiful and strong, both physically and intellectually. I told you she was the volleyball and basketball star. She was homecoming queen the year Judy's boyfriend was homecoming king. Kathy inherited my mother's beauty and my father's athletic talent.

"The thing that made her *The General* was that she *always* knew the answer. Whenever there was a problem in the camp, she would solve it. The campers and Mrs. Birmingham respected that in her."

"I'd like to see a picture of your family."

"OK." Mindy nodded. "I'm sure Mrs. Birmingham has our last Christmas card."

"So … Judy gave you the parachute and the map, anything else?"

"Yes, advice. She warned me about jerks, good old boys, and Prince Charmings."

Jake grinned and wondered which category he fit in. "There it is! There is the sweet gum tree, and there is the bench," Jake exclaimed. He looked over his shoulder to catch Mindy smiling with delight.

Mindy sat on the bench as Jake surveyed the large tree. He looked back at Mindy. "What's the deal with the benches?"

"Bill, Judy, and Kathy were cabin counselors their junior and senior years in high school. Bill loved the forest and working with wood. So he pitched the idea to the Birminghams to map out a "tree identification trail" through Birmingham Forest. He agreed to build these benches as location markers. Each bench was named after the tree it is under."

"That sounds like a great idea."

"It was a great *idea* … but it went astray. In the daytime, the benches worked fine as rest stops for hikers. At night, they got to be make-out locations for kids who snuck out of their cabins."

Jake frowned. "Why didn't the counselors put a stop to it?"

"Some of the counselors were the worst offenders."

"Judy and Bill?" Jake asked.

"Yeah. You see, this sweet gum bench is where the boys took their girlfriends, and the bench behind the girls' cabin, under the giant maple tree, is where the girls took their boys. The other three benches were further off. Few campers hiked that far away from camp. There was an unspoken rule that the outlying benches were for the oldest campers and for counselors."

"Have you ever been to this bench before?" Jake asked with tender curiosity.

"I've hiked here many times. Do you mean with *a guy*?"

Jake nodded as he drew closer.

"No!" Mindy squirmed in her seat. "... Yes."

"Yes?" Jake's reply begged for an explanation.

"I came here with Elliott Rubin." Mindy hesitated. "We were both in seventh grade. He was a brilliant math student, a finalist in the National Science Awards. His parents must have sent him here to broaden his social skills. Elliott's dad and my dad worked together, so I'd known him for years. We were both really shy."

Mindy smiled. Her voice got softer as she shared the memory. "He was shaking in his boots when he approached me outside the dining hall. He could barely speak when he asked me if I wanted to take a walk. We walked to the bench in silence. I could tell that he had been put up to it by the other boys in his cabin.

"So I made it easy on him. I knew he liked me as a friend. In fact, I was kind of honored to have him trust me enough for this right of passage. He was so nervous; he couldn't say a word. I took his face in my hands, puckered up, and gave him a big kiss on the lips. I could feel the burden lift from his body. We walked back up the path, both with joy in our hearts. All he could say was 'thank you.' Ever since that day, his face lights up every time we see each other."

"Just once in the seventh grade?" Jake asked. His playful smile remained sympathetic.

Mindy's face turned down. She turned away. Her face revealed the rejection of every girl who has been passed over for an invitation to the prom. "I was not the kind of girl that boys wanted to take to the benches."

Jake was moved with compassion; the playfulness dropped out of his voice. "I'm sorry." His heart danced as he silently slid beside Mindy on the bench, gently placing his arm around her shoulder. His other hand touched the far side of her face and drew her face to his. He kissed her on the cheek. It was a swift peck; yet it was the kind of kiss that could make things all better. When he pulled away and opened his eyes, he could sense the delight in her face. "There. Now you can say that you have been to the sweet gum bench with Jake Olson, the hot shot from Ft. Wayne, Indiana."

Mindy blushed. "Thank you … that was very sweet of you."

Mindy paused and then said, "Jake, there are a few things you need to know about the camp's past. Judy and Bill were fun counselors, but their love affair set a bad precedent. The year after Judy and Bill left, the camp turned away from a Bible-teaching camp to a party camp. That was the year Carl Birmingham fell sick with cancer. Mrs. Birmingham grew increasingly preoccupied with caring for her husband, and she ignored the camp. Before that year, all of the counselors were in high school, and Mrs. Birmingham worked directly with them. The bad counselors that came in after my sister's generation literally destroyed the camp. You saw the results of their neglect when you arrived."

Mindy turned to face Jake. Her voice resonated with sternness. "God gave Mrs. Birmingham a vision to rebuild the camp. She needed someone she could trust, someone who would look after her and the best interest of the camp and campers. That is why she hired me. She also needed a man who was handy, someone who could fix things. This guy needed to be a strong Christian leader, someone who would be a moral mentor to the kids. That's why she hired you. I know Mrs. Birmingham added the 'romantic entanglements between campers and counselors are strictly forbidden' to the counselors' contract as a result of the mess the kids got in over the last few years."

Mindy drew a deep breath. "Jake, I need to tell you something." She peered directly into his eyes. "Whatever happens this summer, whatever happens between us … we *must* ensure that God is honored. We are here for Him and the campers."

Jake nodded. "I know." He took Mindy's hand and stood up. "Come on, we have other benches to find." They walked hand in hand until the clearing funneled into a single-file path. Jake took the lead. He set a course for the Frog Pond.

Jake wondered if he had imagined that Mindy had hesitated to let loose of his hand. He had never liked holding hands. He associated it with his mom's attempts to restrict his free motion when he was a rambunctious child. Somehow this was different. Mindy's hand was soft and warm. He could not shake the feeling of how snuggly her fingers had felt as they wrapped their palms together.

Jake replayed the kiss in his mind. He liked the way his arm felt around her slender, well-toned torso. He liked the way his palm felt against her face. But he really liked the way it felt when his nose and lips collided gently with her cheek. He savored the moment. Maybe he would turn around and kiss her again … no … maybe not. He couldn't take the chance that she might reject him and go running to tell Mrs. Birmingham that he had made a pass at her in the woods. No, he would have to keep his affection in check. Any further intrusion into the heart of Mindy Brice would be by her invitation.

Jake's blissful contemplation ended as the perception of danger grew more intense, as though a rattlesnake had coiled on the path in front of them. Even though it was unseen, he could sense its presence. He stopped.

One second later, Mindy came to an abrupt halt as she collided into his back. "Jake, what is it?" Mindy asked. She came around to his side. She looked surprised at the expression of deep concern on his face.

"What's the deal with the Frog Pond?" he asked.

"I don't know … rumor has it that it's haunted. Why?"

"A strange image just flashed in my mind of two skeletons lying in a sinkhole." Jake's eyes peered down the path.

"I'm getting a very creepy feeling. Can we go back?" Mindy asked.

"Sure. I think it's time for us to go into town."

They made their way back up the path, through the courtyard, and up to Mindy's car. After a short drive, they arrived at the Tasty Freeze and ordered. Mindy decided on a chocolate sundae. Jake ordered a malted chocolate shake.

As they enjoyed their ice cream, an old friend of Mindy's family walked up to meet them.

"Well, hello, Missy. It is nice to see you back in town. I have heard amazing things are happening at the camp this summer." Mr. Eller stopped at the edge of Mindy and Jake's table.

"Hello, Mr. Eller. Yes, it has been amazing. This is Jake Olson. He is the Senior Counselor for the boys," Mindy replied.

"Nice to meet you." Jake rose to shake Mr. Eller's hand.

"Jake and I were hiking down by the Frog Pond. We got a really creepy feeling. Jake thinks he perceived something evil," Mindy relayed.

"What exactly did you see?" Mr. Eller asked.

"A picture came to my mind … of a sinkhole … and on a rock shelf some ways down in the sinkhole were two skeletons," Jake said.

Mr. Eller stared at Jake. "Would you mind coming with me to the Mennonite church? They are having a prayer meeting there right now. I think they will be very interested in what you have seen."

Jake looked at Mindy. She nodded with approval.

"I will run the errands and catch up with you later." Mindy stood to walk to the shops in the center of town.

Mr. Eller led Jake to the church. They entered the sanctuary to find a small group of men praying.

"Good morning, Pastor. This is Jake Olson. He's the new counselor from camp. Jake perceived a vision of two skeletons in a sinkhole while he and Missy Brice were hiking in Birmingham forest."

The aging Pastor Shillinger turned from his conversation with the plain-clothed Sheriff Brown and placed his hand on Jake's shoulder. "Bless you for joining us on this day. Barbara Birmingham has told me of your fervent prayers the night of the tornado. This community has been plagued by two demons for a number of years. The Lord has blessed me with a word that our town will be the location of a training camp for extraordinary Christian leaders. A number of us have committed, with the Lord's help, to remove the demons from our midst. This must be done before the vision of the training camp can come to pass. Our Lord, Jesus Christ, removed demons by pronouncing commands, not with requests, not with pleas. If you're confident that your prayers will be effective, please pray with us. If you are doubtful, then you must leave this church immediately."

Jake nodded that he was staying.

Pastor Shillinger instructed Jake, "You must not be distracted. Concentrate … whisper this prayer without ceasing: In the name of Jesus Christ, demons be removed. IN THE NAME OF JESUS CHRIST, DEMONS BE REMOVED. If you should get into trouble, call for me immediately."

Jake lowered his head and walked past the men who were already kneeling at the altar and in the pews. He found an open space at the front of the church. Jake knelt down, formed his arms into a cross on the floor in front of him, and laid his forehead on top of them.

Jake prayed, "Lord give me strength. Keep me safe. It is in your name I pray, demons be removed. In the name of Jesus Christ, demons be removed …"

The church was silent except for the occasional moans and prayers of the faithful. Jake had only been praying for a few minutes when he heard what sounded like two large birds crashing into the stained-glass window to his left. A terrifying scratching and gnawing erupted. Jake tightened his focus on his prayer. *CRACK. CRASH.* Something broke through the stained-glass window. Pieces of glass ricocheted off wooden pews. A frantic, rampant swirling motion disturbed the sanctuary. With two loud thuds, like a pair of fists slamming into the wooden cross, the two spirits began to pry the cross off of its steel support bars with an agonizing screech.

Jake was tempted to look up, but he remained steadfast in his prayer. He perceived his fellow prayer warriors tightening their focus on the demons.

Finally, the creaking of bending steel ceased. The next thing Jake heard was the demons slamming into the stained glass window to his right. Again, there was a terrible clawing and scratching; only this time, the demons were trying with all earnestness to escape. *SMASH. CRASH.* Stained glass spewed on to the sidewalk that ran alongside the church.

Peace came upon the sanctuary.

Pastor Shillinger touched Jake on the shoulder. "It is finished. You can relax now."

Jake's shirt was drenched in sweat. He rolled on his side to survey the damage. He wondered if the pieces of stained glass could be collected to repair the two broken windows. The cross had been bent and slanted to one side.

Prayer warriors, each in turn, stood up and made their way to the altar. Pastor Shillinger instructed them to embrace in a huddle formation.

Then he said, "The Lord bless you and keep you; the Lord make his face shine upon you and be gracious to you; the Lord turn his face toward you and give you peace." Raising his hands heavenward, he said, "Go in peace, my brothers."

As the other men shuffled to the front door, Pastor Shillinger and Mr. Eller came alongside Jake. "We think it is time to find your sinkhole," Mr. Eller said.

Sheriff Brown lingered silently behind Jake, and then he paced out of the church.

CHAPTER 5

Sinkhole

MR. ELLER TURNED off Kellum Road and onto an old logging road that ran through Birmingham Forest. A hundred yards into the woods, he stopped his car in front of the shagbark hickory. Jake noticed that the tree had one base and two trunks. As Jake climbed out of the back seat, he snapped a few pictures so he could find the location later.

Mr. Eller pointed into the woods. "The path to the Frog Pond is right over there."

Pastor Shillinger got out of the passenger side of the car. "It's been many years since we've been to this spot."

Mr. Eller nodded his head.

Jake made no small talk; the gravity of the situation weighed heavily upon him. He slipped his left arm through the handles of two large duffle bags and then slipped his right arm through the coil of thick rappelling rope. The three walked down the path to where it forked.

Mr. Eller looked at Jake. "That path goes out to the Pine Grove, and this path leads to the Frog Pond."

In front of him, Jake could see a wall of tall, dense vegetation. *That must be the pond's edge.* A few steps further, the trunk of a huge oak tree became visible through the clearing created by the path. The base of the oak tree was at least nine feet in diameter. *This old giant must be between two and three hundred years old.* The tree's canopy created a natural clearing beneath it. A weathered, wooden bench sat next to the tree's base. Past the bench was the edge of a small pond. Jake paused to study the bench.

Pastor Shillinger and Mr. Eller walked to the pond's side. Jake watched as they stopped abruptly, stunned. Their mouths dropped open. Jake looked past them. He froze.

The pond was empty. The rocks and mud were still wet, but there was no water to be seen. The rock formation that was revealed reminded him of the cascading layers of a waterfall. Every five feet or so, the flat, horizontal planes were met by a one-or two-foot drop off. This pattern of downward stair-stepping circles ended abruptly at the crater, a sinkhole.

Jake tied the rope to the oak tree with a bowline knot. He walked past his guides, who stood on the edge of the rock and mud. "Pray for me?" Jake requested quietly.

Jake stepped carefully down through the rock formations. When he got to the edge of the sinkhole, he looked down. He could see the foot and leg of a skeleton lying on a ridge about twenty feet below the crater's rim. He lowered the rope down the side of the sinkhole to measure its depth.

Jake pulled the rope back. Carefully, he tied a series of knots in the rope, each about one foot from the last knot. He figured this would help him climb down and climb out. Jake prayed, "Sweet Lord and Savior, Jesus, protect me, give me strength, let me have the wisdom to handle these bones with the reverence that your children deserve."

Jake lowered himself into the pit. While still holding the rope, he set his feet down onto the rock shelf to test to see if it would sustain his weight, and then he lowered himself into a sitting position on top of the empty duffle bags. He paused long enough to snap a few pictures as he surveyed the skeletons. Their bodies were lying on their sides, on the floor of a cavity that receded ten feet into the wall of the crater. The toes of the larger body were only a few feet from where he sat. The skeletons faced each other, curled in relaxed, fetal positions.

A rush of tears welled up in Jake's eyes. *These two poor souls must have been holding each other until the very end.* He decided to start with the toes and systematically work his way up the skeleton. He opened the first duffle bag and started gently lifting the toe bones off the rock floor and placing them in the bag. Jake's fingers fumbled with what he knew was not a bone. It was a toe ring. He polished it with his fingers. His work revealed a silver ring inlayed with turquoise; in the blue stone was a pattern of a single, five-point star and two lightning bolts.

Jake placed the ring in the corner of the duffle bag. He worked his way up the skeleton. Tears streamed down his face as he apologized in his mind for disturbing the latter-day Romeo and Juliet. He prayed that they were in heaven … watching him with approval.

Jake zipped the first bag shut and tied the handles together with the rope. He pulled the other bag close to him and opened it. Then he started removing the bones in the hand of the smaller skeleton. Jake felt a second ring on the finger reserved for a wedding band. Wiping the mud off the ring revealed the same single star followed by a pair of lightning bolts. *I wonder what the pattern means?* Jake shook off the temptation to speculate about the circumstances surrounding the deaths of these two individuals. *Only the Lord knows.* He concluded that his job was to recover the bones.

After the smaller set of bones was securely placed in the bag, Jake took a deep breath. He leaned back against the wall of the sinkhole. He studied the crater that angled down and turned black as it curved off to the side. *Darkness was on the face of the deep,* he thought. A disturbing, dreadful fear came upon him. For the first time in his expedition, he realized that the water could, at any instant, come roaring back. *My sightseeing is over.*

Knot by knot, he climbed up the rope. He could hear the small rocks that broke loose as he climbed ricocheting off the sinkhole wall and then falling of into silence. As he poked his head over the crater's edge, he could see Mr. Eller and Pastor Shillinger praying face down on the shore.

As he walked away from the cliff's edge, pulling the rope over the crater's edge, the two duffle bags dragged against the sinkhole's wall. When both bags were securely on top of the ridge, Jake sat down. "Thank you, thank you, Lord, for guiding me and protecting me." After only a moment's rest, he stood, lifted the bags, and started his trek to the shoreline.

The duffle bags hit the dry bank with a thump. Mr. Eller and Pastor Shillinger looked up with great relief. Jake collapsed beside the bags to pray, "Heavenly Father you are the God of life and the God of healing; Jehovah Rapha, let these bones heal the pains and anguish of their families."

Jake had not seen Sheriff Brown approaching.

"What's going on here?" At that instant, the sheriff stopped and looked in horror at the empty pit before him. He walked to the pond's edge. "What in the heck is going on here? Where did the water go?" Sheriff Brown looked back at Pastor Shillinger and Mr. Eller, who sat speechless. Sheriff Brown looked at Jake, who was still sprawled next to the bags. "What's in the bags, young man?"

"Skeletons," Jake replied.

"Where did they come from?"

"I recovered them from a rock shelf about twenty feet below the rim of that sinkhole."

"Who gave you the authority to disturb human remains?" Sheriff Brown glanced at the duffle bags and then watched Jake for an answer.

"The Holy Spirit." Jake's voice stayed calm while his eyes stared directly at the sheriff. The sheriff looked at Pastor Shillinger and Mr. Eller, who nodded in agreement.

"How long has the water been gone from the pond?" Sheriff Brown turned to re-examine the wet expanse before him.

"It was already this way when we arrived," Pastor Shillinger said.

"Jake, why don't you show me *exactly* where you recovered the skeletons." Sheriff Brown walked out onto the wet rocks.

Jake got up and stepped quickly to catch up with the sheriff and then led him to the sinkhole's edge. "All I could see from here was the leg and foot of the larger set of bones. When I got down there, I saw that there were two bodies. They both were in a cavity in the wall of the sinkhole."

"What position were the skeletons in?"

"They were lying close together, facing each other, in relaxed, fetal positions." Jake cupped his hands close to each other. "The larger skeleton was on his left side, the smaller skeleton was on its right side."

"Did you see anything interesting down there?" Sheriff Brown squinted while searching the crater for details. "Geologists say there is a fault line in the bedrock that runs through this part of country. It may run right through the Birmingham's property."

"No. Once I got the bones in the duffle bags, I leaned against the wall to look around. The sinkhole curved down and off to the side. I could see only darkness. The realization that the water could rush in and overtake me made me *very* leery. So I climbed out as quickly as I could." Jake noticed Sheriff Brown drying a tear from his eye as he stood at the edge of the sinkhole.

"When I was about nine or ten, I was playing in the back of my family's property." Sheriff Brown wiped his eyes. "There was an old, overgrown apple orchard in the back corner. I was sneaking around playing army, like I was on an imaginary commando mission." Looking off to the side, Sheriff Brown stroked his chin. "I stumbled across an old man sitting next to an apple tree. It was Wabeno, the Native American medicine man. He was very old, and the sight of him scared the daylights out of me. I froze from fear ... held my breath.

"Wabeno gently smiled, reached down, and lobbed me one of the apples he had in his lap. He motioned for me to sit and eat my apple next to him. Although he didn't say it, I understood that he was not stealing *our* apples; he was sharing *his* apples. So I sat."

"I had heard stories of the wise and mysterious Wabeno. How he was one of the few Native Americans that still lived in the area. I knew that he and a few of his relatives lived on the land behind the far corner of our property. When I finished the apple, I stood, nodded, and quietly said, 'Thank you.'

45

"Have you ever had an experience where you're not sure if it was a ghost or dream?" Sheriff Brown turned to Jake. "I finally got the courage to tell my dad about the encounter. He assured me that it was not a ghost. Wabeno lived with a recluse named Jeremiah Slough, an eccentric artist who lived in the hills behind our property. He told me to show the old man the upmost respect, because there was a vein of Native American blood that ran through our family.

"For the rest of that fall, I returned often to the spot next to the apple tree. On occasion, Wabeno would be there. Sometimes he would tell me stories of his ancestors and of a glade in the nearby woods that was a sacred location for his people. This clearing marked the location of the *healing trees*, where natives of different tribes would come to heal their sick." Sheriff Brown paused and then continued, "Then the settlers came ... and between their guns and their diseases, they wiped out almost every trace of the tribes.

"As the season ended, I took a bushel basket full of the best apples I could find and left it in the spot where we always met. I checked back a few times; each time, a few more apples were missing. Then, on a bright, brisk day, I found the bushel basket had been over turned. I guess that he had finished eating all the apples. When I picked up the bushel to take it home, I noticed there was a leather cross, embroidered with beads, lying under it. Somehow ... out of nowhere ... Wabeno appeared, standing next to me."

"He told me of a time when he was a grown man. That he had fallen deathly sick, and the Slough family took him in and nursed him back to health. It was in that time that Wabeno accepted Jesus as his Savior. He told me that the symbol of the three-armed whirlpool pattern at the center of the cross revealed the Father, Son, and Holy Ghost."

Sheriff Brown pointed to the sinkhole. "Wabeno told me of 'the abyss ... the water well that had no end,' which marks the line of *healing trees*. He told me, 'When the abyss is revealed the years of peace and prosperity will come to an end.' Wabeno spoke, trembling with terror, of the destruction and suffering that the great demon will bring against the earth.

"After a short silence, Wabeno smiled … with tears in his eyes and whispered, 'I am one of the fortunate ones. I will be in the arms of my Savior and will not endure the calamity. Yet in that time of great suffering, the Lord will bring his children to the healing trees as a place of comfort and refuge. My son, if you are to survive during the time of tribulation, you must draw close to the Lord, allow the Holy Spirit to direct your path.' When I looked around … he was gone. That was the last time I saw Wabeno."

Sheriff Brown drew in a long breath. "Has the Holy Spirit given you any insights concerning what I just told you?"

Jake shook his head. "My instructions, as far as the sinkhole, were to recover the skeletons. I did get a vision on the night of the tornado that I was to prepare a training camp for spiritually gifted youth. I'm not sure how to go about it or when it is to be completed. Pastor Shillinger, Mrs. Birmingham, and Mindy have all perceived versions of the vision. I guess I'll keep praying."

Sheriff Brown and Jake walked back to the shoreline to rejoin Pastor Shillinger and Mr. Eller.

"Jake, you have done a great service to the community by recovering these remains. When the deaths occurred, we assumed this was a shallow mud hole. We walked the perimeter and across the center. We had no idea the sink hole was there." Sheriff Brown looked back over the empty pond. "We did know that drowning victims float. We checked back every few weeks and found nothing. The fact that the bodies were trapped in a cavity in the sinkhole wall explains why the bodies never surfaced. We assumed the kids staged the drowning and skipped town to elope.

"This recovery needs to be handled very quietly." Sheriff Brown shook his head. "I don't want any sightseers or reporters to come looking for adventure. It will be better if I claim that I found the remains. That will keep Jake from being tangled up in this mess. I'll turn the remains into the coroner, then drop by Mrs. Birmingham's to brief her on the matter."

Sheriff Brown shook Jake's hand. "Good luck with your camp. Let me know if there's anything I can do to help you."

With a nod to Pastor Shillinger and Mr. Eller, Sheriff Brown picked up the two duffle bags and headed up the hill to his car.

Jake looked over to Mr. Eller and Pastor Shillinger for assurance. They nodded with approval. Jake stepped to the edge of the pond. He started pulling in the rest of the rope and turned around to address Pastor Shillinger and Mr. Eller. "Is that Sheriff reliable?"

"Yes, he has been a member of my church for many years. He's a good Christian man," Pastor Shillinger said. "He headed the investigation when the two kids disappeared. The police could not find the bodies; the mud was too thick. As long as I remember, campers have been hiking out here. Never has there been a report of the pond being empty."

Mr. Eller looked at the young man he had met only a few hours before. "Thank you, Jake, for your act of courage and compassion. Maybe now the feuding families can heal. You see, when no one could find the bodies, we chose to believe that the kids staged the drowning to skip town and elope. Each family blamed the other for leading their child astray. Both of the kids' diaries were filled with schemes to break free."

Pastor Shillinger added, "Ron Montgomery, the larger skeleton, was a hothead. His family had plenty of money. He, unfortunately, used his resources for fast living and drugs. The Capp's girl was from a good Christian family. Julie Capp was a cute, bright kid, but she grew reckless and rebellious in her teen years. Their families could not stand the idea that their kids were in love. The forbidden love affair bore a hatred that tore the community apart. Those two had been a train wreck waiting to happen ever since they met at Camp Koinonia. Their disappearance happened in the fall, after the camp had closed. During the police investigation, wine bottles, drug paraphernalia, and Ron's and Julie's clothes were found on the bank of the Frog Pond. Without the bodies, no charges were ever filed. Everyone knew that the Birminghams had nothing to do with it."

"Let's gather our things and get out of here." Mr. Eller glanced over at the pond. He gasped, "The water! It's back!" The three men marveled at the water that had returned silently in the span of a few moments. "It's a miracle ... the water is crystal clear."

"Praise the Lord."

Mr. Eller backed his car down the logging path and onto Kellum Road, then up the short jog and into Camp Koinonia. He let Jake out next to the path that led from the parking lot to the camp yard. "Thank you, Jake, for all your efforts today."

"You are always welcome in my church." Pastor Shillinger's voice conveyed victorious fatigue.

"Thank you both." Jake walked out of the parking lot and into the tree-lined path darkened by the setting sun. As he entered the camp yard, he consciously observed the tree tops of the sweet gum and giant maple as they protruded over the rest of the forest. His steps slowed, then stopped.

Jake looked around the camp yard that formed an open space surrounded by forest. *A glade in a nearby forest ... a line of healing trees marked by the abyss.* Jake turned and ran back into the center of the parking lot. He searched the horizon in the direction of the Frog Pond, but his line of sight was blocked by the trees at the parking lot's edge. *I have got to get off the ground.*

He searched the opposite side of the parking lot for a tree to climb. *Great, that old pine tree will be easy.* Jake scrambled up the regularly spaced rows of branches. Nearing the top, he scanned the horizon. *There it is! The oak at the Frog Pond.* He searched the forest for the tallest tree in the distance. *And that must be the beech tree in the Pine Grove.* Jake felt in his pocket for his camera. *I can't believe I forgot to tell the sheriff about the pictures I took at the sinkhole. It might be better if I keep them to myself.* Jake climbed to the highest limb that would support his weight. He captured a series of panoramic shots. *It's amazing how those few trees tower over the rest of the forest.*

In his mind, Jake pictured Mindy's map. He drew a line from the distant beech tree to the oak at the Frog Pond to the sweet gum and maple by the cabins. The line cut through the camp yard and then extended through Inspiration Point and ended at Giant Pine. *I need to get a copy of Mindy's map. Wonder how I would get hold of Jeremiah Slough. Wonder what he'll think about all of this?* Jake shook his head as he noticed that pine sap covered his hands. *First things first. I need to climb down, get cleaned up, get some dinner, and then get some sleep.*

CHAPTER 6

Morning Coffee

MRS. BIRMINGHAM CALLED Jake on his cell phone about 7:30 A.M.

"Good morning, Jake. Did I wake you?"

"Oh no, I've been up. How can I help you?"

"I was wondering if you would come up to the house for a few minutes so we can talk."

"Sure, I'm on my way." Jake returned his phone to his pocket and hustled up the path to the house. Champ greeted him with a few friendly barks as he stepped up to the back screen door. With two soft knocks, Jake called, "Good morning."

"Please come in. I'm in the kitchen."

Jake scratched Champ behind the ears, then made his way to the kitchen.

"Would you like a cup of coffee?"

"Yes, please."

Mrs. Birmingham poured coffee into the cup that was already on the table. "Please sit down." Jake complied.

"I sent Mindy to the town early this morning. With tomorrow being opening day, we needed to get an early start." Mrs. Birmingham sipped her coffee. "Jake, I know this last week has been a whirlwind. I want you to know how proud I am of you and the contribution you have made to Camp Koinonia."

Jake beamed. "Thank you. It's been my pleasure."

Her smile faded. "I spoke to Sheriff Brown last night. He told me about the prayer meeting at church and the skeletons you found in the sinkhole." She slouched in her chair as a look of sadness consumed her. "Ronnie and Julie disappeared over ten years ago. With you being new to the area, you have no idea the turmoil and division that fiasco caused. Before the accusations and feuding were over, the entire community was in an uproar."

Mrs. Birmingham sighed. "I want you to understand that we *cannot* allow what happened yesterday to adversely affect our mission to provide a Christ-centered camp for the kids who are scheduled to show up this summer. I am asking you to not let *the sinkhole* be one of those stories that counselors tell their campers around the campfire. I'm not sure how this will all play out, but Sheriff Brown assures me that with the coroner's investigation and the cold-case paperwork, the news of this recovery may take weeks and maybe even months to reach the public. I'm sure you realize we do not need kids sneaking around the property in search of the *sinkhole*." Mrs. Birmingham studied Jake's face, obviously looking for affirmation.

"I understand." Jake nodded.

"Sheriff Brown mentioned how he thought the sinkhole might be related to an ancient Native American legend about a group of healing trees. I have to admit that I don't know anything about it. The natives all but disappeared from this part of the state a long time ago. I do know that this land has been the private property of the Birmingham family for almost 200 years. It was developed as a logging and mining business owned by the Birminghams and the Watsons, who are our neighbors to the west. If my husband, Carl, were still alive, he could give you the family history." She turned her face to the side.

In the pause, Jake took his first drink.

"The Lord has had his hand on this camp for as long as there have been campers. I've seen souls saved, broken bones restored, burns healed, an outbreak of the flu stopped in its tracks, and violent storms vanish. You know as well as I do that our Lord and Savior, Jesus Christ, is the provider of all these miracles. It has nothing to do with the trees."

Mrs. Birmingham looked directly at him. "Jake, let's focus our energy on the future, on the camp at hand, on the campers, and not glorify ancient wise tales."

"OK," Jake concurred.

"I'm sorry this turned out to be more of a lecture than a discussion. I've wrestled with this talk all night. Do you have any questions?"

"I only have one ... what are you going to tell Mindy about the skeletons in the sinkhole?"

"Well, I was going to wait to see if you had told her anything."

"No. I haven't talked to her yet."

"I'll talk to her about it when she gets back. She needs to know." Mrs. Birmingham reached into her purse, retrieved a business card from Sheriff Brown, and handed it to Jake. "I would like you to enter the sheriff's number into your cell phone in case there's an emergency."

"I'll do it right away." Jake took the card from Mrs. Birmingham's hand.

"So ... is everything going to be ready for the cabin-counselor orientation and the shareholder's tour tomorrow?"

"I assure you, everything will be ready."

"Thank you, Jake. I have the utmost confidence in your and Mindy's abilities. I guess you're ready for your breakfast."

"Yes, thank you for your honesty and openness. I'll have a full report ready for our 3:00 P.M. staff meeting. Excuse me."

Jake walked through the house, out the door, and down the path.

Well … that settles that. Guess I won't be tracking down Jeremiah Slough. Not any time soon. It sure seems like there's a lot more going on in this little community than meets the eye.

OK, I have seven hours; better organize my project notes over breakfast and then schedule my top priorities.

Better make sure I have a clean camp shirt, shorts, and clean shoes for the stakeholder's tour … and memorize all their names and all the names for the cabin counselor orientation … and …

CHAPTER 7

Prank

JAKE POINTED OUT to the group of the camp stakeholders the new paint and improvements to the dining hall and shower facility. He took his time at the girls' cabins, highlighting the recently color-coordinated window frames and bunk beds. Secretly, he was stalling to allow the youth time to get the paint spill cleaned up in the boys' cabin.

It was the Saturday before the camp opened on Sunday. Jake wondered if it had been a good idea to let the camp stakeholders, the group of people who had been so generous with their giving to the camp, tour the camp on the same day the six cabin counselors were doing the final painting of the cabins.

Mindy met the group at the girls' cabins. With a wink and a nod, she silently indicated to Jake that the mess was under control. Jake and Mindy led the group of impressed stakeholders to the courtyard in front of the boys' cabins.

Out from the cabins, the team of youth burst. They scrambled into a line, each with a wet paintbrush in their hands. Each bore the insignia of a wet handprint of paint on the upper-left section of their shirts. They stood stiffly, at attention, without expression, with their still-wet palm print testifying to their solidarity.

The group of stakeholders eyed the group of youths with suspicion, smiled, and nodded to each other as they moved to the shelter of one of the nearby cabins.

"The painters' corps is ready for inspection," Zeke barked.

Jake knew Zeke was the self-appointed leader of the six cabin counselors. He was surprised and yet flattered by their gesture. "I want to thank you all for the outstanding job you've done for Camp Koinonia. I can only hope that the kids that go through camp this summer will inherit your sense of dedication and teamwork." Jake started to choke up as he spoke. He was truly moved by the cabin counselors' acts of service.

"Permission to be dismissed, *sir*?" requested Zeke.

"Well, after you clean up ..."

Before Jake could finish his sentence, the group of youth exploded into laughter and cat calls as they threw their paint brushes and rollers in the air. Zeke pitched his paint-soaked roller directly to Jake and then dashed off. The kids laughed and yelled and ran as fast as they could up the hill. The crowd of adults snickered with laughter.

Jake's soul soured. After he had poured out his heart to them, they had betrayed him. Anger tightened Jake's gut. He turned to Mindy. With his back to the parents, he faced her. He could not believe his eyes; Mindy was laughing at him. If she had been a boy in front of him, he might have struck her down. Having the youth act in such a disrespectful manner was one thing. He had reduced them to mere children in his mind. As for Mindy, that was another matter. Mindy's delight over her deliberate betrayal hurt him to the core. *After all I have done for her and the camp. They are all going to pay for this stunt. I'll see to it.*

"Why are you laughing at me?" Jake snapped.

Mindy looked up. "Jake, you are scaring me." Stepping to Jake's side, her hands gently grabbed him by the shoulders. "Jake, snap out of it ... it was just a prank. I am not laughing *at* you ... I am laughing *with* you."

"I'm *not* laughing!"

"Haven't you ever been pranked?" she asked.

"No ... pranks only lead to resentment and to a cycle of revenge. Why did you set me up for this?" Jake asked with troubled disbelief.

Jake saw Mindy's saddened face. He glanced over his shoulder to see that the adults had dispersed into the cabins. He appreciated that they had the grace to give him a little time to work through the misunderstanding.

"Jake, I did not set you up. When I brought the paper towels down, they were all working to clean up the mess and finish up the work before the inspection. I will admit that I knew they were scheming something. My only part was to ensure that you came down to the courtyard."

Jake looked at her as he shook his head. "'I did not set you up' and 'my part was to lead you down the path' sound like a contradiction and an admission of guilt."

Mindy inhaled, "OK ... I was part of the prank. I knew they were planning a prank, and I did lead you down the path. I'm sorry ... I'm sorry that their stunt hurt you so badly." She came around to face him. Their eyes met.

"Pranks are an act of affection," Mindy asserted. "The best pranks are never hostile, never mean-spirited. I will tell you something from the bottom of my heart. They only prank the ones they love, and they devise the best pranks for the ones they love the most.

"Zeke is a master prankster," Mindy continued. "One time, he put a live snake in Bob Peterson's boot. Yes, Zeke had to do a number of extra chores around the camp, but that was the summer that Bob and Zeke developed a bond that is still strong today."

Mindy peered into Jake's eyes. "If you want to develop into the finest counselor this camp has ever seen, you will have to learn how to appreciate being pranked. Jake, before the summer is over, you will be able to smell a prank a mile away. If you fight back, if you retaliate, you will ruin it for us and, more importantly, for all of the campers. Please, Jake, find it in your heart to forgive them." Mindy leaned close to Jake's ear. "Welcome to Camp Koinonia ... your initiation is now complete," she whispered.

Jake coaxed a reluctant smile onto his face. His anger melted away. Little Miss Brutus was reinstated as the most noble Roman.

Then Jake and Mindy led the tour down to the newly renovated beach area and council fire ring.

At the end of the long day, Jake watched Mindy accompany the stakeholders to the parking lot. He turned to Zeke and Lex to discuss the upcoming camp session. "Lex, I would like to offer you the facilities manager's position."

Zeke, in a great burst of exhilaration, grabbed Jake in one arm and Lex with the other and gave them both a rousing bear hug.

"I'll take it!" Lex cheered.

After a series of high fives and back slaps, Jake dismissed the two guys. "I'll see you both tomorrow morning."

"Bright and early," Lex replied.

Jake could see Mindy across the camp yard, waving good-bye to the last of the stakeholders. He made his way down the path to the dock.

He had known Mindy for only one week, and so much had happened. He reflected on the meteor shower, the tornado, the skeletons in the sinkhole, and the incredible amount of money and resources that had poured in from the community and former campers. The last six days had been extraordinary. Jake looked back over his shoulder. He could see Mindy standing at the path to Inspiration Point. Her relaxed, pleasant smile drew him. He walked quickly off the dock and up the path to meet her. As they met, they wrapped each other in a bear hug and held each other for a long time.

Jake whispered in Mindy's ear, "Congratulations, Miss Brice. Your camp is at last ready for opening day. Tomorrow at 2:00, this place will be packed with campers and parents."

"Thank you, Mr. Olson, for all you've done. I couldn't have done it without you," she whispered back.

"You're welcome. It was my pleasure." They pulled only far enough apart to see each other's faces.

"I trust you're going to *rest* for the remainder of the evening," Mindy said with a pleasant assertiveness.

"Well ... I have just enough energy to dig out the box of Epsom salt from my locker and pour myself a hot bath. I think I'll sleep in the house tonight. Those pranksters wrecked my cabin room. How about you?"

"It sounds like I better get to the house for a shower before you do. Then I'll probably read and check e-mails. Oh, I almost forgot. I got a call from Mrs. Birmingham while I was in the parking lot. She planned to cook dinner for us to night. She said she was sorry, but she's exhausted and is turning in for the night. Why don't you come down after you bathe, and I'll fix us something." Mindy's face beamed.

"Great."

Mindy slid her hands from around Jake's neck until they cupped his face. She drew him near and gave him a soft kiss on the cheek. "Thank you for everything."

Jake wanted to hold her … to keep her from leaving, but the gentleman in him let her slip away. He wondered what she was thinking when she kissed him in that way. He suspected that her kiss was her way of letting him know that she was not holding ill feelings over his cross words. He was grateful for that.

Jake watched Mindy walk up the path to the house. She paused to look over her shoulder. She winked as she flashed him a smile, then turned and made her way up the path to the house on top of the hill.

That girl can really get me going. She can launch me off into bliss or grind me into a rage. I've got to be careful. I know she is rebounding from breaking up with her boyfriend. I have to keep reminding myself that this camp is about honoring God and mentoring the campers. Jake glanced up the empty path to Mrs. Birmingham's house. *I need to control my emotions. I'm already starting to like her way too much.*

For Jake, it was a long walk up the path to the big, white house. He was exhausted and sore from the week of physical labor. He thought back to the phone calls he had made just a few hours before. The first call was to Bob Peterson, then one to Mrs. Birmingham, and the last to Lex's parents. Jake had been arranging for Lex to be offered the job of facilities manager. This was the first time a teen had been offered the position. Lex would be a paid staff member. He would be given a written list of weekly duties and a daily schedule of tasks to do. Bob would oversee the initial training, and then Jake would follow up with Lex at the end of each day. Lex would be given a cell phone so he could be in touch with Bob Peterson and the other members of the camp's staff. Lex had worked alongside his father, who was a plumber and handyman. He was now ready to head up his own projects.

Jake climbed his way to the second-floor bathroom. He soaked in the hot tub for as long as he could stand it, and then he headed for the master bedroom. He laid his weary body down across the still-made bed. He had decided to rest a minute before he ventured downstairs for dinner. Deep sleep came upon him.

Through his motionless slumber, Jake perceived a dinner plate and drinking glass being placed on the hope chest at the foot of his bed. Mindy sat gently on the bed and combed his still-wet hair through her fingers. She whispered in his ear, "I made you a sandwich for dinner."

Jake stirred, smiled, and whispered, "You are my angel. Thank you." They sat on the hope chest as he devoured half of the sandwich. "I was really hungry. Thank you again." He picked up the sandwich's other half.

"Jake, can I talk to you about something?"

"Sure." Jake put the sandwich down.

"Did you have a bad experience in your childhood … when someone pranked you?" Mindy asked.

"Yes," he replied reluctantly. "My older brother used to scare me all the time. He used to have a lot of fun jumping out from behind trees and in dark rooms to startle me. My parents didn't think anything of it. I hated it. I hated him for it. It got to the point where I would hit and kick him as hard as I could to make him stop. At first, it only encouraged him to torment me more. It was only when I got strong enough to inflict pain on him that the teasing stopped."

Jake tried to contain the pain and anger that swelled inside of him. "You know, I am really trying to adjust my attitude about the whole pranking issue. But as far as I am concerned, I will be a champion for the victims. Somehow, I will rally them to inflict a few pranks on the stronger, more popular campers. Then we'll see who has the last laugh."

Jake's body tensed like an angry, cornered cat. He wasn't about to let her laugh at his pain, like she had done earlier that afternoon. "I get the feeling that *you* have enjoyed a place of privilege here at Camp Koinonia, with your mother, sister, and Mrs. Birmingham watching out for you." His eyes grew fierce. "How many times have *you* watched with glee while someone else got pranked? How many times have *you* been the victim of a so-called *really funny prank?*" He stood and brushed past her. His words lashed out at her. "'The world is a dangerous place, not because of those who do evil, but because of those who *look on and do nothing.*' I did not make that up; Albert Einstein wrote that." Tears came to Mindy's eyes. He could tell his words had ripped through her heart.

"If there are victims, then it is not a prank. It is something else. It is something horrible, something unacceptable. If there are victims, then I can't tolerate it either." Mindy wiped her tears off with the back of her hand. "Thank you for sharing your heart with me," she whispered.

Jake walked over to the window. "I'm sorry I went off on you like that. I am wrestling with the line that separates humiliation and humility. I know in humility … there is wisdom."

"Jake, I now see you as the protector of the underdogs. 'Blessed are those who hunger and thirst for righteousness, for they will be filled,'" she said. "I now understand that this blessing is not intended for the haughty self-righteous, who are convinced that they are holier than all the rest. Nor is it for the Bible-toting hypocrites, who preach a strict standard of performance, yet whose lives are lived in sharp contrast to the teachings of Jesus. This blessing is for those who *hunger and thirst,* for those who were genuinely seeking the Way. Jake, you may be stepping back and forth over the line that separates humiliation and humility, but at least your feet tread firmly on the path to Jesus."

Mindy walked to where Jake's body slumped with his back to her. She gently slid her hands under his arms and cupped the front of his shoulders with her palms. She laid her head on his back. "I can tell that something has changed. I could tell by the way you looked at me just a minute ago. Something has changed in your heart. I want to understand it. Please ... Jake, let me hear what is in your heart."

Jake took a deep breath. "I feel like a hired hand. I feel like a hired hand who has just mistreated the plantation owner's favorite daughter. I have to keep reminding myself of the job I was hired to do. I came here to teach the youth teamwork, mutual respect, loyalty ... and most of all, to show the face of Jesus in all situations. I have failed at that; I failed in front of the youth, in front of the stakeholders, and now, once again, in front of you. I can't stand the thought of encouraging the kids to excel in horseplay. I cannot stand by and watch the clever ones extract their pleasure at the expense of the few. I am sorry if I hurt your feelings. You don't deserve that. You don't deserve any of this." Jake's head bowed as he wept.

"Jake, if you insist on seeing yourself as a hired field hand, then see me as a handmaiden who milks the cows and bakes the bread. See me as the humble nanny who teaches the children their Bible verses. But please, Jake, don't condemn me in your heart to a sentence as the plantation owner's daughter, not until you know what is in my heart. That is not fair to me. That is not fair to either of us. I want to be on the same side as you. I want to be with you, Jake."

Jake turned around to Mindy. Her face was filled with compassion, with peace, with strength. He would never forget the countenance that shined back at him.

"This evening has not turned out the way I had planned," Mindy pleaded. "Can we go back ... back to the point where I whispered in your ear ... back to the point where you awoke and you called me your angel?"

"Yes ... yes, of course ... we can go back."

Mindy leaned into Jake. She wrapped her arms around his shoulders. Her head settled against his neck as she prayed, "Thank you Jesus for healing the hurt feelings between us. Lord, I pray that all of our actions will be pleasing in your sight. Bless this camp and the campers who will attend it. Amen."

CHAPTER 8

Zeke

ZEKE WAITED FOR Jake outside the tool shed. It was the Wednesday morning of the first week of camp. Each counselor and camper had been assigned a service project. *The other cabin counselors are busy with yard work. I wonder what my chore is going to be?* he thought to himself. *I hope Jake is not going to have me clean out the tool shed.* Zeke peered into the shed's window. *This may look like a mess ... but it's all great stuff. I can't believe the new guy would have the nerve to pitch what he doesn't know the value of.*

Jake seems cool enough, but he needs me. Zeke's ego inflated as he pondered. *I've been everywhere in the camp. I know everything about it. Yeah ... I'll impress him. He'll soon learn who the #1 guy is around here. I wonder if he's still stinging from the great paint mutiny? I guess I got him good. It sure seems that everyone's a little too well behaved. Guess I better stir things up.*

"Zeke, I would like for us to work together this afternoon." Jake rounded the corner with a brisk walk.

"Sure, what's up?" Zeke returned.

"I'd like to check the trails out to the Frog Pond and then onto Pine Grove."

"Great."

"After the campers finish cleaning the dining hall and shower facility, Mindy is going to teach the campers their Bible application session. Mrs. Birmingham has Lex and the other cabin counselors doing yard work. I thought we would walk the trails out to the Frog Pond and then out to Pine Grove. I want to make sure the paths are free of fallen trees."

"Uh ... you might want to skip the Frog Pond," Zeke said with dread in his voice.

"Why?" Jake smiled.

"It's been really weird down there ... you know, haunted."

"You're not afraid of ghosts ... are you?" Jake asked.

"Well, no. I bet you'll freak out before you get all the way down there."

Jake unlocked the tool shed door and walked in. "Choose your weapon." Jake offered Zeke his choice of a handsaw or ax.

Zeke smiled as he lifted the ax out of Jake's hand. Rubbing his thumb over the ax's sharp edge, he asked, "Have you met Bob Peterson? He's the man you have to thank for this well-stocked tool shed."

"Yeah. He's helped me a ton already. He is a walking encyclopedia on the camp and its facilities."

"Mr. Peterson is a great guy. I'm glad you gave Lex the job of facilities manager. I know he'll do a great job." Zeke hoisted the ax to his shoulder.

Jake pointed across the camp yard. "I'll let you lead. You know where the benches are. Take the best path for the campers."

Zeke and Jake walked across the camp yard and entered the path into the woods.

"Benches? How do you know about *the benches*?" Zeke inquired.

"Mindy told me."

"Mindy?" Zeke chuckled. "What does she know about the benches? She's such a sweetie pie. She's probably never been to the sweet gum tree." Zeke tried to ignore Jake's frown. "I've known Mindy for a long time. Our families go way back. She's a few years older, but we were here during the same camp sessions. Mindy really blossomed at Northwestern. I asked her if she had been working out. She told me she swam every morning with her friend on the swim team. Hey, do you think she'll be the lifeguard again this year? I bet she looks great in a bathing suit." Zeke pondered her figure. "Jake, do you want me to show you the sweet gum bench?" Zeke led Jake through the forest. "It's down that path, behind the boys' cabins."

"No. Mindy took me there a few days ago."

They shared smiles.

"Here's the old logging road. It runs from Kellum Road down to the beach area, then weaves around to the back side of Birmingham Forest, then onto the Watson's property. These woods are lined with logging roads. Most of them have grown over." Zeke and Jake walked at a brisk pace down the path.

"OK, here we are." They marveled at the massive oak tree on the edge of the Frog Pond. "That's funny; it doesn't seem haunted anymore." Zeke was astonished. "I can feel the … peace."

"Haunted?" Jake struggled to keep a straight face as he made himself at home on the bench.

"Yeah, a number of years ago, some kids disappeared. Some think they drowned in the Frog Pond; others think they faked the drowning and eloped. Far as I know, no one's ever heard from them. Strange things started happening. Even the camp went through a downturn."

Zeke turned to watch Jake as he stared out over the pond. "Were you the *newcomer* at the church when the demons broke in and bent the cross?"

"Yep."

"You were down here when they found the skeletons at the bottom of the pit?"

"This pit does not have a bottom." Jake withheld comment, and there was a moment of awkward silence. Then he stated, "I recovered the remains of Ronnie Montgomery and Julie Capp from a rock ledge twenty feet down the sink hole that is out there in the middle of the Frog Pond."

Zeke's mouth dropped. He waited for Jake to laugh and tell him it was a joke. Jake's face bore the validity of his claim.

"So … when you got to the Frog Pond, all the water had been pulled back." Zeke's voice quivered. He was feeling shaken. "How'd you get the skeletons out?"

"A rappelling rope and two large duffle bags. How do you know about all this?" Jake asked.

"I overheard Mr. Eller talking to my grandpa. Mr. Eller wanted to know if Mr. Birmingham had ever mentioned anything to Grandpa about the Frog Pond being empty."

"Had it ever been empty?" Jake stood and took one last look at the water.

"No. But this is the first time I've seen the Frog Pond with clear water." Zeke pointed to the cascading rock formations on the pond's floor.

Jake glanced at his watch and motioned for them to proceed to the Pine Grove. A few minutes past the Frog Pond, they came to a tree blown across the path. They climbed on the fallen trunk to observe a path of devastation through the forest.

"Good call on bringing the saw and ax." Zeke sliced the ax into the tree trunk.

"Thanks." Jake kicked the trunk, checking to see if there was any pressure that would pinch his saw blade. "I could see this tornado path from the satellite photo I downloaded after the storm."

"Satellite photo?" Zeke smiled and shook his head in amazement. "You thought far enough ahead to pack a rope and duffle bags the day you pulled the bodies out. And now you tell me that you downloaded satellite photographs of the tornado damage. I guess that's why Mrs. Birmingham made you the boss."

"Why don't you chop off the limbs, and I'll cut the trunk. Then we can swing the log off the trail." Jake positioned his saw on the trunk and began cutting. Within minutes, the tree had been cleared from the path.

"Do you think we're about fifty yards past the pond?" Jake asked as he put his saw down and reached into his pocket.

"Yeah, why?"

"I want to mark the storm path on this trail map." Jake pulled his copy of Mindy's map out of his pocket.

"Trail map?" Zeke studied the map. His eyes widened as they locked on the bottom corner. "Who drew this?"

"Judy Berry drew it for Mindy."

"Judy … so Juice Kramer married Wild Bill Berry. Wow." Zeke studied one corner of the map.

"What is it?" Jake followed Zeke's line of sight onto the map.

"Inspiration Point and Giant Pine, have you ever been there?" Zeke asked.

"Mindy and I watched the meteor shower out there on my second night at the camp."

Zeke grinned, "So … Mindy took you to Inspiration Point in the middle of the night and then to sweet gum bench. She's your ticket to adventure."

Jake's frown warded off any further inquiries.

"Let's go out to the Giant Pine after we finish this path," Zeke insisted.

"Zeke," Jake shook his head, "it's on the other side of the property. You can go there in your free time. It's not far from the camp, and there is a logging road out to the point. You must be able to see the tall pine from out on the end of the point."

"I would have to go with you," Zeke said. "That area is off limits to campers. Did Mrs. Birmingham know you were out there?"

"Uh, I don't know. Mindy only mentioned that it had been a place where her mom and dad would go back to when they were cabin counselors."

Jake and Zeke continued down the path to Pine Grove.

"Jake, what made you decide to come to Camp Koinonia?" Zeke asked.

"Well, it all started when I was handed a case study in my Business Management class back at Taylor. The case presented a summer camp that had failed. It was my job as a consultant to turn it around.

"Anyway," Jake continued, "I spent way too much time and energy on it. Shortly after I got the grade, Dr. Ransokoff called me into his office. He had arranged a phone interview with Mrs. Birmingham. When she made me the offer, something in my soul urged me to take it. I felt like the Holy Spirit handpicked me for the job." Jake looked skyward. "I got here the week before camp started. It's been crazy, to say the least. How about you?"

"You know, Jake, my grandpa is the spiritual giant in our family. He called me over to help him clean out his garage. I could tell he had something on his mind, like he was going to ask me to do something, something important, something between just him and me." Zeke cleared his throat.

"Grandpa looked at me and said, 'The realm of the spirit world is in turmoil. The reins are being passed from the elders to the youth. You are going to be given an opportunity to make a great difference in the service of Jesus Christ. Watch for it. You are the only one that will recognize it; you are the only one who can accept it. Cling to the Lord; listen for the Holy Spirit to lead you. One day in the near future, the evil one will bring a worldwide calamity upon the earth. On the day the cities are desolated, you will find refuge beneath the Giant Pine.'

"Grandpa wept. I couldn't help but think, *I'm just a big, dumb jock, what could Jesus want with me?* I guess I'll understand it better when the Holy Spirit reveals it to me.

"A couple of days later, I got a letter from Mrs. Birmingham, offering me the job at Camp Koinonia. I knew in my heart that this was my opportunity. I too felt handpicked for the job." Zeke looked at Jake. He now knew they were both part of some divine scheme.

Jake said, "You know your Grandpa's advice: 'Cling to the Lord. Let the Spirit guide you,' that's the best advice on the face of the earth. You know, the Lord always reveals his prophesies in parts so that believers have to work together to get it right.

"The Lord has revealed to me that I am to prepare the camp for a group of spiritually gifted youth. Who they are and when they will show up, I don't know. But I am determined to be ready."

Zeke stopped and smiled through his moistened eyes. He held his arm up and pointed down the path, indicating that Jake should proceed alone.

Jake walked to the edge of the dense forest. "Wow ... this is incredible. I noticed this foliage pattern in the satellite photo." Jake called back to Zeke, "Praise the Lord. This is beautiful." A uniform pattern of pine trees stretched before him. At the center of the Pine Grove was an enormous beech tree.

"Pine Grove," Zeke said as he came alongside Jake. "I'm surprised Mindy didn't bring you here. Her dad orchestrated this re-foliation for his Eagle Scout project."

"What's with the beech tree in the middle?"

"I guess it had been dry for a number of years. Somehow a fire started. People like to think it was started by lightning. Anyway, when the fire burnt itself out, the only thing living was the big beech. Mindy's dad and his cabin mates took it upon themselves to haul water out to the tree. The next year, he rolled out a plan to plant these pine trees."

Jake and Zeke strolled into the heart of the Pine Grove. Jake took a deep breath. "I love the smell of a pine forest."

"Yeah, me too."

They walked out of the pines and into the clearing made by the dense canopy of beech tree limbs.

"This is *so cool*. I can tell why campers love to hike out here," Jake said. "There's the bench. It looks like a short, sturdy table."

Zeke tried to hold his comments, but his need to feel important drove him to speak. "Each of Bill's benches was uniquely designed. This one ... was built to withstand the weight of two adults ... at the same time." Zeke looked to the ground, embarrassed as he pressed his open palms horizontally together.

"So this is where they snuck off to at night." Jake shook his head with disgust. "Give me that ax! I'm going to break it up. We don't need it anymore."

"Jake, please hold on. Wild Bill and Juice are long gone. I've been out here a number of times. I've never had a girl *on top of* the bench. It makes a great place for hikers to eat their lunches."

"You know, Zeke, we are going to turn these benches into altars so campers can come here to pray. There is not going to be *any* sneaking out this year, *right*? I fixed all the screens in the cabin windows."

"All right." Zeke was reluctant to admit that it was the end of nighttime shenanigans.

"So, how did they get all the way out here without someone seeing them? Weren't there campers milling around?"

"First off, the campers were afraid to leave their cabins. Wild Bill Berry would spin a ghost tale around the campfire that scared the life out of the campers. His best horror story was about the haunted Gruger house around the corner from the camp's entrance. After the ghost story, he would slip away and put on a camouflaged parachute. He would walk in the woods at night. You could hear him, but you couldn't see him. It was *really creepy*."

"You mean that old shack on the other side of Kellum Road?" Jake asked.

"Yeah, I guess some time ago, old lady Gruger couldn't stand the poverty and her husband beating on her all the time, so one night, she poisoned him, stabbed her two kids, and then hung herself in the kitchen."

"Zeke, I don't *ever* want to hear anything about that house at our camp. *I mean nothing.*" Jake's eyes were fierce.

Zeke knew not to raise even the slightest objection.

"Campfires are for fellowship and worship, not ghost stories. Let's head back."

"If we take the path by the Frog Pond, it's about a mile and a half back, but look at the map." Zeke pointed to a tall tree he could see over the pine tops. The back edge of the camp's parking lot is only thirty yards in that direction."

Jake checked his watch. "Let's cut up through the woods to intercept the service road. We'll follow it back to camp."

"And on to Giant Pine?" Zeke inquired.

"No, let me check with Mindy. If we are *not* supposed to be out there, then we're not going, and you are not going alone ... right?"

"Right," Zeke answered.

"So what's the story on Carl Birmingham?" Jake asked.

"Well, Mr. Birmingham was one of those quiet genius types. He was the mastermind for a group of church friends for all kind of things, like organizing food drives for the poor, helping families washed out by the flood, working with families to get them back on their feet." Zeke's voice tensed. "Rumor has it that there are caves stocked for the end of the world on *his* half of the property."

"His half of the property?"

"Yeah." Zeke pointed in the direction of the Birmingham's house. "The camp half runs from the house to the cabins to the beach and out this way to Kellum Road. Carl Birmingham wanted to keep the rest of the property pristine. So he kept the campers out."

Zeke and Jake walked along the service road until they arrived at the camp's beach.

"Zeke, I greatly appreciate your openness and honesty. When it comes to Mindy, let's remember she is more than just the senior counselor. She is the one everyone is counting on to pull this camp through. She deserves our cooperation. We need to show her the utmost respect. Please be very careful about telling stories about her. All the campers are going to take their cue from you.

"I know how funny it was to prank me the day we painted the cabins. You and I both know camp has to be fun, but let's be sure to make it fun for everyone. Remember, you are one of the leaders now." Jake looked into Zeke's eyes. "Are you OK with that?"

"Aye, aye, Skipper! I read you loud and clear."

Jake extended his hand. Zeke shook it with vigor.

Later that afternoon, Zeke barreled out the shower facility's door and across the camp yard. The firecracker he had taped to the toilet stall door was set to go off with the arrival of the next camper.

Zeke gave Jake and Mindy a delirious, rambunctious smirk. He figured they could tell he had set a prank in motion.

"Well, don't you two make a cute couple?" Zeke bellowed from mid yard.

Jake glared at the wild-eyed youth as Zeke ambled over to where Jake and Mindy were talking.

"Well, if your sister was the General, what are we going to call you?"

In a stern voice, Mindy snapped, "You will call me *Mindy.*" The glare on her face cut through Zeke's soul.

With a quick glance at Jake's scowling frown, Zeke's physique softened. For an instant, Zeke perceived the face of an almost-invisible, Christ-like figure glaring at him from behind Mindy. A shocking pulse penetrated Zeke's body. There was no escape from the pain; it rolled around deep inside of him. The Holy Spirit had come to call.

Apologizing to Mindy would not be enough. At that minute, Zeke Thorne repented of his childish ways. As he stood frozen by the conviction, the Holy Spirit spoke to him: *"When I was a child, I talked like a child, I thought like a child, I reasoned like a child. When I became a man, I put childish ways behind me."*

"I'm sorry," Zeke said. "I have been acting like a child. Mindy, I know you must be wondering why Mrs. Birmingham invited me to be a counselor this year. I am not sure myself. I want you to know, you are my number-one priority. I promise, I'll not prank you or embarrass you in any way. I just realized, I'm not here for my own pleasure. I'm here to serve the Lord. I'm here to see to it that the campers have a positive, Christian experience.

"Excuse me ... I need to take care of something." Zeke glanced at Mindy and then at Jake. Their eyes, full of reassurance, shined back at him.

Zeke turned and headed to undo the prank he had set in the men's bathroom.

Jake smiled at Mindy. "Sounds like the line of humble servants has just increased by one."

Mindy nodded, "Yeah, praise the Lord. Now, as far as what we were talking about before we were interrupted, I'll check with Mrs. Birmingham tomorrow and get back with you about the caves stockpiled for the end times."

CHAPTER 9

Giant Pine

MINDY WATCHED MRS. Birmingham's car pull out of the garage and up the driveway. She snatched her cell phone out of her pocket and called Jake. "Can you help me with something up at the house?"

"Sure," Jake answered. He signaled to Zeke that he was needed up at the house. Zeke responded with a thumbs-up.

Jake hustled up the path to Mrs. Birmingham's house. Mindy stood at the backdoor. She waved him into the house. Without a word, she led him through the house, out the front door, and around the back side of the detached garage.

"Where are we going?" Jake asked.

Mindy searched both ways up and down the driveway. "Come on." Mindy darted into a slender path on the opposite side of the driveway.

"We are going to Giant Pine. Mrs. Birmingham wants me to retrieve her husband's Bible and writing material from his bench that's out there. She wants me to carry the bench back and put it in the garage."

"And my role is?" Jake inquired as he paced behind Mindy.

"To carry the bench."

After a few minutes in the forest, Mindy and Jake found themselves on a rock plateau that overlooked a wilderness vista. Shading the slab of rock was an enormous, majestic pine tree, the Giant Pine. A wooden structure stood in the middle of the slab.

"What's that?" Jake asked.

"It's a chair that Bill Berry designed for Carl Birmingham. It opens up." Mindy unlatched the mechanism to reveal a chair and attached writing table. "Under the seat is a waterproof box that holds Carl's Bible and writing material. Look, you can see William Berry's initials, WB."

"The design of this chair is ingenious. I'm changing my opinion about Bill Berry. He is truly a master craftsman." Jake studied the chair's joints and supports.

"Wild Bill's the stuff that camp legends are made from. He's the one who designed and built the sign that hangs over the camp entrance. He built it all by himself, back when he was still a camper. He was smart. He was funny. He was a highly effective leader."

Jake made himself at home on the chair.

"I just had an interesting conversation with Mrs. Birmingham." Mindy lingered as she faced the scenic view in front of the plateau. "I showed her the map Judy drew me. I thought she was going to have a heart attack when she saw it revealed Carl's bench under the Giant Pine. She made me promise not to show the map to anyone. I told her that I had made you a copy. She just shook her head in silence. I could tell she was praying for guidance.

"After a few moments, she looked at me and said, 'My husband, Carl, was a brilliant man, a devoted and loving husband. The Lord had his hand upon him. He spent many hours alone in prayer. Carl led a Bible study group. They did more than study. They conducted many wonderful projects for the community. Because of his desire for privacy, we kept the west half of Birmingham Forest separate from the camp.

"In the last years of his life, I believe Carl perceived a revelation about the years before the second coming of Christ. Apparently, what he saw was so terrifying that he refused to share it with me.

The one thing he did say was, "Cling to the Lord. Let the Holy Spirit direct your path.""''

Mindy looked back over her shoulder at Jake. "I never got the courage to ask her about the caves that were stockpiled for the end times." Mindy walked back to Jake. She slid onto his lap and slipped her arm over his shoulder.

"She was not sure who all was in the Bible study group. The members seemed to change over time. The fascinating thing was that many of these men were often complete strangers. The only link they had in common was that the Holy Spirit drew them together. Just the right people turned up at just the right time to get the task done.

"She said Bill Berry was in the group. That was when she asked me to come out here and retrieve Carl's Bible and bench. She wanted the bench back, but she wondered if it would be too heavy for me. She thought you could help me."

Mindy noticed that Jake stared off into the distance. *I guess this calls for a little physical intervention. Maybe he hasn't figured out that his presence here is to be alone with me.* Mindy shifted on Jake's lap to get his attention. "Have you been listening to anything I have been saying?"

"Yes, yes, of course. The Holy Spirit pulled men together to do certain tasks, and Wild Bill was in the group." Jake pointed to the far off hills. "I'm mesmerized by the view. God must have smiled when He created this part of the earth. I mean, look at that, rolling hills covered with dense forest, blue sky with white clouds, and around the corner is Inspiration Point and its view … and the massive oak tree at the Frog Pond and the beech tree that towers over the new growth at Pine Grove. There is something very, very special about this place."

Mindy swiveled to take in the view of the far off, forest-covered hills. *I can see why Carl came out here to pray and study.* Bliss overcame her. A thought that had been buried in the back of her mind for years rumbled to the forefront.

Wow ... I know what my dad was trying to tell me the day he brought me out to Inspiration Point. Now I see the connection between his story about Sedona, Arizona, and the camp's lookout bluff. The rock walls around Sedona emit bursts of energy. Dad had felt it when he hiked there as a teenager. Legend had it that braves in the Sedona region would take their squaws to the sweet spot on the wall so they would fall in love.

That energy phenomenon occurs in different spots of the world. The energy makes people feel euphoric. Dad was trying to tell me that Inspiration Point was one of those spots. This must be one too. The energy works like an aphrodisiac. Dad brought Mom to Inspiration Point so she would fall in love with him. These rocks must emit the same energy.

Mindy surveyed the outcrop of boulders around her and noticed the intersection of three enormous slabs met directly under Carl's chair. Mindy bit her lip in an attempt to conceal the theory that had just hatched. She couldn't resist the urge that had welled up inside of her. She leaned in and kissed Jake on the forehead. "I've missed you. It pains me the way we have to avoid being together."

Jake smiled. "I've missed you too. Thanks for bringing me out here. I'm counting on you to call the shots about when we get away alone together. We do not want to get a reputation like Wild Bill and Juice. We are going to have to be wise about the time we spend alone together

"Yes, very careful. We better get back." Mindy stood.

"Should I carry the chair back?" Jake stood and tried to lift the chair to test its weight. It wouldn't budge. He checked the legs. One of the legs was bolted to the rock slab with a metal stake.

"No. Don't force it; it might get damaged. We'll have to *come back*." A faint smirk grew across Mindy's face. She carefully folded the chair back into its storage position. They meandered single file back through the path.

"Jake, I wanted to ask you about something. You know that open weekend when the camp will be empty. It's not going to happen until late in the camp season. My mom wants me to come home. Are you going home that weekend?"

"No. I had not even thought of going home. I'm staying. It'll be nice to get some rest, and I'm sure there will plenty for me to do at the camp."

"You know … I was wondering … if you would like to go home with me." Mindy's blood rushed away from her head. She bit her lip to retain her focus.

Jake hesitated. *I didn't see that peck on the forehead coming, and now it's, "Let's go home to meet the parents?" She must really like me. I can't do it. We have to hold off until the camp is over.* "That was very sweet of you to ask. I'd love to meet your family. But it might be better to do that after the camp is over. Maybe we can plan it for the way home."

"Yeah, maybe you are right. You know, it would be pretty selfish of me to leave you here to do all the work. I think I'll stick around too. There will only be a few weeks of camp left by that time. Maybe in our free time we could have a picnic out here or at Inspiration Point." She grinned. "I don't think Mrs. Birmingham will care as long as there are no campers around."

"Great. So … tell me about Carl and Bill's Bible study," Jake said.

She answered him in a matter-of-fact voice, "They met in Carl's basement. *No one* outside the group was allowed down there. After Carl's only son, Roy, moved away, Carl befriended Bill to go hunting and fishing with him. Do you remember that rocking chair in the basement? Bill made that especially for Carl. It fit his body exactly."

As the trail was about to end, she asked, "Whatever happened to the map I made you?"

"I showed it to Zeke while we were clearing the path to Pine Grove."

Mindy stopped. Her chin dropped. *"What?"*

Jake hesitated as he looked back over his shoulder. "Zeke's grandpa mentioned something about 'On the day the cities are desolated, seek shelter beneath the Giant Pine.'"

Jake and Mindy shrugged their shoulders. Jake didn't know what to make of the statement, and he could tell Mindy didn't either. They shared a glance and then dashed undetected across the driveway, into the yard, and back into the Birmingham's front door.

"On the day the cities are desolated, seek shelter beneath the Giant Pine." What kind of shelter can the shade of the Giant Pine provide? Wonder what else Zeke's grandpa had to say? Jake pondered the statement as he walked down the path to rejoin his campers. *I wonder which cities?*

CHAPTER 10

Nancy

NANCY, THE COUNSELOR from the cabin next to Mindy's, watched as Mindy settled a misunderstanding between two of Mindy's campers. From that distance, Nancy could hear much of the conversation. Nancy observed Mindy as she listened patiently to both sides of the story, making eye contact with only one of the girls at a time. Mindy insisted that she wanted only the facts. She let them know that if they did not arrive at a compromise for themselves, then Mindy would decide what was best, and that would be the end of it. Shake hands or hug; it was up to them. Conflict resolved. No festering grudges would be permitted to spoil the camp yard. Nancy had admired Mindy's insistence on harmony ever since Mindy was her cabin counselor a couple of summers ago.

It was mid-July, and this summer's camp season was half over. Nancy rejoiced in her decision to accept Mrs. Birmingham's offer to be a cabin counselor, even though she knew she would have made more money being a law clerk at her mother's law office. Nancy's aspiration to be a doctor would have been better served as an aid to her father in his family practice. This summer was about giving back. Nancy appreciated the joy of poverty, like that of the monks and missionaries who lived to serve.

Nancy turned to look in the other direction. She winked at the young man carrying a load of wood to the fire ring. Then she slipped over to Jake's cabin. She could hear Jake singing in and out of tune as a camper strummed his guitar.

Good, everything is setting up nicely, Nancy thought. I need to find a candle and a lighter. I'll check with Miss Ella and see if I can help her with the cupcakes. Nancy hustled toward the dining hall.

Later that evening, as the stars twinkled their first lights, Nancy approached Mindy. "I arranged for the boys to make a campfire. Will you join us?"

"Sure, I wondered where everybody'd disappeared to," Mindy replied.

Nancy watched surprise roll across Mindy's face as she surveyed the boys and girls around the fire ring. Nancy noticed the long, affectionate eye contact Mindy made with Jake. She led Mindy to the stump at the head of the fire ring; the location usually reserved for the storyteller or discussion leader.

Mindy grinned. Her easy smile revealed that she knew this was not a prank. Pranksters always held their breath with intense anticipation as they waited for the trap to spring. These kids were filled with eager jubilation. As the boys and girls settled in, Nancy stood. "Thank you for coming to the fire ring. Tonight, we honor Mindy on her birthday!" Mindy smiled as tears welled in her eyes.

Nancy thought, *Fortunately for my plan, one of the campers in Jake's cabin is a gifted musician nicknamed "Maestro."* Nancy, Jake, and Maestro had decided earlier that day that Jake would be the humorous warm-up act, and Maestro would provide a concert for the campfire.

Jake stood and gave Maestro a nod. "Hit it!"

Maestro's perfectly tuned guitar filled the summer evening with music. Jake and Maestro selected songs that Jake knew well. Conveniently for Maestro and the campers, both songs had been featured in recent movies, and everyone was familiar with them.

Jake wasn't a great singer, but he sang the first simple love songs with gusto. He swayed as he danced in front of the girls, letting them know that he would be selecting a few of them to dance with him. They leaned forward in their seats.

Nancy watched from the side of the fire ring as Jake sauntered while he sang until he stood directly in front of Mindy. Nancy could sense Mindy's dilemma. Mindy's expression longed for Jake to select her for the dance. Nancy had suspected mutual interest between the two, even though she had never seen them express it physically.

Jake leaned past Mindy to select the shy girl from the fire ring's back row. Nancy observed, as Jake bent forward at Mindy's side, their legs brushed against each other. Nancy realized Jake's intentional but almost unperceivable touch was a gesture of acknowledgement. She could tell that Jake wanted to pick Mindy for the dance, but his sense of honor and duty forbade it.

Mindy squirmed slightly on her stump, preoccupied by the sensation of the swatch of sweat that had inadvertently rubbed off of Jake's leg onto hers. Mindy had not made eye contact during the encounter. She looked up as Jake waved his arms, motioning for all of the campers to stand and dance. Bedlam erupted.

As the campers reveled, Mindy watched from her stump, hoping her face hadn't revealed her private anxiety or her newfound elation.

Within minutes, the song ended. The boys and girls clapped and called for more.

A number of Mindy's campers noticed that their leader had not joined in the merriment. Above the clamber, they cried, "Jake, Jake, dance with Mindy! Dance with Mindy! It's her birthday! She *wants* you to dance with her!"

Mindy blushed. With her heart pounding, she forced her lips into a nervous smile. She watched the camper's faces for clues. *Could this be an innocent coincidence, or could the campers have discovered my secret affection?*

Jake glanced at Mindy. Her face beamed as her eyes locked on his. He glanced at Maestro and nodded. "Hit it!"

Jake's second song was again a simple love song. Everyone had heard it many times. As he sang, he moved closer and closer to Mindy, who sat across the fire ring from him. Jake bowed and offered Mindy his hand. She rose to engage him in a dance. Their arms were extended, with Jake's hands placed loosely around her waist. Mindy's arm lay across his shoulder. They stepped in time as they waltzed once around the fire ring. As he returned her to the stump, he bowed to her. She curtsied. Mindy sat regally on her throne. Jake returned to join his men. Loyal subjects cheered with glee.

Nancy dispatched three boys to retrieve the tubs of cupcakes and the juice cooler. As they returned, Nancy pulled the single candle from her pocket, lit it, and placed it on the one perfect cupcake. Nancy silenced the crowd and then proclaimed with great pride, "From all of us at Camp Koinonia, happy birthday, Mindy!"

A raucous chorus of "Happy Birthday" erupted.

Like all fairy tales, this too came to an end. When all the cupcakes had been eaten and Maestro had played his last tune, the boys and girls returned to their cabins for lights out.

Early the next morning, Nancy waited for her last camper to leave the cabin for breakfast. As she exited her cabin, she noticed Mindy standing alone on her cabin's porch.

"Good morning," Mindy called.

"Good morning," Nancy replied as she walked to meet her.

Mindy gave Nancy a hug. "Thank you for the birthday surprise at the fire ring last night. That was very thoughtful of you."

"You're welcome," Nancy returned. "Believe me, it was from all of us. I hope you didn't mind that I invited the boys. I hope it didn't cause ... complications ... between you and Jake."

"No. It didn't *cause* the complications." Mindy grinned. With a tender, vulnerable voice, she whispered, "How obvious is it?"

Nancy hesitated. She wanted to be sure she answered the right question. "How obvious is what?"

"That I really, *really* like Jake." Mindy blushed.

"To me … it's obvious." Nancy and Mindy broke into nervous laughter. "All the counselors who see you week after week can see the attraction. The campers are only here for a week. They are more worried about campfires, hikes, crafts, and snacks. They see you and Jake in parental roles, and you fill that role very well."

Nancy stepped closer to Mindy. "There is a big difference between mature, sincere affection and unbridled lust. You know, as well as I, how out of hand the shenanigans got here at camp in years past. It was destructive enough when the counselors would sneak off with each other at night, but when the counselors and the campers started pairing up … that was going *too far*." Nancy turned to hide her disgust from the group of campers that had gathered outside the dining hall.

"Mindy, it's like you and Jake brought Jesus back to Camp Koinonia. Because you and Jake have kept your affections pure, it has set a new tone for the camp and the campers. No one sneaks out at night. I mean, look at Zeke. In all his years at camp, he was a big, rambunctious flirt. Somewhere in the first week of camp, something changed in his life. Now he's thoughtful, courteous, and he can work next to the girl counselors and not flirt with them."

Nancy and Mindy shared tender smiles.

"You've started a great work. I'm glad the Lord let me be part of it. The love that you and Jake share flows from above. It's not just obvious … it's contagious!" Nancy leaned over and hugged her friend and mentor.

"Good morning, counselors. Hey, are you two going to chit chat through breakfast?" Zeke called from the dining hall's door.

"No!" They cried in unison as they walked off the porch of Mindy's cabin.

CHAPTER 11

Lex

L EX LEANED BACK in his chair, locked his hands behind his head, and put his feet on his desk. He smiled. *It's the Friday before midsummer break … at last!* It was a good feeling. For the first time that summer, he felt caught up on his projects. He could relax and enjoy the weekend.

He thought back to the day, earlier that summer, when he constructed his desk out of a four-foot-by-two-foot piece of plywood and a couple of old, two-drawer file cabinets. Lex remembered how impressed Jake was the first time he saw the new arrangement in the tool shed. But what touched Lex's heart the most was what happened the next day, when Jake showed up with a box full of office supplies. The desk calendar, pens, and pencils would have been enough. The fan, calculator, file folders, and notepads had proved useful, but the navy-blue notebook portfolio and the name plate that read Lex Kemple, they were above and beyond the call of duty.

Acts of generosity were what separated Jake from all the rest of the people in Lex's life. Jake had been a straight shooter. He was the kind of guy who didn't care if you wore the latest fashions or how much money your parents did or didn't have. Jake was concerned about two things: how committed you were to your relationship with Jesus Christ and how willing you were to work as a team to get the project done.

Lex stood and looked out the tool shed window. Then he made his way out to the camp yard that was already swarming with campers. *I wonder if Mindy needs me to help her with anything.*

Due to the near-capacity attendance during the last weeks, the midsummer break occurred a few weeks later than the Fourth-of-July weekend. As tradition would have it, the day of fun and sports culminated in the annual counselors vs. campers tug of war. By design, the counselors would appear to put up their best fight, but in the end, the campers would always win.

Mindy was in the front position, leading the counselors' team. Jake manned the back of the rope for the camper's team. Immediately after the horn sounded, a few of the campers stumbled, which caused a chain reaction of campers falling over each other.

Lex, who had intentionally positioned himself directly behind Mindy in the rope line, stepped back to stop his fall. Mindy, in wild excitement, jumped and screamed, *"We won! We won!"* She lunged toward Lex in a spontaneous victory hug. Tumbling backward, they landed on top of their teammates, who laughed and squirmed on the ground.

Mindy's arms were momentarily pinned behind Lex's neck by the body of the person behind him. Instinctively, he wrapped his arms and legs around her to break her fall. He could feel her heaving gently as she chuckled. Anesthetized by laughter, Mindy relaxed completely. Lex savored the moment. He could smell her perfume and the fragrance in her hair. Sweat from Mindy's neck moistened his cheek. Their embrace lasted for only an instant.

Mindy dislodged her arms and sprang to her feet. They blushed at each other. The emotional rush overloaded his adolescent libido.

"Thanks for catching me. Did I hurt you?" Mindy asked.

"No, no, I'm fine," Lex replied. But he was far from fine. Cupid had emptied his quiver into his heart. In their brief tumble, a bond had formed. Somehow … he *loved* her. Somehow, he knew that he would always love her. As he slowly sat up, Mindy stepped over him to direct the untangling of her fellow counselors. She stood directly in front of him. He looked away.

Mindy quickly turned to face the mass of campers at the other end of the rope. Jake had rallied them to demand a rematch. She quickly accepted and turned to snap her team into tug-of-war position.

Lex rolled away from the group and stood off to the side, stunned, aroused, and nauseated. He could barely breathe as he watched Mindy command her troops. She was not even aware that he was no longer behind her. He realized that in her mind, their tumble had been incidental, insignificant. In the excitement of the moment, she might not even remember that it was him. He forced himself to walk to the back of the rope. He played along. This time, the campers won the tug.

For the rest of the afternoon, Lex went through the motions of congratulating the campers, wishing them well, reminding them to come again next year, and of course—to bring a friend. Out of the corner of his eye, he watched for Mindy. He had felt the sparks of love only a few times in the past. This was different. This was a bonfire.

After all the other campers and other counselors had packed up, said their "good-byes," and gone home, he lingered in one of the boys' cabins. He knew Mindy would report to Mrs. Birmingham and eventually return to her cabin.

He would wait and watch for his chance to encounter her, one-on-one, and would probe her for any hint that their brief tumble had revealed Mindy's hidden affection for him. If he positioned himself properly, maybe she would hug him, or best of all, kiss him good-bye.

From his vantage point in the cabin, he could look diagonally across the pane of glass, from the far-right side of the window to the far-left side of the window. He could see the fronts of the girls' cabins and the path that led up to Mrs. Birmingham's house. This was perfect; he could watch for her completely undetected.

After twenty anxious minutes, Mindy and Jake strolled down the path from Mrs. Birmingham's house.

"Darn! I can't believe she is with *him*."

He watched. Jake was explaining something to Mindy. She listened intently; Lex could tell she was more watching Jake's face move than digesting his words. Jake's hand motions aroused his interest. First, Jake held his open hands up about three inches apart, then clapped them gently together. Jake then laid his hands, one on top of the other, to the side. Then, with a teasing smile on his face, Jake rubbed his two hands together.

Panic. The rush of rage and embarrassment pounded through Lex's body. *Jake is teasing Mindy about our tumble*, he concluded. *I hope she rebukes him*. But no, they both smiled.

As Lex watched, he could tell that Jake's kind-hearted lecture was about how inappropriate "outward displays of affection" were between counselors and the staff. He saw something forming on Mindy's face. Her slight but pleasant smile broadened, then it bloomed into a beautiful, mischievous smirk. It was the smirk he had only seen on her a few times in his life at camp. It was the smirk that revealed a perfect prank had hatched in her mind.

Her body drew back ever so slightly, like a kitten about to pounce. Jake nodded and made his first step to leave. Mindy lunged at him, circled his neck in her arms, and planted her lips squarely against Jake's cheek. Jake blushed. As her extended kiss lingered, the smile on Jake's face radiated approval. She rocked him slightly and then pulled her face away. She quickly turned to step away, possibly to insure she would have the last word in the encounter and possibly hoping to avoid another lecture. But Jake caught her elbow and spun her gently back to face him. Without a word, they gazed into each other's eyes as their lips drew near.

Jake and Mindy locked themselves in an embrace, each yielding completely to the other, as though to consummate a passion that had brooded in their hearts all summer. Lex willed himself to continue watching, but he could not. An invisible knife had just plunged into his heart. Nausea tightened his gut. As the kiss finally broke, he slid down the wall.

At first, the heartache set off only a few tears and then a stream rolled down his cheek and then a gush. *How could she do this to me? I love her.* His love might endure forever. But, in the face of the overwhelming evidence, Lex now knew that he and Mindy would *not* be spending the future together.

There's no sense trying to dislodge Mindy's love from Jake. No, my best bet … my only bet … would be to endear myself to them, to be worthy of their friendship, to be their loyal and humble servant. Lex wiped the tears off his face. *This passion play will not turn out like Camelot, where Sir Lancelot's adulterous affair with Guinevere not only destroyed her marriage with King Arthur but also unraveled the moral fiber of the kingdom. No, I will seek unity. There will be peace in this kingdom. As far as my love for Mindy, I'll appoint myself her guardian … for life.*

A puddle of tears stained the worn wooden floor. Lex heaved as he cried. He tried as hard as he could not to make a sound.

Click, clack, the sound of Jake's footsteps marching across the front porch of the cabin next to him arrested his sobbing.

Oh no. Jake is checking the cabins. Oh great, I left my blue portfolio sitting on the table, in clear sight. Lex shifted his body to the corner, moved away from the window, curled up in a ball, and hoped to disappear. Jake's frame made a shadow on the window, then disappeared. Jake stepped to the door. He twisted the knob and opened it.

I'm busted. I forgot to lock the door. Resigned that he would be discovered by the very person he had spied upon, Lex prayed, "Please, Lord …"

Jake's hand reached around the door, twisted the knob to the locked position, pulled the door shut, and walked off.

Thank you, Lord. Lex rejoiced silently from his curled-up position.

The camp yard grew quiet. Solitude gave Lex time to reflect on the past summer's camp. For the first time, he realized how Jake and Mindy had surpassed the roles of the former senior counselors. Through their wisdom, maturity, and compassion, they had matured into true mentors for the counselors and campers. He knew there was a special attraction between them, but Jake and Mindy had kept it carefully hidden from sight.

Ring. Ring. Ring. Lex's cell phone pierced the silence. He scrambled to mute it. The call was from Jake. He was leaving a message. Quietly, Lex switched the volume to low so he could listen to the message undetected.

"Hi, it's Jake. I saw your portfolio on the table in the second cabin. I left it there so you could find it when you came back looking for it. I will be around for a few days … let me know if you'd like me to let you in the cabin to get it. Hey, I know I've told you this a hundred times, but thanks for your hard work and leadership this year. You know, we still have a few weeks left, but I'm already looking forward to next year. Bye."

Lex shut off his phone. Slow shadows crept across the room as the evening wore on. Lex sat imprisoned by his insistence to remain anonymous. He realized he may have to wait until Jake and Mindy had gone to bed to escape unseen.

Lex heard a faint voice. He could hear Jake talking on his cell phone as he walked by the second cabin. He rose slowly to watch the drama. Within minutes, Mindy emerged from her cabin to join Jake in the camp yard. Apparently, their moratorium on dating lifted as the last camper waved good-bye. Gone was her ever-present ponytail, her well-worn but always clean khaki shorts and her Camp Koinonia logo shirt. Mindy's hair was combed out and fell down on her shoulders. Lex studied her face. Her makeup and lipstick had transformed the coed into a beautiful woman. Mindy was dressed in a Khaki skirt and a sleeveless, light-blue oxford.

Mindy and Jake looked much older as they walked hand in hand toward their cars in Mrs. Birmingham's driveway. At the edge of the camp yard, Jake paused and turned around to take one last look at the camp yard. Jake stepped forward, placing his hands on his hips. A satisfied, confident smile formed on his lips.

As Mindy turned to face the camp yard, curiosity stirred on her face, as though some unseen being had pointed over her shoulder, directly at Lex, and whispered in her ear, "Lex is watching you from the window in the second cabin." She scrutinized the cabin's windows. Mindy's eyes locked onto the eyes that peeked out from the corner of the window.

She's looking right at me! She can't be. There's no way she can see me. Mindy's eyes pierced directly into his. The adrenaline rush paralyzed him. He held his breath in an effort to become invisible. *I'm busted!* Embarrassment and guilt raged through his soul. He figured his fate of humiliation was soon to follow. He waited, staring into her eyes. He was at her mercy. *Please, Lord ... let this pass.*

Mindy leaned her head slightly to one side as a tender smile broke on her face, a smile of compassion, a smile of kindness, a smile of mercy. It was a smile that only revealed a person as far as he or she wished to be exposed. Her smile broadened like the smile of a young mother who had discovered her son peaking through her bedroom door as he watched her pray at her bedside.

This was not spying; his intrusion was based on love, a sincere desire for one person to observe and understand the other. Somehow in that silent yet potent visual transmission, they both understood each other, they loved each other, and it was not to be erotic, romantic love. It would be a love based on mutual affection and respect. Lex returned Mindy's smile. He was at peace.

Mindy turned to face Jake. She nodded as Jake spoke. Jake made a step up the path towards the house. She caught his elbow in her hand and then looked back over her shoulder to catch the young man's eyes who stood in the shadows of the boys' second cabin. Mindy smiled and winked at him and then turned to walk with Jake up the hill.

Lex leaned his head against the cabin wall. He knew his encounter with Mindy would be their secret. It would never be discussed in public; yet it could never, never be forgotten. He picked up his blue portfolio off the table and shuffled through to remove the four pages that contained information that he would need during his weekend away from camp, and then he returned the notebook portfolio to the tabletop.

I'll leave my portfolio here as my calling card. Guess I'll give Jake a call tomorrow. Maybe I'll get a chance to see them both for a few minutes. Lex looked around the darkened room. The puddle of tears that moistened the room's corner had outlived the traumatic ordeal that triggered them.

He walked out of the counselor's room, past the four sets of bunk beds, and paused for a moment in the cabin's doorway. Surveying the abandoned camp yard, he brooded. *Alone ... at last.*

Lex scurried across the turf, out to the parking area, and into the last car in the lot. As Lex drove under the Camp Koinonia arch and onto Kellum Road, he shook his head, *So many days are just like every other ... and then one day ... everything changes.*

CHAPTER 12

Sunset

MINDY WALKED DOWN the path that connected Mrs. Birmingham's house to the camp area. She had noticed Jake's car parked next to hers in the driveway. Mrs. Birmingham had mentioned that she was going into town to run errands and would be stopping in to see an old friend.

Mindy passed the dining hall and the shower facility. With it being the Saturday evening of midsummer break, Miss Ella would not be back until Monday morning. No lights were on in the shower facility. Camp Koinonia was at peace.

Mindy longed for Jake. As she made her way to Jake's cabin, she carried in her heart the hope that their eyes would meet with the same degree of interest. Mindy was grateful that the camp's master schedule contained a weekend where no campers would be present. She had phoned Jake at lunch to tell him that Mrs. Birmingham and she were still in town and that she would not be able to see him at lunch. They left the conversation with a casual "maybe we can do something for dinner."

Mindy had endured a long day working out cabin assignments, wrestling with budget issues, and buying supplies. She was starting to understand the complexity of running a small camp. She wanted to get away. Secretly, she longed for Jake to take her to dinner and a movie. This was a lot to wish for, as they were not actually dating and *romantic entanglements between counselors are strictly forbidden.* She knew the counselors were there to mentor the campers and not to find boyfriends.

Mindy saw a notebook page sticking out of her cabin's door. "How about a swim and a campfire? See you at the lake, Jake," the note read. She shook her head with disappointment. The note's signature lacked the expression of affection she longed for. She stuffed the note in her pocket.

Mindy reluctantly contemplated her options, *Swimming in the lake would be refreshing,* but she didn't want to mess with it. *However,* she thought, *Jake is already in the water. I might as well put my suit on under my clothes. That way, I'll be ready for a swim or a movie.*

She quickly slipped out of her clothes and into her suit. She redressed, then walked to the beach area. She could see that Jake had moved a bench out to the end of the dock; his towel was draped over it. Mindy arrived at the end of the dock to find him washing his hair in the lake.

"What are you doing?" Mindy asked, trying to hide her annoyance.

"I am taking a bath, Henry David Thoreau style," Jake replied. "You know … just me and nature. Anyway … the scenery is extraordinary down here at the lake." He ducked under the water and then reemerged to shake the water from his head. "Where is your swimming suit?"

"I don't think I'm going to need one."

"Come on in. I'll race you to the buoy." Jake splashed water on her legs and then turned to thrash his way to the buoy.

Mindy's annoyance festered; this was not what she wanted, but she stuffed her feelings. Jake's playful charm had disarmed her. She watched Jake, who was preoccupied with his swimming, and then kicked off her shoes and dropped her blouse onto the bench. She slipped out of her Khaki shorts and placed them next to her shirt.

She dove in. In two smooth, swift strokes, she positioned herself directly under Jake. She could see that Jake was a lousy swimmer. In all of his thrashing, he had not even made it halfway to the buoy. Mindy was tempted to pull him under, but she convinced herself otherwise.

She debated in her mind about whether or not she should beat him to the buoy. *No,* she thought, *let him win.* In the end, with one swift stroke, she arranged for them to arrive at the buoy at the same time.

"You beat me." Jake gasped for air.

"No, it was a tie."

He smiled as he panted.

Mindy placed her hand on his upper chest. She could feel the powerful, swift, rhythmic pounding.

With a few cleansing breaths, Jake returned his breathing and heart rate to normal. "Remind me to never challenge a lifeguard to a swim race. Hey, will you try the lifeguard thing on me?"

"Lifeguard thing?" She suspected he was hedging for a kiss through a veiled request for mouth-to-mouth resuscitation.

"You know how you come up behind drowning swimmers and haul them to safety."

Still skeptical, Mindy asked, "The rescue maneuver? Are you trying to get a free ride back to the dock?"

Jake looked slightly insulted. "Don't you think I can make it back to the dock?" Jake tensed in a ready position to thrash his way back to the dock.

"No, no ... What is your interest in the rescue technique?" she asked.

"I thought it would be a great way to allow kids who can't swim to experience the water. You know, kind of a piggyback ride in the water."

"That's a great idea. Are you ready to try it? Come on out and tread water." Mindy ducked under the water and came up behind Jake. She slid her arm across his chest and began to pull him through the water.

"This is really nice. I know the kids will love this," Jake said.

Mindy reflected on Jake's "piggyback ride in the water" concept as she pulled Jake away from the buoy. *I bet the non-swimmers would like a ride like this. With a little practice, I know some of the better swimmers could learn to administer the maneuver.* Mindy arrived at the dock. She grabbed the ladder, and she looked back over her shoulder. "Were you asleep?"

"I was daydreaming. The way you held me and your smooth strokes made me feel like a baby in a mother's arms. As I eased into the gentle rocking and the sloshing of the water, I saw myself as a baby still in the womb. Thank you ... that was wonderful." They paused to watch the sunset.

"I'll cherish this day. When I'm off in the mission field, lying face down in the desert, no food or water for days, I will call upon you, and you will refresh me." Jake spoke in a soft voice as he stared into the sunset.

Mindy thought that was an interesting compliment. She turned to thank him only to find that he was facing away from her. She looked to see who he was talking to. She searched the lake, then the far-off shore, and finally the amber sun. She stared into it, searching for what she perceived to be someone whispering her name.

As though an invisible arrow had pierced her heart, she felt a tingling sensation and then a wave of tingling pulsed through her. Somehow the lake was different now. A new understanding was dawning in her soul, a wisdom that was beyond physics and chemistry and the phases of matter. Mindy saw the world for the first time as an expression of love, a love that created and bound the universe together. This was the love of the one true, living, all-powerful, and all-knowing God.

She had experienced the lake hundreds of times but never like this. Overwhelmed by the sensation, she realized that the God of the universe had been watching her all along. It was only after she earnestly sought Him that she was able to feel how close He was to her. When her face met His, He conveyed the mystery of the heavens. He loved her, and He relayed His unique plans to her. Tears streamed across her face.

Mindy now realized her role in God's master plan. It would be to develop a singularly appropriate curriculum for training a group of spiritually gifted youth. Mindy was to love and nurture the yet unseen teens, mentor them, and instruct them in the ways of the Lord Jesus Christ. When their time together was complete, these kids would venture out to bring hope and comfort to a fallen world. She glanced at Jake.

Tears flowed down Jake's face as he stared down at the water's surface. He glanced at Mindy. "I just saw the same barrage of images that I saw the night of the tornado. I realize now that God's miracle of mercy to spare us from the tornado foreshadows the future, where we will be protected under the Lord's wing from a calamity that will shake the world.

"I also understand my role is to construct a safe haven, a hiding place, and that only the faithful, who are obedient to the Lord's instructions, will be admitted." Jake turned to Mindy. "I can't tell how soon these things will happen. All I do know is that the Lord will test me and strengthen me along this journey. One image that is seared on my brain is the face of Jesus, His look of earnest compassion and concern as He said, '*Cling to the Lord. Let the Holy Spirit direct your path.*'"

"I know, I heard that too," Mindy affirmed.

They looked at each other with beaming smiles, their hearts still stirred by their encounters with the divine. The aura of the Holy Spirit lingered with them for only a few minutes.

Jake noticed that Mindy was looking at him, "See, I told you the scenery was extraordinary down here at the dock."

She hugged him. "Now what?"

"You know, all this swimming has made me hungry. Are you ready to eat?"

"Yes." She thought to herself how quickly the spiritual wonder had faded back to the physical world. "There is only one towel, Jake. It's yours."

"No, my dear, it's *our* towel. You go first."

Mindy slipped out of the water, sat on the bench, and pulled the beach towel around her. *How ironic*, she thought, *just a moment ago,*

I was in fellowship with the one true, living God. Now, she hustled to dry herself. All she could think of was how badly she wanted something to eat. *I hope this campfire he's invited me to has a meal included with it. Surely he has chocolate ... I wonder if he would let me eat that first?*

Mindy's thoughts raced ahead to the next evening, to the surprise birthday dinner she had arranged for Jake at Commodore's.

CHAPTER 13

Commodore's

MINDY'S HEART CONCEALED many secrets. She had never gotten around to admitting to Jake that her knowledge of astronomy, which impressed him on the day they met, was based on a newspaper article that she had read while cleaning Mrs. Birmingham's house. Nor had she followed up on Jake's request for a picture of her family. She kept secret the picture that stood on Mrs. Birmingham's dining room buffet.

The photograph was of Mrs. Birmingham; her daughters, Victoria and Elizabeth; Mindy's mom, Catherine; Mindy's older sister, Kathy; and Mindy. Mindy had never actually been called the "runt," but that was how the picture portrayed her. Mindy's mom had requested the picture to commemorate Mother's Day. The framed shot was originally a gift for Mindy's grandmother; yet everyone in the picture had received a copy.

Mrs. Birmingham and Mindy's grandmother had been lifelong friends. It was a great shot for everyone, except for Mindy. She was an awkward ten years old. Her hair was a mess and her camp uniform was mussed and dirty. Mindy remembered how just minutes before the picture was snapped, she had extracted a fitting revenge on little Mick Richards. She couldn't remember what prank he had played on her. Somehow the prank did not matter now.

Everyone cherished that picture except her. She loathed it. Mindy longed for a portrait that would redeem the tomboy standing next to her mom.

She focused her energy on the day in front of her. Judy Berry had stated that if you meet your Prince Charming, you may have to go after him. It was the Sunday evening of midsummer break. Tomorrow morning campers would once again flood Camp Koinonia. It was time for action. Mindy sat at Mrs. Birmingham's dining room table with her back to the rest of the house to conceal her work. She methodically checked her list: the dress shop, the hair dresser, and finally, the reservations at Commodore's Restaurant.

Commodore's Restaurant had been an icon in Norton for many years. It was created when the descendants of Commodore Drake who had been commissioned by President Lincoln to patrol Lake Michigan and Lake Superior during the Civil War, married into a family that owned a small chain of restaurants. At that time, the local museum of Civil War naval memorabilia was infused into an upscale restaurant. In the back corners of the restaurant were two distinct dining areas: the Captain's Table, which consisted of a large, oval table for family gatherings, and the Crow's Nest, which held a single table mostly surrounded by partitions made of ship's sails. The Crow's Nest was typically reserved for intimate occasions like engagements and romantic birthdays.

Mindy realized she could not hide her feelings for Jake any longer. Making a dream come true sometimes requires bold action. *My Prince Charming is going to get a little nudge. I love him, and I'm going to tell him at dinner*. Mindy scurried off to town. She had told Jake to be ready at 7:00 P.M. and that they were to meet in Mrs. Birmingham's back entryway. She only had a few hours; she had to hurry.

Jake dressed and arrived at the house a few minutes early. He strolled around the corner from the pantry, where he had returned Mrs. Birmingham's iron.

Stunned by the sight of Mindy, he stopped in his tracks. She had positioned herself on the stair step, second from the bottom, to slip on her sandals. Her firm, shapely legs jutted out of her navy-blue skirt and around to the side so she could latch the small buckles on her sandals. Mindy's tanned limbs were fit for a goddess.

Something has changed, Jake thought. *No ... everything has changed. There's something about how the lotion makes her legs gleam, something about how her elegant new haircut redefines her face, something about her perfume, her makeup, her lipstick. This is not the cute, young coed I pecked on the cheek under the sweet gum tree. No, this is a beautiful woman.*

Mindy stood to smooth her skirt and blouse. She looked up to catch Jake admiring her. She blushed and smiled broadly, "Happy birthday, Jake."

"Thank you." Jake walked over and placed his hands on her arms, just below her shoulders. "You are gorgeous."

He studied her, his eyes focused on her lips. He yearned to kiss her, not just a peck, but the way a man kisses a woman. Mindy closed her eyes and her lips relaxed and drew open slightly. Jake pulled away. He realized that he would be wearing her lipstick for the rest of the evening if he kissed her now.

Mrs. Birmingham scurried around the corner. "Don't you two look sweet. I need to get a picture for my scrapbook." *Flash, flash,* snapped the camera. "Now, one more picture over here by the bookcase." *Flash.* "Don't stay out too late ... camp opens first thing in the morning." Mrs. Birmingham smiled with delight as Jake and Mindy walked to his car.

Jake opened the car door for Mindy. It had been washed and waxed for the occasion. On her seat lay a dozen red roses. She beamed with appreciation.

Jake smiled as he said, "*We* didn't get a chance to officially celebrate *your* birthday. I'll put them in a vase and will be right back."

After a short drive into town, Mindy and Jake settled in at the secluded Crow's Nest table. Throughout his dinner, Jake noticed a large man, pale with sweat, sitting across the room. His clothes and manner indicated that he was wealthy. The man's eyes were fixed on Mindy. He had been watching her with great interest. He stood and walked across the room.

"Excuse me, I don't mean to interrupt …" asserted the man, "but are you any relation to Catherine Brooks?" His abrupt arrival startled Mindy. She had not seen his imposing figure swagger over to her table. The man towered over her. His eyes twitched.

"Yes," she said in a soothing voice. "Catherine Brooks is my mother's maiden name. I'm Mindy Brice." She extended her hand cautiously to the obviously nervous stranger.

In his instinct to protect her, Jake pulled his chair slightly out from the table, giving him unobstructed access to the intruder. *Something about this guy is not right.* Jake was not afraid of the juggernaut. He was leery of what the deranged man could do to Mindy if he got close enough to her. Jake imagined his first strike would be to the man's Adam's apple and jugular vein. Then, with a swift kick, he would slam the man to the floor. Nervously, Jake watched the man move closer to Mindy.

"My name is Alexander Montgomery. I've had a very difficult week. My son's remains were returned to me on Monday. I buried him next to my wife's plot just yesterday. As I was sitting at dinner tonight, I'd decided that this would be my last night on earth … *then* … I saw the angel of Catherine Brooks sitting before me. Love and compassion radiated from your face. It compelled me to come over here." Mr. Montgomery stared at Mindy for some ray of hope. "I'm sorry. I'm all messed up."

Mindy looked into the man's eyes. She smiled and said, "Mr. Montgomery, please sit down."

Alexander Montgomery complied immediately. "I've never been a church-going man, but something happened at the cemetery. The Capp family must have been burying their daughter Julie at the same time that I was burying Ronnie. I was all alone. The Capps were with a small group of family members. I could tell they were praying. Oddly enough, I could tell they were praying for me. At first, I was outraged. 'Why can't they mind their own business?' I thought. In a few minutes, I felt Mr. Capp's hand on my shoulder. 'God bless you, and may He bring you peace.' That was all he said."

"Something is happening in me," Mr. Montgomery sobbed. "Something is pulling my heart out. Somehow, I'm thinking that you can help me." Mr. Montgomery looked into Mindy's face. Tears streamed down the broken man's cheeks. She slid her hand over Mr. Montgomery's hand. His large, brutal hand was cold and tense.

"Would you like me to lead you out of the darkness and into the light?" Mindy asked quietly.

"Yes," Alexander Montgomery whispered.

"Would you pray with me, Mr. Montgomery?"

"Yes," he replied.

"Pray the words that I am about to say, even if you can only pray them silently in your heart."

Mr. Montgomery nodded.

"Heavenly Father, I am a sinner. I choose on this day to turn from my sinful ways. I want you to come into my life. I want you, Jesus, to be my Lord and Savior. I pray Lord that you lift my burdens and grant me peace."

Mr. Montgomery recited the prayer word for word and then lifted his head. His face relaxed. "Thank you, thank you. How can I repay you?"

"Repayment is not necessary." Mindy smiled as she relaxed back into her chair. "All of our debts have been paid in full by Jesus' blood on the cross."

Mr. Montgomery looked at Mindy with sincerity and compassion. "I feel that I need to confess this to you. In my youth, I had a *big time crush* on your mother, back when we were counselors at Camp Koinonia. She was smart, charming, and exceedingly beautiful. I was large and awkward and not very bright. I knew she was out of my league. Don't get me wrong; she was always friendly to me and even a good friend to me. But secretly, I wanted more. I had dreams of building an empire and of her living in that dream with me. As that never happened, I grew resentful. My failure festered into hatred, an irrational hatred for someone I did not even know any longer. All these terrible feelings I had for a woman who may not even recognize me if I were to see her. Somehow, I built my empire, hoping someday Catherine and I would be united. It's funny how someone you meet at summer camp can effect your entire life."

Mindy flashed a glance at Jake.

"I've harbored many inappropriate thoughts and feelings about your mother. I want to apologize for all of that." Alexander continued, "I may never get a chance to tell her in person, so please know, I've changed my ways. I can't tell you how much your prayers have meant to me. I apologize one more time for interrupting your meal." Mr. Montgomery stood and peeled two one-hundred-dollar bills off the roll of money in his pocket. He placed them on the table. "At least allow me to buy you dinner." Mr. Montgomery turned and walked away.

Mindy drew in a deep breath. As she let it out slowly, she looked over at Jake. "I'm sorry. This dinner did not turn out the way I had planned."

"No apology needed. Watching you lead that poor, broken man to the Lord was the best present you could have given me. You know as well as I do that the angels celebrate more for the one lost lamb that is saved than for the ninety-nine that stay in the fold."

As though the waitress had been waiting for Mr. Montgomery to leave the table, she arrived with a plate full of cake and ice cream that was topped with chocolate syrup, whipping cream, and two cherries.

"The order was for coffee also," said the waitress. "I'll be back in a minute with it ... enjoy."

"Now this is what I'd planned!" Mindy asserted. "I really want you to let me pay for the dinner. What do you think we should do with Mr. Montgomery's money?"

"Why don't you keep it? My grandmother once told me that 'lucky Franklins' only stay lucky as long as you *don't* spend them."

They finished their dessert and coffee and left to drive home. Jake loosened his tie immediately after he closed the passenger door for Mindy. The evening's weather was perfect, warm, and moonlit. Mindy rolled down her window to let the breeze play in her hair. The radio played softly during the ride home. Preoccupied with the turn of events, she gazed out the side window.

"Mindy, are you OK?" Jake finally asked.

"Yes. I'm sorry I've been so quiet. Did you want to talk about something?"

"Yes. I wanted to tell you thank you and that I *greatly* appreciate the effort you put into making my birthday special."

"You're welcome. You know, I've been dreaming about this evening ever since our trip out to Giant Pine." Mindy smiled as she squeezed Jake's hand. She had much more to say, but she held back. Her number-one priority for the evening had not been accomplished. Mindy would hold out for a more perfect location. Telling someone for the first time that you love him was not a casual endeavor. She was not entirely sure how he would respond to her announcement. Nor was she sure where it would happen, but she didn't want it to be in the car.

Jake pulled the car into Mrs. Birmingham's driveway. A halo radiated from the light by the back door. He glanced at her, searching for a suggestion.

"Would you like to take a walk?" Mindy asked as she slipped off her stylish yet obviously uncomfortable sandals.

Jake stared at Mindy's sandals on the front seat. "Yes." He slipped off his jacket, tie, shoes, and socks and plopped them on the seat. By the time he joined her at the front of the car, her hand was outstretched for his. Dim rays from the back-door light lit up her beautiful face. He could see that her eyes were trying to tell him something; yet her lips smiled silently.

Strolling down the path that led to the cabins, Jake felt the soft, warm sand ooze between his toes. A pulsating chatter of crickets, insects, and tree frogs emanated from the dark forest. An ever-present pine scent lingered in the cool, moist breeze. Jake's thoughts raced back to the night he first arrived at Camp Koinonia. He had prepared thoroughly before his arrival. However, he'd had no way of foreseeing the virtuous, young woman whose hand now led him through the midsummer night.

Across the camp yard, Jake could see the outside light shining as a beacon above his cabin door. Jake perceived restlessness in Mindy's soul, as though coals of indecision smoldered deep inside her. *Is she looking for something ... or looking for someplace to go?*

They stopped at the path that led to Inspiration Point. Jake watched Mindy peer anxiously down the dark tunnel created by the trees and then shift her gaze over his shoulder to the dock.

As the full moon broke free of the clouds, Mindy and Jake found themselves bathed in moon beams. She ran her hands gently up his arms to take his face in her hands. Jake closed his eyes. His lips readied to receive her kiss.

Mindy slid her cheek along the side of his face. She whispered, "Jake, I love you. I have loved you since the first day I met you. I will always love you, Jake ... no matter what happens to us or what happens to this world ... I will always love you."

Before Jake could say a word, Mindy drew her head back and then pressed her lips to his. She kissed him with what Jake felt must have been all the love in her soul. Jake's skin tingled; his heart leaped. As she pulled away slightly, Mindy's face revealed a radiant, satisfied smile. Jake could see that her weeks of planning had just come to fruition.

"Mindy, I want you to know something ... I love you too ... more than anything in this world. I fell in love with you under the sweet gum tree the week before camp. I will always honor and cherish you."

They melted into each other's arms.

CHAPTER 14

Pine Grove

SURROUNDED BY THE chatter of cicadas, Jake walked alone through the camp yard for the last time. The mid-August heat brought sweat to his head, arms, and chest. He recalled the story of Julius Caesar, where after his successful military campaign, the Roman conqueror exclaimed, "I came … I saw … I conquered."

Jake shook his head. He was not gripped by haughty arrogance; his heart was filled with joy. He was a humble servant. Jake actually related more closely to the Bible prophet Nehemiah, who not only rebuilt the fortress wall around Jerusalem but also instructed his people in the words of the Lord.

Jake had come to serve and through his toil had found true love. It had been only three weeks since his fateful night with Mindy at Commodore's. He felt confident that his newly pronounced affection for Mindy had not adversely affected the campers' stay.

Jake carried a large suitcase in each hand and flung lightly over his right shoulder was his trusty backpack, which only contained two small items. He stepped over the tire tracks of the golf cart that Lex had arranged to be donated to the camp. Lex had given Mrs. Birmingham lessons on how to start and drive the cart. However, she much preferred to be chauffeured.

He made his way up the wide path that led to the camp's parking lot. Mindy and Jake had arranged to meet there at noon after they said "good-bye" to Mrs. Birmingham. That would leave them time to say "good-bye" to each other and still make it home at a reasonable time. His gaze broke onto the almost-empty parking lot. Mindy was there waiting for him. Her car was pulled alongside his so that the two driver doors were across from each other. Mindy got out of her car and ran to hug him. He dropped his suitcases and embraced her. Their plan was to say "good-bye" under the giant beech tree that stood out in the middle of the Pine Grove.

As Jake loaded his suitcases into the car, he kept his backpack on. They shared smiles. They each had prepared a gift for the other. Of course, the gifts were top secret, intended as a surprise.

They walked hand in hand as they reminisced. They reflected about Alexander Montgomery and how he had arranged to give them both generous cash gifts at the end of the summer, just before he left to dig water wells in the desert of Sudan, Africa.

After a short walk through the pines, the towering beech tree came into view. The bench stood in the clearing caused by the thick canopy of tree branches and leaves. It was as though the bench had been waiting patiently for them all summer. Jake and Mindy walked to the bench and sat down.

With that sweet but mischievous grin that Jake had grown to love, Mindy said, "I have something for you." Jake's eyes watered slightly, but he fought back the tears. Mindy reached into her pocket and pulled out two rings. She held them out to Jake. "An eccentric artist named Jeremiah Slough, who lives in the woods outside of Norton, made these matching rings."

Jake's eyes fixed on the pattern inlayed into the silver rings: a single, five-point star and two lightning bolts, followed by a delicate rainbow pattern. He had never mentioned this pattern on the rings he had seen on the bones in the sinkhole. He had never mentioned to anyone that there had been any rings at all. Jake looked at Mindy with an amazement that begged for an explanation.

"I see the star as Jesus. We are the lightning bolts. The rainbow represents the new work that has been created at Camp Koinonia. You can have either one you like. Because of the fact that you never wear jewelry, I thought that you might prefer the smaller one as a toe ring."

Jake slipped off his hiking boot and sock. She carefully slid the ring onto the toe that corresponded to the wedding ring finger. Jake wiggled his toes with delight. He took the other ring from her palm and slid it onto her ring finger. It fit perfectly.

Jake watched as Mindy's face reddened and then paled, as though she could hardly breathe from the weight of the decorated metal band on her wedding ring finger.

"I will wear this ring forever ..." Mindy said.

It was now Jake who bore the playful smile. He reached behind him to retrieve his pack. There were no bottles of water, no fruit, only two picture frames wrapped in shiny gold paper. He handed one to Mindy. She opened it carefully. It was an eight-and-half-by-eleven-inch wooden frame with Camp Koinonia and the camp's dates inscribed across the frame. The picture was of Jake and Mindy from Mrs. Birmingham's camera. It had been taken the night they celebrated his birthday at Commodore's. It was an extraordinary portrait. Their faces captured the radiant love they felt for each other. Jake had placed a copy of the framed print on Mrs. Birmingham's dining room table as he left the house for the last time.

"Thank you, Jake" ... Mindy said.

Jake's grin widened. "You're only seeing the surface; take the back off, and see what's inside."

With a puzzled look, Mindy slipped the locking braces back and pulled off the back cover. There was a photo collage of scenes from the camp: Inspiration Point, Mrs. Birmingham's basement, a nighttime picture of the master bedroom illuminated only by a small flashlight, the Crow's Nest table at Commodores, and a sunset at the dock. The last picture in the series was a shot of the giant beech tree standing in the middle of Pine Grove. It had been taken from the top of a distant tree.

Mindy grabbed him around his neck and kissed him. "I love you, Jake."

"I love you too. Please dig further," he asserted.

She peeled the collage away to find a copy of Judy's map. Under the map was a handwritten letter, describing how he loved her, how he would always love her, and how just as Jesus' love would always be with them, a distance of miles could never dampen the true love between them.

A light trickle of tears ran down Mindy's face. After sliding off the bench and onto his lap, she held her cheek tightly against his. Jake and Mindy sat motionless as the breeze rustled the leaves above them.

Jake noticed that Mindy's tears formed a tiny pool of moisture that was trapped momentarily between his cheek and hers. It rendered a peculiar yet pleasurable sensation. He made no attempt to wipe it off. The warm pool of tears slowly cooled and evaporated.

Jake and Mindy walked hand in hand back to their cars. After one long, last hug and one long, last kiss, they reluctantly got into their cars and started their engines.

As he settled in for the drive, Jake thought of the one additional picture he had hidden in the picture frame. On the backside of the plate that held the pictures to the glass was a black piece of paper. The black paper was glued to the back of the frame's back panel. Hidden underneath the paper was the picture Jake had taken the afternoon at the sinkhole.

In his rush to take the picture of the skeletons, he had inadvertently included his leg and shoe in the picture. Two small moles on the top of his calf were visible, along with the edge of the sinkhole and the two skeletons. Jake had made only two prints of this rendering of the latter-day Romeo and Juliet, one for his frame and one for Mindy's. He wasn't sure why, but he wanted her to have the evidence in case there was ever any question about who, where, or when the skeletons were recovered. He hoped that he would never have to reveal the picture to her. On the day it had been taken, he had provided her with only an outline of the day's events.

Mindy leaned out of her window. "OK, OK … let me go over this one more time … I'll come to your house for Thanksgiving. You'll come to my house for Christmas. *We'll both* write the curriculum for next year's camp at Mrs. Birmingham's house over spring break." Mindy looked into Jake's eyes for assurance. "So this is not good-bye … this is I will see you later."

"Yes." Jake smiled.

"Promise me, Jake."

"I promise you, Mindy. I will see you later."

They looked into each other's eyes. Jake could tell that Mindy was confident in his sincerity, even though she knew that the vast majority of summer camp romances ended on the last day of camp.

"Why don't you take the lead?" suggested Jake.

"We'll take Kellum Road to Highway 51 and then follow it down to I-90," Mindy returned.

Their cars rolled slowly across the parking lot, under the arch of Camp Koinonia, and then out to Kellum Road. Jake knew that Mindy appreciated his suggestion that she should be the lead car. That way, if they got separated, or if she had car problems, he would notice immediately.

Mindy looked at Jake in her rearview mirror. Sometimes he smiled and waved. Other times he would be in deep thought. Even other times, it seemed that he was talking to someone.

The long drive gave her a chance to reflect on the summer. She would always be grateful that she and Jake had conducted their roles with integrity and humility. She was blessed to be in love with a young man who was committed to abstinence until marriage. Although they had never discussed it, Mindy knew that Jake was the man she would marry. She daydreamed of her wedding day, how handsome Jake would look in a black tux, how beautiful she would be in her white wedding dress. Her mind wandered to their wedding night, then onto their honeymoon …

Mindy looked forward to seeing her mother and father. She would have only a few weeks with them before she returned to

Northwestern. She was determined to make the best of their time together. She looked forward to telling her mother all about the amazing rejuvenation she had witnessed at Camp Koinonia. She knew her mother would be proud of her.

She blushed slightly. Mindy realized there would be a few things that would be omitted from the conversation. She realized that there were a number of stories from camp that her mother and older sister had kept only to themselves too.

Mindy thought of the night that the tornado had passed over Mrs. Birmingham's house. She remembered how safe she felt when Jake put his arm around her as they prayed on the basement floor. She reminisced about the evening she and Jake had gone swimming in the lake. She thought of Jake's birthday dinner at Commodore's, the night she kissed him and told him that she loved him. These acts of sincere compassion and affection had turned out to be the most touching and intimate moments that Jake and Mindy had shared that summer. Jake had been a gentleman throughout the summer, and she had grown to love him because of it. She also could not overlook the realization that the Lord had chosen the sunset at the dock to touch her with His blessing. Mindy concluded the summer with a deep and resilient love for Jake and a peace in her heart about their relationship.

Jake could feel the heart tugs of loneliness tightening in his chest as he followed directly behind Mindy's car. *What an incredible nine weeks it has been.* He thought of his staff, the campers, and his friendship with Alexander Montgomery and how it had grown over the last half of the summer. Jake felt an ever-increasing fascination with Alexander Montgomery's mission trip to Sudan.

The death of Alexander's son, Ron, grew more tragic as the situation became more personal to him. Jake wondered if the situation would be different if he and Ron had been friends. He wondered if he could have intervened to prevent the untimely deaths of Ron

Montgomery and Julie Capp. Somehow, if these two had felt the love of Jesus, maybe they would be alive today. Jake realized that Ron and Julie were beyond his reach. He vowed not to let their passing go in vain. Jake would concentrate his efforts on bringing his campers to a deep and personal relationship with Jesus Christ.

In his mind, Jake reevaluated each young camper who had been under his supervision. Had he done everything he could to lead them out of the darkness and into the light? Jake was beginning to realize that he needed to pay particular attention to the kids on the fringe, the kids who were not the brightest Bible scholars, the kids who tended to sulk off to be away from the group.

Jake could feel his new toe ring. He maneuvered his toes to accommodate the newcomer in his shoe. The ring felt at home on his foot. He thought of the skeletons he had recovered from the sinkhole. He figured that they must have purchased their rings from the same artist as Mindy had. *Guess my encounter with Jeremiah Slough was not meant to be. Wonder how she found him and what they talked about.* Jake pondered the rings as symbols of never-ending love. It was the rings which Jake, Mindy, Ron, and Julie all had in common.

He thought of the contrast between Ron Montgomery and himself. Jake thought of the articles about the Frog Pond he had read in Mrs. Birmingham's scrapbook. It made Jake nauseous when he thought of the young lovers who, on that fateful autumn night, had apparently engaged in an intoxicated orgy before they frolicked in the Frog Pond and stumbled into the unseen sink hole. He wondered what inner desperation would drive them to decadence. Ron and Julie's love for each other could not save them.

Jake realized that it was the morals and values that filled their hearts that separated the two couples. Jake and Mindy had chosen a path of service to their Lord and Savior, Jesus. God had used Jake and Mindy to rejuvenate a fading camp. Ron and Julie, on the other hand, had decided to ramble down a dangerous path, a path that led to death by misadventure.

Jake's mind raced as he continued to follow Mindy's car. He was preoccupied with the notion of creating the curriculum for the next generation of campers. He wondered how he would emphasize to the campers that they were there to learn how to be effective Christian leaders and that romantic entanglements were strongly forbidden. Yet, he was the one who had fallen in love on the first day of camp. Even though they had tried to conceal their relationship from the campers, he wondered how successful they had been. He wondered if the camp would have been better if they had maintained only a professional relationship.

Jake pondered his upbringing in the conservative Lutheran church. He was well aware of the writings of Martin Luther and Dietrich Bonheoffer. Jake knew both of them had written in length about the development of young Christian minds. He thought of the suffering and sacrifice that these men had endured. Jake's plight would be slight compared to these giants of the faith. Jake counted his blessings. He, like Luther and Bonheoffer, would depend on the Lord to guide him in writing the curriculum.

A few miles before the road to Chicago veered from his path to Fort Wayne, Jake pulled alongside Mindy and waved. He saw her tears. Mindy lifted her palm from her thigh, brought it to her lips and blew him a kiss. She entered the exit ramp and faded into the distance.

Through the tears that lined his face, Jake could feel the tingling from where Mindy's tears had pooled on his cheek earlier that day. Jake dipped his head.

No ... no ... no, the summer can't really be over. How could camp go by so quickly?

Well ... at least I can reach her by cell phone.

For the rest of the afternoon, Jake could feel where the evaporated tears had formed a mark on his cheek.

CHAPTER 15

Long Distance

JAKE PUSHED BACK from his cluttered desk, took a long breath, stretched, and glanced out his widow to what was shaping up to be the first major snowstorm of January. *It's 10:47 P.M. I wonder if she's still up.* He hit speed dial and smiled as Mindy's phone rang ... "Good evening."

"Hi, Jake."

"Were you studying?"

"Kind of ... what I was actually doing was sitting here, wishing I *was* studying."

"Course overloads again this quarter?"

"Yeah. Jake, you're lucky Taylor lets you take the month of January off to go on mission trips. What do they call that?"

"Interterm."

"So are you all packed and ready to go?" Mindy asked.

"Packed? No. Ready to go? Kind of. Because of my travel schedule, I need to write most of my mission trip report before I leave. I think I'm going to title my report, 'Living Water: The Blessing Beneath Barren Sudan.' That goes on the assumption that we can actually pull water out of the ground."

Jake stood to pace around the room. "I spent all day yesterday at Purdue with Dr. Karl Branding. Mindy, that man is *the expert* in locating underground water, drilling for it, purifying it, transporting it, and storing it. He's been working with Alexander for months, setting him up with drilling equipment."

"I like the title. So how are you going to write the report *before* you leave?" Mindy asked.

"Well … the report has three parts: the history of missionary work in Sudan, how Africans have located water since Bible times, and how strategically-placed wells can help the Christian aid effort. I just finished the first two sections. I'll have to wait to see how the project works out to write the third part."

"I don't remember reading about Sudan in the Bible. Are there many Christians there?" she asked.

"Oh, yeah. Byzantine empress Theodora commissioned the first missionaries there in 540 A.D. Currently, Christians are about 5 percent of the population. One nice thing about Sudan is that English is one of the official languages."

"That's convenient. So how are you going to find water in the desert?"

"The laptop I'll be carrying has the same software that NASA used to look for water on Mars. Dr. Branding helped develop it. I get the feeling he wanted me to handcuff the briefcase to my wrist."

Glancing at the laptop in the old saddlebag, Jake continued, "I suggested the 'security by obscurity' approach. I wanted to use my old saddle bag instead of his aluminum briefcase—and no handcuffs. No one is going to suspect a business student of carrying highly sensitive software. Dr. Branding loaded the software onto an obsolete Compaq laptop. The whole thing looks like a piece of junk. And that's the way we like it. He's sending a couple of drill bits and some spare parts in a duffle bag too. Just for safekeeping, he's not going to give me the access code until I get over there."

"Why is this software so sensitive?" she asked.

"I get the feeling that if it fell into the wrong hands, it could be used to find gold and diamonds instead of water."

"Mmmmm, so are you going to bring back a diamond for me?" Mindy's voice rang with anticipation.

"Ahhh, yeah … if I find one, I'll bring it back for you." Jake blushed at the thought. He'd calculated for months, trying to come up with money for an engagement ring. But his current budget would barely get him through the school year. Jake knew that if he and Alexander were successful in finding and pumping water to the surface, there would be a substantial cash bonus for both of them. *I'd better not say anything,* Jake thought. *I'll wait until the money is in my hand.* "So guess what Alexander wants me to bring him?"

"I don't know? A souvenir canteen from the Wisconsin Dells?"

"You know, that's a great idea. Do you have one?"

"Sure. It's at home in a box in the basement."

"It's kind of late for it to make it on this trip. We might have to work on that for his birthday."

"So what *does* he want?" Mindy inquired.

"Almond Joy candy bars."

"Oh. I want one *right now*."

"I put them in Ziplock bags, in case they melt. How about I snitch two of them, eat them both, and describe every sensation."

"Don't be cruel," Mindy snapped. "Maybe you should save them for Alexander."

"Right." Jake felt inside his suitcase to verify the bags of candy were still there.

"So how did they find water up to now *without* special software?"

"Divining rods," he replied.

"Divining rods?" Mindy asked in a puzzled voice.

"In ancient times, they used the forked branch of a willow or hazel tree. It looks like an old-fashioned slingshot. You hold the forked sections in your hands as you walk across the land, and the branch twitches to indicate a vein of underground water."

"Yeah, right. The branch twitches when it finds water that is *underground*."

"Yes," Jake said, nodding his head.

"Is that kind of like an Ouija board?"

"I don't know. No one knows exactly how they work. But *I know* the divining rods work. Christians have used divining rods for thousands of years. Pioneers and settlers in this country used them extensively. My granddad used one to help us decide where to drill our well when we moved to the country. He showed me how to do it. As I walked across the yard, I could feel the branch twitching. It was kind of like getting a nibble on a fishing pole."

"Why don't you use a divining rod?" Mindy inquired in a mildly sarcastic tone.

"It's like a lot of things; a few people are really good at it, and no one else can get it to work."

"And for those people … there's drilling equipment from Purdue and software from NASA," she said.

Jake paused. "Yeah. You see, in Africa, the witchdoctors are the ones who can get the divining rods to work. From what Alexander has seen, they are almost 100% accurate in finding underground water. But witchdoctors choose to find water only in areas of demonic oppression. That's one way they draw people in. They might have the edge in finding water, but they are limited in their ability to dig by hand through twenty feet of sand and then three feet of solid rock. We are the ones with the modern drills."

"If we can find and bring the water to the surface at orphanages and Christian missionary bases, we can break the stranglehold the witchdoctors have on the local tribes. That's why my report is called "Living Water." Jake spoke with a twinge of pride.

"Handcuffed to suitcases, witchdoctors … I'm getting a bad feeling about this trip. Jake, are you sure this is safe?"

"Yeah, I think so. We both know there are going to be risks. Most of the trouble is in the Darfur region. That's in the western part of the country. I'll be in the south. Alexander has been there for a while. I'm sure I'll be OK." Pulling his desk chair out, he slouched into it. "Hey, enough about me. What have you been up to?"

"I got another letter from your mom yesterday."

"You mean a letter in the mail?" he asked.

"Yes."

"Wow, she must really like you."

"Why? Don't you get letters?" Mindy asked.

"No, I call home every Sunday. So, what did the letter say?"

"I guess your mom has free time between her swimming and your dad finishing his workout. So she takes stationery and writes letters. She makes it an informal chit-chat letter so we can get know each other better."

"So do you write a *letter* back?" he asked.

"I did the first time. After that, we agreed that I'd send an e-mail."

"Wow, she really does like you."

"I talked to my dad; he's planning a party for Mom's birthday on February 24. Would you like to come home with me that weekend?"

"Sure, I'll put it on the calendar to drive up Saturday and then back on Sunday." Jake searched for his calendar as he sifted through the papers on his desk.

"No, come up on Friday. *Please* ... I hardly had a chance to show you around at Christmas. Maybe we can go on a *date* ... you know, hold hands and sit right next to each other."

"Wow, a date, you mean just the two of us? That sounds great. How about tonight? If I left right now, I could get from Taylor to Northwestern by about 4:00 A.M. There might not be any theaters open, but I really like the idea of holding hands and sitting right next to each other." He chuckled. "What do you think I should get your mom for her birthday?"

"Jake, you don't need to get her anything. She'll be thrilled just to have you there."

"That's great, but don't leave me in the lurch. Help me think of something that's not on her list. Something she doesn't know she wants." Jake shifted to sit up straight.

"Mmmm. Well you know one time after Christmas, Dad took Mom shopping in downtown Chicago. She wore that Taylor sweatshirt you gave me. She *really* looked great in the dark purple and gold. Why don't you get her one of those? I guess a couple of people came up and asked if she was a Taylor alumni. They said she had the 'glow.'"

"The glow?" Jake queried.

"Yeah, I guess people from Taylor can find each other in a crowd because they have the 'glow' of the Holy Spirit around them."

121

"Your mom graduated from the University of Chicago."

"*That's* why she needs the sweatshirt," she quipped.

"OK, I'll pick one up as soon as I get back. So, how's my glow?" Jake asked as he grinned.

"Let me check out the window. Oh yeah, I can see it even through the snow."

"Wow, I must be glowing; your window faces west, and Taylor's directly south."

"Jake, don't confuse the compliment with the facts."

"Sorry. You know spring break is only two months away. Have you talked with Mrs. Birmingham?" Jake stood and leaned his shoulder against the wall to peer out the window.

"I talked to her a couple of days ago. She really liked the idea of the three of us developing a piece of the curriculum. With you developing a koinonia society in the modern world, me investigating prayer ministry and Alexander researching evangelism. Alexander has been sending over the Evangelism material in small packets. I guess the internet connection at the Christian Aide compound in Sudan is dreadfully slow."

"So how did it go at your interview with the lady who heals people with prayer?" Jake asked.

"It was amazing. Her name is Mrs. Matthews. She's been healing people since she was a teenager. She works in the background and never draws attention to herself. She was very gracious and generous with me. I guess a lot of people have come to her to be healed, but almost no one has been interested in becoming a healer."

"So, how *does* it work?"

"She said that in her case and for the other people she knows, it's the intimate relationship with Christ that makes the prayers work. She has studied healing prayer thoroughly over the years. She says that God does give certain people the anointing, but a lot of people don't recognize it or are afraid to pursue it. All true faith healers have traits in common: pureness of heart, absolute faith that Jesus can and will heal the sick, and deep compassion for those who suffer."

"Sounds like you are a good candidate," he said.

"She pointed out that Jesus cured the sick and removed demons with commands. 'Blind man see. Pick up your mat and walk. Demons be removed.' He never used pleas or requests. She asserted that healers pray in His name, through the authority of Jesus Christ. She also shared the scripture where Jesus said that some prayers for healing are only answered after a prolonged season of prayer and fasting." Mindy paused to catch her breath.

"Wow, that's powerful stuff." Jake sat on the edge of his bed.

"She said that her prayers don't work all the time and that some people are better at healing certain types of illnesses than others. She has success with ear infections and sinus infections and headaches, but not with burns."

"How does she know who to pray for?"

"The Holy Spirit brings people to her, or He brings burdens to her heart. It is her job to pray for anyone who asks for it. Jesus decides who, how, and when people get healed. It's all part of God's master plan."

"Is this something you can study?" Jake asked.

"Oh yeah. She told me to start with the New Testament. Read every passage where Jesus heals someone. Then she gave me a couple of books on John G. Lake and Smith Wigglesworth. You know, the most fascinating piece of literature she gave me is an article she clipped from a magazine some time ago. It is a series of interviews with faith healers in Appalachia. These people work in regions where there are few medical doctors. There is something about those simple, intensely faithful folks that really lit a fire in my heart. God gave each of them a specific verse from the Old Testament to help them heal specific illnesses."

Mindy continued, "She went on to say that in the end times there will be an outpouring of the Holy Spirit to bring healing around the world. Have you ever heard of the International House of Prayer in Kansas City?"

"Sure, I know some students who are going out there over Interterm." Jake lay back on his bed with his free arm tucked under his head.

"They have prayer rooms where people's prayer requests are interceded for daily. Another ministry has teams engaged in worship twenty-four hours a day, seven days a week. They've kept it up for over ten years. I'd like to take a field trip out there ... don't think its going to happen before school's over."

"So, how soon are you going to start healing people?" he asked.

"I don't know. Maybe I've already started."

"Really?"

"Before I left Mrs. Matthews, she asked if she could pray for me. Of course, I said "yes." She took my hand and closed her eyes. I couldn't hear what she prayed. But I do remember feeling the Holy Spirit moving within me. Both of us were crying for most of the prayer."

Filled with emotion, Mindy's voice broke, "I hadn't thought about it until just now, but I find myself praying for ambulances as they drive by and even for strangers as they pass by me on the way to class. Somehow I can feel their pain. Mrs. Matthews says for most people, it takes lots of practice. She wants me to come back and pray for the people in her retirement community."

"So you *are* going to pray for me while I'm in Sudan?" Jake asked.

"Yes, every day, all day."

"Thank you."

"How are you coming on recreating koinonia in modern society?" Mindy asked.

Jake sat up. "Well, I don't have anything as dynamic as you have, but I have pulled together a lot of material." Jake stood to resume pacing around the room. "As you can imagine, there are a lot of commentaries written about the early church of Acts 2. *Koinonia* is used nineteen times in the Greek New Testament. It not only refers to a community based on Christ-centered fellowship, service, and prayer but also the way Christians participate in the Lord's Supper, Communion. In many ways, koinonia exists today in every healthy Christian church." Jake caught his breath. "What I am looking for is *why* and *how* some groups thrive for the long haul, while others wither and die."

"So which churches are you studying?" she asked.

"Everything from Willow Creek Church in Chicago to small Amish communities," he said. "I didn't just look at churches. I studied group dynamics in different types of communities, everything from hippie communes in the late 1960s to the International Space Station and the McMurdo research base in Antarctica. You know one of the best case studies on koinonia comes from a tiny town in Indiana."

"Oh, let me guess, Upland Indiana."

"No, but you know I could study the camaraderie of workers at Ivanhoe's ice cream parlor—that's just across the street. The town I'm talking about is New Harmony. Back in the early 1800s, a German immigrant named Johann Georg Rapp led his group of devout Christians from Pennsylvania to the Indiana wilderness. They built a community called Harmony. The Rappites were highly successful at farming, textiles, and manufacturing. They prospered in Indiana for ten years."

Jake looked at the stack of research papers piled in the corner of his bedroom. "When Rapp decided to move his followers back to Pennsylvania, he sold the town's houses, factories, and 30,000 acres to Robert Owen, a social reformer and utopian thinker. Owen recruited intellectuals and free thinkers of the day to join him at what he called New Harmony. Owen had some great ideas about free education and a classless society, but too many intellectuals and not enough skilled labor brought the utopian experiment to an end after only two years."

"What happened to the Rappites?" Mindy asked.

"They prospered for a while in their new community in Pennsylvania called Economy. Unfortunately, Rapp was a tyrant. The skilled workers grew increasingly distraught about not being fairly compensated for their work and left the community. Rapp strictly enforced celibacy among his followers. He believed that Jesus would return in his lifetime and that they needed to be pure for His arrival. With few people from outside the community willing to join a celibate group and the defection of the master craftsmen, the community eventually fell apart."

"So …" she pondered, "if all work and no play burns out the laborers and all brains and no brawn can't make it either, what *is* the answer?"

"The answer is … that it is a whole lot easier to *dream* up a utopian society than it is to find one to live in. If I were going to design a koinonia community, I'd start with those who are followers of Christ. There is something about the way Christians love and care about each other that makes koinonia possible.

"Next, a strong, purpose-driven leadership is crucial. If the leaders don't know where the group is headed, they'll wander and squander." Jake extended two fingers as he resumed his march around his room. "The people in charge have to be forward thinking enough to train the next generation of leaders."

After taking a quick breath, he continued, "Third, but equally important, you have to have *infrastructure*. Someone has to make sure the water runs, the food arrives, and the lights come on. And at the other end, someone has to *take out the trash*. That's one thing I learned from the base in Antarctica and the space station. Garbage will bury a community if it's not dealt with."

"JAKE!" Mindy exclaimed.

Jake ceased. "Yes."

"You *already* have my vote for mayor."

"As your mayor, do I have to carry out the trash?"

"Yes," Mindy replied. "You bring in the water, make sure the lights stay on, and carry out the trash. I'll set the table and prepare the meals."

Drawing great satisfaction from their agreement, Jake smiled as he nodded his head. "OK, I think that will work."

"What would you think about meeting somewhere for lunch before we pull into the camp at spring break?" Mindy asked.

"You mean so we can compare notes before we meet with Mrs. Birmingham?"

"No! So we can be *together* …"

"Oh, yeah. You mean hold hands and sit right next to each other," he replied.

"Yeah. Why does it seem that it's always *my* idea?"

"Oh no. Don't think it's not my idea; I just don't want you to think I'm pushing it. Meeting for lunch is a great idea."

Mindy yawned. "When Mrs. Birmingham called the other day, she asked how my classes were going. She knows about my dream to be the next director of Camp Koinonia. She said that she is praying for the Lord to bring it to pass." She hesitated. "She shared that she feels weak and isn't sure how many more years she has left. She wondered if I'd assume the role of director for next year's camp."

"Mindy, that's great, so that's why you've accelerated your class load. Why didn't you tell me about it?"

"I wasn't sure if the college would work with me. Well, I showed them the report I wrote about improving Camp Koinonia. They wanted to hear about the results. The bottom line is, if I write the report in the form of a thesis, they will count it as an independent-study course. Those three credits will allow me to graduate."

"So …" Jake gathered his thoughts. "You're graduating *this* spring. That does change the equation a little bit."

Mindy continued, "Mrs. Birmingham went on to say that if things develop between you and me, we need to understand that the director lives at the camp all year around. Meaning, I will be moving to Norton at the end of this school year."

"So, in a best-case scenario …" Jake pondered, "we both graduate at the end of *this* school year. You become the Director of Camp Koinonia, and I get a job in Norton."

"Yes, and we live happily ever after!"

"Mindy, I have something to tell you. It's one of the reasons I called. A man named Blake Chapman called me. He's the president of Central Wisconsin Bank. He was wondering if I'd be interested in interviewing for an assistant manager's position at one of his banks."

"What! Why didn't you tell me earlier?"

"I just found out today. I wanted to pray about it first."

"Praise the LORD! Jake, that's great. When do you start?" Mindy's excitement belted over the headset.

"Calm down. I don't have the job yet. Even if this job doesn't work out, I want you to know that I will get a job around the camp. What would any location in the world be if you were not there with me?"

"Jake, get in your car and get up here *right now.* I need to give you a big hug."

Shaking his head, Jake glanced at his watch. "I should have left four hours ago."

"So let's look ahead," she said. "You're flying out tomorrow. You'll be in Africa for two weeks. I'll meet you at the airport when you get back. Mom's birthday is a month after that, and then spring break is the first week in April." She yawned again. "Jake, I miss you already."

"I miss you too. Behave yourself while I'm gone."

"Yeah right, look who's talking. Hold on a minute, I'm pulling back my comforter and sheet … setting the alarm … turning on the night light and the desk lamp off … fluffing my pillow. There … ahhhhhhh."

"Are you comfortable now?" he asked.

"Yes, for the first time today … Thanks for calling me."

"You're welcome; did you think I would leave the country without saying 'good-bye'?"

"No, I knew you would call."

"You know," Jake's voice softened, "I wish we could climb into a chamber and be magically transported to the beach at camp. And it wouldn't be blowing freezing snow and seventeen degrees. It would be summer and the sand would still be warm. There would be a couple of William Berry's custom chairs sitting there, waiting for us. It would be just the two of us, under the moon and the stars. And the crickets and tree frogs would be chattering away."

"Yes, Jake. I'm there with you … and there are Almond Joy candy bars there."

Jake laughed, "Yes and slung on the back of your chair is the souvenir canteen from the Wisconsin Dells full of lemonade."

"And I don't have any homework … and you don't have any projects?"

"That's right."

"Jake ... let's not say 'good-bye,' I can't stand the thought of good-bye. Just tell me ... good night."

"Good night, Mindy. I'll always love you."

"I'll always love you too. I'll never stop praying for you. Good night, Jake."

Jake listened as the phone fell silent. Turning his phone off, he plugged it into its charger and picked up the framed picture that Mrs. Birmingham had taken of the two of them, the one from the night they celebrated his birthday at Commodore's Restaurant. Tears welled up. He carefully slid the picture into his suitcase and turned off his desk lamp.

From his darkened room, he watched the snow blowing outside his window. Jake reflected on Mindy's last words. The absence of "good-bye" left him feeling that their conversation wasn't over. He noted that in the last few minutes, her voice had changed from a mature, college coed to almost childlike.

Fathers never say "good-bye" when they tuck their daughters into bed. "Good night" leaves the bedside with the assurance of security and proximity. With the slightest whimper or cry, she could retrieve her father's attention. Because the father would not be leaving, he would be in the next room or just down the hall. The father-daughter interaction would live on, day in and day out.

"Good night" was, after all, immensely more satisfying than "good-bye."

After a deep breath and a long stretch, he glanced at his over-stuffed suitcase and then back out at the swirling snow. *I wonder if my flight is going to be cancelled. Guess I better get some sleep.*

Wonder if Alexander was kidding when he said it was going to be over 100 degrees when I land in Sudan.

PART TWO

Missionaries to Sudan

He who dwells in the shelter of the Most High will rest in the shadow of the Almighty. I will say of the LORD, "He is my refuge and my fortress, my God, in whom I trust." Surely he will save you from the fowler's snare and from the deadly pestilence. He will cover you with his feathers, and under his wings you will find refuge; his faithfulness will be your shield and rampart.

—Psalm 91:1–4

CHAPTER 16

Rebekah

JAKE STRUGGLED TO open his eyes. He squinted to make out his surroundings. In a dimly lit storeroom, he flinched from pain. *Well, it may be hot in here, but at least I'm out of the desert. Let's start at the top. My head … my head is pounding, front and back.*

Jake's swollen, bruised cheek stung with every move of his face. *Guess I've grown quite a shiner.* The lump on the back of his head felt like an egg. He assumed it came from the butt of an AK 47 assault rifle. *My gut hurts. They kicked me right before they threw me off the back of the truck. My arms and legs … good, I can wiggle my toes and fingers; at least I'm all in one piece.* Jake consciously tried to move his arms and legs, but to no avail. He was a prisoner. Jake drifted in and out of consciousness. He forced a deep breath into his lungs. *Lord, help me!*

Jake thought back to the snow-covered Midwest and his phone conversation with Mindy the night before he came to Sudan. *Mindy … I hope you're praying for me … I hope you keep praying for me.*

He remembered the joy Alexander and he had experienced only a few days ago, when they brought water to the surface at a local village using the new drilling equipment. *After that early success, maybe I was foolish to insist on taking the drilling rig to a remote village. They warned me that the guerilla thugs were out there, but somehow I assumed they wouldn't harm a US citizen.* Rolling his eyes brought a sharp pain to his brow.

Jake forced another deep breath. Alerted by the noise, an elderly black nurse arose from the box she was sitting on at the end of Jake's cot. She came to his side and smiled as she whispered a few words in her native language. She placed her hand on his chest to reassure him. She felt his forehead and checked his pulse. Then with her index finger pressed against her lips, she indicated that he was to remain silent. She tapped the saline bag and then returned to look Jake directly in the eyes. Holding up her index finger, she indicated, in universal sign language, that she would be back in one minute.

The sparse supplies that lined the makeshift shelves told Jake that he was being confined in the closet of some crude clinic in the African bush. After a few minutes, the door to the supply closet opened, and in walked an elderly African man and a teenaged African girl.

"Good afternoon. My name is Doctor Isaiah. We have been praying for you. Can you speak English?"

"Yes. Where am I?" Jake asked.

"You, my friend, are in the Nabutu clinic for orphans in Sudan, Africa." Dr. Isaiah picked the clipboard off the hook beside Jake's cot. "What is your name?"

"My name is Jake Olson. I'm from the United States. I'm here for two weeks, drilling wells with the Christian Aide Organization."

"Well, Mr. Jake, you were looking for water in a very unconventional manner. My daughter found you *face down in the desert.* She said she had noticed a rain cloud off on the horizon; she grabbed a bucket and ran to see if the cloud was giving water. What she found was you. She came back for a cart so her sisters and she could bring you to me. I could tell that you were a visitor to this land, so I cleaned you up to assess your wounds and then started an IV."

"Thank you." Jake nodded slightly as he smiled at the young woman and then returned his eyes to Dr. Isaiah. "How soon can I get back to base?"

"You must rest now, and I do mean *rest*," asserted Dr. Isaiah.

Jake relaxed. He was still tied to the cot, but that did not matter to him anymore.

"Mr. Jake, you are a blessed man. The Lord has blessed you with the courage to leave the security of the United States to come to the African desert to dig wells for the poor children who have little food and almost no water. It is people like you who bring us hope. I commend you for that. The Lord protected you as you lay in the desert. He has also blessed you with this young woman who found you. This child would have likely perished years ago if it were not for the aid and nutrition from your Christian Aide Organization. And finally, my friend, God has blessed you with a tenacious woman."

Jake stared in anticipation as the doctor revealed his clipboard. Dr. Isaiah presented a page-size printout of Mindy's face poised behind her uplifted left hand. The back of her left hand revealed the ring she and Jake had in common. The star and lightning pattern on her ring matched the pattern on Jake's toe ring. In the picture, Mindy's face peered directly at the camera, rendering a life-size portrait. Her eyes stared directly at whoever looked upon the picture. In her face, Jake could sense the love she held for him and could feel her concern for his safety. It was a riveting shot. Mindy's strength, compassion, and resolute determination to find her man were imparted to everyone who laid eyes upon her.

The spot on Jake's cheek tingled, where Mindy's tears had pooled the day they said "good-bye" at the Pine Grove. His hands were bound. He was unable to touch it.

"The instructions attached to this picture/poster were very clear," Dr. Isaiah said. "They read, 'Find the man that wears this ring on his toe. Provide for him. All of the expenses needed for his care will be generously reimbursed. Contact the Christian Aide Organization; they will dispatch someone to retrieve him.'

"There was one more instruction. Mindy wanted this picture to be placed by your bed, even if you were unconscious." Dr. Isaiah continued, "Yesterday, I was in the next town when I walked past the bulletin board and saw Mindy's poster; I was immediately drawn to her face. It was then that I recognized the pattern on her ring was the same one that was on your toe ring.

"Your Mindy was wise not to use your face on the poster. The thugs may have recognized you and gone back to find you for the ransom you may be worth, or gone back to kill you and destroy your body so that you could never be found. Because of Mindy's employing the rings that were unique to the two of you, only through prayer and the Holy Spirit were we able to identify you."

Dr. Isaiah turned to the young African girl. "This is my daughter Kenchassa; her Christian name is Rebekah. She will attend to you. If you give me your word that you will stay on this cot until a transport arrives for you, I will untie your arms and legs."

"Yes, of course, you have my word. Do you have a phone … so I can call the United States?" Jake asked.

"No … Please keep your voice to a whisper. This clinic is restricted for orphans with AIDS. If anyone finds out that we are treating a white man, it would be bad for *public relations*. One other thing, if the thugs find out that you survived, they will seek to kill you so you will not be able to identify them. They will also seek to punish the group of youth that saved you. It is for this security reason that we have you housed *here,* in our penthouse suite."

Dr. Isaiah removed the cloth bandages that bound Jake's arms and legs to the cot and opened a generic bottle of nutrient solution. "Our children prefer the strawberry flavored drink, so I am giving you the lime. You do like lime?" Dr. Isaiah smiled as he placed the straw into the container and handed it to Jake. Rebekah quickly helped Jake sit up and placed a large bag of bed sheets behind him for support. "If you can live without painkillers, I will save what little I have for the children. If you need something, I would like to save it until tonight, so you can sleep."

Jake smiled and raised the cocktail in a toast to his generous host.

"Capture your urine in this jar. I need to check it before you leave." Dr. Isaiah disappeared out the door.

Jake took a long drink, *Mmmmmm … yes,* he thought, "Lime is my favorite flavor." Jake motioned to the young woman to sit on the cot next to him. "Do you speak English?" he whispered.

"Yes," she whispered back.

"What day is it?"

"It is Thursday."

"Thank you. What number on the calendar is it?"

"It is January 20."

He thought to himself, *My plane leaves in two days. Lord, I pray you open the doors for me.*

Jake turned to the girl, "Rebekah is a name from the Bible. Have you ever heard her story?"

"Oh yes, many times!" She smiled. "I know many Bible stories." Rebekah's eyes brightened. "You are like Moses, who was lost in the desert and was found and brought to safety and cared for by a tribe who did not know him. I thought of Elijah and his rain cloud when I saw that small, white cloud over the desert. Do you think a hard rain is about to fall?"

He shook his head at his new friend. "I don't know. Only the Lord can make the clouds and bring the rain." He settled back on his cot. Jake massaged his tender, swollen cheek as his thoughts raced back to the armed thugs yelling and waving their rifles as they drove up in a truck to the drilling site. They insisted that the locals move the drill to their camp. The local elder in charge of the project refused to comply. His refusal provoked the mob to riot.

Jake remembered hitting the kill switch on the drill and locking the laptop right before something hard struck the back of his head. As he faded out, he was punched in the face and then kicked in the abdomen. The thugs threw him on the back of their truck, only later to dump him off onto the hot sand.

Lying with his face in a cavity, which he had hollowed out of the sand, an image came to him: He was swimming … in the lake at Camp Koinonia. Mindy was there, her wet hair slicked back over her head, her eyes and smile beaming at him. Jake felt the cool chill of the water. The peace that passes all understanding permeated his soul. Everything went black. The next thing he remembered was the storeroom he had awakened in earlier that day.

Jake prayed silently, *Thank you, Lord, for bringing me to this safe haven. Thank you for all those who have cared for me, and I especially lift up Mindy. I pray she will somehow know I'm safe.*

"May I hold your hand?" inquired Rebekah.

"Sure," Jake held his hand out.

Rebekah cupped Jake's hand between her two palms. Her hands were small but strong. Her slender fingers curled gently as she formed their hands into a knot. Rebekah closed her eyes and prayed quietly in her native tongue. After a few minutes, a tear ran down her cheek. She opened her eyes, smiled, took a deep breath, and looked directly at Jake. "I see the heart of King David in you. You seek first the kingdom of the Lord, and God favors you greatly. Your angel will bring you much joy and will bear you beautiful children. The youngest one will be wise beyond all the rest."

Bewildered, Rebekah sat back, still holding Jake's hand. "I am perplexed by the things I saw as I prayed for you. I could see Mindy, and yet there was a light shining around her, as though she were an angel. There were two children. The baby was white with blonde hair; the older child was black … and her name was Rebekah. And one day, when she is old enough, she will come to Africa and lead the people out of the darkness."

Rebekah shook her head slowly. "Not everything that I see comes to pass, not at least from where I can see. But I must warn you, a time of great distress is rapidly approaching. Jake, you must take heed. Cling to the Lord. Rely only on the Holy Spirit to guide you."

"Thank you for sharing what you have seen with me." His heart stirred.

Rebekah slid off the cot. "It is dinnertime. You do like goat's milk and rice?"

"Yes, very much."

Rebekah left and returned with two bowls, each with a spoon. "You know we have seven goats and twelve chickens. All the children work to take care of them. We have names for all of them. Would you mind if I named one of our baby goats Jake and one Mindy?"

"No, not at all. We would be honored," Jake replied. "Our names are spelled J-a-k-e and M-i-n-d-y."

"What does Mindy mean?"

"It means a woman of great compassion." Jake flashed his new friend a mischievous grin.

Shortly after they were finished eating, Dr. Isaiah returned. "Mr. Jake, you must be a man of high importance! A government vehicle has arrived with an armed guard to escort you back to the Christian Aide headquarters."

Jake and Rebekah looked at each other. Jake took the picture of Mindy off of the clipboard and handed it to Rebekah.

"Oh no!" she protested. "You need to keep this! It will keep you company on your long journey home."

"The Lord is my strong tower. He will protect me, and my dreams will keep me company. I am not sure when I will return to Africa, and I do not know if Mindy will be with me. So, in the meantime, you keep this picture so you can recognize her if she comes to your village." Jake handed Mindy's portrait to Rebekah.

Rebekah took the picture and held it close to her chest.

Jake turned to Dr. Isaiah, "Could I take a mailing label off one of these packages? I would like to have your name and address."

"Yes, of course."

Jake scanned the information page still on the clipboard. "My information is correct. I will be in touch with you. Thank you for everything."

"You are welcome," Dr. Isaiah said. "I look forward to hearing from you. If you're ready, your transport is waiting."

Back at Christian Aide's headquarters, Jake endured a thorough medical examination. The staff doctors decided that he was healthy enough to be released to leave the country.

Missionaries had access to a special phone. They could call anywhere in the world at no charge for up to three minutes. Jake dialed Mindy's cell phone.

"Hello …" Mindy answered.

"Mindy, it's Jake."

"Jake! Praise the Lord. You are alive. Where are you?"

"I'm at the Christian Aide base. I will be leaving tomorrow to catch my plane to Frankfurt and then to Chicago."

"Are you on the same flight?"

"Yes, Flight 1977, scheduled to arrive at O'Hare at 6:30 P.M."

"Jake, I've been worried sick about you. And then something happened yesterday. A peace came over me. I got the feeling that everything was going to be alright."

"We don't have much time left on the phone. I wanted to tell you that I love you and to thank you for all your prayers and for the picture of your face and the ring." Jake continued, "When they dragged me out of the desert, I was unconscious. The doctor noticed my toe ring. When he was in town, he was drawn to your picture and recognized the pattern on your ring. That was the only way they had to identify me."

"Wait … did you just say that *when they dragged you out of the desert, you were unconscious?*"

There was a pause on the other end of the phone. Jake sensed Mindy's displeasure.

"What about *Alexander*?" Mindy asked.

"Oh, he's fine, I guess. Alexander's driver told me all about it this morning. Alexander was captured the same day I was. Instead of beating and abandoning him, the thugs took him to their leader." Jake continued, "Alexander was interrogated by their kingpin. The henchman was in a rage because he could not understand why the Christians came back year after year, no matter how badly they were treated. The leader wanted to know, 'Why do your people dig wells for children who have no way to pay you back? Those

140

children will all die from AIDS in a short time anyway.' Alexander looked the man in the eye and told him that it was the merciful love of Jesus that motivated him to care for the weak.

"Alexander's comment stunned the warlord, who burst into tears. Alexander got up and placed his hands on the weeping man's shoulder. Alexander asked the warlord, 'Would you like for me to lead you out of the darkness and into the light?'

"'Yes.' The warlord answered.

"Alexander directed him, 'You must pray this prayer with me. Repeat every word. If you are unsure, I will stop and explain everything.' Through the saving grace of Jesus Christ, the once evil monster turned his life to the Light.

"Apparently," Jake paused, "Alexander came back to the Aide compound only long enough to find out that I was safe, and then he packed one suitcase full of clothes and the other full of food and Bibles. His driver was instructed to drop him off at a specific point in the road. 'My new friends will bring me back when I am ready,' Alexander instructed his driver."

"Wow ..." Mindy said. "Sounds like Alexander will be adding a new chapter to his evangelism curriculum."

"Listen, after we are married and have children, what would you think about the name Rebekah?" he asked.

"Is ... that ... a ... marriage proposal?" Mindy asked, obviously delighted yet confused by the question. "Or are you only wondering about whether or not I like the name Rebekah?"

"Ahhhhhh. For this moment, I was just wondering about the name ..."

"Well, to tell you the truth, I've always dreamed of having one daughter named Anna and another named Rebekah. But you know, lately I have been thinking of a third child, a mischievous little rascal named Jacob. Why?"

"Hey, the timer's going off, *I love you.*" Jake exclaimed.

"*I love you too!* I'll see you at O'Hare."

Click.

CHAPTER 17

O'Hare

JAKE'S FLIGHTS FROM Sudan to Frankfurt to Chicago gave him time to reflect. He thought mostly of Mindy, about what a great wife she would be. He was already anticipating sharing his life with her. Jake speculated as to how and when he would ask her to marry him. He knew these things had to be carefully planned. *Maybe I should wait until we are both out of school. I wonder how she will react to my disfigured face.* Jake sighed. *Well, at least Alexander and I were able to bring water to the surface before the ambushes. Thank you, Lord, for keeping the laptop from falling into the enemy's hands. The locals should be able to repair the drills with a few spare parts.*

Somewhere over the Atlantic, Jake's fatigue displaced his discomfort. He closed his eyes.

As Jake made his way from the baggage claim area, he searched earnestly for Mindy. He spotted her in the distance. She looked at him with great joy and then with horror as she saw his black-and-blue face. She scrambled towards him.

"Welcome home …" she said as she hugged him. "It's so nice to hold you again."

Jake's eyes watered under the pain of her squeeze.

Mindy felt the lump on the back of his head. "Why did they do this to you?"

"Oh, you know. Thugs will be thugs the world around. All they know is to beat people up, take their watches and wallets, and then dump them off the back of the truck," Jake said. "I'm really starting to feel sorry for those misfit boys. You know, they've not had the blessing of good Christian homes like we have."

"Jake, you have a knack for seeing the glass that is half empty as being *three-quarters full!*" Mindy chuckled. "You must be exhausted."

"Yes." Jake tried to conceal how extremely tired and badly beaten his body was.

"What do you need right now?"

"I need you, Mindy. You are my number-one priority."

Mindy carefully kissed the side of his face that was not black and blue. "You have me, Jake."

"Mindy, I'm sorry about our short conversation from the Aide Compound. I wasn't very sensitive about how I conveyed the situation."

"It's OK. I'm glad you called … to say you were alive. While you were missing, my heart ached through a full range of pain that I had never felt before. I have a new appreciation for what the wives of missionaries endure."

"How about we go get a large glass of Coke, a cheeseburger, and a slice of Chicago-style pizza?" Jake asked.

Mindy nodded. "Instead of you driving back to Taylor tonight, why don't I drive us to my parents' house? That'll give you a day or so to rest. I can stay home and access my classes tomorrow online. We can't wait to hear about your trip." Mindy smiled her playful, mischievous grin.

"Mindy, I look terrible. I can't go to your parents' house."

"Jake, you *do* look terrible. You must be exhausted. That's why you need to let us do this for you. Would you insist on doing this for me if the roles were reversed?"

"Yes. Do they even know you're planning this?"

"They've already made your bed and have a 2-liter bottle of Coke in the refrigerator."

Jake nodded. He realized everything had been prearranged. Jake and Mindy walked hand in hand as they made their way through the airport. They visited a number of fast-food restaurants and then braced themselves to face the frigid January wind that raged between the terminal and Mindy's car.

Jake leaned the seat back as Mindy pulled onto I-90. He was a little uncomfortable. He figured that the Cokes, cheeseburger, and pizza would have been enough. It was the malted chocolate shake that threw him over the top. It was a misery he gladly endured. He reflected back over the past few days. What a turn around his life had taken. Only a few days before, he was face down, abandoned in the desert. Now, he was being pampered by the woman he loved.

He couldn't help but think of the wild-eyed boys who had beaten him. Jake was starting to realize that the kids who needed him most were not the ones who lived in orphanages. Jake was already feeling the yearning to return to Africa. He thought of Dr. Isaiah's daughter Rebekah and her vision.

Mindy took her hand off the steering wheel and slid it down Jake's forearm. She gently squeezed his hand, and he squeezed back.

"Jake?" Mindy asked. Her voice resonated with a trace of anxiety.

"Yes."

"Can I talk to you about something?"

"Yes."

"Who's Rebekah?"

Jake looked in her eyes for a hint of what might be bothering her. "Rebekah is a teenage African girl. Her father is the doctor who cared for me after she found me in the desert. She can perceive things ... you know, spiritual things. She said that I have been blessed by the Lord. She told me that my angel will bring me great joy and that she will bear me children, one of whom will be wise above all the rest. And another child would return to Africa to lead her people out of darkness."

Mindy drove on without responding.

An uncomfortable silence fell between them. Jake knew, from the look of anticipation on Mindy's face, that "the children" could only come after a wedding and that a wedding could only come after a proposal.

Without looking directly at her, he watched her as she waited nervously for Jake to ask her *the question*. In his heart, a battle raged. Tension constricted the silence between them. He could sense Mindy watching him out of the corner of her eye. He knew she would hold out. He knew Mindy was prepared to wait *forever*.

Jake grimaced. Like a tightening vise, his heart squeezed him from the inside of his chest. A lump grew ever larger in his throat, as though something from deep inside of him was struggling to get out. He suppressed it. *These matters require careful planning. I can't ask her now. I don't even have a ring*, he thought as he stared out the side window, *Assurances have to be confirmed, dates have to be scheduled, parents need to be consulted, and just the right rings need to be purchased.*

The turmoil in his heart refused to give up. So, he gave in. Peace came upon him. He could breathe again. His hard-fought logic had just given way to his heart's command. He took a slow, deep breath. Jake turned. In a soft yet confident voice, he asked, "Mindy, will you marry me?"

Mindy's face revealed the jolt of joy that shot through her. Her face blossomed. "*Yes!* Of course, Jake, I'll marry you!" "So where do you want to go on our honeymoon?" Jake asked.

"An island . . . in the Caribbean. Why? Where do you want to go?"

"I was thinking of something a little out of the ordinary ... like ... Africa ..."

CHAPTER 18

Refugee

MINDY STEPPED CAUTIOUSLY through the refugee camp in a remote region of Sudan, Africa. Sweat dripped from her face as she hesitated under the sweltering early-June sun. She could hear a disturbance escalating a short distance from where she stood. Screaming and mayhem originated from around the corner of a row of squalid huts that stood off to her left. *Giving up my honeymoon to search for Alexander is one thing. Being mangled by a vicious mob is another,* Mindy thought. *Now I know why my guides were so reluctant to bring me here.*

She looked around for her guides. They had vanished only moments before to assist a refugee mother who was holding her bleeding infant. Mindy noticed for the first time that all of the gaunt eyes were upon her. Instinctively, she inched backward as she prayed for the Lord's protection. Mindy's mind drew closer and closer to panic. *Lord, help me! I'm trapped! Why was I so bullheaded to think that I could walk in here and find Alexander waiting for me? Lord, why did you bring Jake and me to Africa? We should be enjoying our honeymoon on the beaches of St. Thomas.* Mindy stepped backward, with her eyes locked on the last hut in the row that separated her from the riot.

Grabbing Mindy's arm from behind, a teenaged African girl pleaded, "I am Rebekah! You are my angel! Come with me quickly!"

Mindy yielded. She followed the young woman through a maze of shabby lean-tos and piles of rubbish. They ducked into a small, mud-walled hut.

"This woman's soul is in heaven. She will not care if you wear her robes." Rebekah stepped past the corpse covered only by a thin veil. The smell of death and human excrement defiled the air.

"Cover yourself with these robes. It will mask the scent of your soap and shampoo. I'll tie these sandals to your feet with these rags and cords; they will disguise the size of your shoes. Let this cloth drag along the ground behind you to disrupt your tracks. Listen, you must walk hunched over. Pretend you are an old woman who is ill. Do not show your face to anyone. I will keep hold of your arm to guide you. No matter how loudly they yell at you, *do not* look up. If you are caught, you will be *badly* mistreated, then held for ransom. The guerrilla rebels who start these riots are evil animals. You *must* remain hidden."

Rebekah froze and then raised her index finger to her lips as the clatter of angry men approached their hut. She motioned for Mindy to enter a small, inner chamber to the left of the main room. She nudged her into the corner furthest from the outside walls. Rebekah positioned her body in front of Mindy.

Mindy curled into a ball. *Lord, deliver me from the evil one.* She could tell that the men were quarreling just outside her hut. She held her breath as the cloth door of the hut's outer chamber swung open. A man's body formed a silhouette in the door. Then the door flapped shut.

Mindy heard the men step around to the side of the hut. Then the blade of a two-foot long machete thrust through the walls and roof of the small chamber. The men argued further, then stormed off, apparently convinced the hut was empty.

"They are superstitious of death. They are afraid to disturb a dead body," Rebekah whispered in Mindy's ear. "We must wait here until the UN truck comes to pick up the dead. Let us pray that the peacekeeper from Australia named Wilhelm is driving the truck. He is a good man. He will help us."

Small streams of light filtered through the machete holes into the small chamber. Mindy and Rebekah shared a brief smile. For the first time, Mindy relaxed. For the moment, they were safe.

"May I hold your hands?" Rebekah asked.

Mindy extended her open palms to Rebekah. Rebekah rolled Mindy's hand into a knot and then whispered a prayer in her native language. Only then did Mindy become distinctly aware that the young African girl had been speaking English during their encounter.

Rebekah positioned her fingers gently around Mindy's ring finger. Something halted her prayers. "Is Master Jake traveling with you?"

Shocked, Mindy stared at Rebekah, "What did you say?"

"Master Jake ... did he return to Sudan with you?"

How would this refugee know about Jake? Mindy wondered to herself.

Rebekah looked into Mindy's eyes. "I am Rebekah. You are Jake's angel. I saw you in a vision when I prayed for Jake while he was here in January. Jake gave me the poster of your face and the ring so I would recognize you when you came."

Mindy felt the young woman's fingers searching her ring finger. "The ring ... the poster, yes ... you are Rebekah ... *the* Rebekah." Mindy reached under her blouse to retrieve the ring that she had tied around her neck with a leather string.

Mindy presented the ring and the leather string to Rebekah, who polished the ring with her fingers. Her face beamed as she held the pattern of a single star and two lightning bolts up to the sliver of light. With a radiant smile, she slid the ring onto her finger and turned to Mindy. Rebekah then positioned her left hand up to her face, into the exact position that Mindy had assumed in the picture poster.

A flood of emotion overcame Mindy. She now realized that this young woman had comforted Jake when he had been beaten by thugs at the remote well. "Yes, Jake is traveling with me. We were married just before coming to Sudan," Mindy said.

"May I see your wedding ring?" Rebekah asked.

"I was advised to leave it at home in Wisconsin. But I can tell you it is very pretty." Mindy peered into Rebekah eyes. "So why are you in a refugee camp? Where is your father, Dr. Isaiah?"

Rebekah's head dropped. "When the thugs that beat up Jake found out we helped him, they raided our orphanage. They killed my father and took all our medicine and supplies. They captured the youth for slaves and left the babies to starve. Days before the attack, father sent me away to study at the Christian Aide base. When I got back, everyone was gone." Rebekah shook her head as tears flowed.

Mindy slid her arms around this amazing young girl who had not only saved her life but also had saved her husband's life only months earlier. A mysterious notion was starting to form in Mindy's heart. Though she did not understand it, she perceived that she was holding her adopted daughter-to-be.

Mindy held her until she calmed down. "Rebekah, you referred to me as Jake's angel. Help me understand what you meant."

"While I prayed with Jake, I saw you in a vision, and there was a light glowing around you. I got the impression I was seeing an angel. Ever since the attack on the orphanage, I have prayed for Jake and you to come. And then today, I heard a voice in my head that told me you were here in this camp and you needed me. Even in the daylight, I spotted you from far away—it was the light that guided me to you."

Perplexed by the story, Mindy sat in silence. *Lord, I pray you reveal this mystery to me.* "Rebekah … I am not an angel. I'm human, just like you. All I can do is thank the Lord Jesus for bringing you to rescue me. Rebekah, thank you for saving my life and Jake's life."

Rebekah snuggled closer to Mindy.

In the hours of silence while she waited, Mindy replayed the last few weeks in her mind—the scramble to complete her school work, followed by the whirlwind of wedding plans. The image she clung to was the moment she saw Jake, standing at the front of the church in his black tux and white boutonniere. With his relaxed smile and his eyes full of love, he was waiting for her and only her. Glancing down at her elegant, pure white dress, she knew this was the moment she had been waiting for all her life.

Mindy adjusted her position on the hut's floor. She wiped a tear from her eye as she remembered how tender and patient Jake had been on their wedding night.

"It's all right," Jake whispered. "We have all the rest of our lives together. I'll be right here when you wake up."

Mindy fell into a deep sleep only moments after Jake carried her over the threshold. Mindy shook her head to clear her mind of the daydream. She would have to stay alert. She was far from home, and the stench from the decaying body in the next room was threatening to make her vomit.

Later that afternoon, when Mindy and Rebekah had returned safely to the Christian Aide Compound, Mindy sat on one of the two metal stools and washed her face with the cloth from the basin of water that had been provided for her by the Aide Organization's staff. Jake had gone to shower. She looked around the storage room that had been transformed into living quarters earlier that day. Their suitcases sat just inside the heavy door. She took comfort in knowing that there were two keys. Her key protruded from the dead bolt on the inside of the door. Jake carried the other key. She realized that if the key were applied to the outside of the room, their room could be a prison cell instead of a safe haven.

The room, which was about the size of a small bedroom, contained a thick rug, which she assumed would be their bed, and a few household items. A large, orange pail that supported a screw-top lid sat in the corner. From the international depictions on the pail, she realized that it was a portable latrine. A small, rectangular window at the top of one wall was propped open by a simple bar.

Mindy relaxed on the small stool. *Finally … a moment of peace and quiet.*

CHAPTER 19

Fredrick

*K*NOCK. KNOCK. KNOCK. Startled, Mindy looked to the door. "Hello, Mr. Jake. It is Fredrick from Dr. Bixon's office." The cheerful voice rang from the other side of the door.

Mindy had been told not to open the door for anyone she didn't recognize.

Knock, knock, knock. "I'm reluctant to leave these gifts in the hall. May I set them inside your room?"

Mindy's intuition felt a peace about the stranger. She rose, stepped across the room, unlocked the deadbolt, and peeked outside.

"Good evening, I'm Fredrick; you must be Mr. Jake's wife," stated the elderly African gentleman. His warm smile and compassionate eyes beamed from his weather-wrinkled face.

"Yes, I'm Mindy Olson."

"I present these gifts and a blessing from Dr. Bixon and his family to you and Mr. Jake." Fredrick maneuvered the two wheeled handcart into Mindy's room. "First, the cots; they are not new, but they are very clean. Next, here are your pillows and blankets. They are from the hospital stockroom. They are not made from fine cloth, but they will keep you warm. These sheets are from Mrs. Bixon. She sends her greetings and will send someone to bring you to her house tomorrow, if you would choose to accept her invitation."

Mindy smiled and nodded in agreement.

"In this cloth bag is a large loaf of bread, two bottles of water, a jar of butter from goat's milk, and a jar of figs. This melon is from the Bixon's garden." Fredrick placed the large cloth bag on the table.

"And now, I have a blessing from Dr. Bixon and his family for you and Jake, his most distinguished guests." Fredrick raised one hand toward heaven, lifted the other palm toward Mindy, closed his eyes, and prayed: "The Lord bless you and keep you; the Lord make his face shine upon you and be gracious to you; the Lord turn his face toward you and give you peace."

Fredrick brought his open palms together in front of his chest. "May your stay with us be joyful and prosperous. If you will excuse me, I have many matters to attend to before I sleep." Fredrick turned and scurried out the door.

Mindy re-locked the dead bolt. *In this land of starvation, brutality, and darkness, it has been the acts of kindness and generosity that have impressed me the most.* Mindy thought about Rebekah and wondered where her newfound friend would be spending the night.

Knock. Knock. "Mindy, it's me, Jake."

Mindy eagerly opened the door. She hugged and kissed him.

"Where did all this come from?" Jake asked.

"Fredrick, from Dr. Bixon's office, brought it."

"Oh really?" Jake smiled at the thoughtfulness of his friend. "What's in the cloth bag?"

Mindy mimicked Fredrick's voice as she accounted for the contents. "One large loaf of bread, two bottles of water, a jar of butter from goat's milk, a jar of fig dates, and a melon from the Bixon's garden."

Jake circled his arms around Mindy's waist and pulled her close. He beamed as he imitated the voice of the over-enthusiastic concierge from their wedding night, "So, Mrs. Olson, how are you enjoying your honeymoon so far?"

She peered directly into Jake's eyes, "As long as we are together, I'll be a happy camper."

"I feel the same way. I love you, Mindy. I always will."

"I love you too."

They kissed.

"Well, my dear, how about some dinner?" Jake scanned the food before them. He pulled the small stool out for Mindy.

"Thank you, my love."

Jake broke off two small pieces of bread, handed one to Mindy, and folded his hands. "Heavenly Father, thank you for bringing us safely to Sudan. Thank you for blessing our search for our friend Alexander Montgomery. Thank you for being our Savior, our Creator, our Provider, our Healer, our Protector, and our Peace. We take this bread in remembrance of you." He then poured a small amount of water in each of the two cups. "Lord, we drink this in remembrance of the new covenant of your blood."

After the meal, Mindy turned to Jake and said, "Jake, can I talk to you about something?"

Jake put down his half-eaten fig. He knew this was her way of introducing something important.

"Yes, Mindy, what is it?"

"What would you think of adopting Rebekah?"

Jake raised his eyebrows. "Mindy, you have been married for three days, and you want to adopt a teenage African refugee? What makes you think she wants to be adopted? Was this her idea or yours?"

"Jake, Dr. Isaiah was killed in a raid on his clinic. All the children are gone."

Jake's face turned grim.

"She is no ordinary refugee, you know."

"Yes, I do. Let's not say anything to her just yet. And you know, I think we should be working *on starting our own family.*"

Mindy could see the playful glimmer in Jake's eyes. She slid off of her stool and onto his lap and placed her arms around his neck. *This may not be a five-star hotel, but at least we have our privacy.* She brought her lips to his.

Later that night, Mindy shifted restlessly on her cot. The scenes from the last few days rolled around in her head: her glorious wedding day; the beautiful, five-star Weston hotel in Chicago, where they spent their wedding night; all the effort that Jake had put into securing the special "aid worker" visas that would allow them to enter a region of Sudan that was off limits to tourists.

She turned on her cot to face Jake, who was sound asleep on the cot next to her. She slid her hand silently over the frame of her cot, over the frame of Jake's cot, and cupped his upper arm in her hand. She admired him for his courage and his selfless suggestion that they spend their honeymoon in Sudan searching for their friend Alexander.

Mindy had gathered from the conversations she had overheard that Alexander had started an underground Christian church deep in the bush, bringing the worker slaves of the thugs to Christ. His efforts to evangelize soldiers of the warlords were met with swift and brutal resistance. Consequently, he had been captured and beaten nearly to the point of death. Alexander's fellow underground believers had rescued him and now were understandably tight-lipped about his location. Any of the locals who cooperated with Alexander would be beaten by the thugs. If the thugs could find Alexander, they would surely kill him to snuff out the leader of the budding church.

She thought back to the night she first met Alexander, the night at Commodore's Restaurant, the night of the intimate birthday celebration she had planned for Jake. She replayed the look on the distraught, suicidal man's face as he loomed in front of them. A tingling once again came over her skin as she saw herself placing her hand gently over his to lead him to Christ. She thought of the tragedy that surrounded Alexander's life, how all his wealth and power could not save his wife from her death in a car accident and how his only son's body had been recovered from the sinkhole by Jake. Alexander had been truly all alone in this world.

A tear moistened Mindy's cheek. She remembered how proud and amazed they had been when they found out that Alexander had decided to act on his newfound faith and leave Wisconsin to drill water wells in Sudan. And she thought of how Jake had eagerly agreed to join Alexander for a short-term mission trip.

She remembered the look on Jake's face, only a week before their wedding day, as he read the e-mail from the commissioner of the Sudan's Christian Aide Organization. He was asking Jake if he would consider coming to Sudan to assist them in their search for Alexander.

The commissioner, who knew nothing of their pending wedding, reasoned that Jake had built a strong rapport with the locals while he helped to dig the wells a year ago. The locals would know Jake as a trusted friend of Alexander and would help Alexander reach safety. The commissioner believed that the underground church would lead Jake and only Jake to Alexander.

Mindy was too restless to lie still. She turned for what seemed the tenth time and faced the wall. There was one other issue that gnawed at her. Was it her imagination, or could she feel something stirring inside of her? She recounted how faithful she had been to prepare herself for the month before her wedding night. Now, in all the chaos and commotion, she had forgotten to take her birth control pills for two nights in a row.

Mindy blushed as she replayed the passionate frolic that she and Jake had engaged in after dinner. *What are the chances? Well … if there is any chance that I'm pregnant, I'll need to be extra careful.* She fidgeted on her cot. *Maybe I should stay close to the Aide Compound tomorrow. There must be something I can do to be helpful while Jake is out with the search team.*

She squirmed one last time, yawned, and settled into the cot that drew her into a dream-filled sleep.

After what had seemed to be only a few short moments, Mindy felt Jake's hand on her shoulder as he bent over to kiss her cheek.

She peeked out of one eye. "Good morning," Mindy whispered through her first yawn.

"Good morning. I have to get an early start. The plan is to travel to a distant camp and work our way back toward the Aide

Compound. I left the rest of the bread, the figs, and the bottle of water for you on the table. I made sure *your* key was on the table." A confident, yet humble smile grew across Jake's face. "Today is the day, Mindy. Today *is* the day."

She reached her hand out of her blanket to caress Jake's hand. "I love you, Jake. I'll be praying for you."

"I love you too, Mindy. Take it easy today." With a kiss and a squeeze, Jake stood and left to search for Alexander.

Mindy listened for Jake's key to lock the dead bolt from outside the door. Then she nestled into the cocoon of sheets and blankets. She was content to sleep for a few more hours. Daydreams of her new life filled her mind. She would be back in Wisconsin by this time next week. The list of things to be done formed in her head. First, she would send the thank-you notes, then unpack from the wedding and make Mrs. Birmingham's house a home for Jake and her. After that, the first batch of campers would show up the next week.

Mindy was grateful that Mrs. Birmingham had insisted that, after the wedding, Jake and Mindy move into her house. She had decided that the house was too big for an old widow to handle all by herself. She would move into the retirement home in Norton. That was where her closest friends lived.

Mindy sighed, *Thank you, Lord, for the blessing of a wonderful home to start my life with Jake.* She was grateful that Mr. Chapman, president of the local bank, had hired Jake as an assistant manager. Their combined incomes would provide a comfortable lifestyle. They would pay rent and be responsible for keeping up the property. The money from Mrs. Birmingham's yard sale was enough to buy a new heat pump and air conditioner, with a little left over to do some much-needed repairs. Mindy had been told that Mrs. Birmingham's children had gone through the house and taken the keepsakes they wanted. Basically, what was left in the house was Jake's and Mindy's to use.

Mindy stirred, turned over, and re-settled on her cot. *Maybe I'll catch just one more hour of sleep.*

CHAPTER 20

Ancient One

MINDY AWOKE TO the soft, insistent knocking on her door. She sat up quickly, recalling that Jake had left quietly a few hours before.

"Miss Mindy, it's Rebekah. Are you in there?"

"Yes, one minute please." Mindy searched the tabletop for her key and unlocked the door.

"Good morning. Are you refreshed?" Rebekah beamed with enthusiasm.

"Yes ... I feel fine."

"We must hurry if we are going to catch the transport truck."

"Ahh ... I thought I would stay in the compound today. I have an appointment to meet Mrs. Bixon," Mindy asserted as she blinked the sleep from her eyes.

"No!" Rebekah stared at Mindy with stern disbelief. "Did you not see the vision from the Ancient One last night in your dreams?"

"Ahh ... yeah, I did have a nightmare of an old woman, clouded by shadows, who said that the 'ring bearer' had been badly beaten and that I must go to him. But I thought she was referring to when Jake was lost in the desert. When Jake was here in January, I had a dream about the same old woman; only that time, the message was that Jake was safe."

"Your dream in January *was* about Jake. Now it is another ring bearer that we seek," Rebekah said.

"But there are only two rings—Jake had his on last night; mine is around my neck."

"Mindy, there are more than two rings. We must go north, to consult with the Ancient One. She will tell us where to find the ring bearer." Rebekah obviously was trying to be patient yet insistent at the same time. "Listen, the visions only go to those who are required to act. Mindy, lean not on your own understanding. Search your soul. If you do not have the courage to make this journey, then I will make it alone. Convince yourself one way or the other at this moment!"

Mindy saw the fearless determination in Rebekah's eyes. "OK, I'm in." Mindy realized that many people had risked their lives to help Jake when he was in need.

"God bless you, Mindy. Please sit down." Rebekah pulled a jar of black pigment from her large cloth bag.

"Cover your face and hands with this. I will start on your feet and legs. This will conceal your white skin from the onlookers we pass along the way. No one will want to kidnap on old African woman."

Mindy recoiled slightly from the black goop's unpleasant odor. "This stuff does come off, doesn't it?"

Rebekah rolled her eyes and gave Mindy a "don't be prissy" glance. "Yes, but hopefully, not one minute too soon."

"You may want to wear your Khaki shorts under this robe. That way, you can carry your passport and your key in your pocket." Rebekah handed Mindy a sash. "This is what we wear for a bra. Your white one would be a dead giveaway that you are from the West. OK, let's pull your hair back into this scarf."

Rebekah stepped back from Mindy and grinned. "Mindy … you make a fine African woman."

"Now, here are your outer robe and your sandals. Remember, you must present yourself as an old, blind, and deaf woman. Walk hunched over. When we get to a village, put these wax ear plugs in so you will not respond to the sounds around you. I will keep hold of your arm at all times. If we are separated, *do not call for me.* Stay put; I will not abandon you."

"OK." Mindy began to process in her mind the danger she had just volunteered for.

Rebekah pulled a small electronic device out of the cloth bag. "This is a GPS device. I have set it to mark the location of the well at the center of the town. If we get lost, this will help us find our way home. I set it to a general location in case the enemy intercepts our device; it won't give away the location of the Christian Aide base." Rebekah leaned into Mindy. "If something dreadful should happen, open this side door on the device. One button activates the loud horn. The other sends a radio distress signal. The man here at the Aide dispatch office knows that this device is assigned to us. They will be able to find us by the signal that this gives off."

Rebekah looked sternly into Mindy's eyes. "Mindy, the enemy monitors these transmissions also. Before you send the signal, be sure that the rescue team will get to you before the enemy. If you are captured by the enemy … you will be severely mistreated. They will then use the settings to address their ransom note." Rebekah stared directly into Mindy's eyes. "Are you ready?"

The spirit in Mindy's soul was emboldened. "Yes." Mindy strapped the belt that held the device to her waist and then pulled her robes down so that they completely covered her body. "I need to do one thing." Mindy picked up her camera from the table. "I want to leave Jake a picture, so if he has to come find me, he will be looking for a white girl who is wearing black face paint and peasant's robes. Step over here. This will let him know we are together."

Flash. Mindy's camera captured the unlikely pair.

On a scrap of paper, Mindy scratched a note:

Jake,
    Rebekah is taking me to meet the Ancient One. Please see our picture.
    I love you,
             Mindy

Rebekah and Mindy hurried to the far gate of the Aide Compound, where an old truck was loaded to make a delivery in the next town. Rebekah had arranged earlier that morning for the driver to make accommodations for her and Mindy. Boxes lined the outside walls of the truck's cargo bed, making a cavern in the middle. The two scurried into the small compartment as the driver placed the final boxes to enclose the two stowaways. He pulled a tarp over the boxes and crates.

"The driver will stop at the banks of the dried-up river. From there, we will go on foot to where the Ancient One is hidden," Rebekah stated.

"Help me understand this Ancient One," Mindy said.

"Legend has it that the Ancient One is the last living descendent of a long line of missionaries that the Byzantine empress Theodora sent here around 540 A.D.," Rebekah answered. "Although they preached the gospel for hundreds of years and converted many villages, they have all died or been killed by the warlords. The Ancient One is exceedingly wise. Priests and missionaries come from all over the country to consult with her. Because she is so old and frail, there is a small band of followers who protect and care for her."

The hour-long ride to the bridge that crossed the now-dry riverbed gave Mindy and Rebekah time to talk. Mindy told Rebekah of the miraculous rejuvenation of Camp Koinonia that Jake and she had witnessed back in Wisconsin and how Jake and she had received a vision to build a training camp for young Christian leaders.

Rebekah recounted the story of how Dr. Isaiah's clinic had fallen under attack by the guerrilla warlords while she studied at the Aide Compound. Rebekah spoke through her tears of how the thugs shot Dr. Isaiah and captured the healthy staff members to be used as slaves. Rebekah leaned into Mindy for comfort. As Mindy held the sobbing young woman, she continued to process in her mind the desperate state of life in Sudan.

As the truck came to a complete stop, Mindy and Rebekah heard a soft knock on the truck's cab window. This was their signal to get out. The driver got out and walked to the back of the bridge to remove a few boxes. Mindy and Rebekah climbed out.

"I'll tie this rag to the bridge," the driver said. "If you get back before dark and want a ride back to the Aide Compound, move this rag to the far side of the bridge. Stay hidden until I come to a complete stop. If it is not safe, I will cross the bridge and then come back for you. If the rag is not moved, I will know that you have not returned to the bridge. I can only wait until just before dark. *Please* seek safety if you cannot make it back by sundown. I will watch for the rag when I make my deliveries tomorrow morning. May God speed your steps. May His angels protect you." He replaced the boxes in the truck, then hurried back to the driver's seat and pulled away.

"We must travel upstream," Rebekah pointed up the river bed.

The smooth rocks on the floor of the riverbed allowed Rebekah and Mindy to travel quickly. Rebekah noted that the dry bedrock left little to no trace of their tracks. They journeyed until midday, and then a small, apparently abandoned village of five huts appeared on the riverbank. Rebekah motioned to Mindy to lie on the ground to watch.

"This is the place. We must watch to be sure it is safe," Rebekah whispered.

In just a few minutes, an African woman carrying a large bowl on her head walked casually from one hut to the next.

"That is a good sign. Let's walk up to the hut slowly so as to not alarm them," Rebekah said.

As they walked up to the largest hut, they could hear the murmuring of voices inside. Rebekah quietly announced their presence. The hut went silent, followed by a flurry of movement. One of the women inside came out to meet them and then motioned for the two to come inside.

"Welcome," said the elderly Caucasian woman in a soft voice as she gazed at Mindy. A gentle smile creased the old woman's face. She was seated on a low chair, situated on a rug in the middle of the hut. "I have been praying for you. I am the one known as the Ancient One. I have been waiting for many years for you to arrive.

There are many things I must tell you. But first, come near me. Let my hands feel the outline of your face."

Mindy leaned in and closed her eyes as the wrinkled fingers moved along her face.

"The Lord has blessed you, my child, with the task to train young Christians for the end times. Although you have labored, your work has only begun. You must cling to the Lord. Pray for the Holy Spirit to guide you. Only the chosen few will be selected as your students. You will identify them by the vision that each of them will receive from the Lord. The vision will be unique to your safe haven." Ancient One cupped Mindy's face with her hands.

"The Lord has sent a powerful guardian angel to protect you. You have experienced his influence many times; although, you may not have perceived his light."

The sight of her own shadow on the back wall of the hut startled Mindy. As she turned her head around to look behind her, she saw him. His eyes were filled with compassion; he neither smiled nor frowned. His robe of brilliant white was bound at the waist by a wide, golden belt. A long, broad sword hung off to his side.

"Pray to our Lord and Savior, Jesus Christ, and He will direct the angel to assist you when you are in need. Be alert. It is with the powers of darkness that we contend." The Ancient One paused. "The Evil One crouches at your door. Although your land is in relative peace, a terrible turmoil will soon shake its foundations. Cities will be desolated. There will be great suffering. You must be swift. You must prepare for the troubles before they begin."

Greatly disturbed, Mindy embraced the hands that held her face.

The Ancient One continued, "You are the one who has been chosen to take Rebekah as your own. She is strong in faith. You are to take her to your land, where she will help you prepare the training camp. You, in turn, will educate her in the knowledge of the West and teach her how to carry herself as a leader among all people.

"You must take great care; the Evil One will send his agents to disrupt your lives and destroy your camp. Remember what I told you," Ancient One said. "Cling to the Lord in prayer. Let the Holy Spirit direct your path. Listen to His quiet, gentle voice. Remember always, He is your shepherd. Rebekah will assist you in your prayer life. You cannot rely on your own strength and understanding. You must learn to bring down the supernatural provision from heaven, to bring forth food where there is nothing to eat, to bring forth water where there is nothing to drink."

Mindy sat in silence, trying to absorb all that she had heard.

Ancient One slid her hands off Mindy's face and pointed to a vial and a gourd that sat on the table next to her. "The ring bearer lies in a hut under the massive tree of vines, just before the stream forks to the east and the south. He is in great distress, and you must go to him. Place this ointment on the cut on his calf. It will heal the infection. We have prepared this gourd with the sweet juice of melon. Have him drink it slowly; it will revive his strength."

The Ancient One slowly reached into the pocket of her robe and pulled out a small, leather pouch that was tied at the top with a drawstring. As a radiant smile beamed from her winkled face, the Ancient One handed the pouch to Mindy. "Present this to your daughter Anna on the day she is born. As she grows in stature, tell her of your encounter with the Ancient One. Although she will have many questions, her questions will lead her to the Truth."

Perplexed, Mindy held the pouch in her hand. "I ... have ... no children."

Small tears of joy rolled down the weathered face of the old woman. "The Lord has revealed to me that He has knit together a daughter in your womb. She has been formed inside you for only one day." Ancient One pointed to the door. "You must go now. You must be swift; the ring bearer will not survive until the next morning without your care."

Mindy nodded as she cherished in her heart all that she had heard.

Rebekah rose slowly and nudged Mindy to follow her out. Without a word, Rebekah motioned for them to proceed up the barren riverbed. The two traveled as swiftly as they could over the rough river bottom. Rebekah climbed to the top of the bank every few miles to check for guerillas on patrol.

In the late afternoon, Rebekah froze in her steps. She pointed to the top of a massive tree. Its branches were covered with thick vines. "Legend tells that this tree's roots tap into an underground lake far below the surface. My grandmother told me of this tree. In ancient times, they called it 'the healing tree.' We must be careful; desperate people come here in search of comfort," Rebekah warned.

They crept to the top of the riverbank and peeked over the top. They could see two small huts and one larger one. There was no motion or sound anywhere in the area. They followed the riverbank to its closest point to the huts. Still no life could be detected.

"If this is a trap, there will be no escape. Are you at peace with our entering these huts?" Rebekah asked.

"Yes."

"Stay low to the ground. Remember, you are an old, deaf woman." Rebekah winked at Mindy.

Mindy nodded as they both rose from the riverbed and inched slowly to the main hut.

Mindy pulled back the cloth door and stooped to clear the low door. She could see a bloody and beaten man on a cot.

"Alexander!"

CHAPTER 21

Steinar

ALEXANDER MONTGOMERY MOANED in pain. Mindy surveyed his leg to locate the cut on his calf. Her eyes locked on his toe ring. She marveled at the similarities of Alexander's ring to the one she wore around her neck. The pattern of a single star and two lightning bolts was unmistakable.

Ring bearer ... so Alexander is the ring bearer. How could this be? Mindy questioned. *So that is what Rebekah meant when she said there were more than two rings.*

"Quickly, you must apply the ointment." Rebekah searched around the hut. "I will gather some things to prop him up so he can drink."

Mindy applied the ointment to Alexander's leg and to the other cuts on his body.

"Alexander, can you hear me? It's Mindy. We've come to help you. We have some liquid. Can you sit up and drink?" Mindy placed her hands around Alexander's face. "Lord, restore this man's strength. Jehovah Rapha, you are the great healer; cleanse this man of infection and heal his wounds. He has been your servant; he needs your healing touch. Please, stretch your hand down to heal his broken body."

Alexander responded with a moan. As he opened his eyes, he could barely make out the image before him. In a weak and dry voice, Alexander uttered, "Mindy, thank God you came for me."

"Let me help you sit up. Rebekah, place that box and a rolled-up rug behind him. We have the juice from a melon for you. Please drink it slowly.

"Holy Spirit, guide my path. Is there anyone in reach of our GPS distress signal that can help us?" Mindy whispered. She perceived a vision of the GPS device hanging from a tall pole. "It's time to activate the GPS," Mindy asserted.

Rebekah nodded with approval.

Mindy walked outside the hut and made a quick scan of the horizon. Sunset would be upon them in a few hours. She opened the back compartment of the GPS device and activated the distress signal. Mindy placed the device on a tall pole, in hopes of extending its range.

Within the hour, Jake, his guide, and their driver arrived outside the hut.

"Thank God you're here." Mindy wrapped her arms around Jake.

Jake stepped back, silently adjusting his attitude about seeing his young bride covered in black face paint. "Are you OK?"

"Yes. Alexander is inside. He's been badly beaten, and a terrible cut on his leg is infected." Mindy led the group inside.

Screeching brakes announced the arrival of a truck outside the hut. The thumps of three sets of boots impacting the ground paralyzed the group huddled around Alexander's body. Jake could hear the footsteps of two men hustle around opposite sides of the hut. The third rushed in the door. In his native language, a man with an assault rifle motioned for everyone to raise their hands. The man with the gun then called over his shoulder to the truck.

In walked an elderly, grey-haired, Caucasian man. He ambled in slowly and then paced around Alexander's body. "I do not want to know who you are," stated the elderly man in a stern voice. "Nor do I choose to reveal who I am." He stopped to address Jake. "I do advise you to leave this place at once. If this had been a trap set by the warlord, you would have been captured by now. If they are monitoring the air waves, they know you are here. So turn off your GPS signal, *now*! If you value your lives, you will leave *immediately*."

Rebekah rushed to turn off the GPS. Jake nodded to his driver to help him load Alexander onto their truck.

The gray-haired man walked over to Mindy, who was sitting on the ground with her robe's hood pulled over her head. She pretended to be asleep. The elderly man gently nudged Mindy with his foot and spoke in a native tongue. Mindy raised her head and looked directly into the eyes of the man standing in front of her. The man gasped and then turned away. He walked out of the hut to Jake's side.

"Is your friend allergic to antibiotics?" he asked.

"Not that I know of. His doctor can be reached by radio."

"Please connect me with his doctor."

Jake nodded for the driver to radio Dr. Bixon.

The man turned his back to the others so he could address Jake privately.

"My name is Steinar Lazlow. I am a physician with the UN Peacekeeping effort here. The UN, the government of Sudan, and the warlords have a delicate and complicated arrangement that is often less than cordial." Steinar whispered, "I can provide your friend with some assistance. The first shot will be a powerful antibiotic; next will be a painkiller that will help him endure the rough ride home, and finally, a saline drip. Please see to it that the drip line stays open."

Steinar looked around to be sure no one could hear their conversation. "It would be better for all of us if you claimed that his saline drip was mysteriously in him when you arrived. I am sorry. The UN has strict rules of engagement. I have only a handful of men who are supported by the UN charter. There are many others that work with me. I must do what I can to take care of them and their families. Earlier today, I delivered a baby son for one of my volunteers. The day before that, I saved a young girl's life by providing antibiotics and other medicines. You must understand … these things are outside the scope of my peacekeeping mission. We are here to act only as monitors. I do what I can. One last thing, I can provide you with the fuel from my auxiliary tank. I pray that will be enough to get you home."

"Thank you, you have been most generous," Jake said.

Steinar's face broke into sadness. "I cannot explain it. Something happened to me when I walked into that hut. I felt the presence of the Holy Spirit. I used to feel it as a young boy in Sweden, when I attended the Mennonite church with my grandmother." Steinar spoke in a quiet, broken voice. "When that young woman … in the black face paint looked me directly in the eyes, something awoke in my heart that has been dormant for many years. I am a good man, but I have strayed far from the teachings of our Lord Jesus Christ. I was wondering … would you ask that woman to pray for me?"

"That woman is my wife, Mindy. She would be honored to pray for you."

Jake motioned for Mindy to join them. "In our Mennonite church back in the US, we believe in laying hands on the people we pray for … would you feel comfortable with our hands on your shoulders?"

Steinar bowed his head. "That would be fine."

"Mindy, this gentleman would like for you to pray for him. He is a good man, but he has strayed from his faith."

Mindy nodded. Jake and Mindy placed their hands on Steinar's shoulders.

Mindy prayed, "Heavenly Father … we bring this humble servant to you in prayer. He seeks your face, Jesus. Lord, reach out your hand and touch him. Wash him with your cleansing Spirit. Jesus, let him feel the guilt and bitterness flow out of his body as your Holy Spirit fills him. Let him walk forward from this day on with your Truth and your Light in his heart. In your Holy Name we pray. Amen."

Steinar collapsed to his knees. As he sobbed, Mindy and Jake knelt down to comfort him.

One of Steinar's men stood stunned outside the hut. Shocked and amazed, he mumbled, "The light ... I saw a ball of light around you. Can someone explain this to me?"

"I will be glad to," Steinar replied. "We can discuss it on the way back to the base."

Steinar turned to Jake and Mindy. "A thought came to me while you were praying for me. There is an old Catholic Mission operated by the Belgians not far from here. You can get there before dark. Follow the river bed for seven kilometers, until you come to a row of low trees and bushes. Pull out of the river and drive along the tree row. It will conceal you from the rebel patrols. When you come to the road that goes north, follow it to the village. Father Hume will take care of you. I will radio ahead."

"It would be safest if I told him that you are Canadians on a safari and one of your party fell out of the truck. If the rebels find out that you are from the US and that you rescued a leader of the underground church, it would be very bad for all involved. There is security in obscurity. Keep the women covered with that tarp."

"Commander, there are rebel trucks coming this way! They are off in the distance, but they are moving quickly," one of Steinar's men called from the hut's roof.

"We must leave immediately! Be sure that you have removed every trace of your existence from this area. You will go west on the river bed. We will follow it east. If you leave first, we will cover your tracks around the huts. My truck tracks will lead them away from you."

"Thank you for everything," Jake asserted. The two men shook hands.

"God bless you, Steinar!" Mindy stated through the squeeze of a gentle hug.

"God speed to you." Steinar motioned for his men to get in the truck.

Jake's driver started their truck as his guide checked the hut and returned with Alexander's shoe. They loaded into the truck and departed.

Jake, his guide, and two men from the Catholic Mission carried Alexander from the truck to the Mission's medical clinic. As Mindy waited by the truck, just inside the fortress-like walls of the compound, she watched a nun emerge from a door twenty feet away. A group of young children followed behind her. They were of mixed ethnic backgrounds, ranging from about five to twelve years old. The nun quickly formed them into a line. One of the youngest beckoned the nun to carry him. She politely but insistently indicated that he must walk like all the others. He persisted.

As the nun became aware of the truck, Mindy, and the driver, she pulled the boy onto her hip to quiet him. Mindy and the nun exchanged glances. As their eyes met, there was at first a sense of shock, then curiosity, and then wonder. They recognized that they were similar in age, with the same build, and both their faces glowed from the presence of the Holy Spirit.

The nun extended a brief smile to Mindy as she shuffled the children down the courtyard. Mindy assumed it was bedtime for the children and that the process could not be interrupted for an intrusion into a stranger's life.

Within minutes, the nun reemerged from the fortress. She carried a small, metal jar and a cloth. She approached Mindy, smiled, and greeted her in a European language. The nun was explaining something to Mindy; although, Mindy was unable to understand the lecture.

The nun reached for Mindy's hand and placed the metal can in it. Mindy smiled, yet looked confused. The nun pried open the jar and rubbed a small amount of the goop on the back of Mindy's hand, and then she wiped the goop and the black pigment from Mindy's hand.

Mindy beamed with joy. "Thank you, thank you," said Mindy.

The nun raised her palms skyward. Obviously, she was giving thanks to the Lord. With a quick and satisfied smile, the nun disappeared inside the mission's walls.

Jake's driver stepped up to Mindy. In broken English, he indicated the nun's name was Sister Mary Teresa. "She had overheard that this truck was part of a rescue mission from deep inside the warlord's territory. She believed that you were the one rescued from the warlords. She thinks evil men kidnapped you and painted your face black to traffic you across the country. She also indicated that this goop is what they use to clean the tarnish off the pots in the kitchen. When you are finished with it, you should return it to the cook. Right before she left, she thanked the Lord for protecting you from the Evil One."

The driver continued. "Her story is a miraculous one. That woman had been raised in her youth in Belgium in the Catholic faith but left it to marry a Lutheran missionary. They came to Sudan, where they labored tirelessly for the poor and unsaved. Her husband was captured, tortured, and then mutilated by a warlord. Most widows return to the safety of their homelands. This grieving woman searched her heart for the Lord's path. The Lord asked her to stay and help the children who had no parents. She became a nun and now runs a special school for orphans. In the morning, she teaches a group of spiritually gifted young adults. In the afternoon, her older students are assigned to service projects in the village. In the afternoon and evening, she teaches and cares for the younger children. As you can see, she has her hands full. The Church gave her the name Sister Mary Teresa—Mary being the blessed mother, and Teresa is the patron saint of missionaries."

"Thank you for sharing her story with me." Mindy noted the pattern of the students studying in the morning and then doing service projects in the community in the afternoon. She stored the idea in the back of her mind so she could use this concept in her training school.

Later that evening, Mindy prayed and meditated alone in the room the nuns had prepared for her and Jake. The thick, stone walls that surrounded a simple bed, table, and chair were lit by a single candle. Mindy's skin stung where she had rubbed it raw from scrubbing the black pigment from her face, arms, and legs. Their evening meal had consisted of a piece of bread and a bowl of thin soup.

"Thank you, Lord, for leading us to Alexander; please restore his strength. Thank you, Lord, for bringing us to this safe haven and for our daily bread. Thank you, Lord, for opening our eyes and hearts to the needs of your servants here in Sudan. Help me to understand all the words from the Ancient One. Help me, Lord, to be ready for the task you have laid before me."

A soft knock on the door disturbed Mindy from her prayer.

"Excuse me, madam. I am Sister Ruth. The sisters have prepared these gifts for you." The voice from the other side of the heavy wooden door spoke slowly and deliberately, as though she had learned the three sentences of English only moments before.

Mindy unlocked the door to the dark hallway that revealed a short, stout, elderly nun. Her bright eyes and warm smile glowed with compassion as she presented a bundle of cloth to Mindy.

"Thank you. Thank you. Jake and I greatly appreciate your kindness and generosity," Mindy said as they shared a smile.

"God bless you in your travels," the nun said quietly and then stepped away.

Mindy unwrapped the bundle. The outer layer was a sheet for their bed; the next cloth was a woman's nightgown; and inside the gown were a small jar of skin moisturizer, a small bar of soap, and two wash cloths. Mindy held the gown to her body. She wondered if the gown was from Sister Mary Teresa, whom she had met earlier.

Mindy eagerly poured a little of the water from the pitcher into the bowl to wash the residual goop from her skin. Mindy applied the moisturizer with its faint scent of lavender. She then removed the old, coarse robes that concealed her from the evil world and pulled the linen gown over her head. It was clean and soft. She felt fresh for the first time in days.

There was a soft knock on the door. "Mindy. It's me, Jake."

Mindy sprang to the door, opened it, and hugged him as he stepped in.

"Well, you look nice. Mmmm, you smell wonderful."

Mindy's smile beamed. She tightened her hug around his neck.

"Let me guess, Fredrick from the Aide Compound ran all the way out to give this fine nightgown to you."

"No, one of the sisters brought these gifts for us."

"Well … Mrs. Olson … I just have to ask you …" Jake conjured up his best concierge's voice.

They recited in unison, "How are you enjoying your honeymoon so far?"

Jake's loving smile soon faded. "Mindy, I feel terrible that we didn't spend our honeymoon in the Caribbean. I want you to know how much I appreciate your resolve to join me on this mission."

"Jake, I have learned and experienced *amazing* things on this trip. Look how the Lord has blessed us: He has reunited us with Rebekah. He led us to Alexander, and He brought us out of the desert to this safe haven." Mindy held Jake by his shoulders. "There has been an awakening in my soul. I feel God sent us here to teach us to prepare for what is to come. Have you noticed that we, on our own, have accomplished nothing? It is the people around us who have forged the breakthroughs. It is through simple people who trust in the Lord, who wait on Him and follow His lead that we have been delivered from the Evil One."

Jake watched his beautiful bride as the Holy Spirit stirred in his heart.

"It has been amazing how these Christians, who have almost nothing, find it in their hearts to be generous to strangers. They give without a notion of repayment. Somehow, through their faith and the Lord's supernatural provision, these Christians thrive. They eat where there is no food. They drink where there is no water. It is the power of the Almighty that holds the Evil One at bay. I have traveled halfway around the world to understand the true meaning of the word that hangs over the entrance of our camp. *Koinonia* ... it is about the deep fellowship between God and His believers and the sharing and caring that the community of believers experience on earth. It's the belief that what we give is more prized than what we hoard."

Mindy led Jake by the hand to the two chairs and motioned for him to sit. "I had an encounter this morning ... Rebekah took me to meet a wise, old woman they call the Ancient One. Legend has it that she is the last surviving relative of a once-prominent missionary family. In her youth, she was a mighty woman of God. Now, in her old age, she is almost blind and can barely get around. Because of the terrible oppression from the warlords, the underground church keeps her hidden."

Mindy slid onto Jake's lap and placed her arm around his shoulders. "She told me many things. She told me where to find Alexander and that he was a *ring bearer*. She told me that I am to raise Rebekah as my own child, that Rebekah is to be educated in the knowledge and technology of the West and thoroughly trained as a Christian leader so that when she is called by the Spirit, Rebekah will return to Sudan to lead her people out of darkness."

Jake nodded as he acknowledged that the words of the Ancient One validated the vision that Rebekah had spoken over him on his visit in January.

"The Ancient One told me that a powerful angel had been working around me. Although I may not have recognized his voice in the past, he would help us build the training camp for young Christians. Jake, I have seen him ... the angel ... he has eyes of compassion and a brilliant, white robe." Mindy trembled as she spoke. Goose bumps swelled on her arms. "Ancient One warned me to be alert. Satan is crouching at our door. We must be swift and deliberate in preparing ourselves for the wave of evil that is about to be unleashed upon our nation."

Mindy handed Jake the small, leather pouch that the Ancient One had given her earlier that day. Jake removed the golden ring from the pouch and turned it over in his hands. A series of symbols lined the outside of the ring. One of the patterns was a single star followed by twin lightning bolts and then a rainbow, just like the pattern on Jake and Mindy's rings.

"Mindy, tell me about the rings you presented to us on the last day of camp," Jake inquired.

"Mrs. Birmingham suggested that I might find an interesting gift for you in the artwork of an eccentric, old artist named Jeremiah Slough. He lives in the hills outside of Norton. Why?"

"I was wondering how you came to the understanding that the star is Jesus and we are the lightning bolts and the rainbow represents the good work we are doing at Camp Koinonia."

"I don't know ... the notion just popped into my mind."

"What made you buy those particular rings?" Jake asked.

"I don't know. I told Mr. Slough about you and what we had been through. He went to the back room and carried out our two rings in a small, wooden box. I tried the larger one on, and it fit perfectly. I told him I would need a larger one for you. That's when he told me that the smaller one could be a toe ring. For some reason, I really loved those rings from the minute I saw them."

"Forgive me for not telling you this earlier," Jake turned to face Mindy, "but I found rings on the skeletons of Ronnie Montgomery and Julie Capp the day I recovered them from the sinkhole. Both rings had the single star and a pair of lightning bolts, but neither of them had the rainbow like ours. Did you happen to see the toe ring on Alexander's toe? It's exactly like the one I found on Ronnie's skeleton in the sink hole. I have a feeling Alexander is wearing Ronnie's ring in honor of his son." Jake examined the ring. "This must be some sort of master ring. What do the rest of the symbols mean?" Jake asked as he placed the ring back into the pouch and handed it back to Mindy.

"I don't know." Mindy shook her head.

"Are you going to wear it?"

"The ring is not meant for me ... it is for our daughter Anna."

Jake's mouth dropped open. "Ahhhh ... did you say 'our daughter Anna'?"

"The Ancient One revealed to me that the Lord has already formed our daughter Anna inside my womb."

Jake was stunned. "How many months have you been pregnant?"

"Only one day." Mindy beamed as she leaned into Jake. "The Ancient One instructed me to present the gold ring to Anna on the day she is born. And as Anna grows in stature and understanding, we are to teach her about where it came from."

Jake and Mindy melted into each other's arms. Jake whispered into Mindy's ear, "Did you say 'our daughter *Anna*'?"

Mindy followed Jake as they climbed aboard the plane to Frankfurt, Germany, and then home to Chicago. *If everything goes according to plan, Rebekah will work as a lay nurse to help Alexander recover at the Aide Compound. In turn, Alexander will tutor Rebekah in writing, history, math, and science. When his strength has been restored, he will process the maze of paperwork for us to adopt Rebekah.*

An unsettling thought haunted Mindy. It was the warning from the Ancient One: *"The Evil One will send his agents to disrupt your lives and destroy your camp."*

PART THREE

Turbulent Times

> Blow the trumpet in Zion; sound the alarm on my holy hill. Let all who live in the land tremble, for the day of the LORD is coming.
>
> —Joel 2:1

CHAPTER 22

Getaway

MINDY WAVED AS Jake's car pulled out of their driveway. Although she had intentionally hidden her anxiety from him, she disliked the idea of having Jake gone for the weekend. She stooped and gently grabbed the aging Airedale behind his ears. "Well, Champ, I guess we'll be holding down the fort. I've always been glad that it worked out for you to stay with us." Champ's tail wagged with approval.

Mindy and Champ climbed the two stairs to the back door and walked in. She turned, locked the doorknob, and engaged the deadbolt. "Why does the bank's annual managers' team-building event require overnight stays?" she asked.

Champ tilted his head as though he sympathized with her.

She walked through the back entryway and across the kitchen to the front entry. Mindy grabbed the door knob, twisted it, and pulled on it. *Good, it's secure.*

Returning to the kitchen table, she opened her planning calendar and scanned the last two months. *Jake's and my gradua- tions, our wedding, a week in Sudan, the conception of our daughter Anna ... now Jake's gone for a team-building event ... and the camp will be opening next weekend. No wonder I feel exhausted.*

Glancing at Champ as he lay on the floor next to her, she wondered why the house seemed so quiet and lonely now that Jake was gone. *It's OK*, she rationalized. *Mrs. Birmingham lived alone in this house for years and nothing happened. Nothing that I know of.*

Champ jolted to his feet. He raced to the backdoor with his fur raised in alarm, ferociously barking as he ran.

Startled by the commotion, Mindy hustled to the kitchen window to see what was in the driveway. "It's OK, Champ. It's just a delivery truck." Mindy walked to the back door and patted Champ on the shoulder. "Sit, stay …" Champ complied. "Good boy."

"I have a package for Mr. Jake Olson," the delivery man said.

"Thanks. I'm Mindy Olson. I'll sign for it."

"Thank you. Have a nice day." The delivery man smiled and nodded as he pulled out of the driveway.

Champ waited patiently at the door. "Free dog," Mindy said. She could hear the kitchen phone ringing as she carried the box into the house. She picked up the receiver. "Hello."

"Hello, may I speak with Mindy?"

"This is Mindy. How can I help you?"

"This is Mr. Watson, with the Watson Trust Fund. My parents and I would like to arrange to make a financial contribution to your camp."

"Wow, that's great. What arrangements need to be made?" Mindy asked.

"I would like to talk to you face-to-face over dinner. Maybe tonight or tomorrow?" Mr. Watson suggested.

"Ahhh, the next few days aren't good. How about next week?"

"My parents will only be in town for a few days. We need to do this right away."

Skeptical of the hasty invitation, Mindy asked, "Are your parents neighbors to the Birmingham's property?"

"Yes. I'm a trustee to their logging and mining fortune."

"I thought they were on a long-term mission trip to China."

"Well, they are. They were. I mean, they're home for only a few days," Mr. Watson said.

Mindy perceived tension growing in the man's voice. "So you're Randall Watson. Is Mrs. Birmingham going to be at the dinner?"

"No. I heard that *you* were the new director. Listen, if you've heard of any *misbehavior* from my youth, I've moved on since then. If this exchange is going to be difficult, I can give the money to another cause."

"Alright, let's go tonight. Your parents will be there, right?" Mindy shook her head. *What can go wrong at a dinner?*

"Sure. Let's meet at Maggy's Restaurant in Brighton at 7:30," Randall Watson asserted.

"That'll be fine. I'll see you then."

"I've been looking forward to getting to know you ... *much* better. See you at Maggy's. Good-bye."

"Good-bye." Mindy hung up the phone.

Feeling apprehensive, she rationalized, *This is all part of being a camp director. What can go wrong? Mrs. Birmingham has mentioned numerous times that the Watsons were godly and generous people. Randall may have been a creep back in his camp days. I can't hold that against him. The camp will need money to make improvements.* Glancing at her watch and then back at the calendar, Mindy sighed.

Alarm bells rang in her conscience. The Ancient One had warned her of pending evil. In the week since returning from Africa, the Holy Spirit had revealed images to Mindy, scenes of occurrences that she could not understand.

Mindy placed her hand on her abdomen. *I need to eat right. I need to get plenty of sleep, and I need to stay positive. Anna deserves a healthy environment.* Mindy closed her eyes. "Heavenly Father, grant me the wisdom, strength, and courage to see me through the next few days. Bless little Anna as she grows inside me. Keep your hand upon Jake as he travels. In your Holy Name. Amen."

Ring. Ring.

Startled by the unexpected interruption, Mindy snapped the phone off the table.

"Hello," Mindy said.

"Hi, welcome back. How was Africa?"

"Hi, Lex. It was great. We found Alexander. He was badly beaten, but he's safe now. He's going to spend a little time recovering, and then I think he's coming home." Mindy relaxed in her chair. *It is so good to hear a friendly voice.*

"Hey, can I talk to Jake?"

"He's gone for the weekend. He went on a bank managers' team-building retreat." Mindy tried not to sound disappointed.

"He's starting his career at the bank by spending all weekend with the bankers?" Lex asked.

"Yeah. You know, going down zip lines, climbing up poles, falling backwards into a crowd."

"Jake should be good at all that. So, what are you doing?" Lex asked.

"Champ and I are home alone, except for the financial donation dinner I'm going to tonight with Randall Watson."

"You are going to dinner with Randall Watson without Jake?"

"Yeah. We're going to Maggy's. Would you like to go with me?" she asked. *Please say "yes." I know it would be awkward, but …*

"No. I need the special oil filter wrench that's hanging in Mrs. Birmingham's garage … I mean your garage."

"Do you need it right now?" Mindy was eager for some company.

"No, but later today would be fine. I'm tuning up my cousin's car tonight so he can sell it. His oil wrench is in Chicago in his tool box. I asked Mr. Peterson if he had one. He said the only one he knew of belonged to Carl Birmingham. It's hanging on the garage wall."

"Well, why don't I unlock the side door to the garage? Would you lock the door when you leave?" she asked.

"Sure. Thanks. Good luck with getting the money. Maybe we can hang a zip line at Camp Koinonia with it." Lex chuckled. "I'll call tomorrow before I swing by to bring the oil wrench back."

"Yeah, that's a great idea. Bye."

"Bye."

From the alley outside Maggy's Restaurant, a man in a black hoody watched Mindy's face pale as she swooned across the table from Randall Watson.

She's in trouble! Looks like she's about to pass out. I'll bet he's drugged her. The man in black ducked back into the shadow of the dumpster as Randall escorted Mindy out the restaurant's front door. Randall steadied Mindy's arm as he helped her into his car. After securing her door, he slipped around the car and opened the driver's door. Randall's body froze for an instant.

Thud! Slam! Randall's head ricocheted off the car's door frame. He had been struck in the back of his neck. As he faded from consciousness, his keys dropped out of his hand and inadvertently onto the top of his attacker's shoe. The hooded man nervously kicked the keys. The thrust of the kick sent the keys flying across the alley, and they dropped into the sewer grate.

Barely able to keep her eyes open, Mindy opened her door to escape. The man pulled his hood low, intercepted her, and hoisted her into his arms. Mindy's body went limp, unwilling, or unable, to resist.

He hustled around the back corner of the alley and placed her in his car. They departed down the alley and around the corner. Peeking around his hood, he checked for witnesses in his rearview mirror. *Nothing. Good,* he thought. *Now just a few quick turns and I'll be out of town.*

He looked at Mindy, who was struggling to stay conscious. "Help me, Lord. Please, Lord, help me," she murmured with a weak, almost inaudible voice.

Jake phoned Mindy from his hotel room. He was only mildly concerned when she did not answer. *She must be out shopping or having dinner with friends,* he decided. He realized that he was expected to be at dinner with the rest of the bank managers in just a few minutes, so he left a quick message.

"Hi, it's Jake. It is Saturday evening. I am sorry I didn't catch you. The team building went really well. We're all going to dinner here at the hotel and then to today's evening session. They still have our laptops and cell phones. They think it helps us to focus on the event. We won't get them back until we leave the event tomorrow evening. I miss you. I love you. I'll call early tomorrow morning from the hotel, before I leave for the session. Good night."

Jake checked his tie in the mirror and walked out the door to join his coworkers for dinner.

Veering his car off the state highway and onto the lonely black ribbon that led into the darkness, the man in the black-hooded sweatshirt decided to keep his hood up and gloves on. The intersection at Potsdam was only a few miles away. After that, they would be alone again in the darkness. He slowed his car as he drew closer to the country tavern that had appeared in the distance. The Post Office, grocery store, and gas station that ringed the intersection had all closed for the evening.

The man slammed on the brakes. "Idiot!" he whispered as he barely missed the pickup truck that careened onto the road from the parking lot of the corner tavern. He instinctively swung his arm to brace Mindy's lunge forward. *I forgot to fasten her safety belt.*

As he came to a complete stop at the traffic light, he gently eased her limp torso back into the seat. He reached over her leg to disengage the latch and allowed the seatback to recline. *Flash! Flash!* Red and blue lights exploded into the interior of his car.

"Busted," he whispered. He jerked off his gloves and kicked them under his seat. With a quick glance at Mindy, he slipped off his hood to appear less menacing. He rested his head on the headrest and readied himself for the patrolman's interrogation.

Out of the corner of his eye, he watched in amazement as the sheriff's car raced past him, through the red light, and down the street. The patrol car disappeared around the corner, apparently in pursuit of the pickup truck that had just left the tavern.

He donned his gloves and hood again. As the stoplight turned green, he pulled the seatbelt over Mindy's body and latched it. They proceeded past the few darkened houses and back into the forest.

Sheriff Brown arrived outside Maggy's restaurant. As he stepped past the restaurant's manager, he immediately recognized the man who lay unconscious in the alley. He handcuffed the man, surveyed the crime scene, and then notified the sheriff's dispatcher.

"I have apprehended fugitive Randall Watson in the alley to the south of Maggy's restaurant. I am requesting back up. There has been an assault. The assailant has apparently abducted a young woman in her mid twenties, average weight and height, light brown to blonde hair, wearing Khaki dress pants and a light-green, oxford-cloth blouse. The manager of Maggy's restaurant thinks he recognized the woman from a recent picture in the newspaper as the new director of Camp Koinonia. At this time, there is no description of the getaway car or of the assailant driving it."

The man drove by Mindy's house to check for activity. Her driveway was empty. He pulled around to the back entrance and stopped the car just outside the house's back door.

He lifted the keys from Mindy's purse, got out, and walked to the back door. He unlocked it, stepped inside for a few moments, and then returned to carry her in. He placed her on the couch in a semi-reclined position.

He debated silently, *Should I stay until she recovers? No … I'm a guardian, not a babysitter,* he concluded. Removing his glove, he touched his first two fingers against the inside of her wrist. Mindy's pulse was slow but steady. Her forehead was warm. "Good, her vital signs are OK," he whispered. He bent his face close to hers.

He could hear her slow, steady breaths. He paused, then pulled his face away.

He slipped his glove back on and returned the keys to her purse. He walked to the kitchen, lifted the mobile phone off the receiver, and placed the phone onto the coffee table next to Mindy.

For an instant, he admired her. *She's like the fairy-tale princess in "Sleeping Beauty."* In his heart, he yearned to kiss her. He whispered the words he had not permitted his lips to reveal, "I love you, Mindy, and I always will … you're safe now." He turned and walked through the backdoor, still ajar. Once outside, he paused just long enough to make sure to firmly shut and lock the door.

I know I did the right thing. Nodding his head, he walked to his car. *I know it. Thank you, God, for that stranger at the gas station who told me how Randall had used drugs to sedate and rape a woman in Madison.* He rolled his eyes and sighed. *Thank you, Jesus, for getting me to Maggy's just in time to intercept Mindy from Randall.* He started his car and drove down the wide path to the camp yard. *If I had arrived ten minutes later … and Randall had driven away with Mindy …* He shook his head. *I don't even want to think about it.*

As he drove back through the camp yard, his eyes riveted on the spot where his life had changed last summer, the place where he fell deeply in love with Miss Mindy Brice. He allowed himself to daydream back, one more time, to the fateful day.

He thought back to the moment when his heart leaped, back to the moment that Mindy Brice had gone from being the competent and charming senior counselor he respected to the woman he loved. Lex replayed in his mind the tug of war and … *his tumble with Mindy.*

Lex kept his headlights off and his window open as his car crawled under the Camp Koinonia arch. *I may be in big trouble, attacking a man, kidnapping a woman.* He hesitated before entering Kellum Road to make sure that no cars were approaching. *Heavenly Father, I plead for Your mercy! I beg for Your protection!*

Sharp gusts of wind whipped and tossed the treetops. Lex could smell the storm approaching. Within the next minute, rain pounded his car. While scrambling to roll up his window, Lex heard a calm, still voice: *"Cling to the Lord. Let the Holy Spirit direct your path."*

Lex perceived a vision that illustrated a route through the back roads. It led him back to the barn, where he had tuned up his cousin's car earlier that day. *Thank you, Lord, for my new understanding of the concepts of … prayer … and concealment.*

Daemon Lynch answered the phone from his bedside.

"Daemon, its Randall. You've got to help me!"

"Where are you?"

"I'm in the county jail in Norton, *Wisconsin*."

"What can you tell me over the phone?" Daemon pulled out a pen and notepad that were close to the phone.

"Somebody nailed me in the back of the head as I was getting into my car."

"And *you* are the one in jail?"

"When the sheriff got there, I was still unconscious … and my car doors were wide open."

"Oh, and they searched your car?"

"Yes."

"I'll leave right away." Daemon checked his watch.

"Get hold of Rox. Tell her I need her," Randall said.

"I'll do that." Daemon retrieved the leather-bound book that contained his essential phone numbers. "How badly were you hurt?"

"Not bad enough to warrant a bed in the hospital."

"You try to get some sleep. We'll sort this out in the morning."

"Yeah. See you then. Bye."

"Bye." Daemon got up to pack his suitcase.

CHAPTER 23

Awakening

*B*UZZ ... *BUZZ* ... *BUZZ*, the low tone of Mindy's alarm clock sounded from the upstairs master bedroom.

The shrill ringing of the kitchen phone stirred Mindy from her slumber. Still dazed and confused from last night, she rallied her strength and picked up the headset from the coffee table beside her.

"Hello."

"Good morning, it's Jake."

"Jake, where are you?" she asked with a shaky voice.

"I'm at the hotel in Madison. You know, I've been at the bank's annual team-building event?"

"Jake, why did you let me sleep on the couch?" Mindy asked, having a hard time making sense of the last twenty-four hours.

"Mindy, why *did* you sleep on the couch? Are you OK?"

Mindy closed her eyes and shook her head. She tried with all her strength to concentrate through the fog in her mind. "Jake, I feel like I've lived through a terrible nightmare. It started when Randall Watson called and said that he and his parents were ready to make a sizeable donation to the camp. This guy was a creep in his youth, but his parents are the most kind and generous souls on earth. My sister despised this guy when he showed up at camp. Everyone who knew the family speculated that Randall was adopted out of the pit of hell. By the time I got to my first camp, he wasn't around. I only knew of him from the stories the older girls told."

"So, you went to dinner with him?" Jake's voice tensed.

"I'm sorry, Jake. He caught me off guard. He assured me that he had outgrown his old ways and that his parents and he would like me to meet them for dinner at Maggy's Restaurant in Brighton. I figured if his parents were there, it would be safe."

Jake drew in a deep breath and let it out, "And?"

"When I got to the restaurant, he was sitting alone at a table for four. I thought it was odd that he had ordered me an iced tea and that a bottle of wine was already opened on the table. He assured me that his parents were looking forward to meeting me and that we should sit and talk for a few minutes until they arrived.

"I was starving hungry and really nervous, so I gulped down the tea. It had a nasty, salty taste. I started feeling sick and really, really sleepy." Mindy paused to hold back her tears. "Randall turned weird on me. He started talking about how my older sister had shunned him when they were campers. For whatever reason, he was taking his anger out on me.

"Randall helped me out to his car. The last thing I remember is a commotion, like a fight or something. And then the phone rang, and it was you."

"Mindy! Are you OK? Have you been harmed in any way?"

"No. I'm fine."

"How *did* you get home?"

"I thought *you* brought me home."

"Mindy, you know I've been in Madison all weekend. Do you have your cell phone with you?"

"Yes," she said as she retrieved her cell phone from her purse.

"Stay on the line with me, use the speed dial on your cell phone, and call Sheriff Brown."

Mindy skipped through the phone menu to dial the sheriff.

"Good morning. Norton County Sheriff's office, Debbie speaking."

"Good morning, this is Mindy Olson; I'm the director of Camp Koinonia. I would like to speak to Sheriff Brown."

"He's on patrol right now. Can I help you?"

"Listen, I was at dinner with a man named Randall Watson at Maggy's Restaurant in Brighton last night. I ended up getting sick, and someone brought me home. I think I may have been drugged. All I can remember is that I got very sleepy, and then I woke up in my house, on the couch."

"Are you OK?"

"Yes."

"Is there anyone there with you?"

"My husband, Jake, is on the other line. He called me this morning from Madison."

"Please stay on the line. I'll contact the sheriff." In a few minutes, the dispatcher's voice returned, "Sheriff Brown is on the way. Are you able to get off the couch?"

"Ah, yeah, I think so."

"Please go to the nearest door; then go to the driveway. Sheriff Brown is on his way. Have you gone to the bathroom or taken a shower already this morning?"

"No, I just woke up."

"Good, please don't. It's important that you stay in your original clothes. We'll need a doctor to examine you. He'll need a urine test."

"Doctor's exam? No, no, please. I'm fine."

"Mindy, please cooperate with us completely. It's for your own good."

"Mindy," Jake broke in, "I'm leaving for home. I'll stay on the phone with you until the sheriff arrives."

Mindy sluggishly climbed off the couch. Champ followed her to the door. Like every morning, Champ was eager to be let out for his morning patrol. Mindy opened the door to let her four-legged companion out of the house. Then she stepped onto the back porch. The morning sun pierced through the fog of confusion that was still rolling around in her head. She tried to remember whatever she could.

In a few minutes, Sheriff Brown's cruiser pulled into Mindy's driveway. He stopped the car with the passenger door in front of where Mindy was standing. He opened the door from the inside. "Please get in. Good morning, Mindy. How are you feeling?"

"Very groggy, but I'm fine."

"Listen, I need to ask you a few questions."

"OK."

"Can you tell me what happened yesterday evening?"

Mindy relayed the story.

"Is there anything else?"

"No. It's all too foggy right now."

"Mindy, when you woke up this morning, were you completely dressed—jewelry, shoes, and everything?"

"Yes." She looked at her shoes. "I remember tying both of my laces with double knots. Right before I walked out the door for dinner, my left shoe was a little too tight, so I untied it and retied it, this time with only a single knot. They are just as I left them."

"How about your makeup? Was it smudged in anyway?"

Mindy pulled down the visor to inspect her lipstick. "Sheriff, this is the same lipstick as last night. It could not have been reapplied because I threw the last of it out in the bedroom trash can."

"I know this is difficult, but sometimes when bad things happen, people choose to block them out. Please be completely honest with me … have you been abused, molested, or mistreated in anyway?"

"Well, I do believe Randall put something in my tea to make me sleepy. If you're asking me if I've been raped, the answer is no. It was like someone gently picked me up, carried me home, and put me on the couch."

"Mindy, who brought you home last night?"

"I don't know. The whole time, I was drowsy. I could hear what was going on. I just couldn't open my eyes. I really felt that Jake had come to rescue me. I remember being afraid when I was alone with Randall. Then after the commotion, I tried to run, and that was when the man picked me up. I never saw who he was. He never said a word. But for some reason, I felt safe. Somehow I knew I was being rescued, not kidnapped.

"How do you know it wasn't Jake?" Sheriff Brown asked.

"Jake left Saturday morning for a weekend team-building event with the area bank managers. They had to turn in their cell phones and laptops at the door. When Jake called this morning from the hotel in Madison, he was not even aware that I had gone to dinner with Randall. When you arrived, I hung up the phone with Jake. He was leaving to come home."

After enduring seemingly endless questions and the humiliation of a police doctor's examination, Mindy sat forlorn, waiting, praying for her Jake to arrive to comfort her. As soon as he walked to the door, Jake and Mindy were ushered into a small room with only a small table and four chairs.

"Good morning. I am Sullivan J. Holt. I'm an attorney here in Norton County. Mindy, I understand you've had a rough morning. I'm familiar with Randall Watson from his past involvement in the area. I would like to represent you on this case."

Mindy and Jake instantly recognized the attorney from his work in the community. "Yes, we would like you to help us," Jake stated.

"Randall Watson is a convicted rapist. He's also been convicted of various other charges. Somehow through the skill and treachery of his lawyer, he's out of prison. When the sheriff found him, Randall was unconscious, and his car door was wide open. They performed a customary search of his car and the area. In his car, they found illegal weapons, illegal drugs, and stolen credit cards. Randall's in custody now. He's not likely to get out for a long, long time. After we're finished with him in this state, three other states have warrants against him."

Sullivan moved his chair a little closer to Jake and Mindy. "Randall Watson's an evil man. And his lawyer, Daemon Lynch, is the devil himself, *in my opinion*. Because of the 'three strikes and you're out' law, if he's convicted on one more charge, he could face life in prison. Randall has filed assault charges against Jake. I know, and you know that Jake is innocent, but with Randall's vicious lawyer, the court case would no doubt get *really* muddy."

Sullivan sat back. "Randall is willing to drop the charges if you agree not to file charges against him." As far as the sheriff can determine, Mindy has not been raped or molested. There is, however, convincing evidence that Randall used a date-rape drug, GHB or gamma hydroxybutyric acid, to sedate Mindy. That is illegal. It may take a long, expensive court battle to convict him. And then you may have the assault charges against Jake to contend with. And if Randall's lawyer can convince the jury that Jake had *any* role in the assault, he could be convicted. It is not a matter of what Jake actually did or didn't do. It all comes down to Randall's lawyer's ability to persuade the jury. Sullivan's eyes were dead serious as he said, "Weigh your decision carefully."

Mindy looked for wisdom in Jake's eyes. She could see that he was deeply troubled. Mindy awakened to the spiritual attack that had ensnared them. Mindy slid her hand on top of Jake's. "It is not flesh and blood that we contend with, but with the powers of darkness."

"So Randall's in jail?" Jake asked, as he turned to Sullivan.

"Yes." Sullivan nodded.

"He is set to stay in jail?"

"Yes, for a long, long time."

Jake turned to Mindy, "So, besides the effects of the drug, Mindy, are you sure you're OK?"

"Yes." Mindy sighed with a hint of relief.

"What effect will the drug have on our baby?" Jake asked.

"The doctor assured me that the baby will be fine." Mindy slid her palm over her abdomen.

"So if we walk away, there will be no further questions, no further charges?" Jake asked Sullivan.

"Yes. That's how I understand it," Sullivan replied.

"Has it been proven that Randall drugged Mindy?"

"Well, he was in possession of the drug that was found in Mindy's urine sample."

"How do we know he won't walk out of jail this time, get out on some technicality?" Jake asked, still skeptical.

"First off, he will not be eligible for parole. Secondly, he will be in custody for his court cases for at least five to ten years. Third, every sentence will have to be served consecutively."

"What about the man who helped Mindy?" Jake asked.

"By the unique circumstances of this case, unless Randall's attacker comes forward to turn himself in, or *you* file kidnapping charges against him, the whole case should pass on quietly. Now, remember, assault is a crime. If you become aware of the assailant's identity, you are required to come forward with the information. If you know who did it and you don't come forward, you could be guilty of harboring a criminal."

Mindy broke in, "Let's not press charges. I'm fine. We and the camp do not need the bad publicity. No charges, no questions, right?"

"That's the way it'll be," assured Sullivan.

Hand in hand, Mindy and Jake walked through the sheriff's station. They exited the side door to the parking lot.

"What do you need right now?" Jake asked.

"I need you," Mindy returned with a smile.

"You will always have me." Jake squeezed her hand.

"Let's go home. I need a healthy meal. Then I'd like to take a long, hot bath and then go out to eat—some place where no one will recognize us. Oh, and *no cell phones or laptops*. I want your undivided attention." A brief smile of relief formed on her face. "My car is still over at Maggy's restaurant. Let's pick it up after we eat."

"Anything you say," assured Jake.

After riding home in silence, Mindy jolted forward in her seat as she spied Champ sitting on their back porch. "Champ!" Mindy cried. "I let him out right before the sheriff came to pick me up, and with all the turmoil, I forgot to let him back in. Wait a minute.

Do you remember what I told you—that I could hear everything last night, but I couldn't see or move?" Mindy, with a puzzled look, turned to Jake. "Champ *did not bark* last night! Champ must be very familiar with the man who brought me home. He would've thrown a fit if a stranger had carried me in."

"Now, Mindy," Jake interrupted, "you've got to let it be. If we figure out who the man was, we'd have to turn him in. Please, Mindy, *let it be*."

Mindy calmed herself. She walked over and grabbed Champ gently behind his ears. She looked into his eager eyes. "You are the *only one* who knows."

On Monday afternoon, Mindy answered the kitchen phone. "Hello."

"Hi, Mindy."

Mindy could tell Lex was nervous and tense.

Lex spoke rapidly to keep from being interrupted. "I am finished with the oil wrench I borrowed from your garage. I was wondering if I could drop it off later today? How'd your dinner go?"

"Uh …" Mindy hesitated. "Listen, there was a bit of a disturbance after the dinner, and someone gave me a ride home. The man I met for dinner was knocked unconscious. The sheriff later arrested him on various charges. Because of the particular circumstances of the incident, there were no witnesses, no suspects, and unless the attacker turns himself in, there will be no further charges."

"Wow. That's … really interesting. So how are you?" Lex asked.

"I'm fine. A little shaken, but fine."

"So if I understand it correctly, you are fine … completely fine."

"Yes."

"The jerk you went to dinner with is in jail, and if your guardian can keep his mouth shut, there will be no more questions or charges."

"That's right."

"Mindy ... the all-powerful, all-knowing, all-seeing God we serve works in mysterious ways."

Mindy perceived a deep sigh of relief emanating from the other side of the phone.

"You know, if you don't mind, I'll hold onto this oil wrench for a few days. There is no need for me to bring it by today."

"That'll be fine. Jake and I want you to know that you're welcome here any time."

"Thanks."

"God bless you," she said.

"God bless you too, Mindy. Bye."

Not far from the house, in a van parked next to a phone tower, Rox pushed the "save" button on the wiretap device. *Daemon*, she typed into the encryption device, *I think I've got something.*

Rox

ROX GROANED. WITH one eye half open, she stumbled out of bed, groped for her bottle of tequila, poured herself a shot, and tossed it down her throat. Tequila was not her usual breakfast, but this *was* her birthday. In her line of business, anything that reminded her of her past had to be deliberately obliterated.

Peaking through the crack in the hotel's drapes, Rox shook her head in disgust. "Another cold, dreary, November day. Wonder if I've missed Thanksgiving?" She looked around for a calendar. *I can't remember. Doesn't matter. I'm glad my job is over in this town. Time for this bird to fly south.* Her past months had been filled with botched schemes and unfortunate developments. She surveyed the room, and then she checked the bathroom. *Good, he's gone.*

She hated sleeping with pawns like Lester Bullick, the "bank dweeb," but for her, sex was an inexpensive and highly effective way to insure the loyalty and compliance of the men she manipulated.

Lester had served her well. He had secured the highly confidential information about the upcoming foreclosures from Jake Olson's desk at the bank. The article Rox had ghost written for the *Oltsburg Times* would already be on the newsstands and in newspaper boxes.

Jake Olson must be scratching his head about why someone would write such terrible things about him and his bank. Rox's article was the latest shockwave from the devastating quake she had been paid to generate.

With a mole like me and Randall Watson's money funding a ruthless lawyer like Daemon Lynch, no one is safe. Rox's exploits rendered her a twisted feeling of satisfaction. *They never see me coming. I just slip into town, wreak havoc on our enemies, and then disappear without a trace.*

Rox smirked as she rolled her eyes. *Honest, God-fearing folks don't stand a chance. They are always so trusting, so naive. That's what makes them so vulnerable. They'll take my bait and then do anything to save their reputations or keep their spouses from learning about their dirty little secrets.*

She poured herself another shot and toasted herself for a job well done. Rox slid the tequila past her tongue. *Now I'm starting to feel better.* She opened her laptop and typed in the website address for her bank in Chicago. *It's 10:13 A.M.; Daemon Lynch should have my paycheck deposited by now.*

Rox had learned to verify that her paycheck had cleared the bank before she left her current assignment. If it didn't clear, she could threaten to blackmail the boss and expose his evil schemes. *Blackmailing the blackmailers, that is dangerous business.* She reflected on the past. *Somebody always seems to end up with a bullet in his head.*

"I hope Randall and Daemon appreciate all I've done for them," she mumbled. "I was the one who manipulated Zeke Thorne into stating into my hidden recorder that he slugged Randall. I know he didn't do it. That doesn't matter. That shred of evidence is all Daemon needed to file an assault case." Rox entered her login ID and password.

It's not my fault that the weasel who actually clobbered Randall cooperated with the authorities in exchange for witness protection and amnesty. She waited for the account screen to populate. *If I had more time, I'd find that little twit. Maybe Randall will pay me to come back in a few years, when it's not such a tightly held secret.* Rox hammered her finger on the enter button, "Come on!"

I'm the one making things happen around here. I'm the one who uncovered the scandal about the two missing campers. I'm the one who juiced up Wilbur Capp to file a wrongful death case for his dead sister against the Birminghams. It's not my job to win the court cases. I just dig up the dirt. Randall and Daemon owe me … big time.

Rox gloated as the tequila rushed through her veins. *Rox, you are a genius. If my childhood wasn't so screwed up, I could have been a detective, a journalist, or a lawyer.*

She laid back on the bed, still balancing the computer on her lap. She drifted back to the small town in the Texas panhandle. Rox could still feel the pain and hatred of growing up with an abusive, alcoholic dad and a promiscuous mom. Her hell on earth deteriorated even further when her older step brother moved back home. The sexual abuse she endured while still in junior high left a scar that never healed.

Rox learned at an early age that she could manipulate men into giving her the things she wanted. From Texas, she hitchhiked to Phoenix and then onto Las Vegas. Each journey forced her deeper into the arms of evil men.

Rox pulled herself up to a sitting position. *Ahhh, there it is, that slippery devil paid up. It's only half what my work's worth. But it'll get me through for a while.* With a few clicks, Rox transferred the money to her account in Fort Lauderdale. "Time for me to *go!* Shower, pack, and motor." Rox closed the lid on the laptop and then rolled off the bed to pour herself another shot.

After her shower, she rubbed her wet hair with a towel. She stared at herself in the vanity mirror. Her once firm and shapely body had grown wretched from neglect. Years of misery had drained the beauty from her face.

I can't keep this up much longer.

Rooting through the jumbled clothes in her suitcase, she retrieved the small, locked jewelry box. She fumbled to open the false bottom and counted the five one-hundred-dollar bills. Placing the money back in the box next to the three vials of white powder, she slipped her index finger onto the trigger of her small pistol. Cocking the gun, she lifted it to her head. *Bet I wouldn't even feel it.* She contemplated *the bullet.* Secretly, she wished that her bullet would find its mark. Being severely wounded would be far worse than death. With little money, no friends, and nowhere to call home, somehow a bullet in the head seemed a fitting end to her lousy life.

I can't do it ... not today ... I just got paid. Daemon has already set me up with at job in Miami. Caressing the pistol with both hands, she peered into the open barrel. *I know you'll be here when I need you.* She laid the pistol on top of the money, closed the false bottom, and relocked it. "I've got to get out of here."

While Rox scurried to pack her belongings, she brooded over her enemy, Mindy Olson. *What gives her the right to be so happy all the time? I wonder what antidepressant she's on ... I need to get some of that. It amazes me, no matter how badly we treat her, there is something in her face that shines. I can't help but hate her and all the good little camper boys and girls. Prison is the only camp I'll be going to. I wish I had more time to destroy her. Maybe when I get set up in Miami, I'll hack into her camp's website and slam it.*

Rox forced her suitcases shut. *What really makes me mad is the way Mindy slipped my business cell phone number out of me the evening we had dinner together, and then she had the nerve to ask the waiter to take our picture together. I wonder if my picture will make the camp scrapbook? Yeah right.*

Rox stumbled out of her room and threw her two suitcases in the back seat. She placed the travel cup in the drink holder and laid the bottle on the seat. With the tequila rolling around in her brain, Rox drove out of the hotel parking lot. She failed to notice the car that followed her onto the interstate. The FBI, armed with her photograph, her business cell phone number, and the fingerprints from her glass at the restaurant, would be stalking her every move. It would only be a matter of days until the tigress of deception would be caught and caged.

Jake held open the door that read "Sullivan J. Holt, Attorney at Law" as Mindy walked in.

"Please come in. Have a seat." Sullivan stood and warmly shook Mindy's and then Jake's hand. "Thank you for meeting with me so late in the day."

Jake and Mindy settled into the sturdy chairs in front of Sullivan's desk.

"I know the last several months have been stressful for all of us. I would like to provide closure on a number of issues before I lock the office for the Thanksgiving holiday. Hopefully we can all rest a little easier after this.

"As you know, I defended Zeke Thorne in the assault case filed by Daemon Lynch. After that, Mrs. Birmingham hired me to defend her in the wrongful death case filed by Wilbur Capp. Daemon was the opposing attorney in that case also. There are a number of things that I can't discuss because of attorney/client privilege. But there are a number of thing I believe you should know."

Sullivan sat back in his chair. "I believe that Randall Watson was the instigator of both cases, and his motive was to discredit and destroy Camp Koinonia. Exactly why he launched this undertaking, I may never know. It was some sort of sick obsession against Camp Koinonia."

"In the first case, the assault charges filed against camp counselor Zeke Thorne were dropped because an individual, who shall remain anonymous, turned in Randall Watson's keys that were lost the night of the attack. FBI and federal investigators placed an extremely high value on obtaining Randall's keys. They believed the keys would unlock a Pandora's Box of incriminating evidence against Randall Watson and his evil empire. The individual who came forward was granted witness protection and amnesty from prosecution for his cooperation.

"In the wrongful death case, the testimony that was supported by Jake's photo, which was taken on the day two members of the

Mennonite church accompanied him to the small Frog Pond, provided a critical piece of evidence. The time-and-date-stamped snapshot revealed the moles on Jake's calf in one corner of the picture and the two perfectly formed skeletons that lay in an indention in the sinkhole. Forensic experts concluded, from the position the bodies were in, that the two that had drowned were highly intoxicated at the time of the tragedy.

"Because the water in the small pond had always been extremely muddy, no one was aware of the existence of the sinkhole. It continues to be a mystery." Sullivan leaned forward to place his elbows on his desk. "Why the water receded back into the earth and how the water that refilled the pond remains crystal clear—well, I'm convinced the Lord played a hand in both of those events."

The wrongful death case fell completely apart when Wilbur Capp's mother turned over his sister's diary to him. Mrs. Capp had attached Julie's ring, which had been recovered from the sinkhole, to her daughter's diary by a ribbon. Wilbur pondered the lone star and twin lightning bolts inscribed on the ring. As he slipped it on his finger, he had a change of heart. Wilbur realized that the case against the Birminghams was ill conceived. Mrs. Birmingham was in no way at fault for the deaths of his sister Julie and Ron Montgomery. Against the vehement objections of Daemon Lynch, Wilbur dropped the case. On the last day of court, federal marshals arrested Daemon Lynch on fraud, tax evasion, and extortion charges."

Jake shifted in his chair. *Julie Capp's ring is now on Wilbur Capp's finger. Alexander Montgomery wears his son's ring. Mindy, Anna, and I each have one. I've got to track down Jeremiah Slough. I wonder what he can tell me about these rings.*

Sullivan continued, "And then there is Elma Willoughby, otherwise known as Rox. Mindy, your intuition was correct. Rox was not a freelance author researching a book on summer camps in America. She was an evil, manipulative pawn of Daemon Lynch. Rox played a critical role in the mayhem that occurred over the last six months.

"With Randall Watson behind bars as a result of his failed kidnapping attempt at Maggy's restaurant and Daemon Lynch taken into custody, we can only hope the federal investigators will follow Rox to her next crime syndicate and nab her before she ruins any more lives."

A warm, broad smile formed on Sullivan's lips. "I do have one more item. Randall Watson's parents, James and Lavern Watson, have returned from their mission work in China. A private investigator for Mr. and Mrs. Watson compiled evidence on the illegal and unethical practices of their adopted son. Mr. and Mrs. Watson were appalled at the width and depth of the atrocities that Randall had committed. Randall was immediately and permanently shut off from the source of family wealth that had fueled his evil obsessions.

"As a goodwill token, the Watson's would like to make a generous financial contribution to the Camp Koinonia trust fund. They have asked me to present you with a check for $100,000.00. They will be contacting you in the near future about a few things that the Lord has placed on their hearts." Sullivan pulled the check from his pocket and handed it to Mindy.

"Thank you. This is incredible. How can I thank them?" Mindy asked, elated by the news.

"As I understand it, they will be reuniting with old friends over the next few weeks. I suspect they will be in touch with you after that." Sullivan smiled.

Jake stood to shake Sullivan's hand. "Thank you for everything. Have we settled up our legal expenses?"

"Yes. Have a restful and joyous Thanksgiving." Sullivan motioned them towards the door.

Jake and Mindy strolled along Main Street.

"Well, I think we should grab a bite to eat," Mindy said.

"Agreed—how about Oma and Opa's diner?" Jake stopped in front of the restaurant's window.

"Jake, look." Mindy pointed to Lex and Zeke at the back of the diner. "No, let's not bother them. Let's keep walking."

In keeping with their tradition, Zeke and Lex met on the night before Thanksgiving at Oma and Opa's German diner. Best friends since childhood, they had met each other with bear hugs.

The secret that Lex was bound to conceal, Zeke had known in his heart all along. Zeke, Jake, and Mindy would ever press Lex for an explanation about his involvement with the knockout punch against Randall Watson. Nor would Lex ever doubt how much they appreciated him.

Late that night, Jake was awakened by a voice.

"On the day the cities are desolated, you will find refuge beneath the Giant Pine."

CHAPTER 25

W. B.

JAKE STOOD ALONE in the cemetery after Mrs. Birmingham's funeral. He had meandered to a private place to satisfy his need for fresh air, silence, and most of all, solitude. With his back to the large crowd of mourners, Jake wept. *Why, Lord ... why did this have to happen right before Christmas?*

"Jake Olson." A man addressed Jake from behind.

"Yes." Instinctively, Jake turned around and extended his hand.

"You have a Bible study at 3:00 on Sunday afternoons."

"Yes," Jake said in surprise.

"Instead of you meeting with the group at that time, let's meet under the Giant Pine. I need to talk to you about a number of things, just the two of us."

"OK ... uhh ... and you are?" Jake asked.

"William, William Berry," he said with a slight smile.

Jake's grin grew across his face. "3:00 P.M. tomorrow, under the Giant Pine, just the two of us."

The two men stood for an instant, their eyes locked. Jake's skin tingled. He knew this meeting was prompted by the Holy Spirit. Divine business of the utmost importance was brewing. Jake watched William walk over to a crowd of mourners, touch a weeping woman on the arm, and then help her into his car. They drove off.

"So that's Wild Bill, and that must have been Juice … the stuff camp legends are made of."

A few minutes before 3:00, Jake walked onto the rock slab under the Giant Pine. William Berry sat in the chair he had made for Carl Birmingham.

Before Jake could say "good afternoon," William asked, "Have you ever sat in this chair?"

"Yes, a few times. It's an incredible work of art."

William waved off the compliment. "Did you ever wonder why this tree grew so huge?"

"It must have something to do with the tree's genetics, the soil. I figured it must have tapped into an underground water supply," Jake replied.

"There's an energy that seeps up through the ground in certain spots around the earth. No one can see it or smell it. Some people can feel it. Energy ports are scattered around this property—Giant Pine, Inspiration Point, the oak tree at the Frog Pond. It's why the beech tree survived the fire." William stood and snapped the chair into its storage position.

He continued, "Ponce de Leon searched in vain for the Fountain of Youth. It wasn't in the water. The energy flux cannot be stored in matter like water, wood, or rock. All you can do is place yourself on top of it."

William turned his gaze to the scenic view. "I first saw this spot in a dream. I'd been fasting and praying. I watched an angel touch down on this spot, where the three cracks meet, with a tiny seedling in his hand. The twig grew into a giant tree. The same angel showed me the other spots. I built the benches to mark the energy ports."

William pulled two flashlight headsets from his coat pocket. "You're going to need this."

He walked over to the face of the rock wall and stooped down, with one hand on the boulder and one hand in the rock's crack.

The rock door opened. "Let's go." William turned his headset on and stepped into the cave. Jake followed.

"Carl and his son, Roy, found this cave while they were hunting. This cave has five main chambers. They developed it as a bomb shelter for the cold war. Then Carl and I and a few others enhanced it in case there was an economic collapse at the turn of the century. Hold out your left hand with the palm up. This cave system resembles the shape of your hand. The entrance is your thumb, the main cavity is your palm, the control room is in your pinkie."

William led Jake to the center of the main chamber. "The two middle fingers house the living quarters and the dining hall. Your index finger takes you out to the quarantine facility, which is located on top of a major energy port. When you get out there, look at the ceiling of the cave. I scratched my initials, W.B., directly above the port. None of these facilities are much to look at, but they are highly functional.

"Jake, I'm going to tell you a lot of information. The most important thing you have to remember is this: Cling to the Lord. Let the Holy Spirit guide your path." William hesitated to let the statement sink it. "Have you ever heard this advice before?"

"Yes. Jesus told me that in a vision," Jake said. "A number of people have stated the same message."

"The Lord has echoed this message around the world. Only the faithful can hear it. The way we will survive the coming calamity is to follow His divine instructions. The devil can't intercept the Lord's messages."

William peered into Jake's eyes. "I'm not sure if you are familiar with Ezekiel 9 and Joel 2. God is marking the faithful in His church. When the wrath of the Lord sweeps over the earth, the followers of Christ will be protected. The chosen will disappear under the shadow of the Lord's wing. After a period of time in the safe havens, the Holy Spirit will prompt us to emerge and be the light to a fallen world. We must labor for the Lord until the day He comes again."

William lowered his voice. "You have to *be* ready. The great and terrible day of the Lord is rapidly approaching. Upon the Holy Spirit's command, *run* to the safe haven, and do not look back. Fire will devour entire cities. Devastation and slaughter will spread across the world. Our proud and prosperous nation will be reduced to a wasteland."

William shook his head. "*Do not share* what you have learned today *with anyone*—not even Mindy. The Spirit will direct her path accordingly. Only those prompted by the Holy Spirit will know about this place. Anyone who has to *ask*, doesn't know. Don't tell them."

"OK." Jake nodded his head in sober confirmation. He concentrated on William's every word.

"So what do you know about *your* role in the end times?" William asked.

"Mindy and I are commissioned to prepare a group of spiritually gifted youth to comfort a fallen world," Jake stated.

"This cave system will be perfect for that. In the coming months, people will come to you. They will *know* your name. The Holy Spirit will prompt them, just like He prompted me to contact you at the funeral. They will arrange to meet you inside the cave; that's how you will know they are agents of the Lord." William motioned Jake deeper into the cave. "In the end times, Satan's attack will come like a thief in the night. Fast and pray. The Holy Spirit will prompt you into action.

"Earlier today, I visited the benches; I anchored two of the legs on each one to the ground so that their positions will be stabilized. They have to be directly over the energy ports to maximize the healing effects.

"In the end times, social order will be in disarray. Electrical power will be interrupted. Medicines won't be available. Hospitals will be closed. The Holy Spirit will direct people to Camp Koinonia to be prayed over and healed. God will energize the ports to facilitate healing. Native American medicine men knew of these energy ports. They referred to this area as the 'Healing Trees.'"

Healing Trees … Wabeno … the Abyss … when the Abyss is revealed, the end times will begin. A grand perception began to form in Jake's mind.

"There are many elements to the Camp Koinonia Prophecy. The training camp and the healing facility are the ones I am most familiar with. At some point, this area will be part of a transit route for displaced Christians. And finally, this property will be a source of the hidden manna, a nutrient substance that will feed a large community of believers. Carl Birmingham could only give me certain details before he died.

"God provides only a portion of His divine plan to each of the faithful on earth. That insures that the Enemy can intercept only a tiny piece from each Christian he corrupts. In the end times, the safety of the multitude of unarmed Christians will depend on prayer and concealment."

William followed the stream of water in the cave as far as his light would shine. "Last time I tested it, this water was pure. You better have it checked before you drink it. If you go back far enough, this stream originates from an underground lake. I don't know for sure, but I bet this lake feeds a stream that flows over to the Watson's property. Let's head back.

"There are a couple of things you need to know about caves. Never go into a cave alone. If you arrange to meet someone on the inside, stay just inside the door until that person navigates through the door for him or herself.

"You'll need a reliable headset and a backup light source. Buy the best lights and batteries you can afford.

"Don't burn anything in the cave. That ancient notion of burning a torch is outdated. Everything that burns poisons the air supply. Caves don't have a mechanism to break down carbon monoxide."

William and Jake arrived at the cave's entrance. "There should be two large spools of bailing twine in Carl's garage. We tied them to this loop in the rock and then let the twine unravel as we walked through the cave. You'll want to buy nylon cord. It's white, and it won't rot. We tied knots in the twine to help us remember where things were.

"And now for the most important instruction; I'm going to show you how to open and close the cave door. Then I am going to let you do it."

After a few tries, Jake could open and close the door from both sides of the wall.

"Thank you." Jake shook William's hand as they stood outside the cave.

"God bless you, Jake Olson. Welcome to the Christian underground. Remember, only those who cling to the Lord and are obedient in following the Holy Spirit's guidance will ever be admitted into the safe haven. We are not alone, Jake. There is a worldwide syndicate of believers preparing safe havens in every nation. Pray hard; stay alert." William turned and walked down the logging road that led to the Watson's property.

Jake's eyes gazed up the trunk of the massive pine tree that towered in front of him. *On the day the cities are desolated, seek refuge beneath the Giant Pine.*

I wonder which cities? I wonder how soon?

CHAPTER 26

Proposal

REBEKAH PUSHED THE save button on her laptop. *Praise the Lord; I'm finished. It's only June 26th, and I've already completed my course work.* She glanced over at Alexander and watched him reading the biography of the great evangelist Dr. Billy Graham. Rebekah and Alexander met regularly at Norton Public Library. Rebekah worked on her homework, and Alexander read as he made himself available for any questions she might have.

She reminisced back to her days at the Nabutu Orphanage in Sudan. *The locals all referred to him as Grand Alexander. His efforts to drill water wells for the Christian orphanages made him a hero to the local tribes.*

She grinned with delight. *So I guess he's been my hero too, and he was my patient as I nursed him back to health after the Ancient One directed Mindy and me to him. Then he was my instructor as he oversaw my remedial studies to prepare me for when Jake and Mindy brought me to America. And for the last year, he has been my mentor, organizing my independent studies at University of Wisconsin.*

She looked around the back corner of the library. *We're alone. It's time to make my move.*

Alexander looked up from his book and smiled. Rebekah left the chair at the desk and sat next to him on the sofa.

"Alexander," Rebekah whispered.

"Yes."

Rebekah leaned to bring her lips close to his ear. "Will you marry me?"

"*What?*" Alexander drew his head back to look her in the face.

"I asked you if you would *marry me.*"

"Aaah, I'm honored that you asked, but do you really want to marry someone who is old enough to be your father?"

"I love you, Alexander. I don't want to marry *someone* old enough to be my father. I want to marry *you.*" Her eyes locked onto his. "If our ages matter to you, I need to know if you think I'm old enough to be your wife and not *your daughter.*"

"*Yes.*" A broad grin grew across his face. I do think you are old enough to be my wife. I love you, Rebekah. I would love to marry you. I have to admit that I've been thinking the same thing."

Rebekah slid her arms around his neck and squeezed him.

"How soon do you want to get married?" Alexander asked.

"Right away!"

"OK. So where do you want to go on our honeymoon?"

"Sudan," Rebekah answered.

"Really? I get the feeling the Holy Spirit has been sending us the same signals. You're thinking we'll go back to stay, until the end, until Jesus returns."

"Yes. Have you been sensing it? It is like something terrible is about to happen, something catastrophic, and God is putting His people in place for the end times."

"Yes, I hear the quality of life has deteriorated in Sudan. It is going to be dangerous to land on a flight from Europe. The last group of missionaries flew first into South Africa, then caught a small plane into Sudan." Clearly dismayed by the danger, Alexander turned to Rebekah. "Are you sure you want to get married? We can face the end together, without ...

"Alexander! Are you afraid of getting married?" Rebekah snapped to cut off his sentence. "I'm talking about holy matrimony.

I'm talking about until death do us part. I'm not talking about having a travel mate."

Once again, a broad, proud smile came to Alexander's face. "Good. Let's get started. I'll check on flights. You check on the church. Who should we invite?"

"Mindy, Jake, and Anna. That should cover it."

"Right. The Fourth of July is a little over a week away, so let's try to be gone by then. Are your passport and papers in order?"

"Yes."

"How about your coursework?" Alexander asked as he pointed to the laptop and pile of books on the library table.

"I just finished it." Rebekah rolled her eyes. "I would like you to proof it, of course."

Alexander nodded his head. "I guess all we need are the rings."

"You know how I hate diamonds," she said.

"Not all diamonds have blood on them."

"Let's get our rings from Jeremiah Slough."

"Jeremiah Slough? How did you hear about him?"

"Mindy suggested I get the rings from him."

"So, Mindy knows about your proposal?"

"I told her how I felt about you, and she said, 'Just ask him.'"

There was a moment of silence. Then Alexander leaned into Rebekah. "What are Jake and Mindy sensing about the end times?"

"They know it's close," Rebekah whispered back. "There's a group of spiritually-gifted youth coming to Camp Koinonia the week before the Fourth. They're from inner city Chicago. Something is stirring in Mindy's spirit. She is not sure what to make of it. She's thinking of sending Anna to Jake's parents in Fort Wayne for that week so she can concentrate on the campers."

"I need to put the finishing touches on the evangelism curriculum later tonight. Let's get the marriage license tomorrow and pay a visit to Jeremiah Slough."

Rebekah cupped his face in her hands. "Alexander, I'm not afraid to admit it to you: I'm exhilarated and terrified about our future together. But with the love of Jesus and you beside me, I'm confident we will run our race to completion."

"Amen."

Alexander and Rebekah sealed the proposal with a kiss.

CHAPTER 27

Peg

JAKE WAITED IMPATIENTLY at the edge of the camp's parking lot. This was the first time he'd made the effort to be at the parking lot in advance of the campers' arrival. Anxiety laced with anticipation wrestled in his heart. He heard the busload of campers winding along Kellum Road. Jake's eyes searched for one individual, Margret Walker. *I have no idea what she is going to say when she gets off that bus, but I'm going to be here to hear it.*

Jake's mind raced back over his life at Camp Koinonia. *By this time three years ago, I hadn't even been to Commodores Restaurant with Mindy. Two year ago, by early July, I had gotten married to Mindy, been to Sudan to find Alexander, and Mindy had been rescued from Randall's rape attempt.* Jake wiped the sweat off his forehead. *It is amazing that Anna is a year and a half old. She is truly an amazing child. It has been a miracle how Camp Koinonia prospered all last year—record attendance and record donations. And now Rebekah and Alexander are married and on their way to Sudan.* He stared across the parking lot and then off into the woods that concealed Kellum Road. *But something is wrong. I can sense it. It's like the heavens and earth are about to be shaken apart.*

Back at the house, Mindy looked in Anna's empty room. *Oh Anna, Anna, Anna, how I miss you. Lord keep your hand upon her as she visits with Jake's parents.*

As she walked through the house, Mindy mused over how smooth Rebekah's transition had been from her refugee camp in Sudan to the lush forest of Wisconsin and now back to Sudan. *This old house is going to be way too quiet.*

Mindy made her way through the camp yard and approached Jake silently from behind. As she stepped to his side, she gently wedged her hand between his arm and chest and gripped him above his elbow. She could tell he was preoccupied, so she stood in silence next to him.

They stood in the summer swelter as the chatter of the midsummer cicada serenaded them. This session of campers would occupy the camp for the week that included the Fourth of July. The air around the camp was absolutely still, no breeze, no rustle.

Jake could hear it far off down the road, like the rolling thunder of an approaching storm. It was children singing—not the half-hearted "Kum Ba Ya" the affluent white kids sang reluctantly around the campfire. This was full tilt. This was powerful. This was worship—hearts and lungs open wide! It was a song that he knew well; although, he had never heard it with such intensity.

The Holy Spirit moved in Jake and Mindy as joyful tears streamed down their cheeks. Their hands tingled as their hearts danced. The praise choir grew louder as the bus rolled under the arched sign that read CAMP KOINONIA.

Jake could tell by Mindy's tears that her fears had been relieved. He knew she had prayed in the weeks before their arrival that this busload of kids from Chicago's Vine Street Baptist Church would not tarnish her pristine camp. After all, these kids were the offspring of murderers, prostitutes, vagrants, and drug addicts.

"These campers are going to be the best thing this camp has ever seen," Mindy whispered as she sobbed.

Jake and Mindy instinctively raised their hands in applause as the bus pulled up in front of them.

The bus fell silent.

"Welcome to Camp Koinonia," Jake and Mindy shouted in unison.

Thunderous applause erupted from inside the bus.

Zeke and Nancy, the two camp counselors that had been selected for this special assignment, arrived at the parking lot to greet the kids and help unload the bus.

The four veterans of Camp Koinonia watched with saddened hearts as the kids filed off the bus with their shabby possessions in nothing more than half-empty grocery bags and old shoeboxes.

As the campers found their places in a straight line in front of Jake and Mindy, the eyes and smiles of the eight young men and eight young women gleamed with anticipation. They looked in awe at the towering pines and the row of immaculate cabins they could see down the path. It was as though they had arrived in paradise. This was as close as they would get to heaven on earth.

Margret Walker climbed off the bus. Her radiant smile barely held back her tears of joy. She nodded politely to Mindy, Nancy, and Zeke and walked straight to Jake and embraced him.

"Peg, it's truly an honor to welcome you to Camp Koinonia," Jake whispered in Margret's ear.

"Praise the Lord," was all she could say.

The first order of business was to feed the troop of hungry youths. Since they had left Chicago with little to eat, they were very hungry. The small group quickly devoured a mountain of hot dogs and peanut butter and jelly sandwiches.

After dinner, a tour of the camp was followed by shower time. While the campers were in the showers, Nancy and Zeke quickly gathered spare sheets and blankets to make beds for each of the new campers who had arrived without sleeping bags or bed sheets.

Jake lit his signature welcome bonfire, while Mindy prepared the chocolate bars, graham crackers, and marshmallows for s'mores.

At the conclusion of the orientation, Margret led the campers in singing a few worship tunes.

Jake, Mindy, Zeke, and Nancy sat stunned at the beauty and intensity with which the youth sang. If demons had lurked in the forest within earshot of the campfire, they would have trembled and fled, dumbfounded by the ferocity of the worship. The notes that projected from the lips of Vine Street Baptist's youth group were unmistakable. Their worship reverberated with the soul-piercing presence of the Holy Spirit. A force had been released from the fire ring's perimeter that night. As the concert ended, the entire group joined hands for a long prayer around the embers. Finally, the kids and counselors returned to their cabins for lights out.

Later that night, Jake went through the motions of getting ready for bed. He could not shake the chorus the kid sang as they arrived on the bus.

It rang in his head. It resonated in his soul. He pondered the prophetic nature of the worship chorus. It had been only a few years since he had received the vision from the Lord that he would be instrumental in building a training camp that would prepare the next generation to lead the world through the darkness.

He pictured the night of the tornado that had threatened to destroy the camp during his first year at Camp Koinonia. He replayed how he prayed for mercy from the storm. He could still feel Mindy, as she trembled beside him, his arm around her shoulders.

So much had happened. Yet, he knew the most intense spiritual battles were yet to come.

These campers would be the first kids to receive the Christian leadership training that Jake, Mindy, and Alexander had compiled. These kids would be the first class of spiritual warriors.

Still preoccupied, Jake shuffled to his alarm clock. After checking the wake-up time, he pulled back the sheet and summer blanket. He smiled at Mindy, who was lying on her back, watching him. After a long, joyous day, he snuggled on his side, next to her, placing his forehead lightly against her upper arm.

"Can I ask you something?" Mindy asked.

"Yes, of course," Jake replied as he pulled back just far enough to see Mindy's face.

"How long have you known Margret Walker?"

"Well, when I *came to* on her couch, it felt like I had a jack hammer pounding on the back of my neck. As I cracked my eye open, I saw that she was sitting on the chair, staring at me.

"She said, 'Are you a choirboy or a preacher or something?'

"'No. Why?' I replied.

"'Because when I picked you up off the floor, you had *the glow* around you.'

"'The glow?' I asked.

"'Yeah, I see it on some of the people who sing in the church across the alley from my window.' She smiled and said, 'My friends call me Peg.'"

"So you were *passed out* on her couch?" Mindy asked, disgusted and horrified.

"No, not passed out—knocked out." Jake tried to sound reassuring.

"She knocked you out?" Confused and bewildered, Mindy rolled her eyes.

"No, it must have been a beer bottle or something," he said.

Mindy glared at Jake. The look on her face demanded an explanation.

"Let me start over." He sat up to face her.

"Remember that time I came up to celebrate your mom's birthday? It was right before midterms. Remember that I told you I had car trouble on the way home? Well, my radiator hose blew out, so I had to pull off the interstate before my engine locked up." Jake shifted a bit. He wanted to be clear and accurate in his explanation.

"I parked under the light of an old corner drug store. The store clerk told me he had coolant and water but not hoses. The car parts shop was two blocks over, then three blocks to the north. The clerk said 'They're closed. It wouldn't be safe for you to walk anywhere after dark. You should wait until morning.' I checked my cell phone, and it was dead. So, I decided to buy a meal at the tavern across the street and then sleep in the car until the car shop opened."

"Where were you?" asked Mindy.

"All I can tell you is that there was a mom-and-pop-type tavern across the street from the drugstore. Howl'n Wolf's Lair was the name of it. I thought it would be a great place to hide out for awhile. I thought it ironic that the Undercover Blues Band was playing that night."

"Howl'n Wolf's Lair?"

"Yeah, you know, Howl'n Wolf, Muddy Waters, Elmore James—Chicago's legendary blues men of the 50s and 60s."

Mindy shook her head. Jake could see she was obviously not in the mood for a lecture on Chicago bluesmen.

"Then what?" Mindy inquired.

"So I went in and ordered a cheeseburger and a Coke and sat back and waited for the show. Somewhere after midnight, a biker gang swaggered in. They were all wasted on something. Somewhere off in a corner, someone started yelling and pushing, and then it all broke loose. A fight broke out, and bottles started smashing against the walls. I was making my way to the door when one of them hit me in the back of the neck." Jake rubbed the back of his neck. "Peg must've picked me up and carried me to her apartment. That's why I woke up on Peg's couch."

"So you slept there?"

"No, not really. I told her about the radiator hose. She knew someone who could help. So I gave her the $27.50 I had with me, and she took off. I was afraid to go to sleep, so I looked around her place. She had *a lot* of interesting books. I took the opportunity to look through Malcolm X's autobiography. Sometime around 3:00 A.M., she came back with a hose. Then she decided to come with me while I installed the hose to make sure I got away safely.

"While I was working on the car, she started asking me about Jesus. I asked her if she would like for me to pray with her."

Mindy shifted on her pillow, unable to relax.

"Peg nodded 'yes,' so I led her through the sinner's prayer. The Spirit moved in both of us in a powerful way. I reached under my front seat and handed her my study Bible."

"You gave *her* your favorite study Bible?" Mindy replied with surprise.

"Without hesitation," Jake asserted. "I wrote on the inside of the back cover 'Genesis, John, and James.' Then I encoded my cell phone number disguised as Scripture verses."

"You gave her your cell phone number?"

I told her, "Call me if I can do anything for you."

"I checked the clamps, dumped in the coolant and water, and started the car up. I gave her a quick hug and thanked her one more time. I didn't waste any time getting out of Chicago."

"Jake, why didn't you tell me this before now?"

"I did. I told you I had car trouble on the way home from your mom's birthday party. When I got back to Taylor, I was swamped with midterms. By the time we had a chance to talk, it was old news."

Obviously relieved, Mindy asked, "Is there anything else?"

"Yes. Last year I was walking down the hall at work. I was on my way to give my presentation to the bank president when my cell phone rang. I assumed it was you and that it must be important, so I answered it. It was Peg. I was shocked, but I listened anyway. She said she was working with the church youth and wondered if my camp had a program for poor kids from the inner city. I encouraged her to get on the website and fill out the application. I stressed to her to state how the camp would benefit the kids and what special funding would be needed. She thanked me and hung up. The bank meeting that followed the conversation was the one where the bank decided to foreclose on three houses in Oltsburg. To tell you the truth, I forgot all about Peg's phone call.

"It was not until earlier today, when I heard you say that the bus from Vine Street Baptist Church had just pulled off the highway and onto Kellum Road, that I decided to leaf through the folder to acquaint myself with the kids. When I saw Peg's face on the youth pastor's page, that's when I walked out to meet the bus.

"You see, until today, I had no idea that the church across the alley from her apartment was Vine Street Baptist Church. I guess when Peg submitted the application a couple of months ago, she inquired as to whether or not I was still with the camp. Nancy told her that I was a bank manager and not involved with the camp's daily operation. Nancy also told Peg that you are the camp's director."

"Is there *anything* else?" Mindy asked reluctantly.

"Yes. During the tour of the camp, while we were down at the beach area, Margret mentioned that all of the kids wanted to get baptized. I told her it would not be a problem. We baptize campers all the time in the lake.

"She looked directly at me and asked, 'Is there a pond in the middle of the woods with a giant tree right on the pond's edge?'

"I said, 'Yes … we call it the Frog Pond. Why?'

"Margret replied, 'The kids and I have been seeing visions of it in our sleep.'"

"Did you say that *all* of the kids had the same vision of being baptized in a woodland pond with a giant tree on the pond's edge?" Mindy asked. "The Ancient One told me that I could identify my students because the Lord would give them a common vision that was unique to our location."

"Why don't I get off work a little early, and the three of us can go down there and take a look around. We can go while the kids are eating their dinner. We'll take the golf cart out to the service road. There's a shagbark hickory tree that marks the deer path that goes directly to the Frog Pond.

"Oh, and another thing, I think we can skip the crafts and concentrate on the new Christian leadership curriculum. These kids are spiritually advanced for their age. I get the feeling that these are the kids that will fulfill the end time's prophecy. These are the gifted children that we must train to be the light in a fallen world."

Jake took a deep breath, and kissed her gently. Then he resumed his position—curled on his side, with his forehead pressed gently against the side of her arm—and closed his eyes.

I guess that's the end of the conversation, she thought to herself.

As Jake passed into deep sleep beside her, Mindy was left to ponder tomorrow's camp. She would double the food budget, order another set of camp uniforms for each kid, and somehow find durable yet inexpensive sandals for the campers.

Yes, she would skip the crafts. Maybe she would get them each a notebook and have them remain silent as Zeke and Nancy led them on a hike to Inspiration Point. There each of them would be asked to describe their walk with Jesus and what they expected to get out of the camp.

Mindy turned her head to look at Jake. She recalled the enthusiasm with which he had conveyed his adventure in Chicago. It was like a young boy telling his mom about the excitement of an amusement park. Their lives together had been a roller coaster. Mindy was secretly relieved that she had not been on all of the rides that Jake had endured. It was comforting to know that when the rides all fell silent and the park closed for another day, Jake would return home to her.

Three days later, Jake stood in the shade of the massive oak tree at the edge of the Frog Pond. Behind him, he could hear the youth opening their sack lunches. In front of him, the pond shimmered in the midday sun. Its surface was still and calm. The Holy Spirit had blessed each of these kids and Margret with the vision that they would be baptized at this tree and in this pond. Jake felt honored to participate in the ceremony.

Jake's mind raced back. He could still see the contours of the rock slabs that formed the pond's bottom. He replayed in his mind the day, only a few years ago, when Pastor Shillinger, Mr. Eller, and he had come here on Jake's premonition that two skeletons were on a rock shelf twenty feet below the surface of the crater.

It was not for Jake to understand how the water had receded back into the sinkhole, exposing both sets of bones, perfectly intact. His mission was to recover the remains. Jake could still feel his hands clinching the knots on the rope as he climbed down the wall of the wet rock face.

At the time, he had no way of knowing the impact the two small rings that the skeletons wore would have on Mindy's and his life. Both rings from the sinkhole bore the symbol pattern of a star and two lightning bolts. Mindy knew nothing of the sinkhole rings when she purchased the set she used to celebrate the end of their first camp together. Jake's and Mindy's rings had the same pattern of a single star and two lightning bolts, with the addition of a rainbow.

The rings Jake and Mindy wore provided the link that allowed Jake to be identified by the orphans who found him, face down, in the Sudan's desert.

Alexander Montgomery had placed the ring from his deceased son, Ron, on his toe just before he went to dig water wells in Sudan. Again, it was the ring that precipitated his rescue.

A mysterious chain of events connected the ring that was found on Julie Capp's skeletal hand to the hand of her disgruntled brother.

By Wilbur Capp's own admission, it was the presence of the ring on his finger that thawed his insistence for the ill-fated wrongful death case.

Jake stood in awe. He knew the Lord deserved all the praise. As white, billowing clouds reflected on the surface of the still water, Jake sensed the face of the Lord smiling at him.

PART FOUR

Ark of Koinonia

Then the LORD called to the man clothed in linen who had the writing kit at his side and said to him, "Go throughout the city of Jerusalem and put a mark on the foreheads of those who grieve and lament over all the detestable things that are done in it."

As I listened, he said to the others, "Follow him through the city and kill, without showing pity or compassion. Slaughter old men, young men and maidens, women and children, but do not touch anyone who has the mark.

—Ezekiel 9:4–6

CHAPTER 28

Vanished

MINDY PULLED THE small stack of envelopes and magazines out of the mailbox. Flipping through them, she noticed a plain white envelope. It said simply:

Mindy Olson
Camp Koinonia
Norton, Wisconsin

She had received a number of letters addressed this way in the past. They were usually filled with inquiries from youths eager to find out about her camp. But this letter was different; this address was in a woman's cursive handwriting. Mindy opened it as she walked back to the kitchen.

Dear Mindy Olson,

It is only at this point in my life that I have the strength to reveal the truth.

You may remember the night you, your husband, and I had dinner together. I presented myself as a freelance writer gathering information about a book on summer camps in America.

You saw through me. I don't think it was the things I said or the way I acted. I believe something in your spirit saw through my disguise and into the pathetic wretch that I really was.

That is, in part, why I come to you now. I believe you might be the only person who can see through to the new person I have become.

I have been saved by the love and mercy of our Lord Jesus Christ. Because of that transition, I am asking for you to forgive me.

I realize that because I was a con artist before, you might conclude that this is just another manipulation. Please let me continue.

Shortly after I completed my assignment in Norton, I accessed the camp's website, intent on hacking into it and destroying it.

To my surprise, I started reading the testimonies of the youths who had visited your camp and how it changed their lives. My curiosity got the best of me. I went on to read your testimony. At the bottom of your page, you made the statement that you teach the truth at Camp Koinonia, and the truth sets people free.

It was as though someone grabbed my heart, squeezed it, and threw it on the floor. Although I could not understand it at the time, within a few days of that encounter, I turned myself in.

Through plea bargaining and my commitment to testify against my former employers, Randall Watson and Daemon Lynch, I received a greatly reduced sentence of five years. Unfortunately, a shorter sentence has bought me little peace. For now, I am the target of these ruthless men.

Immediately upon entering the Illinois State Correctional Facility at Joliet, I started participating in a Bible study. I am sure many people would find it odd that I had to come to prison to be set free. I can't claim to know much about the details in the Bible, but I do know a few things for certain. I am not alone. I have been saved and forgiven by the love of Jesus Christ. I have truly turned from my evil ways. And that led me to write this letter to you.

I ask only for your forgiveness. I remember hearing a story about ancient times, when they would take a young goat and cast all of the sins of the nation on it and send it out into the desert. I am not sure how all that works, but I do know that of all the people I did horrible things to, you are the only person whose name and address I can recall.

Somehow, I don't believe that it is a coincidence that my brief contact with your website lead me to Jesus and back to you. So you see, this letter is my lone atonement goat, my one and only attempt to seek forgiveness from the outside world.

The only other thing I have to say to you is that even though you and your husband were my targets, I had no contact with your husband apart from the dinner. There was a boy, however, who worked for you. It was my manipulation that set him up for a crime he did not commit. If you have any contact with him, please let him know how sorry I am for my actions.

Although I cannot understand it, I know that all things work for the good for those who love the Lord. I have prayed for Jesus to reveal to me what possible good could result from the turmoil that has been caused by Satan's evil schemes.

I was blessed with only a flicker of a vision that the troubles of the past serve only to prepare us for the exceedingly evil days ahead. Heed this warning: you must cling to the Lord, and let the Holy Spirit guide your steps.

Be alert! The great and terrible day of the Lord is upon us.

I do not deserve, and I cannot, in any way, expect return correspondence from you. I have included my address only in case you choose to verify my story. May the Lord bless you and keep you. May the Lord shine his face on you and give you peace.

Sincerely,
Elma Willoughby
(a.k.a. Rox)

Jake rounded the corner into the kitchen to find Mindy weeping. "Mindy, what is it? Bad news?"

Mindy handed Jake the letter and walked out of the kitchen and into the study.

In a few minutes, Jake walked to where Mindy stared out the window. He wrapped his arms around her. She leaned into him.

"Maybe you should go see her. This weekend is the Fourth of July. It's probably not a good time. We could swing by Joliet on our way to Fort Wayne to pick up Anna from Mom and Dad's next weekend.

Mindy nodded silently.

Jake kissed the back of Mindy's head and gently pulled away. He could tell she wanted some time alone.

Jake repeated the troubling line from Rox's letter. "'The great and terrible day of the Lord is upon us.' Why don't we stay home from the fireworks tonight?"

Mindy nodded.

Jake withdrew from the study. "I'll be in the garage."

A few minutes after midnight, Mindy and Jake awoke to the sound of Jake's emergency ringtone. After snatching his cell phone from the nightstand, he paced out of the bedroom and into the hall and then back in.

"Mindy, get up! There've been massive terrorist strikes in Chicago, New Orleans, and San Francisco—this is it! Satan's reign of terror has begun!" Jake pulled on his clothes. "We need to get the kids out of their cabins and into the woods. If this is in line with how the Holy Spirit is directing you, we'll meet you under the Giant Pine. It is important you stay out of sight. Lock up the house when you leave. I'll take care of Champ. I'll reconnect with you later today." Jake disappeared out of the room.

Mindy dressed quickly, yet took the time to find and put on her sturdy hiking boots. She raced to the computer to send the prearranged message to the campers' parents, but the laptop and hard drive had already been removed by Jake.

As she hurried down the stairs, Mindy surveyed the house. The doors and windows were shut and there was no sign of Champ. She checked the safe's door and spun the dial, then lowered the wall panel that concealed it.

As Mindy left the house, she thought of Mrs. Birmingham. Mindy replayed in her mind Mrs. Birmingham's final words: "On the day the cities are desolated, gather the children, and seek refuge beneath the Giant Pine."

Mindy could still sense the instant when Mrs. Birmingham's spirit left this world. Baby Anna had kicked and twisted in Mindy's womb. She could still feel the limp hand of her lifelong mentor and friend. Mindy knew that the hit and run collision that took Mrs. Birmingham's life was no accident. Mindy had detected the presence of evil growing stronger all around her. In the mangled car and the frail, crushed body, she had perceived a metaphor of the world's future.

As she scrambled through the house, Mindy recalled the training Jake and she had attended a little over a year ago that revealed the end times would be ushered in with a massive strike against the US. The strike would be followed by deliberate and brutal attacks on Christians and Jews all over the world. Camp Koinonia would be one of those targets. The camp had already produced a number of highly effective young leaders. The end-times seminar leader revealed how, in times past, Christians had sought refuge in the wilderness and in deserts. Terrorists understood roads and addresses but were far less familiar with the unsettled areas.

Mindy pulled the door to the house closed behind her and ran down the path to the cabins. She prayed fervently for the safety of her daughters and family. Rebekah and Alexander would have already landed in Sudan. Anna would be safe in the care of Jake's parents in Fort Wayne. "Lord, keep them in your arms."

Mindy decided that she would start with Zeke's cabin, thinking the boys would be able to get ready the quickest. Then she could help the girls get ready.

Mindy stopped abruptly at the window of the first cabin. It was abandoned. She quickly looked around. *They're gone.* Panicked, she search the camp yard for any sign of life.

An almost invisible being touched her on the shoulder and pointed down the path to Inspiration Point. *"Run!"*

Mindy raced down the path. *Giant Pine is a little ways into the forest from the Point.*

As she rounded the curve in the path, an arm from an unseen man pulled her into the forest. Her mouth was covered by a large, powerful hand.

"Shhhhhh!" the voice whispered. "Mindy, it's me. Don't move. Don't make a sound."

Mindy nodded and relaxed her body. She remembered that one of the tactics of the enemy was to drop listening devices onto the grounds around a target so that the Christians' movements could be tracked.

"I am going to slide my hooded veil over you so that both of us will be wearing the same veil. Then, I need to put the boot covers on your feet," Zeke whispered in Mindy's ear.

Mindy nodded.

"After that, I'll put on another veil … then we'll crawl silently into the forest."

After Zeke had secured his veil, he brought a binocular device to his eyes. He searched the landscape with a 360 degree sweep. As quietly as he could, Zeke asked, "Did anyone see you?"

"No." She shook her head.

"Did you see anything or anyone in the camp yard?"

"No."

"Hold onto this tether. These veils make us almost invisible. We won't be able to see each other, so tug twice on the tether if you need to stop. Keep the hood over your face. Watch the trail directly in front of you. We will move only when the wind blows. That will mask our movements from surveillance devices. Stay low; be as silent as possible. Remember, pick your feet all the way off of the ground. Walk quietly from heel to toe. Are you ready?"

Mindy nodded. "Yes."

Zeke slipped under the branches of the first pine tree. Mindy followed. He led her into the forest, down the valley, and across the creek bed. They traversed two ridges and then came to rest in a grove of dense pine trees. He motioned to Mindy to stay seated while he let out a length of tether.

Zeke crept to the top of the hill. He had created this vantage point over the last few months. From here, he could see the surrounding area and particularly the path that led from the campground to Inspiration Point. He had intentionally cleared the underbrush to facilitate observation.

He froze. Slowly, he raised the binoculars to his eyes to observe three men dressed in camouflage who were walking down the path. Each man carried an assault rifle, and each of them was searching in the woods for signs of life. Zeke silently, slowly recoiled a few feet back down the hillside. He once again performed a 360 scan with his infrared sensor.

Zeke retraced the tether to Mindy and indicated to her that it was time to go. Swiftly, he led her to where a large outcropping of boulders emerged from the forest floor. He indicated for Mindy to crouch against the rock. Zeke meticulously scanned the surface of the rock and then the surrounding area.

Zeke felt along the bottom of the boulder for the switch. Almost without a sound, the rock slid open, revealing a cave. Zeke went in to secure the area. He felt for the sensor that he had placed in the crack inside the cave's wall. Wiping his hand over it twice sent a signal that two people had entered the cave. Zeke returned to the entrance and motioned for Mindy to enter. Then he shut the rock door behind them.

Zeke motioned for Mindy to sit on the floor of the cave. He placed their veils over them like a tent. Then he positioned them so that they were sitting Indian-style, facing each other. Their torsos were aligned so that their faces were only a few inches apart.

Zeke flipped on a small flashlight, which had been outfitted with a red lens for working in the dark. He cupped his hands and placed them over Mindy's ear. "Are you OK?"

She nodded. "Yes."

"We need to be as silent as possible. We have to assume Satan is watching us, listening to everything we say. Never use anyone's name. Never describe where we are. Do you have any questions?"

Mindy cupped her hands and placed them over Zeke's ear. "Why are we covered with the veils and whispering to each other if we're alone in a cave?"

"The forces of Satan have employed various intelligence-gathering devices—everything from satellites to small surveillance devices that are the size of a large shoe box. A wire as small as a pencil lead can gather and transmit a tremendous amount of information."

"Why?"

Zeke paused; a stern look came to his face. "The attacks this morning mark the transition to the reign of terror. Forces loyal to Satan detonated nuclear devices on Chicago, San Francisco, and New Orleans. Simultaneously, well-organized ground attacks were launched from sleeper cells in the Midwest and on the East Coast."

Zeke cleared the lump in his throat. "Satan's plan was to cripple the US so that it could not come to the rescue of the weaker countries in the world. The nuclear attacks served as a signal to launch the slaughter all over the world. At this very moment, sleeper cells are assassinating church leaders and Christian law enforcement officials. With all of the Fourth of July fireworks going off during the night, most people will never suspect that their neighbors have been murdered. The butchers will use church directories to target church leaders. The forces of Satan will be dressed like law enforcement and the military so that unsuspecting Christians can be led off to prison camps without a fight." Zeke swallowed hard. "There are three armed intruders walking down the path to Inspiration Point as we speak."

"Where are Jake and the campers?" Mindy asked, deeply concerned.

"It's better we don't know. Please don't use their names. Let's refer to them as *our friends*."

"Why did you leave without me earlier?"

Zeke shook his head with disappointment. "Mindy ... I am the one who stayed behind to find you and protect you. The real question is, what took you so long? We had all the campers dressed and in the woods before you made it out of the house."

Mindy's head sank as she nodded. "When will we see *our friends*?"

"The Holy Spirit will direct our path." Zeke paused to wipe a tear from his cheek. "Prayer and concealment are our only weapons now. If the right hand does not know what the left hand is doing, the location of those in hiding cannot be jeopardized by those who get captured. It doesn't surprise me that you are isolated from the rest. You are the queen bee. I am only a bodyguard. If the hive gets destroyed, the queen bee can produce a new one. The two of us will remain isolated until we are sure the safe haven has not been compromised or contaminated in any way. The Holy Spirit will prompt us when it is safe. Until then, prayer and concealment are our only defenses."

"And what if they capture you? It seems like you know a lot," Mindy said.

"I know enough to tell the enemy a lot of *misleading* information."

"How do you know all of this?"

"I have prayed for years for the Holy Spirit to reveal the truth to me ... and I have attended a special end-times Bible study."

"If people knew of Satan's plan, why didn't they do more to stop it?"

"The last three and a half years of peace and prosperity have lulled the government and the church to sleep. Certain people *have* been doing things. These veils and this equipment didn't happen by accident."

Mindy felt the scales of naiveté fall from her eyes. She looked deeply into the eyes of the young man who sat in front of her. She understood the gravity of the day's events. Nausea wrenched her gut. She could no longer see Zeke as a charming, enthusiastic camp counselor. He had matured into a mighty warrior for the Lord.

"Anything else?" Zeke asked.

"So, how do these invisible ponchos work?"

"They take a picture from one side of your body and display through fiber optics on the other side of the veil. So, if you are standing with a brick wall on your left side, the brick wall shows up on your right side. The batteries need to be recharged every couple of days.

"I'll tell you another thing. While a camper was on a cleanup crew in the woods next to the parking lot, he stumbled onto a listening device. That was about six months ago. He showed it to me, and I had someone from the Christian underground come out and take it. The technology is so advanced that these devices are calibrated to detect and catalog human voices from a great distance. That is why we have to be careful to cup our hands and whisper in each other's ears. We never know when a place has been bugged. All these devices give off heat, and that is why I scan the area with these infrared binoculars."

Zeke paused. "We really need to start praying for our protection and the safety of our friends. Let's also pray that the three armed intruders leave this location without finding a trace. Our hope is that they won't find anyone to interrogate. As long as we stay hidden, we'll be safe. Do you have any other questions?"

"No." Mindy shook her head.

"Find a comfortable spot on the rock slab. Be sure the veil covers your entire body. If the door to the cave opens, don't move, don't breathe. I will be the one to deal with the intruders. Let's start praying."

"It is going to be completely dark in here. I would like to rest my hand on your forearm. That way, we'll both know where the other person is at all times." Zeke turned off the flashlight.

Zeke lay next to Mindy on the rock slab that made up their safe haven. As a security measure, they both checked to ensure they were completely covered by their veils.

"I'll focus my prayers on repelling the intruders," Mindy whispered in Zeke's ear. "Lord, bring forth a swarm of hornets to attack these intruders who lurked on our path. Help us, help us.

Keep us safe; protect our friends." Mindy's voice went silent as the intensity of her prayer seemingly overtook her.

Zeke glided his hand under his veil and then under Mindy's veil and placed it gently on Mindy's forearm. He wanted to maintain contact during the long hours that they would be in the silence of the pitch black.

After only a few minutes, Mindy shifted to slide Zeke's hand down her arm so that she could clasp his palm in hers. At first, he passed the gesture off, thinking that she might have been slightly annoyed at being "held on to." Then the touch of Mindy's hand arrested Zeke's attention. He could not help but notice how warm and soft Mindy's hand was or the way her slender fingers gripped his palm. Mindy's hand conveyed the peace and strength that bonded prayer warriors together.

Zeke had never been fond of holding hands. But this was different—far different from the clutch of a panicked woman clinging to a rescuer and even far different from the casual hand holding he had engaged in with his girlfriend. There was an energy radiating through Mindy's body. Even though her grip was firm, her hand in his had a mysterious, calming effect on him. A pleasant warmth consumed his cold, tense hand, then his arm, and then it ran throughout his body.

Zeke remained motionless as he studied the supernatural sensation. He concluded that the hand he touched was connected by prayer to the all-powerful Creator. Zeke's euphoria was interrupted by a vision. In his mind's eye, he could see the armed intruders on the path between the camp yard and Inspiration Point. They swatted and thrashed as they struggled to fight off a swarm of hornets. The vision only lasted long enough for Zeke to watch the three men retreat to their car and drive off.

Mindy loosened her grip on Zeke's hand. She repositioned her body and veil so that it covered her as she lay on her side, facing Zeke. She calmly ran her hand under his veil and placed it gently on his forearm.

Zeke realized that he was no longer merely leading Mindy along. She was now fully engaged in resisting the enemy.

Late into the night, Mindy awoke to the sensation of a small swatch of Jake's sweat on the side of her leg. The sensation was as real as the instant when Jake brushed his leg against hers the night of her surprise birthday campfire. *He must be praying for me.* Although she had perceived it only a few times in her life, she understood that Jake was safe. Somehow Mindy could tell that Jake knew that she too was safe.

In a vision, she could see Jake was on his knees, praying and weeping over the disaster and massacre that was going on in the world outside. She saw her campers sleeping quietly in a cave. Mindy also saw a vision of the old woman she had met in Africa, the Ancient One. The old, wrinkled face was distorted with rage and disgust; yet the Ancient One remained silent. Mindy could sense the prophetess was holding back her anger, for she knew the Lord would deal final judgment on the Evil One for what he had done to the Lord's church on Earth.

Mindy broke in and out of sleep many times as she tossed and turned on the rock floor of the cave. She longed to hold her children, Anna and Rebekah. The prophecies she had been told over the last few years had finally come to fruition. She realized now that the vision that one of her children would go to Africa to lead the people out of darkness was being fulfilled with her adopted daughter's recent flight back to Sudan. Rebekah's unexpected marriage to Alexander Montgomery a few weeks ago culminated a love that had sparked the day Mindy and Rebekah found Alexander lying, near death, in a hut in a remote region of Sudan. Mindy was amazed at how smoothly the adoption of Rebekah had gone and how quickly Rebekah had devoured Western culture.

Mindy's deepest pain was her yearning for Anna, her baby daughter. She could feel Anna's delicate, golden ring on her toe. She remembered the day of Anna's birth—how she touched the ring to the infant's palm and how Anna turned her tiny head to gaze into her mother's eyes. In the silence, Mindy realized the olive branch had been passed from the ancient, to the present, and to the future.

Mindy and the baby had no way of understanding the passing's significance. Mindy remembered the Ancient One's words: "As Anna grows in stature, she will search for answers. Anna's quest will lead her to the truth."

Mindy repositioned her body. She wondered how Zeke could sleep on a hard, cold rock. His slow, soft snoring reassured her that she was not alone. Closing her eyes, she prayed one more time for the safety of her family and campers. Then she willed herself to sleep.

Zeke and Mindy stayed under the rock throughout the night. Early in the morning, of July 6th, the Holy Spirit prompted them to move to the rendezvous location under the Giant Pine.

CHAPTER 29

Ark of Koinonia

THROUGH THE PRE-DAWN shadows, Mindy followed Zeke to the rock plateau at Giant Pine. Once again, Zeke indicated for Mindy to sit by the side of the boulders. After making a scan of the area, Zeke slid his hand under the rock slab to open the cave's door. Mindy slid through the narrow slit between the rocks and into the horizontal pipe. Then she crawled on all fours to where the pipe intersected with a vertical chamber.

An artificially produced voice greeted her. "Please stand in the chamber. Remove your veil. Hold the veil's battery box in your hand, allowing the inside of the veil to be seen. Place the veil into the box at the floor of the chamber. Please stand with your feet shoulder's width apart and raise your hands above your head."

After the chamber's scanner ran from the bottom to the top of the cylinder, the voice came back. "Please exit the chamber. Your escort will be there to greet you."

Mindy saw Jake standing just outside the chamber door. They rushed to embrace.

"Thank God you're safe," Jake said. "Are you OK?"

"Yes. A little stiff from laying on a cold rock all night," Mindy said. "Jake, where are we? What's going on?"

"You're in a cave that Carl and Barbara Birmingham's son, Roy, found a long time ago, while he was hunting. Carl and Roy developed it into a bomb shelter during the cold war. Carl later updated it for the expected economic breakdown at the turn of the century. William Berry brought me here when he was home for Mrs. Birmingham's funeral. He suggested that I upgrade it to serve as a safe haven for us and the campers during the end times."

"Are Anna and our parents in here?"

Jake inhaled deeply. "No. I'm sorry. If we had more time, things might have been different."

Mindy sank into Jake's chest and wept. "Where's Champ?"

"I put him to sleep before I came to the cave," Jake said.

"What ... why?" she asked.

"You know we went to great lengths to train Champ to find us in the woods in case something went wrong while we were hiking with the campers. There is a good chance that if he were set free, he would lead the enemy right to us. We may be in here for a long time. This facility is designed for humans. It would not be sanitary to allow pets in here."

Mindy looked up after a long pause. "Can we call our parents?"

"We will not have any contact with the outside world for at least forty days. I did get a call from my dad right before I came down here. They were safe and on their way to their safe haven. Anna is fine. She woke my parents up, even before the disaster phone call came.

"I called your parents' landline and cell phone. The network in Chicago was not available. Mindy, your parents are wise and devout Christians; the Holy Spirit will direct them in this time of need. I haven't heard from Alexander and Rebekah. You know from their last e-mail that they were preparing for this day."

"Jake, how is it that the enemy could waltz in and nuke three major cities?" asked Mindy, still puzzled by the day's events.

"There have been rumors that forces loyal to Satan refitted old tanker ships. A number of ships came up *missing* in the ocean and in the Great Lakes. Apparently, the ships were used as floating submarine bases. Because of the flood of traffic in the ports for the Fourth of July, small, one-manned subs packed with nuclear devices slipped past the port security."

Jake led Mindy into the cave's control room. She looked around at the array of laptops, monitors, and devices. "Where did you get the money to pay for all of this?"

Jake tapped a command into a computer's keyboard. He studied the screen. "Most of the money for the high tech sensors, batteries-and facilities came from a generous gift by Mr. and Mrs. Watson. Alexander Montgomery paid for the nutritional supplies and training materials. Zeke, Lex, and I put it all together during all those Sunday afternoons that we were at the end-times Bible study."

Jake walked Mindy back out of the control room. "Remember those long weekends when I went off with a few men from the church?" Jake continued. "That was actually a labor-sharing arrangement. Specially selected people helped build our safe haven. In turn, we helped to build theirs. Everything was conducted in secret. Everyone agreed to be blindfolded before they arrived at the worksite. We did not know where the shelter was or who would be in it. In turn, no one knows where our shelter is."

Jake paused to look into Mindy's eyes. "I apologize for keeping all this from you. Do you remember the end-times seminars we went to? That was all part of the Christian underground. The end-times prophecy revealed to us that Satan would lull the world to sleep with three and a half years of peace and prosperity. This peace would be broken by a massive strike on the US and other nations." Jake paused. "We have to rely on the Holy Spirit for everything. Prayer and concealment are the only weapons that we have against the Evil One. The less each individual knew about the whole system, the better it was for everyone. If someone got captured and tortured, he or she would only know a small piece of the resistance. The Holy Spirit instilled each of us with the exact knowledge we needed to make the system work.

"The master plan for the Christian resistance was to use the peaceful time to develop safe havens. The Holy Spirit directed each phase of the plan. Our plan was to vanish into the safe havens without a trace and then stay hidden for at least forty days. At that point, we are to go forth as directed by God to comfort a fallen world.

"Mindy … these campers are the ones that fulfill the vision the Lord gave us the night of the tornado. This is the new Camp Koinonia that the vision presented to us."

Mindy stared into Jake's eyes. She realized the truth in everything Jake had said. She understood that her role had been to prepare the Christian training curriculum. She would now be a mother/mentor figure in the final preparation for the eight young men and eight young women who had just a day ago slipped into the cave.

"Why don't we spend the next twenty-four hours together?" Jake asked as he wrapped his arms around her. "I'll show you around the Ark of Koinonia. You'll need to know where everything is and what every little device and sensor does before you can lead the campers."

"The Ark of Koinonia?" Mindy questioned.

"Yeah," Jake chuckled. "To help the campers adjust to their new home, we told them that they had just entered an *ark*, like Noah's, and that they would be shut off from the outside world for at least forty days. They understood immediately. We *did not* fill them in on all the details of the desolation. We'll do that when the day of re-entry gets closer."

A buzzer sounded, and a light flashed. "Let's get behind the wall. We are never exactly sure who is coming in." Jake and Mindy stepped out of the chamber and into an observation room.

Zeke dropped his pack onto the floor of the re-entry chamber and then stepped in. He held his veil by the battery pack and dropped it into the box. Then he stood motionless, with his feet apart and hands over his head.

The chamber door opened. He smiled as he called out, "Shall I secure the hatch, Skipper?"

"Secure the hatch," Jake returned.

With an almost silent thud, the door to the outside world clamped shut. The great Ark of Koinonia launched on her maiden voyage.

Outfitted with headset flashlights, Jake led Mindy through the underground corridors. He explained that the power for the lights and devices came from the solar panels on the surface that were camouflaged to look like foliage and patches of moss. Other sources of power came from equipment that functioned as treadmills and stationary bikes.

"We get our exercise at the same time that the cave's batteries get recharged. High-efficiency fans keep the air fresh. Water comes from a spring that runs through the cave. We will eat a mix of dried foods that were packed away before the attacks. Nancy has researched low-light foods, like sprouts and mushrooms. They will take a little getting used to, but they are highly nutritious."

Mindy stayed at Jake's side. She had never been fond of the dark or enclosed places.

They made their way to the bathroom and shower facility.

"These toilets are based on port-a-potty technology. We have to store the tanks of waste until it is safe to dispose of them outside the cave." Jake walked to the showers, which were the size of two port-a-pottys connected by an internal door. "The water that comes out of the spring is a cool fifty-seven degrees. We have four showers, two for men and two for women. Each is outfitted with a stationary bike. The longer and harder you peddle, the hotter the water gets in the holding tank over the shower head. It only takes a few minutes to raise the temp of a five-gallon tank to 120 degrees."

"This place gives me the creeps. It's cold and dark, and you can never see more than a few feet ahead. How do we know that something isn't watching us from the cave walls?" Mindy asked.

"Mindy, it'll be OK. This is not just a hole in the ground; it's our new home. Here are your clean *cave* clothes. Why don't you take a shower?" Jake handed Mindy the plastic bags that contained her new clothes.

Mindy lost her composure. "It's dark! I'm cold! I'm scared! I don't want to climb into an oversized trash can and take off my clothes," Mindy exclaimed.

Jake smiled. He pulled her close. "Why don't I sing to you? That way, you'll know that I am right outside."

Mindy's eyes swelled with tears. Slowly, she shook her head. She was reluctant to enter the chamber. Yet she realized how desperately she desired a shower and the clean clothes. It dawned on her that she had skipped her shower yesterday morning during the panic, and then she had slept in a cold, damp hole last night.

Mindy searched Jake's eyes for reassurance. She found in them a deep well of compassion. In all the time she had known him, he had never pranked her and never misled her. If he had asked her to crawl through a black crack in the cave, with the assurance that he would be there to meet her on the other side, she knew she would believe him.

"How about I turn on the light and the chamber heater? They run off batteries. This chamber heater doubles as a hair dryer." Jake smiled with the confidence that let her know he would be there for her. "I'll start peddling so the water is hot whenever you're ready."

Mindy hesitated for a few minutes and then climbed into the chamber to prepare herself for a shower. The water that sprayed from the nozzle was hot to the touch. She stepped in. Simmering rain drenched the back of her neck. Closing her eyes, she thanked the Lord for protecting her, Jake, and the campers. Mesmerized by the flowing water, Mindy swayed to direct the stream from her neck to her left shoulder, then back to her neck, and over to her right shoulder. An impulse from the logical lobe of her brain warned her that her water supply was running out. She dismissed it. *Let it flow.* She knew with a simple request Jake would refill the holding tank.

Mindy lingered, motionless, long enough to allow the steamy fluid to drain the anxiety from her soul. She remembered Jake's words from earlier that day: "This is not just a hole in the ground, it's our new home."

Mindy could hear Jake's voice reverberating through the cavern as he sang. She instantly recognized the tune. It was the love song he sang at the surprise birthday celebration that Nancy had orchestrated around the fire ring.

Tears streamed from her eyes. *How could things have changed so much in only a few short days?* Mindy scurried to wash, dry, and dress. Then she sat motionless on the chamber's bench.

With the chamber door cracked open, Mindy could hear water running in Jake's shower stall. A familiar sensation overtook her, a mild, pleasant, euphoria. It reminded her of the feeling that overtook her one frozen, wind-blown, winter night, after she had trudged through the icy parking lot to her car. In the moment between shutting the car door and turning the key, there was calm, a peace in the stillness, where snarling wind and brutal cold were held at bay. Her world came to rest. There was peace in the solitude.

Like a reluctant butterfly, she lingered in her cocoon. Her transformation was not quite complete. She had stepped into the chamber as Mindy Olson, Director of Camp Koinonia. When she stepped out, she would take on her role as mentor to young spiritual warriors.

She felt the Holy Spirit emboldening her with each passing minute. Darkness was now her friend. Thick cave walls that choked out the sun and blocked out the green insulated her and her campers from the evil and death that haunted the surface. Mindy opened the chamber door and stepped out into her new home.

Jake exited his shower chamber. "Hey, you look great. How do you feel?"

Mindy hugged Jake. "I feel much better."

"Why don't I put your old clothes in this bag? I'll wash them later. Ready for the rest of the tour?"

Jake and Mindy rounded the corner to enter a large cavern. He pointed to its ceiling. "You'll notice there is a skylight. That keeps us in sync with daytime and night. From the surface, the window looks like a large puddle of water."

Throughout the rest of the day, Jake presented the caverns of the cave to Mindy. Late that afternoon, they proceeded down a long corridor. As she rounded the corner, she could see the faint outline of a domed structure with the light from her head lamp.

Jake walked up to the door and entered a numerical code into the keypad. He opened the door, flipped on the light, and then stepped back to let Mindy enter. "Welcome to the guest house," Jake said, flashing her a smile.

Mindy gave Jake a playful smirk as she walked over the threshold.

"We built this outpost for the Watson family. I don't think they will be here anytime soon. I have to think they are safely tucked away somewhere. This facility has two units. This outer one can be used as an apartment. The inner unit can be used as a quarantine facility. We have various pieces of medical equipment and various medicines stored in there in case someone comes down with something contagious."

"Jake, this is the helm calling. Do you read me?" Lex's voice announced over Jake's walkie-talkie.

"Yes, I read you," Jake replied.

"My sensors indicate that the door to the Quarantine Unit has been breached."

"Mindy and I'll be spending the night out here. I'll be finishing up her orientation. We plan to join the campers for breakfast in the morning."

"Will you need any *room service*?" Lex asked with a chuckle.

"No, we'll be fine," Jake answered.

"How about I give you a wake-up call about 6:00 A.M.?"

"Good night, Lex," Mindy remarked.

"Enjoy your stay." Lex chuckled. "Over and out."

"Here's a variety of dried food pouches." Jake opened a large supply drawer. "A lot of these are based on the military's ready-to-eat meals. These cylinders contain fruit juices. Why don't we eat and then settle in for the night?"

Mindy smiled with relief as she realized how tired and hungry she had become. She selected a chicken soup and mashed potato meal and a can of apple juice. Then she ran her hand across the desktop. "Jake, how did you cut all these materials to fit exactly along the irregular floor and walls of this cave? I noticed how the cabinets, tables, and bunks are all flat on top, yet conform to the rock surfaces around them."

"All the work was down here when I got here. I'm pretty sure it's the work of William Berry." Jake pulled out a chair for Mindy. "How about I say the blessing?"

As she settled into bed in the black silence of the subterranean night, Mindy marveled at the complexity of her cavernous home. Ark of Koinonia reminded her of the books she had loved as a child. Her safe haven presented a curious mix of the Phantom of the Opera and Swiss Family Robinson.

"Jake, can you turn on a flashlight so it's not so dark?" she asked.

"Sure. That reminds me; hand me that box. This is a small, digital jukebox. We downloaded a ton of worship music before the fall. How about I dial up your favorite artists and set it to play all night. This thing has an LED night light. It's about as bright as a candle; yet it requires very little energy. We'll keep our headlamp batteries for our walk out tomorrow."

"Thank you. I love you, Jake." Mindy snuggled next to him under the covers.

"You're welcome. I love you too." Jake stretched. "Do you think you'll be able to fall asleep?" Jake curled into his favorite position, with his forehead pressed gently against the side of Mindy's upper arm. He kissed her.

"I think so. Good night."

"Good night."

"You know, this place feels familiar, kind of like Inspiration Point and Giant Pine," Mindy remarked.

Jake sat up. "Really? You can feel it?" He smiled as he pointed his finger to the ceiling. "If you go outside this dome and look up, you'll see a WB carved into the ceiling of the cave. It marks the spot over an energy portal. William Berry had a dream in which an angel showed him a few spots in Birmingham Forest where the rocks emit bursts of energy. He built benches to mark their locations. The energy helps things grow and heal. I get the feeling that it can also work as an aphrodisiac in humans."

"An aphrodisiac?" Mindy grinned playfully.

"Yeah. Think about this." Jake paused. "William finished the benches during the last year that your sister, Judy Kramer, and he were at camp. In the absence of strong leadership, the morals of the camp went downhill. I think the downturn was an unintended consequence of William's benches. I don't think he understood about the energy when he built the benches. Campers were attracted to the "feel good" benches to party and make out. It wasn't until we got to camp and turned the benches into prayer alters that the true purpose of the benches was realized."

Jake shifted on the bed. "Just think, the night we met out on Inspiration Point, I could feel the euphoria."

Mindy sat up and repositioned herself on Jake's lap.

"Then a couple of days later, I was overcome with compassion when I kissed you on the sweet gum bench."

"Yes, that was wonderful." Mindy grinned with delight.

Jake stopped pondering and looked into Mindy's eyes. "Did you know about this energy all along?"

"A little bit."

"Is that why you arranged for us to have all those picnics out at Giant Pine and Inspiration Point?"

"Shhhhhhhhhh. No more talking." Mindy cupped her hands around Jake's face and drew their lips together.

CHAPTER 30

Life in the Ark

THE NEXT MORNING, Jake and Mindy joined the campers in the cave's dining facility.

"Good morning, campers," Jake said. His voice was confident, his smile and eyes bright.

"Good morning, Jake! Good morning Mindy!" roared the youth group as they stood to applaud their leaders.

"Let us open with prayer. Heavenly Father, You are the God of Psalm 91. You are our fortress. Under your wings, we find refuge. Your faithfulness is our shield and rampart. We do not fear the terror of night nor the arrow that flies by day, nor the pestilence that stalks in the darkness, nor the plague that destroys at midday. Help us to prepare for the day when we will come to the aid of a fallen world. It is for your glory that we labor. Bless this food to our bodies. In Jesus' name, amen.

"Welcome to the Ark of Koinonia. Your journey from the Vine Street Baptist Church has been a miraculous one. You have studied hard; you have obeyed the promptings from the Holy Spirit. Jesus is proud of you."

A chorus of "amens" and "hallelujahs" sprang from the youth.

"The Holy Spirit has called each of us here for one purpose," Jake continued. "We are here to prepare ourselves for the day that we emerge from this safe haven to bring the light of Jesus to a fallen world. We must work efficiently. We must work together, perform tasks we find unpleasant, and eat foods we don't like.

"Many years ago, there was an experiment where scientists placed rats in a small cage. Before long, the rats killed each other off. My brothers and sisters ... we are not rats. We are the children of the almighty God. We will thrive in our cave because we will look after each other with love and generosity.

"Our enemy will stop at nothing to destroy us. He's searching for us at this very moment. Satan is executing his plan to slaughter and imprison Christians and Jews around the world. In the early morning hours yesterday, agents of Satan detonated nuclear devices in the harbors of Chicago, New Orleans, and San Francisco. Hidden by the clatter of Fourth of July fireworks, evil sleeper cells labored throughout the night, systematically assassinating true believers from churches, civil services, and the armed services.

"It is imperative that no one leave this cave and no one gain entrance. We have vanished from the surface without a trace. We cannot afford to compromise our position. If at any time you discover evidence that someone has entered this cave, let us know immediately."

Jake softened his voice. "Like Noah and his family, we've been shut off from the outside world. But, we're not alone; we are part of a worldwide system of safe havens. Only those believers who followed the Holy Spirit have found their way to their haven. Each haven is unique, each with its divine purpose. Mindy and I do not know the fate of our daughters, Anna and Rebekah, nor do we know the whereabouts of our parents. We have no way of finding out any information about your families either. All we can do is pray. The Lord will do the rest.

"For the next forty days, your activities will be divided into three, eight-hour segments: study, service, and rest. Mindy will instruct you in a very unique Christian Leadership Curriculum, which is based on Christ-centered leadership, prayer dynamics, and evangelizing in crisis.

"As we settle into our new home," Jake gazed at the barren rock wall of the cavern, "you'll probably find that your life resembles the manual labor of the pioneers of the early 1800s; yet many of the devices we'll be relying on are of the highest technology on the face of the earth.

"A few of the things you took for granted just a few days ago, like sunlight, fresh air, abundant water, and electrical power, are now scarce commodities. We must be thrifty in how we use them and do whatever it takes to ensure that none of these necessities get depleted.

"I want all of us to be aware …" Jake's voice broke as his eyes welled up with tears. "For the next forty days, we'll be the privileged ones, hidden in this safe haven. I urge you to study, train, and pray diligently. The day will come when we'll embark on the most dangerous task on Earth. We will be the face of Jesus in the stronghold of Satan.

"I want to thank you for stepping up and stepping out onto this path. With the help of our Lord Jesus Christ, we will be the Way and the Light until He returns.

"Thank you, and God bless you!"

Jake stepped aside to wipe the tears from his cheeks.

Students and counselors roared into a standing ovation. "KOINONIA!" they shouted.

Each person in the room had his or her own understanding of this term; yet there was no doubt that they were in this mission together.

"Are there any questions?" Jake searched the crowd for a raised hand. Yes, Krista."

"So, how soon, after the forty days, *can* we call our parents?"

Jake took a deep breath. "As I understand it, the Holy Spirit will prompt each of us with a task. During your journey on the surface, you can try to locate your parents. Please remember that security is of the utmost importance. The act of finding your parents may lead the enemy to them and their safe haven. We will understand more as the days go by. That was a very good question. Are there any more? Yes, Jay."

"Do we have any guitars down here?"

"Yes. We packed a guitar, a flute, and a tambourine. Lex can help you find them. We are taking readings all around the cave. As soon as we know the cave is clear of any of the enemy's surveillance devices, we will pipe in worship music over the intercom."

"Andrew, what would you like to know?"

"Do you know if there is any gluten-free food down here?"

"Mmmmm …" Jake glanced at Nancy.

"The good thing is that a lot of our food is naturally gluten free. There is a box of gluten-free nutrient bars. I know it's down here," Nancy said.

"We'll put our heads together," Jake stated. "I'm sure we'll find it." Jake looked through the crowd of campers.

"Dallas, Blake, I can see the lightbulbs going off in your heads."

"Is there any way we can set up a basketball hoop down here?" asked Blake.

"Well …" Jake looked at Lex and Zeke. "We didn't pack a basketball or hoop. But you know what the US Marines say: 'Improvise and overcome.' I'm sure we can come up with something."

"Misty," Jake called.

"Is there anywhere in the cave that we can sing?"

"Misty, that's an excellent question. At the moment, no singing outside this section of the cave. Let's stay as quiet as possible until we get a chance to scan all of the rooms for hidden listening devices." Jake looked at Nancy, Zeke, and Lex. "We'll work on it. Give us a few days."

Mindy signaled that the breakfast was ready.

"Ladies and gentleman, let's eat."

Jake stepped to Zeke's side. "Well, it seems the campers have adjusted pretty well to the news of the biggest mass murder in the history of modern man."

"These kids know Revelation, Daniel, Joel, and the whole end times prophecy by heart," Zeke said. "They know what's going on. We all spent the night praying and crying. They understand that the Holy Spirit has been prompting the faithful to prepare themselves for years. I think they knew what was going to happen as soon as they got off the bus two weeks ago. Like true spiritual warriors, they have placed their mission for Jesus as their #1 priority. I have to admit, I never would have thought of a basketball court and a choir room in the Ark of Koinonia, but I think they're great ideas."

Lex and Jake shared nods.

"You know, I have a feeling that pick-up basketball games and impromptu worship concerts are going to be potent evangelistic tools when they get back to the surface," Lex stated.

Jake nodded in agreement. "I want to stress that we need to keep the storeroom and all the supplies locked up. As everyone gets more comfortable, I want to make sure that we keep strict control over the inventory. And as we trained, no one but the three of us and Mindy will be allowed in the control room. Now, let's not forget about the gluten-free food. Do you guys remember when that box came down?"

Lex and Zeke exchanged blank stares as they shrugged their shoulders.

"Nancy, can we see you for a minute?" Jake inquired.

"Sure, what is it?" Nancy replied.

"Think about the day you packed the box of bars. When was that? Where did you see it last?"

"The gluten-free bars came down with the tub of alfalfa seeds."

"I remember putting that whole load against the wall about halfway back in the storeroom. I can help you find it," Lex said.

"Lex, as soon as breakfast is over, you and Nancy go *find* the box." Jake was gentle, but insistent.

"Thank you." Nancy smiled with relief.

"I think we can convert that deep cavern in the back of the cave into a gym/choir room. Zeke, why don't you and I string an electrical power wire back there after breakfast."

"We'll have to seal off the back end and make a soundproof door at the entrance," Zeke said.

"Yeah, I'll have Lex set up sound monitors outside of each end of the cavern. That way, we can monitor how much sound is getting out."

"What do we have that we can use for a hoop and basketball?" Zeke asked.

"We have plenty of five gallon buckets. Don't cut the bottom out of one yet. For the ball, maybe we can roll up rags and stuff them into a plastic bag. It won't bounce, and it won't make much noise when we shoot it."

During their stay in the cave, everything was shared in the truest sense of the word *koinonia*, the Greek term for things held in common. Everyone in the cave understood their roles. They, for the most part, mimicked their past lives at the camp. Jake oversaw the operation of the safe haven. Mindy administered the Christian Leadership Curriculum. Zeke and Nancy served as counselors and instructors for the youth. Lex labored as the facilities manager. Sixteen youth studied and trained diligently. They realized that at the end of their term in the cave, they would transition to roles as missionaries, leaving the safety of the Ark to bring comfort and light to the fallen world.

On the thirty-eighth day, Jake approached Mindy. "Mindy, I'd like to show you something. You'll need your veil, a flashlight, and your hiking shoes."

Silently, they walked through the cave, taking a left turn, which led them down a passage she'd never been in before. At the end of the passage, a rope ladder ascended up the rock wall.

Jake tugged on the rope. "Let me get to the top before you start."

As Jake cleared the ledge at the top, he flashed his light to signal for her to climb. Once they both settled onto the cliff's plateau, Jake whispered, "Let's make sure our veils are working." They checked their battery packs and slipped the veils over their bodies. "From here on, we'll need to cup our hands over each other's ears when we talk."

Jake slid his hand along the edge of the boulder slab in front of him. The rock wall slid open, and cool, moist air rushed in. They could smell the pines from the forest around them. Jake crawled slowly out of the chamber and onto the floor of the shallow cave that led to the outside. Mindy followed.

The cave's exit was directly below Inspiration Point. They both lay on their stomachs, admiring the sunset over the vast valley of forest. They could see the lake that extended up to the beach at Camp Koinonia. From this vantage point, nothing in the scenery had changed. They had only been underground for a little over a month; yet they realized that the whole world had changed around them.

"We're facing south." Jake pointed. "To the west of here is an old road made by lumberjacks about a hundred years ago. It runs from the lake to the west side of Mr. and Mrs. Watson's house."

Jake spoke with a soft, tender voice, and tears welled in his eyes. "I believe … *you* … are going to take the girls over to the road and then follow it west until you see a gazebo. It is important that you and the campers stay hidden. If someone is in the gazebo, do not go up to it. Remain hidden. If all is clear, go up the outer edge of the structure. You will see a series of ground lights. The light fixture that is on the east side of the gazebo will have an on/off light switch on it. Don't worry, the switch works only as a signal; it doesn't turn on any lights. Flip the switch on and off three times, and then return to the woods. When it is safe, someone will come out from under the gazebo. That person will have been prompted by the Holy Spirit, so that person will know your name and where to find you. Remember, if anyone comes down from the house, *do not* reveal yourself to them. Do you understand?"

"Yes." Mindy's head sank as she sobbed. "I've seen this path and the gazebo in my dreams for the last few nights. Following the Lord's plan is not the hard part. It's that I will be making the journey without you." Mindy yielded into Jake's arms. "I know now that we are to be separated, possibly for the rest of our lives.

The vision that defines our paths forward will be given to us one destination at a time.

"Jake ... I love you. Do you remember your first year at camp, the night we celebrated your birthday at Commodores Restaurant? I told you that I loved you ... and no matter what happened to us or to this world, I would always love you. I meant it then, and I mean it now." She wept. "I am afraid, but above all, I trust in the Lord."

Jake pulled back only far enough to peer into Mindy's tear-soaked face. He spoke tenderly. "I love you too, Mindy ... forever and ever ... and ... I'm afraid too. But I have to keep thinking of something your dad told me. He said, 'Every good day is one less bad day.' We know the Lord has our days numbered. Each day that is a good day ... leaves one less day to be a bad day. Mindy, we have been blessed abundantly. Our good days are rich and many. Our bad days have been few. I know the Lord will keep us under His wing. You know I will be praying for you without ceasing."

"What do you see ... about the future?" Mindy sobbed.

"There have been attacks on safe havens like ours. All those who were found were brutally tortured and murdered. Zeke is taking the boys to another facility. Nancy, Lex, and I will hold down the Ark for as long as we can while we wait for further instructions." Jake drew in a deep breath and let it out slowly. "Do you know when you will be leaving?"

"Soon. I need to get the campers ready." Mindy's voice rang with confidence.

Jake and Mindy watched in silence as the sun set. They quietly reminisced over their few short years together: how the Lord had spared them from the tornado on the night the Holy Spirit had given them the vision of the training school for spiritually gifted youths, how the Lord had pulled the water back from the Frog Pond to reveal the skeletons and rings that Ron Montgomery and Julie Capp wore, and how the rings had played a role in their lives. Jake and Mindy had been blessed abundantly by their daughter,

Anna, and their adopted daughter, Rebekah. They were ready to face whatever tasks the Lord would place in front of them.

The great and all-powerful God smiled down from heaven upon His humble servants. He and only He knew the plans He had laid out for them.

CHAPTER 31

Gazebo

ON THE FORTY-FOURTH day, Mindy gathered the eight young women she had been mentoring into a small huddle. "The time's come for us to leave the safe haven and go out into the world. All of you know that we'll face a world much different than the one we left. Always remember: cling to the Lord, and let the Holy Spirit direct your path. Jesus loves you, and He'll never forsake you. Jake and I love you too. No matter what happens, we'll all be united in heaven."

Mindy made eye contact with each of the faces of the girls who stood around her and then prayed, "Lord, we yield our lives into your hands. You are our shepherd, our protector, and our provider. Guide our paths for the glory of your kingdom. Amen."

After a deep breath, she instructed, "Let's check the batteries and our veils."

The girls checked their batteries and slipped their veils over their heads.

"You've all been well trained. Stay close; stay low. Pray without ceasing." Mindy led the group up the ladder, across the plateau, and out the cave's door. The autumn night was brisk and windy, which allowed the group to move quickly through the forest.

The gazebo stood dark and abandoned in the night. Mindy crept forward to the prescribed switch and flipped it on and off three times.

Before she could return to the woods, a veiled body came out of the hidden door under the gazebo. A hand from under the stranger's veil gripped Mindy around her shoulders while the other hand covered her mouth. "Be silent. We are in great danger. Move your group into the gazebo immediately. Make *absolutely sure* that those who enter are the members of your group."

Mindy complied. When the last girl passed the threshold, Mindy stepped into the darkness underneath the gazebo. She felt a gentle but persistent hand ushering her through the darkness along the corridor. Behind her, she could hear the scurrying of bodies as they closed the door with a quiet thud and the clanging of what sounded like chains and locks. Each member of the arriving party was processed through a chamber similar to the one in the Ark of Koinonia.

Out from the observation room walked Margret Walker. "Welcome to Gazebo." Margret walked over to a very surprised yet relieved Mindy. "It's so nice to see you and the Vine Street youth group again. You gals look great. The food must be pretty good back at camp."

"Yes, we've been blessed. The guard spoke of danger; what's happened?" Mindy asked.

"Evil forces have been amassing around Norton. A few minutes ago, hand-to-hand combat broke out in town. We suspect the enemy will fan out to search for the safe havens here and at Koinonia. They do not know exactly where we are, so they will be patrolling the area to find us."

"Hand-to-hand combat. Who is fighting for the Christians?"

"The Christian resistance has enlisted ex-military and law enforcement officers to defend the safe havens. They are loyal and fearless, but they're badly outnumbered."

"So what are we to do?"

"Our role is to pray and to teach the children. When all this clears, I'll be taking the Camp Koinonia students out to their assignments."

"And for me?" Mindy asked.

"I don't know exactly, but I do know you won't be alone." Margret Walker motioned for Mindy to follow her down the hall. Margret opened the door to reveal a small group of young women. "Say hello to your new safe haven mom." A warm and enthusiastic chorus of "Hi, Mom!" reverberated out of the group.

From the middle of the pack Mindy heard, *"Mommy! Mommy!"* Anna sprang to her feet, raced to Mindy's side, and dove into her arms.

"Anna, my precious child! Praise the Lord you're safe." Mindy squeezed her daughter.

"Mommy, I want you to meet my friend." Anna directed Mindy to a tall, stocky, red-haired youth. This is Christen. She's teaching me karate, and I'm teaching her how to pray."

"Hi." Christen moved to Mindy's side. "I've been assigned to bring your daughter to you. Anna's grandfather was wounded in the fighting when our safe haven was raided. Mrs. Olson stayed behind to care for him. We've been praying for them and you."

"When I get too tired to walk, Christen carries me," Anna blurted.

Mindy embraced Christen. "Thank you."

"You're welcome. It was really my pleasure." Christen smiled as she looked upon Anna. "You see, when I met Anna, I was lying on a stretcher; my arm had been mangled in the first wave of attacks. When Anna walked up to me, I was amazed at how intelligent and wise she was for a toddler. It's like she is a mature adult in a child's body. She knew I was in great pain. As she prayed for me, my hand, my arm, and then my whole body all were completely healed. The Lord spoke to me. I knew my task was to bring Anna back to you. Through our time together, I've learned to pray at a whole new dimension."

"I look forward to working with you and the rest of the team." Mindy's eyes panned back across the group of young women.

Margret stepped up next to Christen and addressed the assembled group, "I'm going to give Mindy her Gazebo orientation tonight; she'll be joining you tomorrow. Anna, why don't you come with your mom and me?"

The group smiled as they jockeyed back to their relaxed huddle.

Margret shut the door to the dorm. "It'll be safest for everyone if they refer to you as mom. You won't know their real names until you reach your final destination. Only the Spirit knows where that is."

"How were these kids selected as my group?" Mindy asked.

Margret smiled. "They have each received the vision of being baptized in a woodland pond shaded by an enormous tree."

Several days went by. The safe haven where Mindy and Margret were stationed received dozens of injured Christian resistance soldiers. The youth groups from Camp Koinonia and Gazebo took turns caring for the injured. Mindy's group studied in the morning and then assisted the injured at night. As the fighting in the area came to an end, Mindy felt the prodding of the Holy Spirit to move her new group to the next location.

CHAPTER 32

Night Quest

JAKE WALKED THROUGH the remote quarantine facility with only the light of his headset to guide him. He stopped at the back of the chamber and pulled out the heavy, metal trunk.

He palmed the padlock. *Mmmmm ... let's think ... First Samuel 17:49. "S" that's the nineteenth letter. So it must be 19, 17, and 49.* Jake twisted the lock's dial back and forth. The lock popped open.

A pair of survival knives, two pistols, their holsters, and their ammo were housed in the trunk's lid. A compound hunting bow with arrows lay on top of the partially disassembled assault rifle and shotgun in the trunk's base.

Jake slipped the pistol harness over his shoulder, dislodged the first pistol from its retainer, and dropped the magazine out of the pistol's grip. "David chose five smooth stones from the stream and put them into his bag," Jake whispered as he loaded the shells into the magazine and then slipped the magazine back into the pistol's grip. He pulled the pistol's receiver back and released it. His first shell chambered—it was ready to fire.

Jake pressed the gun's safety lock button to the no-fire position. He holstered the gun under his arm. *What else will I need?* Jake thought. Jake strapped the survival knife to his leg. Out of another box, he pulled out a small flashlight and a tube of black face paint.

Then Jake carefully closed the trunk, locked it, and walked back through the remote facility.

I will have to pick up some food sticks, a canteen of nutrient solution, and of course, a veil with a couple of battery packs.

"Lex, Nancy, will you both meet me at the re-entry chamber in a few minutes?" Jake asked over his walkie-talkie.

"I'm in the control room, and I think Nancy's reorganizing the store room," Lex said.

"I heard you, Jake. I'm on my way," Nancy replied.

Jake rounded the corner into the re-entry chamber area. Lex dropped his lower jaw in disbelief.

"What's with the camo suit? And the *gun?*" Nancy mumbled.

"The Holy Spirit has prompted me to secure a supply of mushroom spores and seed sprouts." Jake could tell his young colleagues were uneasy with his unexpected departure. He was confident they could manage the Ark of Koinonia. His deepest concern was that they would feel abandoned.

"You're going *out* of the cave?" Lex asked.

"Yes."

"Where exactly are you going?" Nancy snapped. Her eyes frowned with obvious disapproval.

Jake smiled; he knew he could not tell anyone his destination. "It's not far; I should be back by daylight." Jake checked the battery pack on his veil and stuffed an extra battery pack in the pocket of his camouflage fatigues.

"Are you going to see Mindy?" Lex asked.

Jake stopped, instantly saddened by the thought that Mindy was out on the surface. "No. I don't think so."

Lex's face began to register the seriousness of the situation as he obviously realized Jake might never come back.

"What can we do for you Jake?" Nancy asked, in a pensive voice.

"Pray ... without ceasing." Jake covered his face and hands with black face paint and then slipped on his veil. "How do I look?" Jake tried in vain to break the tension. He knew he was invisible to them.

"You look fabulous," Lex replied.

"Is there any chance you'll see Zeke?" Nancy inquired.

Jake lowered his veil hood to expose his head. "I don't think so."

Nancy stepped closer. She rose onto her tiptoes and reached for Jake's face. He yielded to what he suspected would be a good-bye kiss.

Nancy pressed her lips to Jake's ear. "If you see Zeke, tell him I love him. I'll always love him. I'll be waiting *here* for him."

"If I find him, I'll tell him. I promise." Jake studied the face of the beautiful young woman in front of him. Her eyes were piercing, resolute, her chin firm. Her face reminded him of the countenance Mindy displayed on the poster she had sent to Africa while he was missing in Sudan.

Jake glanced at Lex, who stood behind the control room window. Lex grinned curiously as he watched Jake and Nancy's intimate encounter.

Jake said, "Lex, can you come out here for a minute? I'd like to pray for us."

Without hesitation, Lex and Nancy each grasped one of Jake's hands.

"Almighty and most merciful God, You are our Savior, our strength, our light. Protect us as we serve You. Guide our paths. We pray that we can serve you completely. Lord, we pray that you reach out your hand and touch Zeke and Mindy. I pray you bring them and me back home safely. In your Holy Name, Amen." Jake looked into the eyes of his young friends. "Cling to the Lord. Let the Holy Spirit direct your path."

Lex and Nancy responded with silent nods.

"Leave the hatch open only long enough for me get out." Jake gave Lex and Nancy one last look for reassurance.

"Aye, aye, Skipper. How are we going to know it's you when you get back?" Lex asked as he returned to the control station.

"I set my entrance code to thirteen, seven, and seven."

"To thirteen, seven, seven?" Nancy asked.

"You know, Matthew 7:7. Knock and the door will be opened to you."

"Got it." Nancy smiled. "M is the thirteenth letter."

"Hey, just to let you know ... It's 10:17 P.M., the air temperature on the surface is sixty-two degrees. There is a quarter moon, it is partly cloudy, and there's wind gust up to twenty-five miles per hour," Lex reported.

"Sounds like a great night for a hike in the woods." Jake turned and waved as he crawled into the exit tunnel.

Outside the rock door, Jake sat motionless, immobilized by the tranquil beauty of the forest at night. Crickets and tree frogs chirped all around him. The smell of the pines and breeze through the forest sang their lullaby. *This is a perfect night for a campfire,* he thought. *How could I have taken for granted all those nights around the fire ring, full of campers and hot dogs and marshmallows and worship songs and late-night swims in the lake with Mindy.* His heart ached. A throb of loneliness immobilized him. He wept. Through his tears, he could feel the spot on his cheek that trapped Mindy's tears the afternoon they said "good-bye" after their first summer at Camp Koinonia.

From what he could see, with his back resting against the rock door of the cave, nothing had changed in Birmingham Forest. It was all the things he could not see that disturbed him. The evil that conspired to destroy him was watching, always watching. From sophisticated, ground-based surveillance devices to ultra-sensitive, low-orbiting satellites, the army of Satan had one objective: to obliterate all traces of true believers off face of the earth.

Jake knew that many great minds in Satan's army were now aware of the Christians' veils. He hoped that they hadn't figured out how to detect them. *Lord, I pray this veil renders me invisible to the enemy.*

Tales of valor that he had read in his childhood raced through his mind: James Bond, Asian ninjas, US Marine commandos. The one he identified with most intimately was the legend of Running Bear, the Shawnee warrior, who lived in the generation before the rise of the great chief Tecumseh. Traveling alone, Running Bear had maneuvered through hundreds of miles of Great Lakes wilderness to rescue his squaw, Little Feather. She had been captured by a Winnebago war party and taken back as a slave.

For Running Bear to trek undetected through enemy territory for hundreds of miles would be an arduous task, but to liberate his squaw from her captor's camp would be all but impossible. If at any time he was discovered by an enemy tribe, he would be killed. Running Bear endured many hardships; yet in the end, he prevailed.

My mission is like Running Bear's. It's all about evasion, not invasion, Jake thought. *I have a job to do. I will make it work, no matter what. If Running Bear could evade detection for hundreds of miles, I should be able to make the two miles over to the Gruger house and back. The quickest way to that deserted house would be to take the path from Inspiration Point into the camp yard, out the camp entrance, and then down Kellum Road.*

As much as Jake wanted to check in on the Birmingham's house and Camp Koinonia's cabins, he suspected the enemy had those routes bugged with surveillance devices.

No … My best bet is to stay off the paths. I'll zigzag through the forest to the Frog Pond, then cut up to the road. Just in case someone is following me, I'll swing wide on the far side of the road, then cut around the back side of the Frog Pond, he reasoned as he crawled out of the crag in the boulders. Jake moved across the forest floor silently, in spurts, always moving when the wind blew.

Jake stopped at the edge of the Birmingham Forest. From his spot, he could see Kellum Road as it curved in front of the Gruger house. Rapidly moving clouds caused the house to wave in and out of the moonlight. Instinctively, he knew that once he stepped onto the road, he was treading on enemy territory.

I can see why this old, nasty wreck of a house was the subject of ghost stories. Jake's heart raced. He dreaded the thought of going into the shack. Jake recalled Zeke's tale about how Mrs. Gruger had poisoned her husband and stabbed her two children to death before she hung herself in the kitchen.

Jake couldn't help reconsidering the sanity of his mission. *What if I misinterpreted the Holy Spirit's vision? Why would God select such a horrible place to hide the seed packs? What if I fall through the floor? No one would ever find me. Or even worse, the enemy would capture me and the seeds. What if this is the enemy's trap?* He shook off the distracting doubts. *There are no cars on the road and no life in the house.*

He took a deep breath. *Lord be with me. Keep me safe. Let me find the packages and make it home safely.* He exhaled silently, lifted his body from the ditch, and crept across the road and into the forest on the other side.

Jake approached the back door. His left hand gripped his flashlight so that the lightbulb was clenched in his fist. By opening his pinky's grip, he could allow a controlled amount of light to escape. He was careful to slide around the screen door that had been busted halfway off its frame. Then he moved the wooden door just enough to slip past it. He noted the holes that exposed the rafter in the kitchen's ceiling had been chiseled out just big enough to loop a hangman's noose through. He made his way into the front room, which housed only a dilapidated couch. *No sign of the seeds.*

Headlights! The flicker of light rays through the room's side window cast his shadow on the opposite wall. Jake froze. *Don't move; don't look.* Adrenaline boiled inside of him. *If I look at the car, the red reflection of my retinas will give me away.* He slid the pistol out of his shoulder harness and pressed the safety button to "fire." *This is war.* He was ready. He would have to kill them all, first the driver, then the passengers. *Dead men can't radio back to the enemy command what happened or whom they've seen.*

The car passed without slowing down. Its rear tail light disappeared around the bend.

Thank you, Lord! Jake sighed. He realized the army of Satan had elaborate schemes for capturing, torturing, and dismembering prisoners. Satan's forces ignored the Geneva Conventions when dealing with the prisoners that his army captured. The devil's generals, however, insisted that the conventions be followed to the letter for all of their men in Christian captivity.

Jake looked around. *Jesus, you've got to help me.* Jake shined his light at the potbelly stove. He walked over and pulled the metal spiral tab on the stove's door.

A *screeeeech* that could have startled the demons in hell pierced the silence. Jake pulled the stove door open. "Thank you, Lord." Jake whispered.

The seeds and mushroom spores were packed in what resembled an old-fashioned life vest. There was one thick, plastic pouch in the back of the vest, and then there were two smaller pouches in the vest's front.

Jake knelt down. He felt the packet for a hard object that might be a tracking device. *None.* He slid his head under the veil, making it a tent that draped over him. Then he slipped off his pistol holster, slipped the seed vest on, and refitted his pistol harness.

Jake allowed himself to relax for only an instant. Then he glanced over his shoulder and out the front window. *Well, I guess it's time for this Running Bear to find his way home.*

Stepping carefully over the debris, Jake made his way through the front room and kitchen and out the back door. *I think I'll go down the road on the Gruger side, until I find a spot where the underbrush is dense on both sides of the road.* He waited for a wind gust to make his move across Kellum Road.

From around the bend in the road, a motorcycle whisked past Jake as he stepped over the center line on the road. The driver slammed on the breaks, throwing the bike into a skid and then onto its side. The driver fired a series of shots as Jake lunged across the road and into the forest on the Camp Koinonia side of the road.

Darn! He must have seen my shadow. Jake dashed into the woods. He could hear the biker pull up his bike and race off the road into the woods. Within seconds, Jake heard the front wheel of the motorcycle strike a stump, flipping the rider off the bike. Jake listened as the driver landed on the ground with a thud. The bike's engine sputtered and died as the driver scurried to orient himself.

For a few brief seconds, the forest was silent—no wind, no crickets, only Jake's pounding heart reverberating in the night.

One on one, Jake thought. Jake could hear the enemy stepping across the forest floor. *I have got to get him in the open, at short range, to pick him off with this pistol.*

Jake suspected the enemy's bike was a hybrid gas/battery motorcycle developed for the military, capable of cruising almost silently. By employing night vision goggles, the rider could travel through the darkness without headlights. Jake looked behind him. The Frog Pond was only a short distance from the tree he was hiding behind.

Jake dashed toward the pond. As he rounded the massive oak trees that stood at the water's edge, he bent down and swooped up a rock the size of his head.

He heaved the rock into the Frog Pond and disappeared into the thick vegetation at the edge of the pond.

Jake sat resting his arms on his knees. His left hand pinched together the top and the bottom of his veil's hood, which allowed only a sliver big enough for his right eye to aim down the pistol's sights.

Motionless, Jake sat as his enemy stalked closer and closer. The enemy advanced a few steps at a time, until he surveyed the pond from behind the trunk of the massive oak tree. With his rifle to his shoulder, the enemy walked slowly to the water's edge.

Bang! Jake's bullet pierced through the enemy's head, splattering its contents into the lake. Jake tackled the man's body into the water, shoving the enemy's torso under and forcing the air out of his lungs with his foot and free hand. *Once I get all the air out, this guy should sink and stay on the bottom.* Jake aimed his pistol up the path that ran behind the oak tree. As the bubbles and gurgling ceased, Jake found himself once again in silence.

He dragged the body through the water, around the corner, to where deep vegetation overhung the pond's edge.

Jake felt around the bottom for rocks. He shoved a large, flat rock between the corpse's body and his body armor. Then Jake loosened and repositioned the dead man's belt far enough up his chest to strap the man's arms against his chest.

Jake scurried to retrieve his spent shell from the pond's edge and the enemy's rifle from the clearing. Then he moved back to the cover of the overhanging brush.

This might come in handy, Jake thought as he held the enemy's rifle in his hand.

He contemplated his next move. He could hear the crickets and frogs. He focused his ears toward the road. *No cars, just crickets. That is a good sign. Any woodsman knows that the crickets go silent when danger is near.*

Jake pulled the corpse to the far side of a log, which had fallen into the water. *This is a good spot. If enemy reinforcements come down the path to the clearing under the oak tree, I can hide behind this log. I'll leave the seed package, the enemy's rifle, and the rest of my gear here, under the veil. On second thought, the pistol and the ammo are waterproof. I'll take them with me. I wonder if there's a tracking device embedded in this rifle … I think it's going down with its soldier.* Jake stuffed the rifle between the dead man's body and his belt.

Moonlight illuminated the pond's edge. Jake could see the small hole his bullet had made just above the enemy's ear. He noticed the enemy was about his age. Jake could not bring himself to check the enemy's left hand for a wedding ring. His body armor was lightweight; the enemy's belt was void of warrior-class devices. *This guy must be a low-level courier, a delivery man.* Jake realized that the similarities between him and his foe were too striking to ignore.

Jake waded out to the center of the Frog Pond, dragging the dead weight behind him. He could feel stinging on the side of his thigh. *One of the shots must've grazed my leg.*

He knew where the edge of the sink hole was. When he felt the edge of the underwater cliff, he grabbed the enemy's belt and shoved the human log as hard as he could toward the center of the sink hole. With one last thrust against the man's boot, Jake released the corpse into the deep, black well. Not a bubble, not a ripple marked the fallen warrior's grave.

"Heavenly Father, forgive me for what I have done. Jesus, I pray for the soul of this man and that you may comfort his loved ones." Jake prayed from a heart saddened with remorse.

He returned to the shore, slipped into the seed vest, then his pistol harness, and finally, his veil. *Maybe this would be a good time to switch my veil battery.* He reached down to pull the spare battery from his pants pocket, and his hand came back sticky and red. *Blood! I've been shot.*

Jake cut off both sleeves of his camo shirt—one to be used to pack the wound, the other to be used as a wrap to keep the bandage in place. *I can't wait for this to clot. I need to get out of here. I'll need to immobilize my leg so I can get the bleeding to stop. I need to find a couple of tree limbs to use as crutches.*

Jake knew the enemy had a technique of wounding their prey and then following them back to their safe havens. He would stick to his original plan to take the long, rough path around the far side of the Frog Pond.

His leg began to ache; his joints stiffened. *Poison bullets!* Jake thought. *I need to keep moving.* Hampered by his makeshift crutches, Jake was forced to walk along the flat planes between the pond and hills of the deep forest. With each step, he could feel the poison moving up his body. With each ten yards of progress, the twenty-five pounds of seeds and sprouts caused an ever-increasing drain on his strength.

At the far end of the pond, Jake took cover behind an uprooted tree. He scanned the perimeter of the pond with his night-vision binoculars. *Nothing. Good,* he thought. Then he did a 360-degree scan with the device set to detect heat. *Nothing. So far, so good. No enemy in sight. Those devils are probably monitoring me from above. I wonder if their satellites can see me.*

As he moved away from the tree, he noticed his hips were almost locked. *This poison must work like rattlesnake venom, slowly paralyzing its prey.* Jake estimated that he was less than a half mile away from the cave entrance at Giant Pine, but the terrain was steep and rocky. He could not risk collapsing from exhaustion in the open.

He glanced at his watch. *It's 3:37 A.M. I'm not going to make it. I've got to find shelter within the next hour.* Jake could smell an approaching rain shower in the wind gusts that whipped through the trees. He knew he was close to where a tornado had snarled a half dozen trees on top of each other. Jake hobbled up to the pile of uprooted trees and stumps. He had been there a number of times before. He had used this landmark as an orientation destination for campers armed with only their maps and compasses. On the far side of the pile was a cavity big enough for his body. It had been used as a makeshift fort by the campers.

He poked his crutch around in the cavity and then surveyed the abyss with his flashlight. *All I need is to crawl in next to a rattler or a skunk or a swarm of hornets.*

Pulling himself across the dirt with only his elbows, Jake grimaced. He dragged his dead leg into the log and dirt shelter. *I better save the veil batteries for tomorrow.* He slipped the veil over his head, turned it off, and made a curtain over the hole between the log and ground. Jake flipped on his small flashlight. *I guess I'll need to take the seed vest off too.*

The heavy plastic vest slid easily off of his sweat-soaked torso. He pulled his canteen and food pouch out of his backpack. *I wonder if this vest is really full of seeds and sprouts. This could be an elaborate setup. What if the enemy intercepted the original shipment, and this one is a fake? The car could have verified my presence in the house, and then the motorcyclist could have been dispatched to wound me. Sophisticated satellites can read a number of criteria: temperatures, infrared radiation. They can distinguish flesh from vegetation, rock from metal. Satan was watching. At least the enemy won't be following me back to the Ark.*

Jake pulled the seed pack closer for an inspection. It felt like long bags filled with tiny granulates. He searched the edges for a zipper. There was an irregular pattern on the external seam. He squinted to make out the pattern. *Scriptures. The device that sealed this pack left an imprint of Bible scriptures along its seam.* Jake raised his eyebrows. *This is the real deal.*

He decided not to open the two food bars. He was losing the use of his arms to the onslaught of rigor mortis. He allowed himself only one mouthful of water.

With the mobility he had left, Jake squeezed the pistol's safety button to the no-fire position. He'd been contemplating using his next bullet to end his misery. *Suicide is of the devil. It's for cowards, not for the children of the almighty God.* He would endure the last few hours of pain. He would wait for Jesus. His neck was now paralyzed. *Breathe in!* He commanded himself. *Breathe out!* He willed himself to fight death with his last ounce of strength.

Lord, help me ... Lord ... help me. I can't make it. I need you. Almighty Jesus ... send your angels to help me. Help me. Help me ...

Jake leaned his head against the log and closed his eyes. There was only darkness. He had been in the shadow of death before, in the desert of Sudan. He was past caring about the pain now. He let his mouth drop open. *Sweet Jesus, I am waiting on you.* Throughout his life of service and prayer, Jake always knew that God's will would be done. *How many believers died to bring the seeds to the Gruger's house? How many will give their lives to carry the seeds to their final destination?*

He held the image of Mindy in his mind.

A gentle, soft voice came to him. "My good and faithful servant, this affliction will not end in death. It will be used to show the glory of the almighty Lord."

A mighty, radiant angel of the Lord touched down on the rock outside of Jake's log haven. Arrayed with the full battle armor of heaven, the angel drew his broad sword and readied his shield.

Death would have no victory over Jake Olson.

The Almighty Lion of Judah dispatched His angels throughout His kingdom on earth. Upon His command, His army of angels would launch their assault on the forces of evil.

CHAPTER 33

Sniper

"MOMMY! MOMMY! WAKE up! Daddy's in trouble. We must go to him," Anna exclaimed.

"Yes, Anna, I could sense it too." Mindy sat up. "Get the rest of the group up. I'll get our equipment. We'll leave as soon as we're ready."

Gusty winds outside of the Gazebo safe haven permitted Mindy's group to travel at a swift pace. Christen carried Anna in the middle of the single-file line that was connected by a tether rope. As they rounded a hill, Mindy sensed the presence of evil crouching in the forest. Immediately, she signaled the group to drop to the ground and flatten their veils over the top of themselves. They were being watched. Motionless, they waited, like fawns stalked by a tiger.

Mindy knew Satan's tactic was to kill the group's leader and then wound and scatter the rest of the group. Instinctively, the wounded and frightened would race back to the safe haven. Eager to help the wounded, those inside would open the doors of the safe haven from the inside. At that point, the enemy could rush in and destroy the haven and all of its inhabitants.

BANG! Thud! A rifle's bullet found its mark. Mindy's heart stopped. She could hear struggling in the forest. Her group stayed motionless on the ground. No one moved. No one made a sound.

In a few minutes, Mindy sensed a disturbance in the brush around her. Fervently, she prayed, *God protect us!*

Ever so quietly, the calm voice she'd heard many times over the years came to her ear. "You're OK. It's safe now. The Holy Spirit will direct your path. May our Lord and Savior Jesus Christ bless you abundantly with mercy, peace, and love."

The paralyzing fear and anguish melted from Mindy's body. As she breathed in slowly, her guardian angel slipped back into the woods.

This was not Satan's trick, Mindy thought. *The enemy would be not able to claim the Lord Jesus Christ as their Savior. An enemy scout must have been shot and killed.*

Mindy crawled back along the tether rope. One squeeze on each small hand, two squeezes in return. Everyone was safe. Mindy, shaken but not deterred, led the small group to the rendezvous spot under the Giant Pine.

Mindy scanned the area with her sensor in a 360-degree sweep. *All clear.* She slide her hand against the bottom of the rock, just as Zeke did the first time she entered the cave. She knew that if the door would not open, then something had gone wrong, and they would be stranded outside the safe haven. She wondered, reluctantly, if anyone still inhabited the Ark. She longed for Jake's embrace.

To her great relief, the rock slab opened. She ushered the seven young women into the cave. Mindy slipped through the crack between the boulders and felt the door close behind her. By the time she cleared the entrance chamber, she saw the group of new campers eating and drinking at a table just inside the re-entry chamber.

The mechanically-altered voice came across the intercom. "Group leader, please enter the door where the green light is flashing."

Mindy entered the open door. It closed behind her.

"Mindy! You're back! Thank God you made it in time." Lex and Nancy sprang to embrace her. "Where'd you find Anna?"

"She was with the group when I got there." Mindy's face turned from joy to distress. "Where's Jake?"

Lex's and Nancy's jubilation dropped to sadness.

"Jake's been wounded. He's back in the quarantine chamber. You know, the guesthouse you stayed in your first night in the haven," said Nancy.

"I'll take you to him," volunteered Lex.

"Mindy," Nancy asked, "are all these kids *safe*?"

"Yes, I've been working closely with them. They *are* the new campers. Thank you for providing them with a meal. After they've finished eating, ask them to pray for Jake."

"Are you hungry?" Nancy offered Mindy a container of water and a bowl of sprouts and mushrooms.

"I'll take the water, thanks. I'll eat after I see Jake."

Lex led Mindy through the cave labyrinth. "Jake received a vision that the Ark of Koinonia would be a bread basket for this area. Nancy has developed a process where highly nutritious mushrooms and various sprouts can be grown in alternating cycles in the cave.

"Jake left the Ark about a week after you and Zeke took the campers to their next destinations. He was gone for a couple of days. I had a dream that he was lying outside the haven in a shallow cave, directly under Inspiration Point. I remember Jake was working on escape routes back in that corner of the cave complex."

Lex caught his breath and continued. "Nancy and I got back there, and sure enough, there was a rope ladder that led up to a ledge of a shallow cave. The cave mouth looked out over the forest and lake of Camp Koinonia. That is where we found Jake. He was badly wounded in the leg and burning up with a fever. We did all we could for him: antibiotic injections, saline drip, and finally nutrient solution. After a few days, he was strong enough to talk."

Lex stopped to face Mindy. "I asked him how he got to the cave entrance with the leg wound. He looked at me and said, 'I was under the log pile, on the far side of the Frog Pond. Right before I blacked out, I had a vision. A bright light came upon me. A tall man in a brilliant, white robe picked me up and carried me to the cave under Inspiration Point.'"

"Under the log pile, on the far side of the Frog Pond?" Mindy snapped. "What was he doing way out there?"

"Jake's task was to retrieve the package of sprout seeds and mushroom spores from the abandoned Gruger house that sits down the road from Camp Koinonia. On his way back, he was intercepted by an enemy soldier. Shots were fired. Jake nailed the guy after the enemy shot Jake in the leg."

"So how was Jake, a mild-mannered gentleman, able to take out an enemy soldier?" Mindy asked.

Lex stopped once again to look Mindy in the eyes. "He shot him in the head. He had to. Enemy soldiers wear body armor. If they have their protective hood on, there is only a hole around the face as big as their eyes, nose, and mouth. It's the only place they're vulnerable. Jake must've used one of the high-powered pistols he had stocked away. You know, in case the enemy broke into the Ark."

Mindy gasped in horror. She'd heard enough. She motioned for Lex to lead on.

Lex and Mindy rounded the rocky corner to find the domed quarantine facility. They could see the light in the cabin's front chamber. Lex entered the code to open the door, momentarily blocking Mindy's entrance. "I'm only a sports trainer," Lex announced. "Nancy's in pre-med. We did all we could. We think the bullets the enemy used were poisoned. I just want you to know that Jake is not doing well." He opened the door.

Mindy walked in. Jake was asleep. He was pale and had obviously lost a lot of blood.

Mindy walked to his side and sat next to him on the bed. She rubbed her hand gently against his. "Jake, it's Mindy; it's time to wake up."

Jake peeked out of one eye and then opened the other. He smiled. "Mindy, thank God you're safe. I've been praying for you."

"Lex and I are going to pray for you," Mindy said in a calm, reassuring voice. "I want you to concentrate your energy on Jesus' healing power."

Jake nodded.

"Lex, place your hand on Jake's shoulder. Pray with me as hard as you can for Jesus to restore Jake's health." Mindy clasped her hands firmly around Jake's hands. "Heavenly Father, I bring before you this humble servant. He seeks your path and your ways. We cry out to you for healing. Through your stripes, we are healed; through your atonement at the cross, we are purified. *You are Jehovah Rapha.* You are the great healer. Stretch your hand down and touch this injured body. In Jesus' name, Jake Olson, be healed. In Jesus' name, Jake Olson, be healed. In Jesus' name, Jake Olson, be healed!"

Mindy's prayer continued for several minutes. Lex said later that he could feel the power and strength entering Jake's body and that he'd perceived the evil presence fading away from Jake's body.

Mindy pulled away from Jake's bed, exhausted. She could see that the natural color had returned to his face.

"Wow, that was incredible!" Lex stood in stunned amazement. "How'd you do that?"

"I didn't—God did. You know as well as I do that some poisons only come out with prayer."

CHAPTER 34

Rapture

THE ALMIGHTY AND everlasting God watched over His faithful servants on the earth. He blessed the Ark of Koinonia and all of its inhabitants. Its cave system under the Giant Pine became the food source for the Christian resistance movement in the area. And through the prompting of the Holy Spirit, Jake and Lex were able to discover an underground passage to the neighboring Gazebo complex.

The Ark served as a training camp for missionaries who, in turn, labored to produce and distribute spring water, mushrooms, and sprouts. The Gazebo group thrived as a modern-day underground railway for displaced Christians who were seeking safety in Canada. With the underground route of transit open between the two safe havens, the flow of people and resources remained undetected by enemy surveillance patrols.

As the months passed, the enemy tightened its stranglehold on all the people of the earth. Trade routes were shut off, safe haven after safe haven was destroyed. Times became exceedingly treacherous.

One day, Jake and Mindy called the inhabitants of the Ark into a sacred assembly. At the end of the worship, Scripture reading, and meal, they offered each member of their group Holy Communion. Then each in attendance was encouraged to enter into a time of fasting and prayer.

Jake retreated to the control room only long enough to verify that the Ark's monitors had been set to autopilot. As he returned to the group, he stepped quietly over his friends who were praying on the floor, face down.

Jake knelt and kissed the back of Mindy's shoulder, and then he assumed a curled, face-down, position next to her. As he had done on countless occasions since the first time they prayed together, he placed his arm over her shoulder. He whispered, "He will come like a thief in the night."

Mindy yielded into Jake. Her opposite arm rested over the delicate shoulder of their daughter Anna. Together, the inhabitants of the Ark of Koinonia fasted, prayed, and waited upon the Lord.

The Lord descended from heaven with a shout and a blast of a mighty trumpet. First, the dead in Christ rose, and then those who were still alive were called up to the clouds to be with the Lord.

Jake awoke in a cloud of brilliant, white fog. As the haze of the cloud parted, he perceived Jesus walking towards him with His arms extended to greet him. Although he kept his eyes locked on the radiant face of his Savior, Jake could sense that he carried his daughter Anna with his left arm and held Mindy's hand with his right. Jake perceived Alexander, Rebekah, Lex, Zeke, and Nancy had gathered around him.

"Well done, my good and faithful servants. With you I am well pleased." Jesus smiled, opened his arms, and drew them in.

Jake, his family, and his friends clung to Jesus, their Lord and Savior.

Back on earth, the once vibrant Ark of Koinonia decayed into an empty, dark, and silent jar of clay.

THE END

Endnotes

1. Holy Bible

    I am forever grateful for the Bible's scriptures, parables, prayers, and inspiration.

    Excerpts from the Bible—Acts 2, Psalm 91, Joel 2, Ezekiel 9, and 1 Thessalonians—were taken from the *New International Version* of the Bible.

2. Wikipedia.com, online encyclopedia

    Wikipedia was the source for various definitions and information.

3. Chapter 29: "Life in the Ark"

    "Every good day is one less bad day." Personal philosophy of Don Kellum. My father in law believes that the Lord has our days numbered. Every good day excludes a bad from happening.

    Camp Koinonia is a work of fiction. Any resemblance to actual people—living or dead—events, or locales is entirely coincidental.

About the Author

JOHN E. OLT lives in Noblesville, Indiana, with his wife, Krista, and their two sons, Jay and Andrew. They attend Grace Communiy Church, where John participates on the Grace Prayer Team and in the Men of Grace ministry. They enjoy hiking and camping. John graduated from Indiana University's Kelley School of Business in Bloomington and works as a production supervisor in the automotive industry.